ALLIANCE UNBOUND

C. J. CHERRYH AND JANE S. FANCHER

ALLIANCE UNBOUND

The Hinder Stars II

DAW BOOKS

New York

Jacket art by Micah Epstein
Jacket design by Katie Anderson
Map by C. J. Cherryh and Jane S. Fancher
Edited by Betsy Wollheim

DAW Book Collectors No. 1967

DAW Books
An imprint of Astra Publishing House
dawbooks.com
DAW Books and its logo are registered trademarks of
Astra Publishing House

Printed in the United States of America

Library of Congress Cataloging-in-Publication Data

Names: Cherryh, C. J., author. | Fancher, Jane, 1952- author.
Title: Alliance unbound / C.J. Cherryh and Jane S. Fancher.
Description: First edition. | New York : DAW Books, 2024. |
Series: The hinder stars ; 2
Identifiers: LCCN 2024017410 (print) | LCCN 2024017411 (ebook) |
ISBN 9780756415969 (hardcover) | ISBN 9780756415983 (ebook)
Subjects: LCGFT: Science fiction. | Novels.
Classification: LCC PS3553.H358 A795 2024 (print) |
LCC PS3553.H358 (ebook) | DDC 813/.54--dc23/eng/20240419
LC record available at https://lccn.loc.gov/2024017410
LC ebook record available at https://lccn.loc.gov/2024017411

First edition: October 2024
10 9 8 7 6 5 4 3 2 1

To Our Patient Readers . . . you know why.

THE HINDER/FIRST STARS

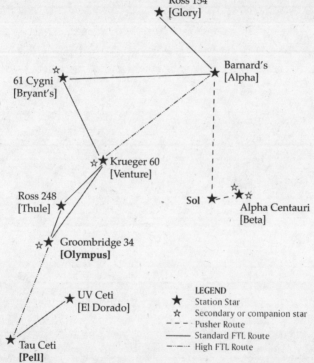

Ross 154
[Glory]

Barnard's
[Alpha]

61 Cygni
[Bryant's]

Krueger 60
[Venture]

Ross 248
[Thule]

Sol

Alpha Centauri
[Beta]

Groombridge 34
[Olympus]

UV Ceti
[El Dorado]

LEGEND
★ Station Star
☆ Secondary or companion star
--- Pusher Route
— Standard FTL Route
-·- High FTL Route

Tau Ceti
[Pell]

NOTE: Distances are not what they seem. The chart does not portray vertical distance.

For Our Fellow Nerds

STELLAR COORDINATES

Alpha/Barnard's Star
17 57 48.49803   04 41 36.2072

Beta/Proxima Centauri
14 29 42.94853   −62 40 46.1631

Glory/Ross 154
18 49 49.36216   −23 50 10.4291

Bryant's Star/61 Cygni
21 06 53.940   38 44 57.90

Venture/Krueger 60
22 27 59.4677   57 41 45.150

Galileo/EV Lacertae
22 46 49.7323   44 20 02.368

Thule/Ross 248
23 41 55.0361   44 10 38.825

Olympus/Groombridge 34
00 18 22.8850   44 01 22.6373

El Dorado/UV Ceti/Luyten
01 39 01.54   −17 57 01.8

Pell/Tau Ceti
01 44 04.08338   −15 56 14.9262

Viking/Epsilon Eridani
03 32 55.84496   −09 27 29.7312

Mariner/Van Maanan's Star
00 49 09.89841   05 23 18.9931

INTERSTELLAR DISTANCES IN LIGHT YEARS

Sol to:
Alpha: 5.958
Beta: 4.244
Glory: 9.703
Bryant's: 11.398
Venture: 13.15
Galileo: 16.472
Thule: 10.290
Olympus: 11.620
El Dorado: 8.7
Pell: 11.905
Viking: 10.446
Mariner: 14.1

Alpha to:
Beta: 6.554
Glory: 5.54
Bryant's: 9 .318
Venture: 12.873
Galileo: 15.905
Thule: 11.328
Olympus: 13.097
El Dorado: 12.483
Pell: 15.531
Viking: 15.653
Mariner: 16.434

Beta to:
Glory: 8.246
Bryant's: 14.399
Venture: 16.978
Galileo: 20.050
Thule: 14.119
Olympus: 15 .533
El Dorado: 10.244
Pell: 13.372
Viking: 12.362
Mariner: 16.623

Glory to:
Bryant's: 12.232
Venture: 16.789
Galileo: 18.677
Thule: 14.766
Olympus: 16.499
El Dorado: 13.420
Pell: 16.059
Viking: 17.586
Mariner: 17.396

Bryant's to:
Venture: 5.201
Galileo: 6.865
Thule: 5.583
Olympus: 7.076
El Dorado: 13. 741
Pell: 15.695
Viking: 16.861
Mariner: 12.989

Venture to:
Galileo: 4.829
Thule: 4.586
Olympus: 4.936
El Dorado: 15.03
Pell: 16.72
Viking: 16.904
Mariner: 13.463

Galileo to:
Thule: 6.574
Olympus: 6.249
El Dorado: 16.27
Pell: 17.184
Viking: 18.521
Mariner: 12.445

Thule to:
Olympus: 1.824
El Dorado: 10.62
Pell: 12.2
Viking: 12.64
Mariner: 9.347

Olympus to:
El Dorado: 11.09
Pell: 12.307
Viking: 12.573
Mariner: 8.943

El Dorado to:
Pell: 3.53
Viking: 5.115
Mariner: 12.492

Pell to:
Viking: 5.462
Mariner: 6.081

Viking to:
Mariner: 9.693

Danger!

Echo in the raging cacophony.

Adjust!

Fingers fly without conscious thought.

Shrink the field. Change the parameters of the bubble.

3-2-

[Fifth decimal adjustment.]

-1: Now!

Implemented. Phase-shift spits them free.

And the universe heals.

✿   ✿   ✿

God. What *had* he done?

Ross Monahan, senses reeling, stared at the screen in front of him. Graphs. Numbers.

Gibberish—

—that *should* make sense. That *would* make sense, dammit . . . once the auto-drip drove the last of the trank from his system.

It had damn well *better* make sense. His fingers had just *input* those numbers, as crazed, as *insane* as those numbers might be in retrospect.

He focused—hard—on one graph in particular, convinced his drug-laced brain to remember . . .

. . . *color* . . . Yes. Color.

Ought to be five lines on that graph. Red, green, magenta, gold—

Where was blue? Blue line was *his* input.

Where the hell was blue?

Adrenaline, natural and real, surged. The numbers and graphs swirled, swam in and out of focus. He blinked repeatedly, desperate to see those lines . . . but when it cleared, his first impression held. *There was no blue line.*

So what had he done? What the *hell* had he just done?

Comp didn't lie. His input wasn't there. But he remembered the drop to realspace, the bubble, the crazed buffeting that defied all logic. He *remembered* pounding those numbers in, dammit!

God. Had he frozen? Bad enough to read the system entry as crazed as memory held it, but not to put the numbers in at all? Even wrong numbers?

He didn't know which was worse.

Dropping the ship was Nav 1's job. Green line. *Kate's* line. And red, Nav 1.2. Bucklin. Perfect echos. Not so much as a pixel of separation. The magenta and gold lines, Nav 1.3 and 1.4, were right alongside green, separated on entry, but within the margin of error, and slowly dropping closer to green.

It all *looked* right, and the graphs now described a ship in normal space, as they ought to be.

But there was no fifth line. Not even a blue border, top or bottom, that would indicate his reading of the drop and subsequent input would have put the ship literally off the charts.

Only one answer: he'd hallucinated his input. And that was, for a Navigator, for his ship, lethal, if his had been the Nav 1 line. The only way the computer would disregard Nav 1 was if 2, 3, and 4 were together and 1 was the anomaly.

He'd frozen.

Even worse: his gut instinct, his *read* of the situation, had been right. *Right*, dammit! His hallucinated input would match what he saw evidenced in that graph. Up to and *including* that last instant change in the fifth decimal. He'd read the entry dead right . . . but he'd frozen, had failed to trust that chaotic input . . . and not keyed anything. Not one damned—

The universe turned inside out as the ship made her first V-dump, a quick dip into a partially formed bubble. He wasn't ready, and his mind was reeling as they exited at a markedly slower pace . . . and with all four lines in perfect synchrony.

All but his. Second failure. *Dammit!*

His hands shook. His fingers tingled. When he rubbed them together, skin sloughed, but that was just what it did. In realspace, *weeks* had passed since the ship had jumped . . . at Helm's command and on Nav's numbers, her crew tranked down against the insanity that ruled inside an FTL bubble. Now the physical debt came due. Throughout the ship, crew would be coming out of that drugged state gently, sanely, slowly; but on the bridge,

Nav, Helm, and Scan had to hype up on a second drug that chased the trank. Hype left them all buzzed, nerves jangled.

Ross took one final glance at that betrayal on the screen. Reality and inexperience had played tricks on his memory. That was all. Never mind it had never, *ever* happened before. Not even his first time sitting at a shadow board . . . almost a *decade* ago, ship-time. Face it, he told himself. It happened. Move on.

But he had to confess it.

As if Kate wouldn't notice.

And if it happened again—if it *ever* happened again—he'd be out of Nav. Permanently. That was the reality of his chosen profession. Nav errors meant death, not just of the ship, but of the entire Family that crewed her. At the moment, on this ship, he was a guest, still a trainee, still only shadowing the real boards, which were in expert hands. Fortunately. Thanks to that fact, the ship, the legendary *Finity's End*, and her equally legendary crew of Neiharts, was safe.

No thanks to him—a Monahan and Nav 1.3 on the Monahan's *Galway*— they were where they needed to be . . . and there were still two V-dumps to calc.

So get your damn brain online, boy! Fallan's voice rang in his head. Fallan, *Galway's* own legend, Nav 1.1 and Ross Monahan's mentor, might not be here, but damned if *Galway's* Nav 1.3 would do anything more to embarrass the old man.

The shakes he was experiencing . . . that was normal, as bodies began communicating properly with brains—as was sight tending to monochromatic.

Red this time.

Gut-churning flash of deja vu. A nightmarish drift through space.

. . . streaks of black-red. Blood. His blood. Beyond the streaks: a metal monster glowing red with reflected sunlight.

Finity . . .

Dammit. He thrust the memory away. Food. He needed food, that was all. He fumbled a nutrient packet from the chair arm storage, tore a careful hole in the top, squeezed the supposedly fruit-flavored contents into his mouth, swallowed: and *tasted* velocity and distance . . . as the numbers on the screen spooled along. A mark from Helm indicated a requested course correction as the ship approached its second V-dump.

He shoved self-doubt out the airlock, and his hindbrain began calculating that dump as he finished the packet and shoved the empty back into the armrest. Hands free, he input without hesitation . . . and the fifth line was back, reassuringly near the others. As routine as such things ever were.

Dump came. He concentrated on those red lines, at the other graphs and numbers that would *tell* him if anything went wrong—

And suddenly, as the ship phased in and out of hyperspace—*it* was back. He recognized it now for what it was: a mass . . . huge. More, it was a color. A nature. A presence that defied common sense. Wave after buffeting wave of gravitational force warping everything in reach.

His mind insisted: *Finity's* entry shockwave reverberating off the Ardaman limit, the outflowing event waves of Pell's gravity well.

His gut said: Pell was pissed. The star was furious as hell at the massive intrusion into—

The bubble dissipated, unformed. The numbers reasserted realspace around them and the monster receded.

He blinked, dazed, at the readout. Was *that* . . . his mind searched for a memory, a word . . . what a G-class star . . . *felt* like?

Fallan had told him, *promised* him that one day soon he'd feel it, and if it were Fallan's grey head at that Nav 1 seat, he could ask him about it. But Fallan, his lifelong mentor, was far, far away, on *Galway*, where Ross himself damnwell should be . . . and wasn't. Fallan, along with *Galway's* whole First-shift, was on his way to Ireland, trailblazing the once-fabled, now-God-willing real, FTL route to Sol and Earth. The holy grail of trade for every Alpha spacer ever born. The hope for the future of the entire First Stars loop.

And a damned scary ride to get there. Two very chancy gravity wells into a final one that would make the monster outside seem tame. He'd seen the numbers, run the sims. And if he'd frozen on *those* boards . . . God.

Maybe it was a good thing fate . . . with a little help from Fallan himself . . . had thrown him out *Galway's* airlock.

Advisement came. Another marker on the chart. *Third* V-dump. Coming fast.

Another calculation; he keyed in; they went *up* . . .

And the monster, the center of that violence, was waiting.

Quieter. Saner, this time. But undeniably there.

He deliberately sent his mind spiraling back to those first moments of flux, trying to understand what he had felt, sorting the tamer *Now* from untamed *Then*, still not resolving what he saw/felt/tasted, but accepting it as legitimate input. Reference for his reality.

And wondered . . . as the half-formed bubble dispersed like a remembered dream . . . was it truly a first, or simply the first time he'd noticed . . .

whatever it was he sensed. It was his first time into a G-class. The numbers of its violence were off the chart of anything he'd ever calc'ed, real time. He'd only known M-class stars like Alpha, little, red, and moody, flaring off from time to time.

This star, this monster, was Tau Ceti, a yellow G-class, locally known as Pell's Star, and it had one prevailing mood, white-hot and angry.

The monster faded away. They were *down* again. Safe. His blue line ran near the others: conservative, but well within parameters.

And blue. Solid, true blue . . . as all other color had returned to him.

Job done. They'd be releasing to Second-shift soon. Which left him too much time to try and figure . . . not what had happened, but why. *Why* had he frozen? Worse, *why* had he hallucinated putting in those numbers?

Before making this final jump into Pell, he'd run the numbers according to the data he'd been given, calc'ed the bubble and the phase-flux and input the code . . . fundamentally no different than he had dozens of times before. He'd matched Kate then. He was relatively sure he'd matched Kate *and* Bucklin at the outset. So had Ty and Jim, all four live Nav posts in agreement on the easy part. Those numbers might have been unlike any he'd run for real before, but over the years, Fallan had tossed him thousands of different scenarios, including Pell's, and he'd run sims of every conceivable situation . . . on *Galway*. Always on *Galway*. A beauty of a ship, in her way. *His* ship. His home. But a fraction of the mass and power of *Finity*.

Galway was smooth on entry—*polite* compared to the behemoth that was *Finity's End*.

Still . . . he *did* know what he was doing. He was Nav 1.3 on *Galway*. Still shadowing, but not, so Fallan threatened, for long. He'd long since lost count of the number of times he'd sat jump on *Galway*. It was First-shift's job to bring *Finity* into a populated system . . . as it was Fourth's to bring her in to dock. He'd felt *Finity's* power before, coming in to Bryant's and Venture, systems he knew well. He knew there was range beyond anything he'd ever imagined under his hands.

But this . . .

This . . . *feel* . . . on system-drop had not been what he'd expected from the numbers, and memory still *insisted* he'd changed his instructions to the ship on the fly, on that barely sane downside of trank.

Had he? Had his screen somehow failed to show just that blue line? God, a mechanical glitch would be far and away better than the alternative.

Is this what you meant, Fallan? He longed to ask.

Is this what it means to feel *a star?*

Since he could remember, Fallan had claimed he could feel them. His fellow Monahans laughed and called it *Fallan's Fancy*, and with Fallan's sense of humor it was hard to tell . . .

But Fallan's discipline never kidded around when it came to sitting ops, and Fallan's voice in his head right now sternly told him to quit nardyfardling and get to work. He'd been given the opportunity of a lifetime, to sit *Finity's* boards. So quit whining. Absorb every moment, every right choice . . . and learn from every screwup.

I'm trying, Fallan. Trying to learn all I can, but grand as it all is, I should be there. With you. Should have felt that squirrelly jump-point. Should have—

Nardyfardling.

He'd had a blank spot, was what. Caught by surprise. Own it. Be done. Be glad his Family wasn't counting on him. Rookie mistake. He could have killed them all had he been sitting Kate's chair. But he wasn't in her chair, thank God, only shadowing. Mistakes like that *weren't* unexpected from the shadow-boards. First time out of the First Stars was some excuse, if not an excuse that sat well with his pride. He just had to reset his memory to accept what was on the display, and never blank out again.

So he analyzed the numbers, the memory, discovered he viscerally *agreed* with what Kate and Buck had done, and what Ty and Jim had done. He *understood* it. If he really had done what that same memory recalled, he would have been proud of that answer.

Old stuff, to Kate, this star. To all the Neihart Nav. To them, to *Finity*, this was home port.

Another rub of his hands, more dead skin. His entire body would be shedding like that. His clothes were rank, and dusty with shed skin cells. Everybody's were. Fans and filters on each chair worked constantly. Silent in normal operation, the fans picked up speed as he and those around him began to move: painful cacophony to senses peeled raw. A shower was in the offing once they'd settled, once the all-clear came down from the captain and Second-shift came up to take over the bridge. He yearned for that. Hot, steaming water to banish the chill and silence the rattle that the entry had set into his nerves.

"Nav. All clear?" The query came on Nav-com from Kate, four rows forward of his, on a bridge crowded with ranks of chairs and operators, most only beginning to stir from trank. He answered in turn, behind the three seats in front of him: "Nav 1.5, clear."

Special designation, that "5" at the end. Fifth seat, a position, on *Finity*, for trainees, teen-aged kids, which he was not . . . never mind he'd just blown his first truly major test on *Finity*.

Stop nardyfardling!—Yes, sir, Fallan, sir!

"Nav reports," Kate's voice again, on general com, *"all well, all respon-sive."* And a moment later, directed to her own: *"Nav 3 through 5, clear to release."*

Ross flipped the clamp on his elbow and pulled the needle from his arm, still feeling a little queasy. He grabbed another packet and swallowed fast before attempting to stand. Around Nav, other stations had been coming on line. Nav, Helm, and both Scan posts, Scan and Longscan, were first to get the hype flowing, right along with the Executive of the shift, roughly plunged into awareness ahead of others of the crew, ahead of the rest of the ship. Critical stations were hyped out of trank hard and fast. Minds had to come clear. All the stations were computer-managed during jump. Frail humans did their work at the start of a jump and at drop-down, but in the latter there could be issues, either the star or the ship, one or the other, that took a little finesse.

Or a lot.

Memory said—there had been an issue on this one. Memory said he'd input the changes.

But memory lied.

And that, for Nav, was the scariest thought possible. Nav *depended* on memory, infallible and absolute. Tracking truth from fantasy was Nav's primary job.

Damn it. First panic and then a memory lapse.

Worst of all, Kate would have seen what he'd done. Or, more critically, not done. Kate would know he'd frozen, for whatever reason; and among the sensors he'd just disconnected would be his heart rate, a record which *had* to be embarrassing, and would probably get him a query from Medical.

A hand landed on his shoulder. He jumped. Turned his head . . . a little too quickly.

It was Kate that came into focus. She'd disconnected and left Nav as Second-shift began to move in and take seats. There would be a nineteen-year-old *Finity* kid wanting his.

"All well?" Kate asked.

"Fine," he said, and he moved to get up. Kate stayed him with a hand held in his way.

"Sure of that?" Kate was not alone. Bucklin, Nav 1.2, was with her, now, Ty and Jim moving up on his other side.

"I'm *fine*," he said. "Just a little . . ."

"Spooked?" Kate asked. "Up there? Spooked?"

He didn't know how to answer. *Up there.* In hyperspace, he'd functioned.

But coming out, coming down, conjured a shape, numbers in his head. A monster of a sun. A monster that shook with force he had never met. No, it wasn't *up there* that spooked him. He had spooked at the edge of realspace. And *still* felt it here. Maybe it was just memory . . . but maybe it wasn't. And that maybe . . . that spooked him now.

"The old girl hiccupped," Kate said. "That's all. You felt it, Galway?"

Felt it. She'd said it first. Didn't mean she meant it the way Fallan did.

"I felt . . . feel—" There was no expressing it. It *was* still there, that monster. Even as his head cleared . . . he felt it. He just wasn't sure *what* he felt.

Kate's hand landed on his arm a second time. "You're seriously lagged. Get to the showers. Are you all right for that?"

Rotation had almost gotten them to 1 G. Not quite. It took a bit after shutdown. And it was the effects of trank, maybe. But the spooked feeling lingered . . . increased, if he were honest. A sense of threat, as if he'd touched something that didn't want to be bothered. And Kate kept asking.

"Just a little shaky," he answered Nav 1.1. "I'll be all right." And he got up, eased past Kate and made his way aft, to the next takehold on the way to the showers.

Book I   Section ii

JR Neihart, senior captain, watched Ross Monahan leave, watched the slight stagger, the reach for the next bulkhead—a reach aborted.

Pride. Determination. And a likelihood of falling on his ass.

"We had a hiccup," Kate said.

"Noticed that," JR said, with a shift of the eyes from Kate to the young man from *Galway.*

"He input," Kate said, meaning Ross Monahan had keyed in on arrival— as he should, shadowing the working boards.

"Was he right?" JR asked.

"He *felt* it," Kate said, and her eyes flicked to meet his. "*And* adjusted on the fly. First time facing the Old Girl and he matched my numbers and Bucklin's close enough you couldn't see his line for ours. Blew the first V-dump—nerves, likely. But not the second and third."

That was interesting. *Finity,* when she dropped into realspace, and when she blew off *V*, was no inconsiderable force plowing into a stellar environment, and Tau Ceti could be cranky when poked. Force met force, *Finity's* shockwave and the unpredictable flux of Pell's recent activity, first at the heliopause, far, far out, where *Finity's* near-light mass dominated the encounter. Then with each V-dump, that initial shockwave came back to haunt them until they crossed the Ardaman limit, after which their speed, legally speaking, had to be low enough their bow wave ceased to matter to the star.

At smaller stars, like the M-classes Ross Monahan was used to, and for ships the size of his *Galway*, the heliopause and the Ardaman limit were little more than mathematical navigational markers, but young Ross, who had only ever met red M-classes, had *felt* the situation and reacted so close to Kate's numbers he'd been *inside* the computer's curve.

The Ardaman limit, that elusive boundary at which a star's outgoing energy—shock waves, solar wind, gravitic forces and the like—were dispersed enough for an FTL ship's realspace disruption not to wreak havoc . . . was Nav's number one nemesis. One never knew exactly what one would meet on arrival in-system, and calcing the V-dumps to minimize the disruption and still bring the ship as close to the Ardaman as possible approached an art form.

Instinct, pure and not so simple. Remarkable. *Galway* had themselves a treasure in that young man.

Truth was, *Finity's* effect at run-in was not *Galway's*. At several times *Galway's* mass, *Finity* was her own major dimple in spacetime when coming into realspace at just under lightspeed. Ross had had a taste of that difference coming in to Bryant's and Venture, but Tau Ceti was a G-class. He'd told Kate to give Ross the charts and let him work it out the hard way. He'd wanted their *Galway* navigator to internalize the numbers—and then see what he'd do in the entry.

Not uncharacteristically, Tau Ceti had obliged them all with its own little surprise, shed a few days ago—one of those things a master Navigator adjusted for on the fly.

So. Test passed. If Ross Monahan hadn't had a Family and a ship counting the days until he returned, he'd be a welcome addition to any crew, never mind the blown V-dump.

But Ross *did* have a Family, and hopefully, in the not-so-distant future, that Family would get their ship back to Alpha safely and *Finity* would send young Ross and his fellow Galways back to their own region of space.

On that hoped-for day, the Galways' collective lives would change forever.

But then, on the day *Galway* dropped back into Alpha system . . . all of human space would change.

Forever.

The shower helped. It didn't solve the wobbles, but at least the grime and the red haze were gone. Ross managed to dress as far as loose coveralls, grey, and scuffs, likewise grey as the walls, and got to the lounge, where there was a supply of drink-packs, a wide choice of mostly empty reclining chairs, and in one of those chairs—

What was *she* doing here?

Jen Neihart, who by rights should still be waking up in her cabin, was already there, her dark hair wet and eyes bright. *Waiting* for him, dammit. Not unusual for her to join him, after a jump, but usually he had *time*. Time to get his head together, get his electrolytes in balance, to, God help him, *debrief* with his Nav 1.1. Of all times, he needed—and dreaded—that debrief more than anything.

But there she was, and there was no dodging her, however much he might, for the first time, want to.

He flung himself down, let his head fall back, and breathed. That was all, for at least a moment or two.

"You don't look so good," said the young woman, who probably never had a bad hair day in her life. "Everything all right?"

He thought about blaming it on the drugs, thought about denying there'd been anything unusual. That he was always a bit green at this point. But that wasn't how they were. They didn't keep secrets . . . not important ones. Not since their first few meetings.

"I blew a calc," he admitted, reluctantly, keeping his eyes closed. It was safer now, a comforting stellar dark without flashbacks lurking in the shadows. "Good thing my board wasn't live."

"Tau Ceti's a big star," Jen said, as if she actually knew. "Different."

Jen was Security, and in training. She knew a lot, was good at what she did, but somehow he didn't think she had a clue just *how* big Tau Ceti really was.

"Good try," he said, and half-opened the eye nearest her. "What are you doing camping out here, when you have a warm bed to be in? You're up and walking with Nav and Helm, woman. Who does that, that doesn't have to?"

"True love," Jen said, with a hand dramatically to her heart.

"Yeah." He let his eye drift shut again, as if that could wall out the situation. "Right." He and Jen joked about love. It wasn't for spacer folk, or at least not forever-love. Lasting love was for kin. Romantic love was for station-calls, and meeting people you were glad to see again—some more than others, but everybody dockside was transient, even the best.

His attachment to Jen, while special from the start, was . . . different. *Monogamous,* was a word Jen had found and embraced.

All he knew, it was a station-side attachment come aboard for a while, which meant sharing parts of life reserved for sharing with Family. Except up there on *Finity's* boards . . . well, he was still a guest. Still something . . . apart. On *Finity's End*, he was hers, though there were others who wanted to discuss that issue, but in truth, he wasn't interested. Getting himself entangled with multiple Finitys in ways that could challenge what he had with Jen was just not the way he wanted to go. He'd decided that for himself, long before she brought up the m-word, as she called it. The other Galways aboard *Finity*—there were eight besides him—were free and easy and all ordinary about their shipboard relationships. Certainly none with the specialness of Jen, so far as he knew.

And she was.

Special.

Maddening at times.

Younger than he was.

Not all *that* younger in years. Two, maybe, in ship years. But younger in never having been poor. Never having had to nurse a drink or sit talking with cousins about how they were not going to make a payment on a debt this run. She had a kind of innocence, this constant assumption that everything was possible, everything was affordable, everything could be handled.

On *Finity's End*, it probably could be. In the Beyond, with its bounty of resources and trade goods, it probably could be.

Not so, for a First Stars freighter, even the newest and best of them, which *Galway* was.

He felt her presence but he appreciated her silence. Input . . . was not something he wanted at the moment. He drifted a glance in her direction, wondering if he should say something, found a rather vacuous, half-lidded gaze looking through him, and figured the need for quiet went both ways.

Anchor. That's what Family provided, and right now with his Family, the Monahans, scattered in every direction, Jen's . . . *monogamy* . . . was damned precious. As was her can-do optimism.

He wondered, even if all the luck went *Galway's* way and if the future turned as bright as they all hoped . . . if he would ever, *ever* feel that way.

That safe. That secure. That eternally hopeful of good things to come. And the flip side was the concern that this extended association with *Finity's End* might instill an expectation in him that his own future would never, *could* never, meet.

There was a reason spacers didn't think in terms of forever love. No two ships were alike. No two ships plied the same route at the same speed. Sleepovers were, by their very nature, ephemeral. Ships purposely staggered runs in an effort to get the best trade deals on either end of a run. You could go years between one shared dock and another.

Still, back in the First Stars, Alpha, Bryant's, Glory, and Venture—everybody did meet again, eventually, so you said, *Until next time.* And you expected it, on endlessly circular routes.

For *Galway,* a loyal Alpha ship, the chance of meeting a Pell ship like *Finity* was, quite literally, a once in a lifetime event. So better, for a whole different set of reasons, that he *would* have to say goodbye to Jen someday in the near future, and face the hard truth that they might never meet again, depending on where the ships went.

But when that time came (and it *would* be "when," not "if") that anchor Jen provided could become a treasured memory. When that time came, the Monahans would be reunited, running a new, lucrative route that included Sol, and newly refit engines that would maybe, just maybe, put Pell on their regular route.

"You upset?" Jen asked, at last. "You shouldn't be. Mistakes are how we get better. You don't make 'em, you're not pushing."

Damn. He really, truly did *not* want to talk about that.

"Yeah," he said, "well."

There was a stir around them. He slitted his eyes to test focus and discovered the whole rest of First-shift was coming into the lounge, moving to the showers, as others came out. His Monahan cousins, Maire and Siobhan . . . twin sisters, both Scan, had shadowed the ride as well. He heard their voices among those coming in from the showers, registered a greeting from them to him, and lifted a hand in acknowledgment. Anything more could wait. The ship was entirely in Second-shift's hands now, and everything safe, everything fine with the ship, or they'd have delayed shift-change. He thought he'd have about two more packets of that yellow electrolyte stuff without throwing up and then he'd be right again. He moved to pull one from the dispenser on the table, and saw Patrick, *Galway's* Helm 3.1 coming in behind Senior Captain, JR Neihart. Standing order was *not* to stand for officers in the lounge, for which he was, at the moment, extremely grateful.

He sensed someone behind him, and looked up to find a shower-damp

Kate Neihart standing at the side of his couch, sharp as if she hadn't just come off shift. Her eyes were on Jen, who gave her a cheeky grin, before setting her hands on her chair arms to lever herself up—only to thump back down again, eyes a bit wide and startled.

"Sit," Kate said quietly. Senior among seniors of the shift, Kate could have asked Jen why *she*, not bridge crew, was sitting in proximity to her trainee, but Kate just rested a hand on Jen's couch-back and one on Ross's shoulder.

"How's the stomach doing?" Kate asked, shifting her gaze to him.

"Fine." He forced the word out. "Doing fine."

"You know what you did, don't you?"

That almost did it. Ross choked down hard. "Froze," he said, trying to look at her without seeing her.

"Why do you say that?"

God help him, she was going to *make* him explain. And there was the rest of Nav 1 behind her, listening. Adrenaline surged.

"Because there wasn't any—" He mended his intended language. "I don't think I input."

Her chin lifted. "Adjust that. You definitely did input."

He swallowed hard as the adrenaline failed again.

"That bad?" He tried not to mutter.

"Spot on," Kate said. "Ace job, Galway. Perfect line with me and Bucklin."

"No lie. Seriously, no lie?" He tried desperately not to *sound* desperate, but Kate would know, better than anyone aboard, just how important the answer to that question was.

"To seven decimals." Kate looked entirely on the up and up, and . . . seven decimals. That *could* explain the missing blue line: Kate's and Bucklin's would have completely masked his.

Kate waited, maybe expecting an answer, but no brilliant words came, and the corner of Kate's mouth twitched.

"Question is," she said, with a slap on the chair arm, "can you do it as good again? But then, it always is, isn't it? Get some rest, Galway. You're excused from the sims today."

"Yes, ma'am." Ross managed not to throw up, and Kate walked away to take a seat over near Jim B, Helm 1. Ross forced down another gulp of the yellow stuff, which was not as good as before. When it wasn't, you knew you'd had enough. But he'd pushed it fast. He'd squeezed for an extra dose of the wake-up juice, wanting to be sharp on entry, and it was still running races in his veins.

"So you *didn't* drop us into the star," Jen said, and swept the back of her hand dramatically across her forehead. "Whew!"

"God." Was all he could manage. Jen could joke. He couldn't. He'd tried to revise his memory so he *hadn't* input, but now Kate said he had, had told him to adjust the hard won revision, so now he had to remember he had, and reality was still dancing back and forth, like the focus of his eyes. "I really don't think it was much other than luck. *Couldn't* be, could it?" *But I felt it. I felt it. Different than anything ever.* He breathed a moment, trying hard *not* to feel those waves, whether for real or for memory. Finally, out of that struggle, he hazarded a question to Jen: "Do you feel a difference between, say, Venture, and here? Do you feel the pressure? The star?"

"Pressure?" Jen gave a shrug. "I don't know." Her brow wrinkled in thought. "Would I know where I was when I woke up, without knowing where we were headed?" Another thinking pause, then: "I think, maybe, yes. . . . but I couldn't say why. And that . . . sense of place is just as I'm coming up out of trank. Once my brain kicks in . . . I just *know* where we're supposed to be, so that might be all that's going on."

He hadn't thought of that. Maybe that *was* all he was feeling. Like tasting velocity or seeing the world in monochrome. Numbers transformed into sensation. Maybe, if he worked at it long enough, he'd convince himself.

"Speaking of brains kicking in . . . how in hell *did* you get up here so fast?"

"Security can get the high-powered juice. Thought I'd try it. Once. Just to know what it's like, waking up while we're still up there. Curiosity, mostly. I rode it out with Fletcher. He always hypes, just in case."

Fletcher. Head of Security. Office just the other side of the section. So she hadn't had a long hike. *That* was how she'd beaten him to the lounge. He'd damn near gone into a trance in the shower.

Curiosity, she said. A curiosity about ops that just *happened* to manifest on this run, his first run into Pell space?

Not bloody damn likely.

They were lovers. And exclusive. He was hers. She was his. And he liked that. But he wasn't sure he liked her pushing into his duty-space, asking what he felt, when he wasn't damned sure himself, and turning up when his stomach was taking a poll on whether to keep what it had or return it, using her pretty eyes to get him to talk about stuff he really wasn't ready to say.

He took another swig of the yellow stuff. It tasted fully vile. Which meant he could well and truly begin to trust his mind, could begin to put his universe into perspective.

I did it, he told himself firmly. *Kate was here. I didn't imagine it.*

Kate was here . . . and so was Jen. He glanced sideways at her, without turning his head on the back rest.

"You did it," he said, "to keep tabs on me. To see if I'd spook . . ."

"Hey. Cheering squad here." She held up her hand.

He just closed his eyes. They both knew better.

"Besides." She finger-poked his arm, which sent shock waves to his toes . . . not in a good way. "Nav's fairly important. And it *was* your first time into the big system."

As if every other place in the cosmos was minor. In her eyes, it probably was. So she'd parked herself in the security office by Chief of Security Fletcher's permission, because the kid from Alpha might have a breakdown, a serious thing, Nav being what it was, critical. And she got that permission because Jen Neihart, the Senior Captain's niece, and Fletcher Neihart's watchdog, could go where she pleased.

And, give her credit, he knew damn well she thought she might have helped, if that breakdown had happened, and more credit still, likely she could have. Still . . .

"Vote of confidence, Jen. Give me a little."

"Plenty of confidence. Besides, didn't Kate just say you aced it?"

Additional confirmation: Kate wasn't a hallucination.

"Luck," he repeated, fighting overconfidence, which could be as deadly as ignorance, but he knew it hadn't been. He'd figured it. He'd been sane enough in that moment to know he wasn't on *Galway* but not sane enough to remember his input didn't count.

If he were honest, he'd not been *that* far from the breakdown in question. Had he not been capable of holding it together, he might have been very glad to have Jen there. He'd been starkly terrified in that nanosecond of arrival, and the feeling was still resident, a black beast still sitting on his shoulders. Maybe it was just hyped-up nerves, but he'd never felt so naked as when he'd felt that presence out there, like a living fire.

But he had held it together, he'd walked off the bridge under his own power and made it here, where Kate had found him and confirmed his input.

Kate was real, Kate had praised him, but he wasn't any blazing success, either. He'd blown the next operation. He'd screwed the first V-dump. He was sure of that. And Kate hadn't mentioned it. He had to wonder what Kate really thought. That he was damned lucky, probably. That he was a ragtag small-ship wonder who might be too dim to learn.

Well, there was nothing ragtag about *Galway*, and damned right he could learn. He'd relive that entry in sims until it was nothing more than—

"You're not mad, are you?"

He wasn't. Not really. It was just . . . he was all raw nerves at the moment, and she was just Jen, Jen who shed whatever fell on her, stainless steel and not giving a particular damn. But Jen didn't deserve to be on the receiving end of his temper, no matter she had pulled favors to get here, to be sure her *Galway* lad had gotten through all right.

In front of everybody in his shift, where he most of all didn't *want* to be special or made over, but was. The youngest Galway aboard, invited to sit critical boards on a shift that handled the most technical jumps, for reasons even *he* suspected . . . Hell, it wasn't Jen's fault. He was an object of curiosity just being here.

"Damned good job," Ty said, voice from somewhere to his right.

He turned his head carefully. Kate had said *his* numbers were on the curve with hers and Bucklin's. She hadn't said, with Ty's and Jim's, Nav 1.3 and 1.4.

"Kate's impressed. So's JR."

Ty's image doubled, swirled. He swallowed hard, and willed him into one body. "Didn't know I'd done it. Thanks."

"We were all close enough not to fry the old girl," Ty said, self-vindication on a grin.

He was glad to know that.

"Spooks?" Ty asked.

"A little," he said.

"Not unusual," Ty said. "Still get them myself, now and then. One reason Security always backs us up, coming into Pell." He leaned forward to look around Ross. "Thanks, Jen. How was your first time hyped?"

Jen pretended to gag. "I've had more fun."

It took a minute for that to register. "Backup?" he asked Jen, and she lifted her eyebrows.

"You think I'm here just to see a cute spacer-boy puke up his cookies?" She smiled then, that smile he'd swear she used just on him and against which he had zero resistance. "SOP, Ross. We're basically emergency runners with keys to every door. I wanted to be up here, but I didn't ask, precisely because I *don't* have experience, and I'd hate myself if you or anyone else needed help and I was too busy puking up *my* cookies to provide it. It was Fletcher's idea that I take the bridge on this run, *his*, normally, and the fact he suggested it means to me that he and Senior Captain had every confidence in your ability to handle it . . . and be ready to hold *my* hand if I needed it. So we both passed."

"Yeah. Right." He grunted and leaned back, as if it didn't matter one way or another, but when her hand found his, he interlaced their fingers and squeezed lightly before releasing her, because, dammitall, that touch was as painful as her earlier poke.

There was quiet for a time, everybody in slow recovery, with the juice ebbing down. Helm and Nav had been the talkative ones for a while. Then it was everybody else settling in, talking to each other. Med came over general com, asking if anybody was *not* doing all right.

"You all right, Jen?" Ross asked, Jen being the one who was not where she was routinely supposed to be. "You okay?"

"Fine," she said, and beyond his closed eyes, a fingertip very lightly traced his, where it rested on the chair arm. And very quietly: "What y'thinkin', Galway?"

"No more than I have to."

"Truth, Ross."

"Sorry," he said. "Stressed. A bit tense. Fallan. All the others. Trying to run the numbers, figure where they are. Could be all the way to Sol, by now. Wondering if they're still alive. Those jump-points . . . God, they were hellish."

"Figured," she said. Another finger touch. "It's okay, Ross. You've run the sims. You know the points are viable."

"Points don't matter if those Earth Company bastards . . ." He swallowed hard. ". . . took out First-shift and tried to take the ship through themselves."

"Abrezio says they couldn't have the coordinates."

"And they'd never get them out of Fal." Wasn't the first time they'd had this conversation, but damned if it ever got any easier. "Still . . . should be there with them."

"Soon as this stuff wears off, I'm gonna punch you," she said lazily. "You know damn well Fallan was right to throw you out. *We* needed to know what happened, and those EC bastards might have finished breaking your head if you'd stayed."

He took a deep breath, trying hard to ignore the memory of that heavy blow from an EC baton, the blood-blind drift between *Galway*'s emergency exit and *Finity*'s service entrance.

"Must be at least a year station-time now. Can't imagine how the rest of the cousins are doing. Going stir, likely."

"We left sims. They'll be smarter than you, time you get back."

"Hope so." And another breath. Shaky, that one. "Honestly thought I'd blown it," he said.

"Don't be thinking about that," she said. "We're at *Pell*. Beginning of the Beyond. Think about that, spacer lad."

He did. It felt surreal. He'd left the First Stars, and he'd arrived at the beginning of the Beyond.

Where everything changed.

"Lots to show you," Jen said.

"Trees," he said, and she giggled.

Book I   Section iv

Finity was inertial now, en route to Pell Station on an ordinary approach, all sound, all in order—beautiful job from Second-shift Helm, JR thought. People could move about, open lockers, see to duties or pursue their own off-shift business as *Finity* took stock of herself from life-support down to safety checks and start-up in the galley, not to mention starting one massive load of laundry.

JR slid into his chair in his own bridge-side office and found Tom had put a dry coffee packet and a granola bar into the keep-safe. There was hot water for the coffee—synth, instant, and bitter, near the bottom of their supply, but it served. JR stirred the coffee, opened the wrapper on the bar—real grain with synth-flavored fudge—and ate and drank slowly, reacquainting his body with actual food. He'd dropped mass on this trip: a lot of jumps, very little dock time, and hell-for-broke run-outs there and back again. He planned to put on a kilo or two on Pell dockside. He *hoped* to have the chance . . . but the job ahead of him had gotten complicated, way more complicated than the local authority was going to want to hear.

What Pell truly, *truly* didn't want . . . had happened, and *Finity*, at the head of the information wavefront from Alpha, was about to drop that news along with the rest of the black box data.

And since station-time stretched long over the condensed months they'd run . . . there was no knowing yet what ships might have dropped in here from Cyteen-side, and what changes of direction local politics might have taken.

Always a challenge, at this dynamic hub of interstellar trade.

It was a safe run-in, however, so far as operations went, and barring relativistic surprises propagating invisibly between here and the station . . . they could relax. They were in the grip of a generally well-behaved star, headed for a well-regulated station, where the local traffic politely stayed in the ecliptic and the miners operated far from the approach lane. The jump range at stellar zenith was wide and clean, reliably clear of any debris of size. There were no worries such as there had been even at Venture, the Hinder Stars being painfully short of robotic sweepers. Theoretically—they could relax for days. Local law said they had to.

Relax. Eat. Sleep . . . all of which left too damn much time to think about questions which would have no answers until they docked—not to mention those questions they might not have answers to for years.

Madison was captain of record, now, Second-shift being in charge. Com would be busy receiving and sorting the local data stream from the outer-system buoys, bringing the ship records into sync with local conditions, everything from Pell Station's clock to ship arrivals and departures. In a typical merchanter's situation, they'd have a few days running-in, a few days running-out—and a precious week or two at dock, enjoying freedom of movement in a massive structure that, short of something extraordinary, was never going to go up, down, or sideways without warning. Unlike stations locked in their steady, predictable orbits, ships while underway saved themselves with very little care to the safety of the occupants. You got, at most, a blast of the takehold siren, and you grabbed the closest takehold, because you always had one in reach if you were not a fool. That was a condition of life, a subtle awareness any time you were underway and carrying V.

They'd had a fair number of those blasts this trip. Unswept lanes aside, *Finity*, all along her course, had been running fairly hot, there being no witnesses and no traffic on most of the path they'd taken, a route that had involved Hinder Stars stations none but the oldest Neiharts had ever seen. A jaunt to Viking and Mariner and back to Pell was *Finity's* ordinary routine, but some two years ago, station-time, in an unprecedented joint operation, four ships had left Pell for Venture, an operation that would ultimately take them clear to Alpha. Of those four ships, *Finity's End* was the first to return, and when *Finity* linked her black box to Pell Station's computers in a few days, information about that operation would flow—there was no stopping it.

Pell's Stationmaster, however, *could* put at least a temporary hold on the general dissemination of that information—and had to do exactly that. Which request coming from *Finity* was going to raise its own questions.

And that data they needed to put on hold? Explosive news from Alpha, not all of which was in a form the ship's black box could relay. Face-to-face meetings with Pell's Stationmaster, Emilio Konstantin, would be required, along with as much silence in the system as they could manage.

It also made critical their meeting with another ship they hoped to find in this port, a small merchanter named *Estelle*, Quen Family, Cyteen registry.

They knew her schedule, and while nothing involving FTL was ever exact, it was possible *Estelle* might still be here. That was one, though not the only, reason for the massive push to get back here. If they *could* not, if *Estelle* had, in fact, already come and gone, well, that was the way it was: they would have done their best. The sneaker-net might need another set of legs to get the news from Alpha to the Reillys of *Dublin*, but get there it would.

One hoped, sincerely hoped, that *Estelle* would manage to leave them an update from the Beyond, in code, if nothing else there being politics involved: Cyteen and Pell did not have official contact. Given *Finity's* news from Alpha, Pell might need the assurances *Estelle* could give them.

Hell, *he* would be upset, in their place. So much, so very much, depended now on speed of communication.

JR sighed, and began to scroll through the information incoming from Pell Central, routine business . . . ships in system, ships recently arrived, ships recently departed . . .

And there she was:

Estelle. Left system two days ago mainday.

Two friggin' days. Damn it! Missed them by a whole week.

He tapped his desktop, and a red light flashed.

"*JR?*" came back, and JR answered absently, staring at the readout: "Fletch? Are you free?"

"*Problem?*"

"*Estelle's* been here and gone."

"*Well . . . damn,*" Fletcher said.

"She may have left a message for us," JR said. "I'd expect she has. If it's written, it'll probably be in my personal queue. Whatever it is, it is. We can't hurry it or improve it. Or ask it questions. If it's coded, it's probably on Konstantin's desk, waiting for us."

"*If it's good news . . .*"

"Let's hope it is. We've still got our own last two shadows to catch. I'm hoping *Nomad* and *Mumtaz* caught one or the other at Glory and got a signature."

"*Maybe we won't need them.*"

"Maybe." If they were missing any ships from *Dublin's* signature-gathering, or if Cyteen was waffling, absolute unanimity on Pell's side of space could be persuasive, and, damn it all, their two holdout merchanters, *Miriam B* and *Come Lately,* had managed to be inconveniently absent, just left or not expected there, all the way from Pell to Alpha and back.

"*Minor fish,*" Fletch said. "*A creaking liability, as far as repairs go, most likely to be in need, and it's on their own heads. They'll reach some port and sign, or they won't—and end up broke on Glory dockside, but they're hardly worth more search. We tried across five stations and back."*

"I'd still like to be able to tell Emilio it's unanimous."

"It's, for God's sake, Emilio's own brilliant idea. —Hold that thought. On my way."

Ironically, the notion of uniting the merchanter Families as a third power, balanced against Cyteen and Pell, the notion that had sent them kiting off to Alpha, had indeed *originated* with Emilio Konstantin. *If Cyteen gives you grief,* Emilio had said to JR, one late meeting on Pell, *hell, cut them off. The lot of you merchanters can have a party out at Tripoint until they agree to behave.*

Tripoint being a treacherous little triple mass jump-point on the way to Mariner and Viking stations . . . that nobody liked to visit.

They'd been sipping Scotch, he and Emilio, discussing shifting economics and the impact on longhaul trade of the two functioning megaships, *Finity* and Cyteen-built *Dublin.* Those two ships, the prototypes of an unacknowledged technological race between Pell and Cyteen, were a next logical step up in power, carrying capacity, and range. Independently developed, they were nonetheless very similar, extrapolated out of identical technology and constrained by the same fundamental laws of the universe. JR and *Dublin's* John Riley had compared notes more than once, though how honest *Dublin's* captain had been in that exchange of stats was a matter of speculation.

JR knew *he* had hedged *his* numbers.

But which design held the edge would likely never be tested, because no merchanter captain would risk both ship and Family to find out. The reality was, the viability of concept was proven, and that was all that really mattered.

They were two highly specialized ships and thus far, they were only two. Problem was, a handful of megaships thrown willy-nilly into the interstellar economy could wreak havoc on the smaller merchanter Families, and the possibility that Cyteen, with their seemingly endless resources, would make such a move was worrisome to everyone. Not that the Neiharts or *Dublin's* Reillys would begrudge other Families the luxury . . . and the headaches . . . of a megahauler, but the possibility that those ships might be handed over to a Cyteen-born azi crew, cloned-men, machines created with human biology, taking massive amounts of trade away from hardworking Families . . . that would be a problem.

I don't think you need to worry, Emilio had said on that occasion. *At least for now. Cyteen could build merchant ships, but the crews to run them, the* training, probably the programming of azi, with all those attendant problems; and decades to get it all moving—that would be one hell of an effort, even for them.

In point of fact, Cyteen had never made shipping a priority. What, exactly, Cyteen did prioritize was something of a mystery to the rest of humanity. They'd discovered FTL, but for its theoretical interest, for the science rather than trade or even monetary gain. Rather than run the sublight pusher-ships out of business, they'd handed out FTL technology for free. They'd converted pusher-ships to FTL, housed and trained their crews . . . also for free, in return for the Families' promise of impartial service, not even seeking to cut trade off from Pell or make demands regarding routes. That had been a good deal all around, a public relations triumph.

It had also been a cold, calculated deal. And an absolutely brilliant strategic move, as the ships had come with a map of jump-points linking every station . . . except Sol. The lack of jump-points to Sol effectively cut the EC there off from the rest of humanity, give or take the light-speed information Stream and the occasional pusher ship load.

The fact is, Emilio had said that day, over their imported Scotch, *their interests lie elsewhere. Merchanters are more than a convenience to the Carnaths of Cyteen—at least right now. You're a necessity for them to maintain their pace, to build up the population, the industry, the reach, so they can tell Sol go to hell for good and all. That's their dream, you know. Maybe they'll tell Pell the same, someday. But right now they won't.*

Emilio had made a weird kind of sense in that argument, as much as anything that had to do with Cyteen ever made sense. Emilio was right. Cyteen's interests lay elsewhere, once the technological puzzle had been solved.

They need you, Emilio had insisted. *Hell, we need you. So long as you exist and maintain your independence—we don't have Cyteeners coming here, and they don't have Pell crews invading their space. This way, we each have our own bubbles to manage—in peace. Bad things can't happen, that way.*

Of course, it also meant that few people outside the Cyteen sphere of influence ever really encountered the enigmatic azi. According to the merchanters who dealt with them on a regular basis, there was little to differentiate them from born-men, other than mathematical infallibility, speed with answers, inability to appreciate jokes, and an annoying tendency to extreme good looks.

According to rumor, Olga Emory, the most notorious of Cyteen's geneset manipulators, did like her eye candy.

"If I were you," Emilio's final observation, in retrospect, was disturbingly prophetic: "I think I'd be more worried about Sol finding their own way out *of their sub-light bubble and owing no one. The EC isn't into sharing, especially where there's profit to be made. They've been hungry for a real return on their investment for a very long time. And we've annoyed them."*

It was indeed a now overriding concern. In the opinion of the EC, every station ever built was the offshoot of the ships and station cores the EC had built at Sol centuries ago and pushed out to the Hinder Stars. In the EC mind, the spacers and stationers were all just EC employees. If stationers, impatient with answers that took decades to get—and then made no sense— found their own solutions in the interim, well, stationers were simply displaying the cleverness for which they'd been hired in the first place. Any innovations stationers made were on company time, and therefore company property.

God . . . *that* was a notion that would never fly out here. Hope, *hope* that Abrezio could help finesse that initial contact, when and if it came.

Because as it turned out, the threat to trade, as they'd found out at Alpha, might be imminent—-and if that was the case, the Earth Company was coming. *Maybe someday* had become very possibly tomorrow.

When *Finity,* along with *Little Bear, Mumtaz,* and *Nomad,* had headed out to Alpha, first and oldest of all star-stations, their sole intent had been to talk to other ship-Families regarding a long overdue attempt to organize— to create what amounted to an insurance company funded by merchanters, for the protection of merchanters and merchanter interests. The idea had been to help all merchant ships handle the shifting economics of FTL trade, a shift that had disproportionately hurt the Hinder Stars, but to which no ship running was immune. Protections included sanctity of the routes themselves. A major part of the agreement was that *only* Family ships could carry cargo.

Meanwhile, a serious challenge to that agreement had been under construction at Alpha for over two decades, station-time.

If it hadn't been for the Earth Company's attempt to copy *Finity's End* from stolen plans, *Finity* might well have left the Alpha run to *Little Bear* and the others, but when they discovered at Venture that the EC's copyship, one *Rights of Man,* had made . . . and aborted . . . a test jump, the Neiharts had decided to go to Alpha and see firsthand what was going on.

They had thought, back when the plans were stolen, they knew what the EC intended to do with their megaship. There had been a theory floating about—still was—that a megaship's jump capacity could top 7 lights, if running empty, and if true, that would indeed get Sol, at about 6 lights from Alpha, out of their isolation.

He could attest it was *not* true, but that hope might well have prompted the EC to steal the plans and build that ship. But between cost overruns and that aborted test jump, that hope was rapidly dwindling when *Finity* arrived and turned Alpha Station on its ear.

The possibility of the EC eventually finding *some* viable FTL route to some star in its highly cluttered region had been a given, requiring only the discovery of intermediary jump-points. Alpha was closest. Alpha-based merchanters had long dreamed of that day. They saw such a discovery as their own salvation—and exclusive control of exotic Sol trade as their just reward for keeping the Hinder Stars alive all these years. Outside the Hinder Stars, however, the arrival of the EC at FTL speeds would be greeted with far less joy. The influx of luxury goods would be welcome, but the EC getting involved in trade was a direct threat to the merchanters, and the EC arriving with EC notions of station ownership was equally unwelcome to the stations. That looming possibility had been no small impetus to the effort to organize.

While Cyteen's founders headed off to harvest yet another viable planet, populate it with birthing labs, and invent FTL . . . competition and individuality had taken over in the rest of the star-stations. Now, every star-station had its own rules, every Family on every ship had its own unique culture and in many cases, their own language. None of them, not even Alpha . . . now . . . would willingly bend again to the EC's ancient notions of ownership.

The flip side of that resistance was that no single station or ship could fight EC tactics on their own . . . which gave the fledgling Alliance a whole new importance.

The specter of the EC horning in on FTL trade had been bad enough, but the situation *Finity* had discovered at Alpha proved far more ominous. The moment *Finity*'s crew laid eyes on *The Rights of Man,* parked in royal isolation on Alpha's A-mast, they'd known they weren't looking at a cargo hauler. Her exact purpose became clear once *Finity* docked and began recruiting merchanters to the Alliance. The EC rep in charge of the *Rights* project, one Andrew Cruz, objected, slammed down martial law on Alpha Station, and tried, twice, to force a look aboard *Finity*, the working version of his failing copy.

The EC, they'd realized, was building *Rights* not for trade, but for transporting personnel: EC Enforcers and their weaponry, sending them up the chain of stars—Alpha-to-Bryant's-to-Venture-to-Pell.

Control. Regimented control.

Taking advantage of the conflict on his own dockside, Alpha Stationmaster Ben Abrezio—who had seen the *Rights* project rob his station of necessary supplies for two decades—had made his own countermove. Using information he'd sat on for years—coordinates for jump-points on the longed-for FTL route to Sol—he'd asked their best local ship, *Galway,* to attempt that route and prove its viability. If they succeeded, fame, fortune . . . and a chance to convince the EC to change tactics. If they failed, well, Senior Captain Niall Monahan had signed with the Alliance, had committed his ship to keeping Alpha independent, and damned if the Alliance wouldn't see the Monahans were taken care of, if *Galway* didn't make it home.

Which possibility loomed painfully large very fast. When *Galway,* with only her First-shift crew aboard—a skeleton crew—had pulled out of dock, Cruz, having guessed the plan and having no crew capable of piloting a jump-ship, had been waiting aboard with an Enforcer squad. Cruz had seized *Galway* at gunpoint and left for Sol, intending to return to Alpha in absolute glory, himself the hero of the EC and a kingpin of the new EC trade loop.

Of the Monahans aboard, *one* had gotten clear to warn Alpha what had happened . . .

Young Ross Monahan, their youngest Navigator . . . the kid who'd just *felt* the star. A kid in limbo . . . as were they all until the fate of *Galway* came clear.

So much, so very much, depended on who was in control of *Galway* when and if the ship ever got to Sol. It was possible that the jump-points they thought they had would not prove out . . . and the ship and all aboard could be lost, which could leave the whole Beyond back where they had been before, with Sol trapped in its isolation, and with every other star-station fired up with new and major grievances against the EC.

If, however, those mass-points proved viable; and if *Galway* got through . . . So much depended on who was at her helm.

If Cruz survived despite Niall Monahan's intent to incapacitate the inexperienced intruders, if Cruz retained control and survived the jumps despite all odds . . .

If all that happened, all bets were off. The Monahans would be floating in space and Cruz would hand the EC everything they needed. The EC knew how to build jump-ships, could, for all anyone knew, have ships waiting for jump-points at which to aim them. They would bring officials demanding to take charge, the way they had back in the days when only pushers plied the star-routes . . . bringing Enforcers to back up their demands. The EC would try to lay down rules and make decisions the way they'd made them back when they had controlled the economy, but they'd arrive with no comprehension of what a complex, potentially dangerous situation they were trying to take over.

If on the other hand, the Monahans won back control of *Galway* . . . if Cruz and his minions were incapacitated by the guts-puking jump-exits

Fallan had promised to give them, they'd be overwhelmed by functioning Monahans and stuck in lockup somewhere chilly and uncomfortable for the duration. Once they arrived at Sol, the Monahans would demand agreements—in writing—before any numbers were exchanged. They'd bring a small group of EC folk back with them and use a gentle return voyage to educate them to the realities of life in the FTL universe.

The Monahans could be a charming lot, given half a chance.

But they had no way of knowing which scenario had won. Niall Monahan had sworn to take time at those two jumps to prudently map the systems ahead. And if *Galway* was lost, for whatever reason, and never arrived? The coordinates would still get to Sol. Stationmaster Ben Abrezio had transmitted them to Sol, for good or ill, to arrive there in six years, light-speed. What the EC did at that point, possibly having built ships, but having no trained crew and no assurance of viability . . . no one could foretell: but in that third case, they could be looking at a decade or more, if ever, before they had to worry about the EC.

He hoped, they all hoped, for a safe return of *Galway* under Niall's hand in, oh, another couple of years, station time.

So, yes, the automatic download of logged information—which would include *Galway*'s Sol-bound venture . . . and the official report of Cruz's hijacking of the ship—was potentially explosive, and the Pell Stationmaster absolutely needed to hold it secret for a bit. At least long enough for said Stationmaster to prepare the populace for deeply disturbing news.

JR did not envy Emilio that bit of finessing. Too much news too soon could breed its own problems. The fact was, even at FTL speeds, it would be years, by stationer reckoning, before the EC came anywhere near Pell's docks. They had time to prepare . . . if they were smart enough.

The Neiharts' own concept of an empowered merchanters' organization had, unexpectedly, become a whole lot broader issue than they had thought they had when they'd headed out to Alpha. Broader, and far more imperative.

They'd managed, with stationmaster Abrezio's help, to put the EC at Alpha on hold, at least for now. Cruz and his hand-picked crew were off to Ireland (as their determinedly optimistic Monahans put it) and as of *Finity's* departure from Alpha, most of the Enforcers and Cruz's second-in-command, Enzio Hewitt, were stranded off Alpha Station in a stalled-out *Rights of Man*. Do the man credit, Ben Abrezio was working to get his station in order in hopes of meeting the incoming EC with something approaching a stable economy and with his people solidly behind him.

Part of *Finity's* job here at Pell—possibly the hardest part—was to convince Emilio to release the cargo vital to that resurrection, never mind Alpha could by no means cover the cost . . . yet.

Emilio was a Pell stationer, many generations a Pell stationer, descended from one of the original builders, with a Pell stationer's view of the universe—namely that the star-stations rightfully ruled everything within their star's gravity well, including the occasional planet and all between . . . to hell with the EC.

But in the spirit of keeping the goods flowing, and evening out the distribution of metals, with which Tau Ceti was not greatly blessed, and of foodstuffs, which Tau Ceti produced in quantity—the Konstantins of Pell were decidedly in favor of ships going and coming frequently to all the star-stations, those founded by the Earth Company, those founded by Pell, and those founded by that *other* outcome of a hijacked station core, Cyteen.

The ship-Families were decidedly in favor of Cyteen trade, too, and of keeping Family-run ships in the black. No one in the Beyond argued with the merchant ships that kept goods moving from points of abundance to stations in need.

And should any government, station or planetary, try to screw all that up . . .

Cut them off. Hold a party at Tripoint . . .

The moment he'd heard Emilio's suggestion, only half in jest, JR had sensed the possibilities. It *could* work . . . but only if every merchanter moving agreed to such a ban. And that took organization.

Difficult when the necessary signatories were typically lights years apart.

But the idea had taken root, a major behind-closed-doors topic at every station from Pell to Cyteen. Fortunately, the Cyteen-side megahauler, *Dublin*, agreed immediately. Without *Finity's* and *Dublin's* initial financial input, the idea was doomed from the start. Together, JR and John Reilly had hashed out certain important principles.

They'd kept the language simple, the goals clear and unequivocal.

What was the Families' overriding interest? The same as it had ever been: ships. Their ships.

And corollary to that priority: survival. Which meant maintenance to a standard.

Square dealing where it came to trade.

Finally—and the principle most likely to meet resistance from the EC—immunity from interference on ships from anything that sat locked in orbit—station, moon, or planet. That meant *no* unauthorized boarding, *no* internal inspections of ships or cargo in hold, and *no* detention of crew excepting on felony charges.

It was a good plan. Convincing ships to sign had its challenges. But they'd managed, all but two ships and maybe one station. If *Dublin* had had similar success, or better . . . God, they might just make it work, might just have it all in place *before* Sol turned up on Alpha's doorstep.

So here they were, fastest of all available ships, to spread the word to the beyond. *Little Bear* was running a vital part back to Alpha, and *Mumtaz* and *Nomad* were headed to poor dwindling Glory Station with some vital supply. They hoped to sign the station and, of somewhat greater importance, the final two Hinder Stars ships, *Miriam B* and *Come Lately.*

The coffee grew cold, the cup too long in hand. Eyes saw things not present. People. Events. Situations.

They were home, such home as *Finity* had. They would dock at what was by far the most luxurious station they knew. Overtaxed bodies and minds would get a sorely needed chance to slow down, hyped nerves would adjust to Pell's scale of things, and eat, sleep, recover. Things as simple and as ultimately necessary as that. The kids aboard—there always were—could play and antic about. Juniors could resume duties.

Himself . . . well, he'd know a lot more once he could access a message from *Estelle*. That most of the Family ships on Cyteen's routes would sign was almost a given, and John Reilly of *Dublin* had been confident of getting Cyteen's cooperation. But then John Reilly was . . . well . . . John Reilly. He was also a slick-tongued bastard, and knew the Carnaths and Emorys personally. But he had his own worries.

A red light flashed above the door. *"JR?"*

"C'mon in, Fletch," JR said into the com.

Fletcher came in, dropped his lanky frame into the interview chair, and tilted his head in that way that asked a question without asking it.

"I wish I knew. Won't get a message until linkup. But the fact they've been and gone . . . one has to assume *Dublin* finished ahead of schedule."

"John Reilly wouldn't give up until Cyteen agreed," Fletch said. "He's good at politics."

"I hope you're right." JR sipped his synth coffee, and Fletcher, with an envious glance, pushed himself to his feet to fetch his own cup.

"Obviously easier if *Dublin* got everyone," Fletcher said, taking the cup back to his chair, "but we have enough signatures as is to make our point and draw in any holdouts. Stations giving preferential treatment to Alliance ships will change minds in a hurry. And since *we* were able to get the Hinder Stars—the Deep Beyond will feel compelled to match us. Cyteen might hedge, but there's history, and they aren't that eager to cut ties; I think

Emilio was dead-on there. Trust John Reilly to convince the Carnaths." He took a cautious sip, hissed, and blew across the top to cool it. "What would we do without crazy relatives? Reilly has Carnaths. Alpha has Sol. We deal with Pell. Pell deals with Alpha *and* Cyteen. At least Konstantin's not crazy. He's a stationer through and through, but he's on our side."

"First on my list is to talk with him."

"Are you going to tell him everything?"

"We have to," JR said. "Our secrets have come close to ruining us. This time we have to lay it on the table."

"Do I get to come?"

"You. Madison . . . but I might ask you to sit outside to start. I think Emilio might say things in private he wouldn't say with witnesses. Maybe consider things he wouldn't like to consider in front of witnesses. I'm going to try to get him without his aides."

"Good luck with that."

"If you two arrive with me, but voluntarily stay out of his office, I think I can do it."

Fletch dipped his chin. "What's our run-in time?"

"Five days, four hours, and fourteen minutes."

"Wish we could fast track. I'm anxious for this one."

"So am I," JR said, "but let's not set Pell on edge any more than we have to. We'll have queries from Commerce, but we won't take on cargo until we know which way we're headed, which I hope is back to Venture with that load we promised Abrezio. I *hope* there's nothing from *Estelle* to worry us. But we're making no commitments in any direction until we know more. Meanwhile soon as we're near realtime in the local feed, I'll send Konstantin a coded request for an exception on *Finity's* feed, get him to hold it until we've had a chance to discuss what's in it. There's information in that feed *he* won't want hitting the station until after he's had a chance to prep the stationers. I'd send the request now, but there's no need for him to worry before he has to."

"I'm happy with that," Fletcher said, downed two gulps of coffee and started to get up, then changed his mind. "Regular rules on this one, upcoming? If we're going to have to restrict everybody, I want to tell them early, before they build up expectations."

"I don't look for any problems dockside. Shore time for everybody. Even the junior-juniors. The only caveat is keep coms on receive, no exceptions, no off hours, and read your messages as they come in. Everybody."

"I'll put out the bulletin," Fletcher said.

"Jen showed up in the lounge."

"Sorry about that. Had her do post-jump. My suggestion, not hers."

JR shrugged. "She had to start sometime. Hyped wake-up is part of your job. Might as well start her now when she's got something else to think about."

"My thoughts, too. Fact is, she's worried about young Monahan."

"Reason?"

"Nerves, she said."

"His or hers?"

"Hers," Fletch said, "about his."

"First jump to a G-class. Reason enough," JR said. "I'm watching him, too. And she's good at teasing him out of his head. He tends to overthink everything."

"Something *you* know nothing about," Fletch said with a grin, and JR snorted.

"Part of *my* job, cousin. But this lad . . . he's got a load on him. Part of him I'm sure is with *Galway*. He was fully prepared to risk his life along with the rest of their First-shift crew, and instead, he finds himself living a life of luxury he's never known before. The wait for news of *Galway*'s fate is particularly hard on him. But that situation with Jen is another part of the load. I can't imagine what it's like to have that kind of personal tie. Who among us has ever had more than a handful of days in the grip of that chemistry? Things have gotten stranger and harder for him, the further he travels from Alpha. Skating the points to get here—that's something *Galway* just wouldn't do. But it might have spooked him. And we hit a wavefront, don't know if you noticed, but we did."

Fletch winced. "I noticed. Lose it, did he?"

"His input matched Kate's."

Fletch's mouth opened, shut, then: "Shit all."

JR nodded. "If he survives the next few years, he'll be a Family treasure."

"The Galways certainly watch out for him."

"I'm sure they do. Like a little brother. He's their youngest. In love. And confused. Jen and I have talked on the matter, but between you and me, she's young, in love, and confused, too."

"Damn." Fletch gave a reluctant shrug. "We *could* hold all the Galways aboard. But we'd better make it clear before too much longer."

"God, no. More than Jen would complain, and she's been hyping the wonders of Pell, since before we left Alpha. I'm sure there are no fools among them. And Ross has been steady thus far. But I do want her right with him day and dark, I want her to tell us where they bunk, where they're going, and when they get back. And I don't want her taking him too far from other Finitys. If any other Galways try to go off on their own, I want somebody with them. I don't want them to feel watched, but they don't know the customs here, they *know* too damn much, and they can reference places we've been that we really don't want referenced yet. Sorry to mess up your leave, Fletch. It's been a godawful run."

"We can do that," Fletcher said. "Arcades. Bars. Restaurants. We can get volunteers. No problem."

Book I	Section v

"I wish First-shift was handling docking," Ross said, breaking another long silence.

Jen blinked at him. "No you don't. Trust me."

"You sayin' Jim B can't handle it?"

"Only sayin' Vickie's the best. Wouldn't want to scare the newbies." She winked and closed her eyes again.

"You're so full of it." He closed his own eyes. "Still . . . never seen a ring-docking. Might be a little curious."

"I can get you a pass to watch."

Damn. He should have known she'd take it as a request. Still . . . tempting. So tempting. He didn't like to pull privilege on *Finity*. He was only a passenger, in one sense. The Finitys gave the Galways they were training most anything they asked for, and it was not pity—it was hospitality, and he understood that.

He just wasn't inclined to ask for it.

But, damn, he so wanted to see that operation. And it was, technically speaking, one of the major changes *Galway* could face in the future . . .

"It's no problem, Ross. Really. Give Vickie a chance to show off and all." Resistance wilted.

"Yeah," he said. "Yeah. I'd like that." And he plunged ahead. "All us Galways would. If only on vid. We don't need to be underfoot."

"I'll work on it," Jen said. Jen, who had no compunction whatsoever about calling in favor points. Or making them up on the fly. Jen was a fixer, par excellence. The sort who could make both sides feel they won. And she was smart. And on his side, all through this whole voyage.

"Thanks," he said and reached for her hand, eyes still closed, just knowing, somehow, where it was. She took it, gave a little squeeze, and relaxed without quite letting go.

She was good, really good, at keeping him from taking life too seriously. He was going to miss her, *really* miss her, when—

He stopped that thought cold. Parting from *Finity* was not only a given, it was the future he very much wanted. He was here, along with eight other Monahans, at Senior Captain's invitation. His *job* right now was to take advantage of the opportunity JR Neihart had given him, to absorb everything a ship like *Finity*, one of the two largest ships ever built, could show him over the next few months or even years. Things like the ring docking which, with luck, *Galway* would one day get a chance to employ. His *job* was learning, keeping sharp, while the majority of the Monahans necessarily waited back on Alpha Station, for Niall and Fallan . . . and the rest of First-shift . . . to bring *Galway* home.

It was hard, really hard, to realize, coming out of every jump, that it was months more, station-time, that *Galway* had been gone. Back on Alpha, his cousins and aunts and uncles, and nieces and nephews . . . they'd all be checking days off on a calendar. God . . . he couldn't imagine. Over a year now. He'd never, *ever* spent so long away from a ship, let alone without jumping.

To a point, the longer *Galway* was gone, the better, because Niall had promised JR to delay as long as he could, to give the fledgling Merchanter Alliance time to prepare. But the success of their mission wasn't a given, and there was no way to know until *Galway* broke triumphantly into Alpha system. If Niall and Fallan didn't show this year or the next or the next, they'd all count themselves lucky, but if that absence continued much longer, the Galways would be down to facing the grim possibility that they had lost not only the ship, but the people that were the heart and soul of *Galway*.

Life would go on, if that were the case. *Galway*'s name would live, even if it came to the building of a new *Galway*, at Venture. *JR* had promised. There'd be a new ship . . . and a new generation to rekindle that heart and soul.

He was here to hold JR Neihart to that promise and secure the Monahans' future.

"Chilly." Jen's voice pulled him out of that pit of concern and near-overwhelming responsibility. She'd tucked her arms around her ribs, trying to warm her hands. He reached for the nearest, discovered it no longer hurt to touch, and sandwiched it between his own.

"Food?"

"Not yet. Just got the fourth packet down. 'Bout to fall asleep."

"Best not to, until your stomach settles." Which she knew as well as he did, but she just nodded.

"Mmm. Just thinking about my list. All the things you've got to see on Pell. Places we've got to eat. Things we've got to do."

"Looking forward to it," he said, just a touch mechanically. Most of him *was* looking forward to it, but a part of him was a little scared. So much new, coming so fast. So many expectations. A lifetime of wild stories about this place, and now theoretical someday had arrived. Would it live up to expectations? What if it did? Could he go back to his life . . . before . . . without regrets?

Dammit, he chastised himself, don't go there.

Galway was Alpha's hope. *Galway* and the Neiharts' Merchanters' Alliance. *Galway*'s mission to Sol, to prove a newly discovered FTL route Sol *could* take, was Alpha's best hope of bringing the First Stars into the modern interstellar trade . . . *if* Sol didn't take that new route and try to monopolize the potentially lucrative Sol trade, using their own ships, denying that opportunity to the ships that had remained loyal despite Sol's decades of neglect.

The Merchanters' Alliance was key to keep that from happening: a still-solidifying agreement that united merchanters large and small into one potent force, with stations agreeing to trade only with Alliance ships. If it held, if the stations agreed, it was hope, where hope had lately seemed very thin for the oldest merchanter Families, running little ships, old ships, serving the stations left behind. If it held—they could present a united front to Sol . . . a future of trade benefitting everyone.

If that future held . . . if that message their *Galway* carried got a positive response out of Sol, this might be the Monahans' first visit to Pell . . . but it wouldn't be their last. *Galway* could be trading here, in the not-so-distant future, with *all* her crew aboard, right alongside *Finity's End* and *Little Bear* and *Mumtaz* and all the rest.

And Jen would be waiting.

Lower decks, where the Galways bunked, were the dropdown row where bridge crew and trainees berthed, accessible by step-lift, easy enough, Jen thought, if you weren't coming down off hype, which she was, and hype and a stint of mind-jarring duty, which Ross was. It was a ride down the little lift-belt, one foot on, and a handhold, then a hike to Ross's cabin, and inside. . . .

Inside, against the door, they hugged clumsily, and bumped foreheads in a wordless exhaustion, let hands drift down, interlocked.

"Stay or go," Ross muttered. "I'm good for nothing. Hype's running out."

"Mine, too." She tipped her head back. Lips met lips, energy lacking. She gave up and just leaned against him, arms around his waist, content just to stand there a moment.

"Are you all right?" he asked, a hint of worry in his voice.

"I'm fine." She squeezed him and rubbed her cheek against his chest. "Just not used to this stuff."

Which was only partially true. If she were honest with herself, it was more than just the hype that made her content to stay right where she was . . . maybe forever. She wanted him so bad, didn't want to take him back to Alpha and leave him for a ship that may or may not return, and even if it did, would probably jump at the chance to dominate the Sol import trade. The Monahans would be fools not to.

Which might mean . . . never seeing him again, or maybe, like Ross's Fallan and *Finity's* Fourth Captain, Mum, not meet again until they were old. Really old. Forever was a scary thought . . . a prospect of losing everything as well as gaining. Her heart took up a panic beat that wasn't the drug, wasn't just being here, wasn't just the attraction they'd celebrated, oh, way many times. It was the thought of forever. And never never after.

"Easier if you have a job to do," Ross said, still talking about the hype. "You wake up fast to do a job up there. All you had was me. No emergency."

"I *had* a job," she said, and pushed herself away. "It was time for me to learn, and Fletcher wants to put me on the regular schedule now. *You* were an excuse. Fletcher had doubts. Was worried about you. I *knew* you'd make it all right. Knew you would."

"Knew more than I did, then."

"'Course I did." She put on a grin, took a step back . . . a knee gave, and he caught her elbow, held her steady until she could trust her legs again.

"Going to make it to your cabin?" he asked. Hers was downspin of here, two sections removed.

"Think so," she said, gave her head a little shake then wished she hadn't. "Stuff's way wicked."

"How much did you take? You *do* know you don't keep squeezing that stuff."

"I'm all right. Nasty stuff."

"Debt comes due," he said. "Keeps us sane, at least. Long enough to react."

She stared up at him, giving her eyes a reason to focus, felt his quiet calm replace the churning in her gut. He was funny that way. He seemed so lost at times, desperate in his desire to do his job right—never shaking that guilt at leaving his Family behind. She'd heard him once or twice recording his ongoing account to his mentor Fallan, who was *on* that ship taking that never-before jump-route to Sol—soulful things he'd said, talking to the man who'd brought him up and trained him. He poured out his troubles to someone absent—but *he* was the emotional touchstone for all the Galways, the youngest of them, the hero of *Galway*'s report to *Finity*. Everyone close to him . . . herself included . . . knew what a heart he had. Uncle-captain said she was good for Ross. She had news for Uncle-captain, sir: Ross was good for her, too. And as a Navigator, well, it seemed he was pretty damn good at that, too.

And she was good as drunk. Hype was running down. Suddenly. Spectacularly. She looked up at him. "You ever—want—to see what's up there? In hyperspace?"

"Idea comes to me sometimes," he said, and gave a lazy grin, eyes drifting to half mast. Green eyes, he had. He said blue. "Used to, anyway. Then Fallan told me about this guy he knew who did that. Told me what he saw. Don't want any of that, nope, nope, nope."

She waited. And when he failed to elaborate, eyes shut . . . she poked him. "So?"

Eyes blinked open. "Said it was hoses and pipes." The grin froze, and Ross gave a little shudder. "Winding all over, only alive."

"You're having me on."

"Hoses and pipes. God's truth. Said he just *knew* you could go down them and not come out." Another shudder, all over. "Sheez! Not something I want to have in my head, going to sleep."

"Fallan was having *you* on." The old man had a wicked sense of humor, she'd met it head-on herself at Alpha.

"Maybe he was." But Ross didn't sound convinced. "Pipes to everywhere, maybe, if you didn't come down from jump."

"God, what an imagination. Think about this instead." She caught his face for a second kiss on the lips, light but letting it linger, fought the urge to make it more. "Go 'way."

"It's my cabin." But for a split second, his eyes said he *wasn't* quite sure.

"Technicalities," she said with a grin, knowing that his hold on whereabouts-and-when reflected that very desperate hold on reality so vital to Nav. Fletcher had warned her about it, told her never to mess with it, and she'd seen the truth in that firsthand, more than once since Alpha. He'd had a few memory lapses back at Alpha, in the days just following his head injury, still had flash-backs to his desperate escape from *Galway* to *Finity*, and part of her job of watching him, so Fletcher and Uncle Jim insisted, included helping him steady down and regain his confidence. Something she'd do, job or no job. She was to report any serious doubt. She had *never* had that.

"You staying?"

"I'm going. We're in system transit and unlike you, *I'm* on call now and I have to haul myself out of this and function for the rest of the watch. See you. Soon."

She slipped outside and shut the door, then walked, mostly without staggering, two sections on, to her own quarters.

A message was waiting for her, green dot on the wall display.

Fletcher.

Damn. She'd missed the beeper. Had it in her jacket pocket, not on her wrist. The see-me call had a star for *text attached,* and she hauled out her com.

Re your question: it's a go for station leave, but keep Monahans together and safe. Particularly Ross.

Why, damn it, single out Ross? And she would have asked Fletcher that, if the message had ended there, which it didn't, Fletcher not being one to give arbitrary orders. It went on: *Precaution, not judgment. Ross is self-starting, we know that. He took action back at Alpha. Remember the raid in the bar. Doesn't start things, but he's Nav and he's fast. He's juniormost, and the Galways protect him for what he is and what he did. He carries personal trauma from what happened at Alpha. You reported that yourself. And he doesn't know the culture here. Don't let him play the hero, especially not to protect you—or his cousins. Get between him and trouble if he walks into it.*

That seemed silly at first, until she thought of the antics to which some of the Beyonder Families were inclined, little pushes she was more than accustomed to handling, but which might head straight for the Galways.

Here's the issue. We won't ask the Galways to wear Finity *colors. That's too much. But the Galway patches will rouse curiosity and they can't satisfy it beyond saying they're taking a lift to their own ship and, no, they're not from Cyteen space. They're free to say Venture registry, but I'd really, really hope you'd divert the conversation away from port of origin in one of your very clever ways. Senior Captain is relying on you to keep them entertained and away from too much contact with locals. Backup won't be too far, but please don't spoil anybody's docktime by needing it. Senior Captain is relying on you, Jenny.*

God. Only Fletcher and Senior Captain-Uncle-sir needled her with *Jenny*, Fletcher being Uncle's closest friend and an almost-uncle too.

She leaned against the wall, punched buttons and dictated, to Fletcher: *Received your message, sir. Understood. Shore leave. Nine people to watch. Unlimited budget. I'll manage. Hank expressed intentions to help guide, and nobody messes with him.*

Hank . . . Twofer, fellow Security, came by his nickname honestly, and not an ounce of it was fat.

No need to check out security kit for Pell . . . local law saw to things. She was just a guide. Hard duty that was going to be, guiding the Galways through the attractions of Pell. Getting them back undamaged.

But it *was* an official duty. She'd wear her arm-band, she'd go that official, to help Fletcher keep up with the group's movements. The arm-band had a service locator and universal id, so she'd be treated as official by Pell's own security, who were trained police, and could request help keeping a Situation under control. She was oddly a little embarrassed about the idea of swaggering about Pell with it, when she wasn't licensed to arrest anybody and wasn't certified for weapons. Worse, where a lot of the people they were likely to encounter at her favorite hangouts . . . were likely to recognize her.

Thanks to the crazy EC enforcers at Alpha, Fletcher had been pushing her to take the tests, while they were here. A Pell weapons certification would transfer to most other stations. Fletcher and his number two, Parton, were certified, but at Alpha, by local regs, ship's security hadn't been able to carry anything. Not so much as a taser. Stationmaster Abrezio, anticipating the potential problems that could be coming in from Sol, had been working at getting that regulation changed, when they'd left.

It was just . . . weird . . . that she had to be thinking of fast-tracking her certification—damn the EC anyway. She'd declared officially for Security

years ago; had been Fletcher's unofficial assistant almost from the start . . .
mostly because Fletcher hated paperwork. On board *Finity*, security meant
tracking down some junior-junior initiation prank down in the deep of the
ring—she'd done that. Stationside could get a bit more exciting, answering a
call to haul a cousin back to the ship, or doing a little trade espionage to
discover what some other ship was offering, or what a local shop could use.
She liked people, liked talking about their products, and knowing what different stations produced and how—meant knowing options to offer. Then
there was inviting some local drunk trying to access the ramp to leave. No,
fella, no access here, this is a ship, not a bar. That was a joy yet to come.

At Alpha, EC Enforcers had swaggered about with lethals she hadn't
even recognized at first sight—because . . . who was going to need stuff like
that? It was not as if a criminal was going to *escape*. It was hard vacuum
outside the walls of a ship or a station. There was always time to find them
without endangering everyone around you.

And what happened to the Monahans aboard their own ship . . . that was
downright scary. Overnight, Security had gained a whole new meaning.

So had the need to counter that kind of threat. Fletcher and Security
number two, Parton, were licensed for everything *Finity* had, taser, needler,
pellet. Twofer was licensed for the first two. Ever since Alpha, at Fletcher's
request, she'd been working seriously on level ones and twos, prepping for
those certifications here at Pell. She had the written exam down pat—that
was the hardest part, in her opinion—and Fletcher had told her he'd arrange for her to take the tests during their layover. Not that a taser was much
use against Enforcers carrying lethals, but it was a statement, rightly applied.

For this stay, however, she would at least have the arm-band, and she
shouldn't feel it was pretentious. Its locator meant that wherever she was,
Finity could find her and so could Pell Security. And if she had to track
down somebody, and had to get cooperation out of random strangers, there
it was in plain letters, *Finity's End Security*. So people would know she had
authority. The Galways wouldn't give her trouble intentionally, but she didn't
want any of them to stray off into it. There were a few places on Pell you
could get into trouble—she'd heard about them, at least. Uncle-Captain
would have a word if any Finitys went visiting there. But *they* would know
better. Coming from where they did—

—well, coming from where they did, the Galways could probably handle
the rough spots of Pell better than some of the subtler problems they might
encounter, and do it with gusto. But that wasn't among the experiences she
wanted to give them on Pell.

Tests. She really hated tests. But she needed to make time for that in all the fun there was to be had. She had some few days before docking: time to do a little crash study. She could pull up the manuals now, but her eyes were getting heavy.

Hype's all run out and I'm wasted. Ross is tucked in his space. I'm in mine. All snug and accounted-for. Second-shift's up. No duty til supper. Do it tomorrow.

She acknowledged Fletcher's message: *Got it. Sounds great. Looking forward to it*—pushed send, then started to pull off her clothes, casting a slightly sleep-fuzzed eye toward her bunk. Clean sheets, turned down and immaculate—with a little cutout paper tree silhouette tucked under the pillow strap, that was not, she was certain, housekeeping's idea.

Trees. Pell and trees. Her promise.

Her thoughts turned to a lazy kiss, an easy-on-the-eyes *Galway* navigator, and endless hyperspace tubes . . .

Sometimes her job was easier than others.

Book I   Section vii

Bed. Bed was good. Lie flat. Let the adrenaline ebb down. Later for Jen. Lots of time for Jen. She was going to show him Pell. They all were going to see Pell.

Pell was just another station. With trees, yes, but . . . Ross wondered . . . could anything the station offered compare with what he'd sensed today, in those moments teetering on the edge of hyperspace?

What he felt, even now, if he gave in to it? That feeling, that awareness changed everything he knew. About himself. About the profession he'd chosen.

"Memo," he said to the recorder. "Fallan. Add to."

"Adding to: Fallan," the recorder said.

"Fal, sir, just back from my shift. And hype's fading. We're just in at Pell. At Tau Ceti. And I felt it. I swear I felt it. Never felt Barnard's, nor Kreuger or 61 Cyg, but I felt it here, oh, my God, Fal. I could almost see it through the hull, white-hot and huge and outputting—output I could feel, and a wave—big one—right off the Ardaman.

"What are the chances? We skate through cranky, touchy little reds one after the other and the stable G-class hands us *that* on entry. We were hot. Godawful hot. We'd skated the points between Venture and Pell. Never calc'ed anything like it. But we couldn't have caused it. Scared hell out of me, I'll tell you.

"But I still input, I did that, and Kate says I was right on. So 'on' I couldn't see my line. But she said hers was on top of it, and hers took priority, of course."

Deep breath. Remembering it, eyes shut.

"I don't know whether I'm still feeling it or remembering feeling it. I was so stupid I froze, Fal, I absolutely froze on first dump, and if I'd been sitting Kate's seat, God knows where we'd have dropped, that I know. Coming down off the hype, now, shaky as hell, a little sick at my stomach. I guess you can tell by my voice. I've got something to make up for on that blown dump. A lot to make up for.

"I try to do you proud, Fal, I really do try. I guess it was kind of a mixed bag this run. Maybe that's useful—so I can't say to myself, Self, you could take charge, you're that good already. Now I have to say, Fool, you were still looking around when you should have been acting, so don't get all high on the freak moment you felt the star.

"I don't know, Fallan. I can't say it was pure guesswork. But it was a thorough spookout. Can't have been that clear-headed in the calc' either, can I? Anyway, we're at Pell now, safe and sure. And I haven't seen the station yet. Just the schematics. I'm looking forward to it.

"But it's weird, Fal. Remember Pru saying she regretted drinking good wine, the once, because it would spoil all the wine she'd enjoy from then on? But I thought, at the time, I'd rather try it . . . just once. Now . . . I'm not sure what side I'm on—whether I'm looking forward to Pell or scared stiff of it. Really don't want the highlight of my whole life to come before I'm thirty."

He was starting to drift, losing his train of thought, scary slide toward a deep dark with a blazing sun trying to suck them down.

It was all right, though. He was in his own bed, flat on his back, job done. He could slide all the way down now. Second-shift was at the controls, and the ship wasn't under his hands.

Never *had* been: Kate had been between him and the white hell he could still feel. Still see—with his eyes shut.

Kate and Bucklin. Ty and Jim. He was just the trainee on this ship, aiming their huge mass in arrival at that unthinkably massive hell—his boards had never been live. And there were no tricks such as making them live, and not telling him they were. That was graduation stuff. That was when your first-seat was sure you were ready, though Fallan had threatened him with it . . .

But that was *Galway*. *His* ship, *his* boards. He damned sure wasn't ready to go live on *Finity's*. Not with the hellbent course they'd run and a bow-shock that, dropping out of hyperspace and hitting a star's energy, could do damage to more than their fragile selves.

He wasn't ready . . .

But he was getting there.

Coming into Pell for docking, *Finity*'s crew ring had coasted to a stop. Down ceased to be down. That was no novelty, and Ross just did the normal things, using the handholds, following Jen through the ship, headed for the bridge . . . with a feverish load of excitement.

Any spacer from the First Stars was used to zero-*G* mast-docking—a simple matter of shutting down the internal ship rotation and mating their exit tube up with a tube from a, relatively-speaking, stationary mast. *Down* in the mast didn't exist except as a referent to the direction the lift took. You made it to the lift, the lift started, and you made a slow, sane, and head-first progress toward the midpoint of the mast, which you could call "up"—or "down"—your choice. If you were a kid, you played mental games, trying to imagine the geometry that had your feet on the floor and your head aimed at the ceiling, which could be rightside-up or upside-down depending on whether you were coming in from A-mast or B-mast, until that sense of direction slowly vanished as the lift reached the station's gimbaled, rotating mast-core, and slid into one of the outward spokes, where the station's rotational velocity took over and the lift began to go down in an even queasier way.

But there'd be no mast-dock here. At Pell, the mast was for ore, water, or service-craft docking. Larger insystemers and incoming jump-ships docked directly to the outermost ring of the station. They lined up with the docking probe—he'd seen engee diagrams and vid of the process—and when the grapple had made solid contact, it would ease the ship gently and entirely into the station's referent, then move them around and down into sync with the ring itself where the specially designed airlock of the ship would lock into its ring counterpart, making *Finity* essentially an extension of the station itself. Hard to imagine, with something of *Finity*'s size, but then there was the monster scale of the station—no small part of which was the outermost ring added especially to accommodate the megaships and their massive cargo canisters, which required special handling.

Harder still to imagine—as they swung through the bulkhead marked Bridge and drifted into the vacant lounge—Alpha station expanding to accommodate such a ring. There'd been talk of that happening, but he couldn't help wondering about the Alpha he knew—had *known*—all his life: the Strip, the civilian section . . . the venerable old hotels that had accommodated pusher crews since the beginning of interstellar travel . . . what would become of those? A moot point, considering the EC would never allocate the raw materials for such a project, but still . . .

All the more reason to take advantage of a chance to observe a ring-docking first hand. Besides, even if Alpha never got a ring, there was nothing, *nothing* to say that *Galway*, victorious and refurbished, wouldn't someday catch this very same docking probe . . .

Well, maybe at least one at Venture's soon-to-be-finished ring, Ross thought, as he sailed through the lounge, skimming above the seats. He followed Jen's shapely rear to the bridge, where all the stations were vacant and a small gathering of other swimmers floated, shadows in the light of the massive center screen.

The majority of the crew would not see this. They would ride out docking in the lower corridor, an area of the ship not visited in ordinary travel, being part of that specialized and stationary docking bow. That corridor had been warming for days, so Jen said, even while the crew ring had still been rotating—and most everybody would be there, waiting to leave the ship, nobody to be left aboard but the littlest Neiharts—there were six—and their minders, up in the loft, that section of the ring locked high and inaccessible, to get a reliable *G* once *Finity* grappled in. The junior-juniors would be let out on the docks, but with a designated sleepover, and strictly under governance of their appointed minders. The junior-juniors would get a daily hour of dockside freedom, but back they would go to the same sleepover. The junior-seniors were given full liberty, but given to fear the wrath of God for causing a scene; and the seniors and senior-seniors were just expected to report upright, clothed, and self-propelled at board-call. That was the way Jen had explained it, and it was not too different from any ship anywhere.

Except having the loft available and the littlest kids staying aboard.

Except *not* having Earth Company customs sure to wander through the ship at will while they were gone, opening personal lockers and disarranging bunks.

Finity didn't allow that. Hadn't from the start. And now *no* Alliance ship was going to. Ever, on any Alliance station.

That was a new freedom, at the largest, most powerful station on this side of space. Confidence that your shipboard stuff was going to stay where you'd left it, at very least, and nothing was going to go missing . . . that was a whole new universe.

Jen spidered carefully past the two operations seats where Fourth-shift now held sway, and Ross followed.

"Late," Captain Mum's voice greeted them. "Have we got all our Monahans, now?"

"Yes'm," Jen said meekly. Ross slipped into the second-trainee spot at Nav, behind a teen-aged kid who was occupying his First-shift seat. Jen slipped into the matching trainee seat beside him, and buckled in. Across the rows all his cousins were here, eyes and ears for the entire Monahan Family.

"Belt and tether," Captain said, which wasn't usual, in Ross's experience, but if a belt clip failed in an unplanned vector-shift, a free-faller on the bridge would be a hazard to the ship—not to mention the damage to the luckless missile. Ross pulled the tether from its socket beside the belt and clipped it to the reinforced strip around his waist, according to procedure. The big screen forward was all Nav telemetry and they were close. But that display was a little disappointing, when the invite had been to come up and *see* the ring-dock.

Fourth Captain, Lisa Marie, old as Fallan, remained adrift, maintaining at a takehold on the front row of consoles. The legendary Captain Mum, as the Family called her—the last Senior Captain of the legendary *Gaia*. Captain Mum, who stepped down only when the next-generation ship *Finity's End* demanded a next-generation senior crew. And in that seat at which Mum was maintaining, was Helm 4.1, Vickie Neihart, who generally handled *Finity's* docking. Vickie herself was a legend, Ross had found out at Venture, for having worked out how to mast-dock a titan like *Finity*. Most of Fourth-shift were like that, retired from First-shift, but teaching the trainees sitting with them *finesse*, giving the youngers a final polish before getting any permanent seat. *That* was who they were, this Fourth-shift, and a Nav 1.5 needed to keep his mouth shut and watch the screen he had.

"Well, Monahans." Fourth Captain's habitual warm tone was back. "What do you think?"

As the screens came alive.

Theater. It was that. A set-up.

The set-up of all set-ups.

Venture Station had been a curious sight, with its half-completed ring under construction a few kilometers off from the current main ring. But that separation failed to provide any sense of scale.

Pell's docking ring was—mind boggling. He'd heard its dimensions, seen the technical diagrams and tried to conceptualize it—but it was the sight of a handful of small merchanters in dock, looking like toys against Pell's ring, that brought the reality of those numbers home. God—the ship farthest on, smallest of the lot, was the same class as *Galway*.

In overall design, Pell was no different from any other station: central core, masts on either end, and varying numbers and sizes of rings rotating about that core, the angular velocity of that spin being dependent on the size of the rings. All technicals, all the dynamics of it were familiar—and Pell's outer ring, the one where *Finity* was set to dock, seemed barely to move at all. That was the sight that brought the chills. To a spacer accustomed to coming into Alpha's mast with a full view of the station ring below, Pell's outer ring, now making a wall in front of them, was a scary sight. And the lack of apparent motion—

He knew, intellectually, how they'd be coming in, and his heart still picked up its beats in a queasy feeling they were about to ram the station. Mast docking meant a comparatively easy approach: station rotated, but the mast, through a complicated arrangement where ships needed to grapple on, above and below—didn't. There was a simple hatch to hatch tube hookup, lines to keep the ship from drifting and freezing. Utility pushers accessed the hold and moved cargo to a separate lift on the mast . . .

"Grapple extending," second Helm said.

One quadrant of the display zoomed in, and a red crosshair appeared on the edge screen. Part in shadow, partly sunlight, and flashing with green lights, the docking grapple was extending out from the ring. Nav's job had gone from finding a star on the scale of the visible galaxy to finding a blinking light on the scale of a man-made object. And there it was. Ross saw it, watched, heart pounding, as Nav locked on, visually, and there wasn't a thing he could do.

There was back and forth chatter—the ordinary mixed with the new and strange as Nav began to shut down and active control automatically shifted to Helm.

Helm talked to station, and now it was waiting and feeling the little shifts as *Finity*'s fine adjustments shed residual *V* to make safe contact. It was Helm's job and the station's job, a lengthy process to coordinate contact and lock, after which—just the slightest tic of the inner ear, the slightest feeling of one's body meeting the seat cushions and getting rapidly heavier, as down asserted itself.

Then . . .

Thump, bang rang through the hull.

New sound. Ross's heart jumped. None of Fourth-shift so much as blinked.

"We're in," Jen said.

A distant whine of hydraulics, their own.

"Bundle's in," Engineering said.

The bundle. In the First Stars they called it the *lines*. They were preparing to connect the cables that the ship needed to do business, while the ship's main was shut down. Power. Fuel.

And shielded information.

"Shift to station power," Captain Mum said.

"Aye, Mum-sir," Engee 4.1 said.

"As of now," Captain Mum said, "we are part of Pell's ring, snug and locked in. Thank you, Vickie. For our guests, we are in. We are secure. Pell will have been making its own adjustments . . ." Moving its entire water supply, that was, in compensation for *Finity's* mass; Ross had read about the process. "You will have noticed we have a slightly heavy G. Our guests are free to make their way to the downside corridor, but stay if you choose. We note the presence of Security. Jen, show our guests the way down."

"Aye, Mum," Jen said, and, already unbelted and unclipped, gathered herself to her feet. "Galways?"

Ian, *Galway's* Helm 3.1, was still paying attention to process as Helm shut down. Other stations were already shut down or shutting down, except Com—Com was madly busy, all occupied, and cousin Patrick was listening closely, jotting notes. Ross unclipped and unbelted and followed Jen back to the lounge and the lift outside, with the others following.

The bridge and the loft would be topside, the docking corridor would be bottomside, and everything in between would be inaccessible by ordinary means, and anything not properly stowed—the Galways had gotten the junior-juniors' warning—would not be where one expected. Possibly violently so. They were used to gentle drift of such items in dock, so Ross had done a last-moment reexamination of his housekeeping . . . but Vickie's docking had been soft as a pillow.

"So," Jen said, walking beside him. "Was it everything you expected?"

He couldn't answer for a moment. He'd seen wonders. Amazing things. And then he'd heard the probe engage, and knew that information was starting to flow to the station, things that were going to upset what was, and change things that part of him never wanted changed, and part of him thought—*we have to. It's too late to go back. We're in it.*

A moment of panic. The black box had never been scary, but then the black box had never held secrets to change the universe . . . not in his lifetime.

The instant the bundle had locked in, the black box system started spilling to station everything it had—absolutely everything it had—as station returned the favor, a massive dump containing all Pell's relevant business and everything other ships had fed into it. Too late to rethink or make exceptions. Time and distance jumped immediately into Pell's reference, and their paths, their status, their knowledge, their history jumped to Pell's data banks.

And that was it: station admin was going to get . . . everything. Beyond that, information easily traveled on sneakernet, over beers or cocktails. It would instantly be all over this huge place . . . who they were, where they'd been, and what had happened out there, on a net that moved to every ship bound in every direction. Pell wouldn't have heard it from Venture yet, because *Finity's End* was the fastest ship going. And from here—ships went to Cyteen. To that scary side of space.

Change . . . was going to happen. But not, they were assured, while they were still in dock. Word had come down from the Senior Captain in no uncertain terms: keep your mouths shut.

Which was fine by this Alpha-based spacer.

"Hey, you! Finity to Galway! Was it everything you expected?" Jen's voice yanked him firmly back to real time as they reached the lift. Not the first time she'd caught him staring stupidly into space.

"Yeah," he said, and put enthusiasm into it, because he couldn't undo anything the universe had done, and he couldn't go back to what he'd been. The Monahans were relying on him, among other things, to *get* this shiny new technology, to understand it and to bring it back and teach them to survive the changes that were coming. "Yeah," he said again. "It's *something*, isn't it? Just a little stunned at the size of it."

They were stuck there a moment, waiting for the lift to round-trip. Jen's hand landed on his shoulder, and he looked at her. "You all right, Ross? Is this all right?"

She had this uncomfortable knack for reading him. "It's a lot," he admitted.

He caught Uncle Connor's eye, among other Monahans awaiting their turn at the lift, and read the same thoughts: *We're in it now. This is real.*

"Ross?" Jen asked.

"Glad to have seen it," he said, avoiding her real question. "Now we'll be begging the chance to be there for undock."

"I'll work on that," Jen said, but from her tone, she knew there was more. Something he wasn't saying.

"Yeah," he said. He *was* grateful to have seen it. And tried to wish the cold out of his bones. "God. Pell's big, isn't it?"

"Bigger on the inside," she said, straight-faced, and Ross found a laugh to reward her efforts, as the lift returned. They crowded in . . . then held the door as Ian and Patrick came running up to join them. It whisked them down and down, further than the sub-deck of *Finity's* ring. And on.

"This way," Jen said, as the lift slowed and stopped, and beckoned all the Monahans out into a chill corridor. "Everything's arranged. Keep together until we get to the sleepover. It'll be a short trip. Then . . . sights to see. Things to do."

"You promised me trees," Ross said, as if she'd need reminding, grasping at that singular wonder she'd described to him way back on Alpha, their first night together.

"Did. And I'll deliver. I got us a room. Got us some funds. I'm responsible, you know. For the lot of you. I'm supposed to make you all enjoy this."

"Hard job," he said, half seriously, and she grinned.

"But somebody's gotta do it."

"Looking forward to it," he said. "We all are." And it was truth. It was the dream, Pell, being here, seeing these sights. Jen Neihart was his personal added benefit.

"Have had to get pictures," Netha said. "Lots of pictures."

To share it all with the rest of the Monahans not so lucky as to be here. Like aunt Peg, who was waiting at Alpha, and his mother, halfsister to Connor Dhu. Most of all for Fallan and Niall and Aubrey, who were on *Galway,* wherever she was.

God, he wished they were here.

Book II   **Section ii**

Finity's downside executive office was a steel and plastics sort of place—a wide desk that doubled as a conference table, with chairs on tracks and oriented to that surface, and a selection of computer screens that reported on cargo, routine information from station, scheduling, trade. One screen had exec-level communications. JR slid into the primary chair and looked at that screen, whose electronic eye stared back.

Messages waiting, the screen said.

Of course there were. Most were cargo and orders, but one from Blue

Section said: *Emilio Konstantin, Stationmaster to Captain James Robert Neihart. Your earliest convenience. See me.*

Convenience. When it was perfectly clear that Emilio had been stewing all through their days of run-in and hours of docking, wanting a meeting and wanting news he was not going to get until they were in private, no matter what chaff they put out for general consumption. Emilio was a priority. Oh, indeed, Emilio Konstantin wanted a meeting.

So did one other:

Requesting a meeting, your convenience. —Nielander Quen.

Convenience in either case meant now.

Emilio Konstantin was a given. He didn't know the other, personally, but the surname was Quen. *Estelle* crew, a man he very much wanted to talk to.

Konstantin had agreed to the temporary hold on the outgoing auto-feed from the black box—an unusual request, but not unheard of. The station feed arrived as usual, but until Konstantin lifted the hold . . . or *Finity* undocked . . . all that went out was *Finity's* navigational data, and that was exotic enough. An information-hold like that was station's choice—enough to make futures markets jittery for as long as the hold lasted, and enough to send a deluge of questions through news services.

That controlled feed at dock had been announced two days ago, but it wouldn't stop them from getting questions.

The black box system *was* tamper-proof, but the ability of the stationmaster to disrupt that otherwise automated process had been part of the tamper-proof black box system from the start. Even Cyteen, who had integrated that data-transfer inextricably into the new FTL systems, had recognized the possibility of incoming information being too volatile to hit the station without some preliminary preparation. The usual exceptions involved the common sense of permitting company-to-company and station-to-station confidentiality, and among things transmitted but remaining encrypted were copyrighted works and patents that had to be bid upon. It was *not* a way to avoid attention, and heaven help the ship that tried to hold off and delay the feed to play the market.

Matters of diplomatic mail, personal mail, copyright, patent, trademark, and proprietary information—those messages flew back and forth the moment the secure hookup had been established, each at its own level of security.

Ships' records—those were privileged in particular ways, but to put one under executive wrap and a total shutdown of trading information? That was fairly noisy. Speculation took hold where facts were scarce. You could have ten layers of security and permissions on a thing, but sneakernet still sneaked.

Which meant Emilio was going to want answers in his own hands soonest, and fewer delays meant Emilio in a better frame of mind.

So the message he sent to Emilio, even before that to Nielander Quen, said: *First thing when I leave the ship. Estimate: one hour.*

Book II   **Section iii**

The tube was in place. They were all present, in the large room with the rows of takeholds and the low overhead, and safety lockers for the bags they were taking ashore. There were the senior-seniors, all able enough, and the shift officers, who kept order; and the active crew, and the active staff, then the slightly rowdy juniors, and the overawed junior-juniors—the whole Family was there, all the Neiharts excepting the babies and the minders and a handful of cargo crew and top-level execs. Ross, with Jen, joined the rest of the Galways in the aisle to the side of the takehold bars, as Fourth-shift ops crew filed in, last to arrive.

"*It's not all a lark out there,*" Fourth-shift Security said at the front of the room, the amplified sound stopping all milling-about a moment. "*You know what you can say and what you can't say. Remember that at all times. You juniors and below, you stay in sight of your minders and you don't talk out of turn and you know what you don't talk about. You act up, you spend the next six station-calls up in the loft with the one- and two-year olds. Got it? Say got it.*"

"Got it, sir," came the fervent answer from a dozen youngsters.

"*Rest of you,*" Security said, "*stay semi-sober and remember what's at stake. Or vice-versa. Now . . . get your gear and go have fun.*"

Mesh gates on the baggage lockers rolled up, giving access to the row labeled row of duffles they'd stowed before dock. Names rang out and duffles were passed overhead to hands waiting to receive them.

Ross waited for the rack to thin, uncertain where to look. Housekeeping had brought his bag down, and the slots *seemed* to be in alphabetical order. There were *Galway*-green duffles among the *Finity* black, lumped together, from what he could see between crowding shoulders and heads. Patrick, taller than most and with bright red hair, was working his way toward that lot. But among them was *not* the blue bag that was all he'd been able to put together before leaving Alpha, his regular gear having left with *Galway*.

Damn, he was thinking, they didn't get it down. Now it was out of reach.

Jen, who had somehow darted to the front, returned hauling two duffles. She dropped one at his feet. "Sorry it's *Finity* black, but your blue one is in it. You need room, friend. Maybe two bags. Buy a green one. You're coming back with *stuff.*"

"I've got everything I—"

"For the Monahans back at Alpha. Official order from the captains. *Finity* can bring needfuls, but *you,* sir, can pick out stuff that's a little more personal, and you have just docked at one of the truly best shopping strips outside Cyteen. So you and all the rest of the Monahans among us are charged with finding those particular things that you know the rest of the Monahans would like, consumables and personals. And you're not to be worrying about the tab, hear?"

Monahan pride flared. "We've taken charity enough just in—"

"Yeah, yeah, and put in hours of work and all. This is on *Finity's* conscience and *our* honor, so just make us happy and pick out *stuff,* all right? Latest games and pretties and some nice souvenirs."

He moved, he had to, because people were supposed to migrate out and down the corridor to the connector, and he was blocking people behind him. He took the mostly empty duffle, too light to swing to his shoulder. He carried it by hand and moved, just a little upset by the notion of *Finity's* charity, but likewise, he couldn't say no to the idea of souvenirs and treats for the Monahans who weren't here. Jen was rattling on about where they could go and how everybody would be visiting the shops and all, but he couldn't answer past the lump in his throat. He focused his attention on the corridor, and the cousins, a small green knot of them, ahead of him, wondering if *they'd* been told about souvenirs, or if that revelation was being left up to him.

God, he hoped not.

Finitys were kitted out in their grey jackets with the *Finity* patch on the sleeve, nothing but an unrelieved black spot, space itself, and nobody else could claim their aristocracy, offshoot of the first-ever interstellar colony ship, *Gaia.* That was who they were, the oldest, the richest, the biggest. All of that.

His own jacket—the Family had seen to it he at least had that before he left—was green and grey, and the patch on *his* sleeve was the Monahan Celtic knot. Togetherness. Unity. They weren't the oldest ship, not near it, but they *were* old, the Monahans were. They were also Alpha Station's finest and most trusted. They had those *mosts* to their credit.

They walked past the downside offices, where the captains could do business throughout their stay, and headed for the airlock that would cycle them not into space, but into the connector, which was given to be cold as hell's hinges—no different in that sense than *Galway*'s exit corridor into Alpha's mast-dock. The wonder was that instead of floating along that connector, they had their feet on the deck at a good 1 G, and locked through to the corridor in groups of ten or so, as if they were already on the station strip. It felt weird. It looked surreal.

And when it was his turn and Jen's, along with half the Monahans and a few Neiharts besides, it was quick through, pressure being equal—just a hell of a chill in the passage, where it was not so much the thin jackets as body warmth that kept them safe enough. The cold there stung noses and throats and quickly numbed fingers, though it was given to be a heated passage, and everybody moved fast to get to the next airlock, no hesitation in that cold.

The lock and lift combination let them out into another short corridor leading to another airlock and a sign that said: *Welcome to Pell Station. Docking bay 32*. And *Caution: ramp ahead. Please use the hand rail. Boot soles may be slick due to cold.*

That lock let them into a terrifying large space . . . and well above dock level. A steep ramp with a ribbed surface ran out past a skein of giant hoses, two massive hazard-orange machines, and a towering secondary structure of girders painted yellow.

And, yes, there *was* a handrail.

"Those are the can-handlers," Jen informed him, pointing at the machines. "Cargo comes out below us, hits the cradle, gets moved over to the cargo ramp and then onto the carriers."

Noises echoed in that vastness, and looking up, he quickly discovered, was a mistake. He grabbed the handrail and, with somewhat better inner ear cooperation, managed to look out across the vast open space between them and the neon lights of, God, was it a restaurant across the deck? He tried looking up again, where lights shone like groups of A-class stars. Blinding bright. Impossible to see above them, though common sense said there was solid structure at the tops of grey standing girders. But he couldn't *see* that boundary between him and infinite space, and for a terrifying moment, he found himself flashing on a downward view of *Finity* herself, a distant haven in an endless sea of stars, an image so vivid in memory that his equilibrium failed him *again*. Stifling a curse, he tightened his death-grip on the hand rail, forced himself to look ahead rather than up—though that distant view of the restaurant was only slightly less unnerving—and started down the ramp.

He was relieved to note he was not the only one gripping that railing. Glances passed between Monahans, all sharing the same slightly dazed look. The open dock felt unsafe, recklessly unsafe. Human places weren't *meant* to be this large. Were *never* this large. Even at Venture.

Worse, there were *no takeholds*. Just the thin rail he was expected to let go of, and, he supposed, walk out onto that vast expanse. Like decks he knew, it curved upward, but—so broad and so gradual a curve it boggled imagination, and tricked the inner ear.

Jen's arm found his elbow as they neared the end of the ramp, a curiously reassuring anchor, for all she was no more attached to the deck than he was. At least if rotation failed, they'd fly off together. Nor were they the only pair to take hold of each other.

A machine thumped, like the crack of doom, echoing into other echoes. He jumped, glanced about for the source, and Jen gave his arm a little pat as they walked out into the echoing vastness. Ahead of them, a transport rolled up, slowed, gathered up a number of passengers, who just stepped on and gripped its handrails, and trundled off.

"Want to walk?" Jen asked, coming to a halt. "Or ride? It's free."

"Walk," he said. His inner ears were giving him trouble enough. He didn't want to add speed to the equation. "I need to get my feet under me."

"Sure," she said, and reached out to stop Ian and Netha, before they walked in front of another transport that rolled by, its quiet hum lost in the ambient echoes.

"Damn," he said.

"Up-ring, they go on this side of the dock, down-ring they're over by shopper's row," Jen said, and with a glance aside, started walking again. "Just look to your left, always your left, until you cross the yellow midway line, then it's look right. Always give them right of way. They'll stop rather than hit you, but the riders won't thank you."

"I'm not going to argue," Ross said. His eyes were drawn to this, to that, to the far spaces and moving vehicles and flashing lights—distraction was everywhere, around and above, and it was an effort to screen it out.

He'd have walked in front of that damn transport if not for Jen . . . as the cousins just behind him, Maire and Aidan, would have, if not for the Finitys walking with *them*. So he wasn't the only Monahan under escort, which Jen most definitely was for him.

And glad he was to have her.

There were people everywhere. So *many* people. People milling about the shops, on the people-movers, even people waving to them from the front of those shops, trying to entice them in.

He avoided eye contact. "Is it all like this?"

"Pretty much, though *Finity's* a big arrival. There's always food and lodging sharks, who'll try to steer you to their dive. Be just a little careful getting on a trolley that's got a sleepover advertised on it. They're apt to whisk you off God knows how far to some place at the edge of the section, and not the best, either. We have our own list, where we'll be—all in the vicinity of the Versailles—so we're not scattered. I've got the lot of us booked at the Purple Pagoda, otherwise known as the Royal, which is just way less tight-assed than the Versailles. The damn Versailles is just too wonderful to be polite to anybody under fifty, while the Purple Pagoda, only two doors on, has a happy hour with free pizza in *its* bar."

The chaos and dock-noise thinned out as they crossed into the up-ring traffic and even more so as they made it all the way to the commercial frontages. There were people who were clearly stationers mixing with spacers on the strip—the dockside, Venture called it, and probably that described it here. The neon colors pulsed like a heartbeat, music added itself to the echoing racket—it was a bath in chaos, and Ross thought of Rosie's, cozy, dark, with scarred tables and the drain that always had a trail of water going to it; Rosie himself, genial and large and sympathetic to often-credit-short customers—who'd give tips when they had it, and got a free beer when they didn't. The likes of Rosie's certainly wasn't here, in these vid displays and this pricey confusion.

"Let's get signed in first," Jen said. "Get registered at the sleepover, so we have a package drop, and then we'll go out on the docks."

It was reasonable. Establish a handhold somewhere in this chaos, where they could reach each other. A place with a name people would know, if they got lost. Grey-and-green jackets and the *Galway* patch were a minuscule presence here. On Alpha they'd been the biggest, newest ship going.

He cast a look back the way they'd come, where the orange can-handler was the most discernable feature, except . . . except a big holographic sign that probably said *Finity's End,* but they were too far and there were a couple of the big girders in the way. There were other signs for other ships, hanging, like magic, in the air, looking the same no matter the angle.

He'd heard of such things. Knew from vids that holo-signs were common on Sol and in the Beyond . . . but he'd never actually seen them. He tried to imagine one of those signs reading *Galway* . . . and failed. Which didn't stop him from being determined that he *would* see that sign someday. *Galway* would get here and those eager solicitors would greet Monahans with credit to burn.

Damn right they would.

Jen waited for him as people passed them. Waited. Said nothing. Just let him look. Jen had the plan. Jen knew this place. Knew things and places he couldn't even paint in his mind. Viking. Mariner. Stations not as big as Pell, but far, far from Alpha and Bryant's and Venture.

And a living world was under their feet, brilliant blue and white in the blindingly brilliant light of this violent star. He'd seen the planet closeup on vid as they approached. A planet that had intelligent beings who sometimes came up to the station and moved through the service tunnels. Who were employed to maintain such passages as their own habitat, where they lived and worked and dealt with humans. Downers, humans called them, their world being Downbelow. Hisa was their word for themselves, but one shouldn't speak to them unless they spoke first. He knew that. And he looked, as he gazed about the moving traffic, for any figure near the edges who might be smaller and different, but chances of seeing one of them were few. Jen claimed she'd seen one. Once. In all the times she'd been here.

"Trees," he said, lest anyone forget.

"We'll get tickets," she said. "First thing on my list."

Book II   Section iv

While the cargomaster's office, forward, had its own share of people coming up the ramp and into *Finity's* downside corridor, there was one visitor in-bound who wasn't headed for Cargo.

"He's here," Fletch said over com, it being perfectly clear what *he* needed to be reported on.

"Copy that," JR answered. "Thanks."

It didn't take long. The light above the office door flashed an advisement and JR keyed it open.

The man walked in—brown jacket, the *Estelle* patch and the stylized sword that meant ship's security, two bars. JR rose, offered a hand, warmly and strongly taken.

"Captain, sir," Quen said.

"Welcome," JR said. "I hope *Estelle's* well."

"Well and on her way. Apologies from us, that she had to move—granted I could stay to tell you, from the Reillys, that their job is done."

Job done, from *Dublin,* relayed here by *Estelle.* It was a vast, resounding yes.

"And Cyteen?"

"Will sign if Pell does."

A signature that, God willing, he'd get in the upcoming meeting with Emilio Konstantin.

"What percentage could they get?" JR asked.

"Hundred percent, sir, in theory. Every ship signed. Including, obviously, *us.* Viking and Mariner in theory, but also contingent on Pell."

"Not surprising. Reservations? Comments? Requests for amendments?"

"None that I know of, other than, in at least one case I heard personally, what took us so long."

"Splendid. Absolutely splendid. We're *nearly* there. We've got two stand-outs in the Hinder Stars. Unless *Dublin* got them. *Come Lately* and *Miriam B.* You wouldn't know anything about them, would you?"

"I know the names. Met a Come Lately once, here on Pell. Years ago. Chatty, but pleasant. It was her first time beyond Venture. Exclusively Hinder Stars, by what she said. That's a hard lot to track."

"She say what brought them here?"

Quen shook his head. "Lots of innuendo and bravado without substance. If I had to guess, it was a special commission that gave them an excuse to visit Pell. They certainly couldn't make the jump fully loaded, by what she said. Wouldn't be the first time a marginal ship like that looked for an excuse to make the run, every ship-time decade or so."

JR had met a few of those himself, out at Mariner. "Well, we'll hope that *Nomad* and *Mumtaz* found them at Glory. We split from those two at Bryant's. But Alpha *has* signed, without reservations. So has Bryant's, with provisions about Pell's participation, and Venture, also without reservation—if Pell should ask."

"Three *stations.* Outstanding."

"I think we can safely say four. Glory's in no position to argue. We're in good form, provided Emilio signs. I'd offer you passage, but I'm afraid our course is back to Venture, and *Estelle's* on to Mariner?"

"Mariner and Cyteen. No, I've already got a way. The Olvigs' *Hammer.* They'll be here another five days, and if you hadn't shown in system by then, I'd have found another. One thing about Pell, there's always another. But *Hammer's* on to Mariner, so I'm in good shape."

"Excellent. Are you here alone?"

"Well, not quite alone, so to say."

"Anything you need from us, just ask. I'd like to comp you and a companion those five days of dinners, if you'll accept, places of your choosing, plus your lodging. No charity about it. We owe you."

"I make it a point never to turn down a free meal," Quen said with a grin, then pulled a stick from his pocket, and handed it over. "Here's the lot, everything *Dublin* gave us."

"I've got one for you and *Dublin*," JR said, and pulled two from his pocket. One, he handed to Quen. "My one request: you can share this with *Hammer* and any other ship, but only after you're underway and out of here. With so much depending on Konstantin's signature, we need to keep a low profile until we have it. This one—" He raised the second stick, then slipped it back into his pocket. "Is for Konstantin. It's his discretion how he deals with it locally, but you can trust he'll sign the agreement. My word on it. I'll hope to get his signature before you leave. If I don't, you'll get word."

Quen pocketed the stick. "If he hasn't signed before *Hammer* breaks dock, I'll be staying until he does."

"We'll personally be beholden to you for that favor. Truly."

"Deal," Quen said, and rose and offered his hand. "An honor, sir. An absolute honor."

JR took it. "You're going into *Finity's* log. Eternal debt, Quen. In my personal book as well. Thanks."

Quen left. JR stood there until the door closed, then sat down, ran a safety check on the stick on the isolated slot, then switched it over to the general system.

"JR Neihart," he told the computer. "Ship's log. Security Second-shift Neilander Quen off *Estelle* delivered the following report from Captain John Reilly of *Dublin*. Insert time stamp. *Estelle* is away, but Quen stayed on his own to bring the report, saying the tally stands at a hundred percent of ships on the Cyteen reach. Recording a debt owed to him and *Estelle*. We tendered our own report to him, which Quen will carry to *Estelle* via canhauler *Hammer*, outbound on the thirtieth. Log a debt to the Olvig's *Hammer* for that passage, no matter if *Dublin* and *Estelle* also handle it. Debts are many on this voyage. I am moments from meeting with Emilio Konstantin with that report and with our own. Computer, sign off log."

He drew a breath then, and several more. "Computer, copy the inserted file onto an unstamped stick, and eject."

Two sticks came out. One had a stripe that would ID the machine that created it. One had no stripe.

He pocketed the one with no stripe, the same pocket that held the other data stick. And called Fletch and Madison.

The Royal, aka the Purple Pagoda, was an extravagance of gilt, purple in all hues, and a broad touch of whimsy, including the glittering gilt statue of an elephant in the reception. Lifesized, the plaque said. It was impressive by any standard.

Ross tried hard not to gawk, as Jen went up to the marbled counter, laid down the credit voucher. "We have to go to the exchange," she said, "to get some pocket currency. For little stuff. But it's just down the—"

Flash of movement from behind him; Ross jumped aside from a rush of—*monkeys?* Jen laughed, and gave him a little poke in the ribs. Another dash through the lobby, and this time he saw it was, indeed, wiry little monkeys, jumping and leaping over one another in vigorous play, and overhead were some sort of birds—more of that holographic tech. Real, except a slight transparency. It was fascinating. And strangely upsetting. Monkeys and birds . . . even a tiger lurking behind a semi-transparent forest. Ross knew what they were from still pictures, even entertainment vids, but they really didn't belong in a hotel lobby, and he eyed the massive gilt elephant suspiciously, for all it looked very solid. The sleepover on Venture had been a bit too fancy for a lad from the Alpha run to be entirely comfortable. Fancy . . . but sensible. With no holos.

Sensible was out the airlock here. Evidently.

"This," he said to Jen, when they had indebted themselves for whatever this place cost, "this is fairly scary. What did we just spend?"

"Not as much as we would have at the Versailles," Jen said with a grin. "Last chance: rest or roam?"

"Roam."

"Good answer. If you go back to *Finity* less than pie-eyed with exhaustion, I have *not* done my job!" She clipped a tag to her duffle and another to his, then slung her duffle onto a passing low carrier. "Quick, toss yours on. It'll get them to the room. Then . . . follow me! I have so *much* to show you! Twofer's in charge of everybody, but I'm stealing you for a couple hours! I'll let him know."

She fairly vibrated with excitement, as they walked out together, past that monstrous elephant. He felt its presence even with his back turned. A body just couldn't forget it was back there. Up there. Looming over them.

At least the monkeys had not repeated.

They walked a safer track along the frontages of restaurants and sleepovers—he wondered how all of them found customers enough, until he remembered that sight on docking, remembered just how big Pell was. How big. How rich. How incredibly rich. How many ships were docked . . . but even those would have a hard time accounting for the number of people he'd seen out there.

"Are these all spacers?"

She looked up at him. "You mean do the stationer folk keep to their own side, like at Alpha?"

That wasn't quite what he meant, but close enough. He shrugged and she shook her head.

"Fifty-fifty . . . ish. At least for those you see, shoppers and such. Lot more stationers, if you add in those who actually *work* dockside."

God knew there was room in this enormous ring for station population to grow. Room. Jobs. And if the EC, for once, played fair . . . Alpha might experience a comparable boom. He wasn't certain he was really ready for that.

He dared not imagine the room that awaited their return. He hoped for basic: a bed, a place to wash and change clothes. Somehow he doubted *anything* in that place would be . . . basic.

Fortunately, Jen would be there. That would make up for the cost, not to mention any . . . creepy holographic monkeys.

Still, it was overwhelming. *Galway* wasn't rich. It never had been. *Waste* was not what they did, ever. But then, neither was Alpha rich. Alpha, like *Galway*, survived. A beer at Rosie's, sidestepping a leaky pipe . . . that's just how life was.

Pell was beyond anything he'd imagined, let alone experienced, and try as he would to relax and enjoy the hospitality offered, it was all just . . . disturbing. The elephant, the eerily realistic monkeys, even the knicknacks on shelves, and the fancy chairs . . . it was just . . . too much. And . . . wrong. The entire station defied the rules of his universe. Like the docks, with trolleys whizzing past and the bright lights and tiny people scattered across a scary great distance—

All he could think when he looked out there was . . . what the *hell* would happen if they ever suffered a takehold emergency—a disaster with a big ship like *Finity*, maybe—anything that caused that steady rotation of the ring to falter . . . God help them.

Maybe the elephant was bolted down, even if the chairs weren't, but size didn't matter much, when the gravity went. What happened when some poor fool didn't dodge a flying chair because he'd grown so accustomed to bounding monkeys that passed right through you? So many things not secured, depending on gravity to keep them from becoming missiles flying through that great overhead out there. People were just not meant to be in big spaces like that.

At least, he qualified—after a moment's reflection on life on planets, a life more alien to him than Pell's dockside—not in space, they weren't. Jen stopped to look at a display. He saw their reflection in the window. On the far side, trinkets hung from strings, fancy globes like miniature worlds, and their reflections were giants gazing down on them . . . like a station hovering above a living planet.

Maybe it was Downbelow that distorted people's ambitions here: a living world, so rich, all marbled with oceans and clouds, where trees grew and gravity was a given. Down there, where people looked up . . .

And up. Maybe that was what they were trying to create on Pell Station, which never had experienced a vector shift: a fantasy of life on a planet.

Except Pell *wasn't* a planet, no matter how stable her rotation. Being on *any* station meant hazards, and God knew that Alpha *ran* on risks, dilapidated as it was, and with the basics under constant repair, but Alpha's hazards weren't so evident or so challenging to the eye. In Rosie's, he could reach up and, with bit of a stretch, touch the ceiling. The tables and chairs all ran on tracks and locked in place.

All his life, he'd halfway imagined Pell Station from a combination of pictures he'd seen, but something those pictures could never capture was the sheer size, the sense of . . . newness. The variety of input, things he'd never imagined, much less seen. . . . The people walking tens of meters from the nearest possible takehold, where a sudden vector shift of the ring could send them hurtling to intersect that unseeable ceiling beyond the lights.

Alpha was little, now that he'd seen this. Forever little. And old. Even Venture was. All he'd wanted, when he'd accepted *Finity's* offer, was to see a Downer, a single tree, which would be something to tell, back in Rosie's. How would he ever describe this place when he got back there? Even with pictures, he'd never find the words to explain the physical sensation of being here, never be able to explain the occasional shudder some memory caused. His cousins, unless someday they were able to come here and experience it for themselves, would never understand. And for a moment, he felt very, very lost, and a little unhappy.

Jen, with a puzzled glance at him, left the window, to just stand beside him: there, if he needed to talk. She was like that. Solid. God, he loved her for it.

"Does it bother you?" he asked, and she tipped her head. Puzzled. He knew the look. "So many things not tied down. Those monkeys, appearing out of nowhere and running right through you. *Real* where nothing like them should be. But . . . not."

He'd never been all that good at describing what he felt, and this was one of his clumsier attempts, and do her credit, she didn't answer right away, just looked at him, frowning just a little. He felt a touch on his hand, and turned his to accept hers.

"They aren't, you know," she said, very quietly, and with a small smile that would fool any casual watcher into thinking they were having an intimate conversation, which they were, just not the kind any stationer would understand.

He met her gaze and stifled a shiver. "Aren't? What . . ."

"Real, Nav 1.5. Those monkeys."

"I *know* that!"

"I know you know. In your head. But convince your gut, right here and now."

He got, then, what she was about. Reality. Nav's most important touchstone. And she was right. Pell itself was a constant assault on, at the very least, his personal reality. He drew a breath, squeezed her strong, slender hand. "I hear you, Security. I'm working on it."

Her smile returned, and she lifted their clasped hands to give his a quick kiss. "Have every confidence in you, spacer-lad. —As for all the loose chairs and such . . ." Jen let their hands fall apart and shrugged. "Yeah, it bothers. Doubt it'll ever not. They're smarter at Viking and Mariner. But you'll never convince this lot, until disaster actually happens. I'm just glad the odds of us being here when it does are pretty low."

"No kidding."

"Now, quit stalling!" She jerked her head toward the exchange and started walking. As he turned to follow, a glint of gold behind them caught his eye. The Royal. Down-spin of the direction they were headed, and suddenly, as he fell in beside Jen, he realized they were walking, just as with any station, up-spin. You went up-spin or down-spin, and it was still, no matter how big, how busy, how noisy, how strange, just a case of up-spin and down. Even if he got separated from Jen and didn't have a map, he could always find his way back to *Finity*.

It was never more complicated than that. Up-spin and down.

He could find his duffle. And Jen. Easy as finding a gilt elephant.

"What's funny?" Jen asked.

"I just got my bearings," he said. "Shaky for a bit, but I think I'm situated now."

"You're feeling the star?" She sounded entirely impressed.

"Not this time," he said. "No. Don't need to. I got an elephant, don't I?"

She blinked. Twice. Then her eyes lit up, and she laughed. "It's the dead easiest place to find in the whole universe, that's sure. Probably creates its own gravity well. Not to mention there's a *Finity*-sized berth opposite. Only one ship ever takes that one."

He drew a deep breath, put his hands in his jacket pockets as his spine relaxed, and looked ahead with eyes that began at last to make sense of the chaos. "It echoes. That's the thing. There's so much sound from all over. Makes me a little dizzy."

"Me, too, sometimes. Kind of hard to hear yourself think in some places. But there's sound baffling back in the Royal. Do you want to go back and find the room, just maybe get some quiet?"

"Hell, no. I'm good, now. Let's go up and down a bit. See what's on offer that's weirder than where we're staying."

Book II   Section vi

The receptionist in Emilio's office didn't get the chance. Emilio popped out of his office and waved them all in, where a decanter of liquor, with four glasses, awaited them on the desk. The office was otherwise empty.

Fletch caught JR's eye—it wasn't what they'd agreed on—but JR tipped his head toward the door, letting Emilio set the tone. Another couple heads taking in the proceedings couldn't hurt, but unless directly addressed, Fletch and Madison would just sit and listen. Convincing Emilio was JR's job.

"Is this to be a celebration," Emilio asked, as JR, Fletcher, and Madison took seats, "or fortification?"

"A bit of both," JR said, propping the all-important briefcase he'd brought in against his chair. "Are we secure?"

Emilio raised a brow, as he gently worked the stopper out of the decanter.

"I'll cut right to it, then," JR continued. "We got Alpha, Bryant's, Venture, and probably Glory by now, all signatory to the agreement, and every ship we could find that operates on this side of space, which is all but two."

Emilio nodded, and poured the first glass. "Excellent news. Excellent."

"The bad news is—Sol may be about to escape the bottle."

The pour hesitated on the second glass. Then resumed.

"I knew," Emilio said, "when you didn't want the data link, that we had a problem. Tested?"

"Not yet. Not even a robotic probe. Just potential jump-point coordinates a retired historian pulled out of masses of pusher data. Our Nav's run sims; says doable, but dangerous. We should know for certain soon: a merchanter is making that run stone cold blind from Alpha."

Emilio passed him a glass with an admirably steady hand. "That's . . . a little crazy. Why the rush? Why not a robotic probe?"

"Major power struggle at Alpha involving the *Rights of Man* project. Project director, man name of Cruz, is EC to the core and a militant ass. Sending a probe would have alerted him that the coordinates existed. Stationmaster Abrezio kept the coordinates secret, waiting for the next pusher ship from Sol. Figured to send them in a secure packet—make sure the station and the old man got credit for finding them, but let the EC handle the testing from their end. Didn't even trust the numbers to the Stream, until circumstances forced his hand."

"'Until,' you say." Emilio handed glasses to Madison and Fletch before sinking into the chair behind his desk and picking up his own for a lingering sip. Hard to read just how he was taking the news. Calmer than JR had expected. "So he did transmit them?"

JR nodded, and Emilio's eyes narrowed as he digested that bit of information. The Stream, Alpha's ancient communication link with Sol, was limited to the speed of light, unlike the merchanter ships' black box system that let the rest of humanity communicate at FTL speeds. Emilio was the only stationmaster outside of Alpha who might truly understand that long delay, Pell having maintained its own Stream to Sol in this post-FTL era.

Mainly because Pell never trusted Alpha as the information gatekeeper to the EC. One of several points of distrust between the two stations that they would have to overcome soon, possibly in the next half hour.

"Which means Sol will have the numbers in, what, six years?—No, wait." Emilio shook his head. "Less your return travel time. So . . . four? Four and a half?"

"More like five. We . . . made good time." He didn't elaborate. "And that's only if *Galway* doesn't get there first."

"*Galway*. —That's the merchanter who's making the trip?"

JR nodded.

"Heroes? Glory seeker? Money-grubbing idiots? All of the above?"

"Good Family with a solid ship and outstanding crew. They saw opportunity for themselves and all the Hinder Stars, and took a gamble with their ship and their First-shift crew, a gamble that could end up saving all of us."

Emilio's hands, folded atop his desk, tightened at that, but he said nothing.

"I'll be honest, Emilio," JR continued, "what we uncovered at Alpha was disturbing, to say the least. If *Galway* makes it through and can convince the EC of certain realities of life beyond Sol, it could go a long way toward keeping EC enforcers from flooding in and taking over Alpha . . . possibly every other station they can reach."

Silence. A swallow that wasn't a sip, on Emilio's part. Then:

"What—in—hell," Emilio asked, "what in bloody *hell* did you stir up out there?"

"Nothing that wasn't already agitated. Their precious megaship, on which they've lavished materials and man-hours for years, can't make jump."

"The Rights of Man, you mean. Their copy of *Finity's End."*

JR nodded. "Without the modifications *we* made. And I have to say, you stopped the leak very effectively. —Part of the reason *Finity* herself went all the way to Alpha was to have a first hand look at her."

"You said you might go." Emilio's hands relaxed. That compliment about the leak had done its job quite effectively. "What tipped the scale?"

"We heard rumors at Bryant's that she'd powered up, even tried to jump . . . and failed to initiate. Fairly common opinion on Alpha is that it was the ship herself that aborted, which is why she's in one piece."

"Aborted? Why?"

JR allowed himself a slight smile. "Local spacer opinion holds the ship sensed fools at the helm and refused to jump in self-defense, but there's no real data, yet. The EC in charge of the project kept those records tightly password-protected. At the time we left, Stationmaster Abrezio was still trying to get at them. I can think of several reasons the ship's systems might have overridden human input, but whether or not she is or ever will be safe to jump is, at the moment, a minor concern. *What* she is, the changes *they* have made to the design, is far more concerning. Cruz may have started with *Finity's* blueprints, but *Rights* is definitely not *Finity,* not in configuration, not in capability, and not in crew. From the reports Abrezio could give us, we can definitely say she's fundamentally the original drawing board version. She lacks all the system modifications that make *Finity* operational, changes we made as production proceeded. She also lacks the new bow. Not because they only use mast docking out there, I'm quite sure, but because the entire ring-docking system was under development at the time those plans were stolen."

Emilio nodded, a bit smugly. JR had often suspected those initial, first-draft plans, stored in files "carelessly" left on a desk, were bait for the Pell-based Earth Company reps that had become a serious pain in Emilio's ass. Once those were stolen and sent on to Sol, the theft became grounds for throwing the EC presence off Pell's deck completely. The EC had since been allowed back, but only under strict regulation: effectively, the EC office on Pell had been politically and operationally castrated.

"More significant," JR said, before Emilio could get too satisfied, "are the modifications they've made on their own. The hold is way smaller. The crew space is way larger. *Rights* was built to move people. A lot of people. And people-scale equipment."

Smug turned utterly grim. "Going where?"

"There aren't a lot of directions they can go, are there? But it says volumes about their intentions and their attitude."

"How are they crewing it? Certainly not merchanter Families?"

"No. From what I got, they didn't even try. Such is EC distrust of merchanters that they were recruiting unemployed stationers, plentiful in the economic situation at Alpha, and training them with sims."

Emilio's eyes widened. "As a *megaship's* crew?"

JR shrugged.

"Good . . . God. Could they do that?"

"That remains to see. We all start on sims. The first Family FTL crews had never jumped and they all learned."

"From *azi*, who had actual jump experience! Of course *azi* could learn with sims. That's how they learn everything. I mean, some of those Cyteen clones are walking, talking computers! But those early converted FTLers weren't *Finity*, not even remotely."

"No argument here. And from someone who actually made the transition, standard FTL to a megahauler . . . damned if I'd trust *my* life to a sim-trained stationer crew. If they don't turn *Rights* over to a Family for a real shakedown, I doubt she'll survive. But what's truly concerning: all of her crew are also certified Enforcement. Desperate, disenfranchised stationers recruited, trained in weapons, a thuggish hand-to-hand—and a very bad attitude."

"Excuse me." Emilio raised a hand, extracted a small box from a drawer, and slipped a wafer taken from it under his tongue. A moment later, he sighed and waved for JR to continue.

"When we arrived at Alpha, the *Rights* project was horrifically over budget and behind schedule—the failed run being only the most recent and devastating blow. The project manager, so-called *Admiral* Cruz and an enforcer-type, Hewitt, a support goon sent on the last pusher, had been pushing Abrezio hard, trying to diminish his authority, exerting enforcer control on the Strip, where they could get their young stationer recruits to push merchanters around. Between them and in the name of the Project, those two have confiscated *everything* brought in on the last two pushers from Sol, *twenty years'* worth of essentials, which has left the station increasingly unable to keep the merchanters *or* its own operations up to snuff. The stationers are hurting, badly, and so are the merchanters."

Emilio's brow twitched. That last had struck a nerve. JR registered that twitch for future use and continued:

"I suspect, but have no proof, that the EC has been trying to get some Family so desperate they'd sign on and solve all the technical problems with *Rights.* Cruz and Hewitt certainly didn't like our presence and *really* didn't like the notion of merchanters organizing. So I don't know whether it was our presence that pushed the situation over the edge or whether it was already headed there independent of us. It says something about local politics that Abrezio didn't tell the EC about the jump-points. He'd kept the coordinates in his pocket for years, waiting to send them in a secure packet on the next pusher. But shortly after we docked, in response to overt power plays by Cruz and Hewitt—which *were* triggered, if not outright caused, by our arrival—Abrezio risked transmitting them on the Stream, so that *he'd* get the credit with Sol, and Cruz and Hewitt wouldn't."

"He's always wanted a place in the history books." Cynical tone: there *was* history between these two stationmasters: Abrezio, newly assigned stationmaster, *had* been the one responsible for transmitting the stolen *Finity* plans to Sol, and relations had gone downhill in the decades since. But in this case:

"Maybe," JR said. "But I suspect his main motive was undermining Cruz and Hewitt with their handlers back at Sol. Those two are poison and, say this for him, Abrezio's sincerely got *Alpha's* interests at heart, above the EC's. Besides, as I understand it, that transmission made a point to ensure the old scientist, who actually found the points, got full credit and *his* place in history, which is more than the EC men would have done."

Emilio flipped a hand, dismissing the issue: no interest to Pell, the internal politics of Alpha. "The point is," Emilio said, "it's a done deal. The coordinates are en route to Sol, where there's *every* chance the EC has been building jump-capable ships—God knows they've got the resources . . ."

"No question."

"Fool Abrezio should have stuck with that. Hell, given, say, six plus years for the data to reach them on the Stream, a couple of years for probes to verify . . . We could have been looking at decades to prepare. But if that damned merchanter actually makes it through—" Emilio broke off. Coughed. And met JR's frown squarely. "I didn't mean it that way and you know it. Bad, *bad* choice of words. We all hope for the best for the ship and crew."

"Indeed." JR controlled his expression . . . and granted Emilio the benefit of the doubt. A lot of *what ifs* were running through the stationmaster's head right now. Questions and possible answers JR had had months to process. And damned if he had the leisure to take offense. Too much depended on Emilio's being on board with them. "To Abrezio's credit, he transmitted before fully understanding what we were there for. He was facing an imminent coup by Cruz, who would co-opt those coordinates, and the credit, and use his EC contacts to take control of Alpha. Abrezio getting the coordinates, along with an honest account of the situation at Alpha, on its way to *his own* EC contacts seemed Abrezio's best chance to stop Cruz. Once he understood the potential of the alliance, becoming *the* conduit for the EC gained a whole new importance for him and his station. Time became critical, and tested points and a sane *new* power arriving from Sol could ensure Abrezio's hold on the station: hence the decision to send *Galway*. He sees both the merchanters *and* Sol trade as the future for his station, and he was doing his best to make sure one of *his* ships got the credit for trailblazing. The idea in sending *Galway* was to get there ahead of the Stream, prove the route, get the EC to listen to them, convey their point of view, support the Alpha stationmaster, and undermine Cruz and Hewitt in the process."

"Regardless of his reasoning," Emilio said, "sending that merchanter still cuts buffer time before the EC descends on us down to . . . how many jumps? Could the round trip already have happened? How soon before the EC turns up on my doorstep?"

"Two points, but with luck, longer than you think." JR held up a hand, and Emilio clamped his lips on his next question. "It's complicated, Emilio. And it's important you understand the kind of people we're dealing with. The ship to station relationship is . . . different . . . in the Hinder Stars. *Galway's* Alpha's newest ship, good Family crew. Abrezio engaged them to make the run untested, yes. Promised them fame and fortune, yes. But it's more complicated than that. These Hinder Stars ships are deeply loyal to the stations they serve, who are their livelihood, and vice versa. One can't help but admire them. Loyal, but not stupid. Had Abrezio not been desperate, he wouldn't have asked, and if we hadn't been there to give them an option for the Family, should the venture fail, I doubt *Galway* would have accepted. When Abrezio made the offer, *Galway* immediately came to us, to sign, yes, but *not* before telling us the whole situation. They asked us to take care of their Family—the Monahans—if they didn't make it, and in return, they offered to give us as much time as possible to solidify the alliance. They planned to laze through the jumps, mapping the points . . . And they'll have to come in on the edges of Sol system, take their time getting to the station. That's a damned messy system, and our maps are centuries old. They could pull an Oort Cloud avalanche in with them. Plus, they've got to come in far enough away not to induce panic at Sol. Once they do make it to Sol station, they've got to deal with the EC, and since they plan to keep their doors closed until agreements are reached, that could take a while. Then it depends on whether the EC at Sol *has*, and is willing to risk, its own ships and sim-trained crews—or whether they'll use common sense and settle on a minimal investigative team sent back on *Galway*. In many ways, *Galway*'s testing the jump-points may be the *safest* part of their trip."

Emilio swallowed the last of his Scotch, then stared into the empty glass. JR sipped his own, waiting. Finally:

"You said . . . with luck." Emilio's eyes lifted, met his. "What happened?"

"That's the truly bad news: Cruz twigged to the deal and hijacked *Galway*. Hid his men until she'd released and spun up, then moved in with clubs swinging and guns blazing."

"Oh, good God." Emilio pressed fingers to his temples.

"And we'd have been none the wiser until Cruz showed up missing—if a *Galway* Navigator, with a head injury that nearly put him in hospital, hadn't taken a hardsuit route to *Finity* and alerted us what was going on. There was damn all we could do to stop them without killing the Galways aboard, but at least we were a jump ahead of Hewitt, who was aiming to take us on and take control of the station."

"Insane. The lot of them. Which means we're back to worst case and the EC on our doorstep."

"Not quite. Granted the *Galway* crew left under armed duress—to our knowledge, the only one on board with the numbers for the jumps is the Monahans' Nav 1, and those numbers are only in his head. Before shoving his Nav 1.3 out the airlock—Ross is the young man's name—Fallan gave him the paper with the coordinates and told him that the Family is going to try to take back the ship as they exit the first jump. That exit from jump can be rough or smooth depending on Nav and Helm, and merchanters are hell and away better able to handle the phasing than stationers who've never experienced jump. With luck, the EC aboard will be caught heaving their guts up and we'll be back on the Monahans' proposed schedule, with a piracy charge to add to Cruz's list of failings once they do arrive at Sol."

"And if the merchanters don't manage to regain control?"

JR drew a deep breath. "Then Nav 1 will slip a decimal or two on the second jump, and we'll have at least four and a half years before Sol even knows the points exist."

Emilio's eyes widened. "They'd scuttle their own ship in jump?"

"To stop Cruz? Yes."

A pause, then: "Damn. Just . . . damn."

JR added nothing more to the mix of sentiments running races behind Emilio's stare. Just waited for the stationmaster to ask:

"These points. You have them?"

"Yes. From Ross. Ultimately Abrezio also gave them to us, not realizing we already had them."

"How reliable are the numbers?"

"Their senior Navigator is one of the best. An old-timer named Fallan—known to our Fourth Captain. He told young Ross they were doable when he saw them. Our Nav agrees . . . and after six sim runs, *Finity's* computer agrees."

"Young Ross. He's the Ross Monahan on your visa list?"

JR nodded.

"Credible?"

"Very."

"Good. Pell Council might want his testimony."

"No problem. He knows it's a possibility."

Another pause as Emilio digested the ramifications—and poured himself another Scotch. No offer to refill the Neihart glasses, but JR didn't take offense. Wouldn't have accepted if offered.

Fletch's and Madison's were still full.

"And if this Cruz *has* the numbers, if he has his own crew commandeer the boards?"

"Then our problem will be solved," JR said grimly. "And we'll owe the surviving Monahans a new ship, because numbers or no numbers, an inexperienced crew will fry the ship going into Sol. Sol's one hellish, messy system. After that . . . even if Abrezio could talk another Alpha ship into taking the risk, he won't try for years."

"He knows about the plans to delay?"

"He was profoundly relieved, especially given the rest of the plan."

"There's more?"

"Just say, if Abrezio is going to stand up to the EC, he needs help."

"Of *course* he does." Disbelief in that tone, but the brow twitch returned, and JR judged it time to push.

"Truth, Emilio. The situation at Alpha is far worse than we thought. EC management has run Abrezio's station dangerously low on just about every resource they have to import. He's got a cadre of hundreds of newly unemployed EC-trained kids with police skills and no jobs, with beer and food running low, and no future in sight. He needs supply to get the factories going, get some jobs open, get a stable food supply, get the printers and the vats up and running—in short, he needs everything. Hewitt is stuck aboard *Rights of Man* for the time being, effectively under arrest until the next pusher comes, at which point they'll toss him aboard and let him stew another several years back to Sol. If we are extremely lucky, Cruz has gone to a hot hell and the Monahans have taken back control of their ship. But at least we've got Hewitt in a bottle. He's not going to age well, I'm afraid."

Emilio choked on the sip he'd just taken. "That is *abysmal* humor, sir. What about this EC-trained crew?"

"Currently bottled up with Hewitt, but Abrezio is working to repatriate them. They're stationers, a lot of them kids, but some old enough to have very bad attitude. There's going to be some stress. They're unemployed and all of them are trained to violence. But Abrezio has the support of the Strip, and he's never lost the support of the stationers—he's been a good administrator, and we're backing him."

"We. As in, this alliance of yours." Emilio did not look altogether pleased with that information.

"Ours," JR confirmed, firmly, unsubtle reminder of just who had suggested the Alliance in the first place.

Emilio's sour look confirmed the hit, but he didn't give in easily. "So *you're* going to hold the line against Sol, at Alpha."

He raised a brow. "Better at Alpha than here."

"Your alliance."

"It might not be all *that* difficult. I *don't* think we'll be flooded with traffic direct from Sol in any near future. Points or no points, Sol does *not* have an easy route in *or* out. Sol has an uncommon lot of rock. Their planners may have anticipated the problem and taken steps to clear a path at the zenith, but unless they've dedicated the last two centuries to the problem, traffic in *and* out is best left to experienced crew, a fact of life it might take some expensive losses for them to figure out. But their influence out here, their cachet—their supply of luxuries—" JR slightly lifted his own Scotch glass. "That kind of economic influence can move ships. Stations. Organizations. Which is why *we* organize first, to make sure their organizations can't get a foothold."

"We. Your alliance."

"*Our* alliance, Emilio, no matter how drunk we were when you first suggested it. It's a sound concept. It's *already* working. Alpha has tilted far over to our side, wanting only badly needed resources to stand firm. And in accordance with the agreement, and to prove exactly what we're about, we're already handling one desperate case: the merchanter *Firenze*, Galli Family. A ship in pretty dire straits, the fact the Gallis are still alive a testament to their skill and ingenuity. We're arranging their refit. They're grateful. They'll be operational again within the year, but in the meantime, they're stuck at Alpha, which means, with the Monahans, two full Family crews added to Alpha's bio needs. *Little Bear* is running pieces and parts and technicians from Venture to Alpha for *Firenze*, and meanwhile we are hoping to *pump* supply back to Venture, which means much needed business for ships like *Santiago* and *Qarib*, of whom you've probably never heard. They've been the bottom end of the supply chain, but they'll carry supply from Venture to Bryant's and Alpha and Glory. These stations need everything, and they're depending on Abrezio's signature on the Alliance agreement to help them get it. Just sufficient to replace all the blown lights and leaking hose is all Abrezio's really asking for, but a few new games and vids and food varieties will make the stationers and the Strip a whole lot less vulnerable to EC bribes, when they arrive."

"And prop up Abrezio," Emilio said. "I find a certain irony in that. He does *not* like me."

"Respectfully, Emilio, yes. I know you two have history. But—"

"History? He stole the damned plans for your ship! He's been pouring everything into a martial counterpart! And you trust him?"

"You know very well *he* didn't order that theft. And while he's technically EC, a fact that compelled him to send those plans to his superiors, what he really is, is Alpha stationer. Believe me, he'd *love* not to have that giant ornament on his A-mast, sucking down resources. Yes, I trust him to follow through on his promises to us. Yes, I believe he *wants* what we're offering him. I've met him face to face. I've *talked* with him. And as you have very wisely pointed out many times in the past, it's that direct contact that humans need for *real* agreement. It's that direct contact with other places and people that gives merchanters the advantage, and *makes* us such a valuable buffer between stations."

"You pick the damnedest times to quote me."

"They're wise words, Emilio. True words. Trust me: you *want* Abrezio between you and what will one day be on its way from Sol. Those supplies will enable him to offer jobs to people that won't be wearing the EC uniforms any longer. And granted the Sol connection does work out and trade starts running through Alpha at FTL speeds, Abrezio's popularity on that station will mean a station in far better case to hold its own. He's smart, he's local, he detests the EC at this point, and he's in a mood to ally with you. He's not exaggerated the need. If anything, he's downplayed it. He *needs* to have those supplies. At near cost."

Emilio took a drink of his Scotch. And stared off into the possibilities.

JR took a sip of his own. Two. Fletcher and Madison kept very still. Emilio followed his glance toward his cousins and frowned at them.

"You two have been pretty damned quiet."

Fletch and Madison looked at each other and Madison tipped his head at Fletch, whose mouth twitched in a half-smile. "*His* job."

Emilio grunted. "Yeah, well, I'm asking you. Truth?"

Fletch grunted back. "You don't want to know about the plumbing in the bathrooms."

Emilio closed his eyes, tipped his head back, then said quietly: "God help me, I've believed for years he was exaggerating the need. I mean . . . we still get the occasional case of Scotch. Even coffee . . ." Emilio heaved a deep sigh and met JR's eyes. "Shit. Fire me off a list of what he needs and I'll see what I can justify with the Board. Maybe even swing you a humanitarian discount to bolster that buffer against Sol you're promising. I'll send a love note with it."

JR felt the knot in his shoulders relax at last. "The Alliance will appreciate that."

Another, more prolonged silence. Then:

"You think I pretty well have to sign at this point," Emilio said. "Don't you?"

"It *was* your idea. Sir. And you can bask in the knowledge that by signing, you're also committing Cyteen."

Emilio rolled his eyes. "As I recall, and just for the record, it was a simple *party at Tripoint* I suggested. A simple boycott of Cyteen if they tried to muscle in on your trade routes."

JR let his mouth soften into an almost grin. "You've known what we were about."

"Hell if. I still haven't seen the latest version of this document you want me to sign."

JR felt a touch on his arm, reached to accept the printout Fletch was handing him, pulled from the case he'd brought in, placed it on the desk and pushed it over.

"Take your time. It hasn't substantially changed. Not for *Galway*, not for *Firenze*, not for the little ships or for big ones."

Emilio made a quick scan, then flipped back to the beginning to read with more care.

"How many ships did you say you've signed?" he asked.

"All the ships but two, *Miriam B* and *Come Lately,* which we're still hoping to lay hands on."

"Old," Emilio said. "And small. What about the stations?"

"I've got signatures from Alpha, Bryant's, and Venture Stations. We're hoping to pick up Glory."

"I doubt an act of God could resurrect Glory Station. We can't."

"If Alpha's stable, it's going to help them until regular trade from Sol keeps it there."

"Quen visited you. I take it he brought news from *Estelle?*"

"All Cyteen-side ships have signed. Mariner and Viking have signed provisionally on your signature. Cyteen will sign if you will. If Cyteen signs, she brings all her stations with her."

"I know their ways. Of course they will. Not sure I believe it. *Cyteen* wouldn't shed tears if the EC ate us alive. They'd pull any maneuver to deal us foul."

"Not if it means giving the EC a straight path to their own backside. Besides, you said pretty much the same thing about Abrezio, not so long ago."

Emilio scowled. It wasn't really the same, they both knew. Alpha was damned near dead; Cyteen had power. A lot of power. Emilio didn't and never would trust Cyteen.

"Can't say I trust them," JR qualified. "I haven't ever dealt with them. But John Reilly of *Dublin* does deal with them. *Has* dealt with them. Directly. For years. He knows names, and he's certain he's capable of bringing the Carnaths *and* the Emorys right on an issue." He paused for effect. "Reilly says they feel much the same about you and trusts *me* to bring you right on *this* issue."

"Trusts *you.*" Emilio gave a disgusted snort. "Captain James Robert, is it?"

JR winced. "How did *that* get here?"

"*Get* here? It was *born* here. I take it, then, they've said it of you elsewhere."

Abrezio had saddled him with that history-charged name that he pointedly did *not* go by—tagged him on their last night on Alpha, and his own Family had cheerfully picked it up, for all the wrong reasons. He was the second captain of that centuries-old name, that Mum had had the audacity to lay on him. Captain James Robert Neihart: *Gaia's* first captain, the one to defy the EC and give ownership of the interstellar ships to the crews. He wasn't that man, for all Abrezio had meant it kindly enough.

From Emilio—it was a tactic meant to rattle him.

"Unfair shot, Konstantin."

"Hell if. *Empathy.* I know something about the weight of inherited names."

"So sign the damn agreement. We have a responsibility."

"My ancestor was a pirate. Yours was a flaming hero. Screw responsibility; we both have job security."

"God," JR rolled his eyes. "Just sign the damn paper."

Silence as Emilio took the time to read the contract, again, and as he reached the last page, where the signatures went: "So basically, you're saying throw this agreement at the EC, whenever they show up, and tell them they have no choice: sign or go home empty-handed."

"The truth is, they *don't* have a choice. Not unless they can manufacture a merchant fleet *and* crew it . . . and then somehow convince the stations to betray the agreement they've just signed with us, and—at the cost of cutting themselves off from the rest of the stations—to do business with people they don't know. People in the hire of a company that's been dead set, historically, on its own interests rather than the fair trade we've all become accustomed to."

"And if some Hinder Star decides Sol is the better option?"

"We stop supplies until whatever station is involved throws the EC ships out. —Which means the stations should stockpile for their own needs, because a shutdown *could* happen."

Emilio frowned. Hard. "That's not a threat, is it?"

"No. It's an ability we *will* have. We don't want to, but it's the teeth behind the agreement and it's our defense if Sol comes rolling in with more presence than we think likely at this time. We're working out ways to work in concert with the stations. To protect *you* as well as us. We intend to preserve every station we've got."

"Even the Hinder Stars."

"*Especially* the Hinder Stars. We've got to prove *to them* they can survive without Sol if they're to be an effective buffer against Sol's own-it-all attitudes. If we succeed, if we can make Sol see the possibilities, the *money* to be made . . . God, *three living worlds* trading products and ideas. What can that do for us? *All* of us—including Sol. Sol with its history and luxury goods from the planet that birthed humanity, Cyteen with an entire populace run by insanely brilliant scientists pouring out tech—and Pell being the pin that holds it all together."

"Us—in the middle of this doubtful sandwich."

"You—who are set to be the invaluable buffer, if you're moved to do so. You're independent, but unlike both the EC and Cyteen, you are *not* territorially inclined. The Konstantins have dealt with both the EC and Cyteen for generations. No one else can make that claim. Whether this side of space can ever be *comfortable* with Cyteen and their azi and their expansionist notions, I don't know. What Sol itself is like by now, we'll only begin to see with the first-in from there. But Pell *is* the bridge. The point of reason. Pell can mediate. I have every confidence you can negotiate with them, with merchanter help and backing. It's our best chance to control and moderate Sol's re-entry into our affairs—and to define their role for them in ways actually useful."

Emilio's eyes went from him, to Madison, to Fletch and back. It was not a happy stare.

"You're a dreamer, JR. You're also a golden-tongued, manipulative bastard trying to turn me up sweet. You hand me a situation with Sol inbound into our affairs and a prime reason for them to be damned unhappy with us, and say 'Make it work, Emilio.' Thanks. Thanks *ever* so much."

"Well, we were bound to stir up a *little* turmoil."

Silence, as Emilio just looked at him, tracing the lines on the paper with one fingertip. A very long silence. Then: "All right, all right." He tossed off the last of his Scotch. "I'll sign your agreement. I've got to convene the board and notify them, but I'll make the case for what I've done. Understand . . . they *can* veto."

"We depend on your eloquence and reason."

Emilio gave an . . . eloquent . . . snort. "*We* depend on your silence, all of you, across the docks. I'll keep that feed under a temporary security lock until you break dock to go do—whatever you do from here."

"Currently, I expect to go back to Venture in two weeks, to make sure the supply we're asking for gets to Alpha."

Emilio nodded slowly. "I'll bring the Board along. Somehow." A long pause. "God, should I tell them about the jump-points before or after I secure your lading? It's not as if we have alternatives."

"Well, you do, but if the Board wavers, you might point out that if they ignore the Hinder Stars, they make them completely reliant on the EC, and if the EC does in fact make it outside their gravity well . . . in not that long a time, you lose Alpha, you lose Bryant's and Venture . . . and have the EC on your doorstep, in force."

"You've fairly made that point," Emilio said. "We do still have an EC office, you know. Getting their orders on the Stream, same as ever, twenty-four years out-of-date. Basically, we ignore them." He gave a little shudder. "FTL's going to change that. Big time."

"Even FTL can't make EC orders relevant to anyone other than their own reps," JR pointed out. "That's what Sol needs to learn. That's what they need to understand, more than anything. Stations and ships are independent for more than just preference. *Real* decisions have to be made in *real* time."

"I plan to bring their local agents along slowly, lead them to *our* point of view," Emilio said. "I'll give them the basics before I release your feed. Let them feel Significant. The current set—there are three of them—are decent and sociable, Pell-born, and Venture-born before that. We invite them to official dinners. We share information. They play the EC's word games more for the paycheck than any real loyalty. When the Sol contact becomes imminent, who knows? *They* might have their own reason to worry. They're stationers. More to the point, they're from *here*. Earth's more foreign to them than Downbelow."

"Just—don't trust them."

A steady gaze. "I don't." After which Emilio opened the contract to the final pages. An impressive collection of signatures. All the ships. All the stations.

Excepting two.

"*Miriam B,* you said." Emilio continued to scan the names. "What was the other?"

"*Come Lately.*"

"Contact would be in their interest," Madison said, out of his long silence. "Their best interest, in fact, if you have any information on them."

"Put in the records request to my office. I'll priority it. You should have an answer."

"What we need is executive access to Pell's records," Madison said. "Such as they exist. We discovered, from Venture's records, that those two ships are on the old first-issue black boxes. Still do their cargo trades in the offices, in person, and turn the boxes on and off at will."

"Hinder Stars compliance, in other words." It was an old proverb, objectionable in the Hinder Stars themselves, describing an attitude about inconvenient rules; an attitude definitely *not* limited to the Hinder Stars—and certainly not foreign to the near-hereditary directorates of Pell and Venture. Emilio tapped up computer function on his desk, and asked it, "Display all station calls for ships *Come Lately* and *Miriam B.*"

There was a few seconds' delay. Then: "If their systems are as old as you say, the Venture to Pell jump string would be rough on them, loaded. We've seen *Come Lately* twice in the last twenty-five years, *Miriam B,* once. Nothing recent."

"We'll find them eventually," JR said. "Hinder Stars stations all have a message waiting for them, when they do show. They may have gotten word we're looking for them, and aren't trusting our reasons."

"If they turn up here," Emilio said, "I'll sign them up, myself. Give everybody a share of this, so Sol can't call any of us innocent." He flipped to the last page, firmly, and took up the pen on his desk. "Now shut up, the lot of you. Let's get this done."

Book II   Section vii

The first shop Jen dragged Ross into, utterly disregarding his protests, was a clothing store, when what he wanted was a beer or two in a comfortably small dim bar. True, he was under-equipped, since all his gear other than the bloodied jumpsuit he'd escaped in was on its way to Sol. True, he'd been living in borrowed *Finity* greys. He'd managed to cobble together a bare minimum of necessities at Alpha before boarding *Finity*, and in *Finity's* haste, he hadn't had time even for practical shopping at Bryant's. At Venture, it had all been: wait for Pell. Jen had promised him better deals at Pell, practical clothes he could afford with the credit *Finity* insisted on giving all the Monahans—but new clothes were hardly his top priority, and somehow he doubted that this place, where holo models changed clothes and genders in confusing succession, would be a source for any kind of *bargain*.

But Jen insisted he at least give this place a try, and from the cheerful greeting between her and the owner when they arrived, she was something of a regular.

Customers were expected to undress for a rather embarrassing full body scan and then stand too long, in his opinion, at the click-and-model kiosk to see what he'd look like in various over the edge offerings. And after an embarrassing argument with Jen over her gift of a dress jacket for high-dining— an argument he lost—he placed an order for three basic green jumpsuits, a pair of pants, a shirt, and a jacket that would be delivered to his room by dinner time.

Tailored to his body. He couldn't imagine.

He had a few minutes, then, while Jen disappeared into a fitting room, to wander among the true luxury pieces on display, garments claimed to be made of actual woven plant fibers and, according to a fancy tag, hand-embroidered on Pell. He ran his fingers gingerly over the soft fabrics, felt a ragged nail catch, and pulled his hand away. A quick check assured him he hadn't damaged it, but he moved immediately away from the item.

"Like it?" Jen asked, coming up behind him.

"It's different than printed stuff, that's for—" Words failed him as he turned to face her.

"Wotcha think?" she asked with a teasing grin, and twirled around to let him view from all angles. The silvery one-piece gracing her slender figure was *almost* Finity-grey, he could say that for it. She laughed. "I have absolutely *no* excuse to get it, but I just *had* to try it on. Isn't it fun?"

"Um . . ." He tried not to stare.

She laughed aloud. "Good answer, Galway." She headed back to the fitting room. "Back in a flash."

He took a moment to appreciate the retreating view, then cast a second look at the woven-fabric clothes and a weave-patterned jacket he did covet, but couldn't conceive an occasion to wear it. Woven fabrics weren't unknown in the First Stars—time was, shipments of basic plant-fiber fabrics had arrived on the pushers from Sol—but like everything else not destined for *The Rights of Man*, those shipments had ceased before Ross had ever escaped the minders. One non-printed jacket he owned had known at least one or two owners before him—soft through years of use, but nothing to compare, visually, with the clothing on these racks. And *it* was on its way to Sol.

The Neiharts' shore-leave jackets were made of the same durable, printed fabric as every other ship's, if somewhat more standardized. He knew now, from the sartorial splendor in *Finity's* off-hours lounge, that the crew's simplicity dockside had been deliberate care not to flaunt their wealth in First Stars stations. And what he'd seen in the *Finity* off-hours lounge only hinted at the variety he found on the racks of the store. As he carefully sorted through the hangers, he suddenly realized that, beyond the holo signs and immensely high ceilings, the noise and the sheer number of people walking the docks here, the wild diversity of clothing out there was itself a challenge to First Stars senses.

Those twice-sold fabrics from Sol that were available in the First Stars were solids, basic colors, with none of the exotic prints available in this shop, certainly nothing like that jumpsuit Jen had just modeled and was probably going to leave with. In his experience, embellishment, such as there was, tended to be in the form of embroidered patches of all sorts, transferable when clothing wore out. He'd seen the machines working, once, when he'd gone after more *Galway* patches. There'd been an amazing array of colored threads there to choose from. But those were just spools.

In this shop, this assault on the senses, a kiosk screen said a certain vibrant red was a dye from Downbelow, processed from plants, complying with statute . . . whatever that meant. There was a list of sources, foreign words, excepting the minerals; and the colors derived from them were too many to count.

It was color you saw in vids, not in clothes you could buy. There was an option to have the file downloaded, and he opted for that in his handheld—you had to be a *little* careful, *Finity*'s shore-orders advised that; but Jen had told him at Venture that high-end shops were all right. He put his name down to receive ads for the store, for all the good that would do him, but the Monahans at Alpha would be fascinated just with what he could upload.

Which put him in mind of their mission to find special souvenirs. The clothing itself was too expensive, though a scarf or two might be possible. A search for small items brought him to the children's clothing, which wouldn't be much appreciated by any of the younger Monahans, but it made him think of Winslow, a tiny, multi-jointed doll—hand-carved of precious wood and passed down through generations of Monahans—for whom various Family members made detailed clothing and in-scale paraphernalia out of whatever bits and bobs they could find.

Buy an entire garment to be ripped apart to make something new . . . for a doll? Except it wouldn't be for the doll alone, but for the whole ship. The doll, Winslow, fragile with age, was kept in a clear case in one of the ship's lounges, a mascot for generations, his pose and outfit, even his setting, changed "mysteriously" from time to time, to the endless delight of the youngest—nobody would be so low as to tell them the magical secret.

Winslow would justify at least the price of a scarf.

Provided, of course, the little guy returned from his trip to Sol.

Ross squelched that painful thought and was thumbing through the catalog, looking for tiny prints that would work for the doll, when Jen returned. "Going back after that shirt?" she asked, and he explained, hoping she'd have an idea.

Before he was done, she was grinning.

"Scraps," she said, and headed for the sales desk.

"Jen, what—"

"Hey, Kiara!" She waltzed up to the woman at the desk and flashed her friendliest grin. "Got a question for you."

"Certainly." The woman smiled back. He'd yet to meet anyone who could resist Jen's grin, the best part of which was that it was absolutely real. The

Finity patch didn't hurt either, he imagined. And the clerk had, no doubt, tracked Jen's foray into the fitting rooms.

"Do you make all these?" She waved her hand vaguely about the room. "They're really great."

"Not personally." Another smile. "But we're a consignment outlet for locals, in addition to the on-demand printed stock. Some of these are sewn entirely by hand. No machines involved."

"That's what makes them so different! That and the fabrics. Local? Downbelow?"

"Natural fiber. Entirely."

"Mmm." Jen picked a frilly shirt off a rack and appeared to examine it minutely. "This woven stuff . . . it's done in big long strips, right?"

"Yes . . ." the woman said slowly, obviously beginning to wonder where this conversation was headed. And over at a rack, the owner, who had called Jen by name, had stopped what she was doing to listen, a little grin on her face.

Another glance up. "So they cut pieces out of that strip?"

The woman nodded, looking as puzzled as Ross felt, and her eyes made a quick dart to her boss, whose was immediately busy again, apparently oblivious to the exchange.

"Must make for a lot of waste," Jen continued. "I mean, printed stuff can always be recycled, right?"

"We recycle, yes." The woman shifted into friendly sales mode, patently relieved to be able to fall back to familiar territory. "As for the fabric, the computer calculates the most efficient layout and lasers cut the pieces, so there's little left over."

"But there's still *some* left over, right?"

"A very small amount."

"I wonder . . ." Jen leaned an elbow on the desk. "You know I'm a merchanter."

"*Finity's End*. Of course. No question."

"I have a notion. Pure spec. Not sure anything would come of it. But we just got back from the Hinder Stars, and they've got nothing like these fabrics. Actual clothing is out of the question and even the large pieces of fabric would be too much for spec, but those scraps . . . as trim, they might have some resale value. How much would you sell it for?"

She named a price that sounded reasonable to Ross. Jen winced. "Well, maybe a little steep for our margin. Can you maybe do a bit better?"

"I'm sure we can work something out." That not from the clerk, but from the boss, coming over to join them, and fifteen minutes later, they left with a large bag filled with bits of locally-grown fabric, scarves for Peg, his mother and his sister . . .

And one glittery silver-grey jumpsuit.

Book II   Section viii

"We're signed," JR said.

It was a staff meeting, Madison, John, Mum, and Fletch, in the downside office, the common meeting space.

"Difficult?" John asked.

"After we explained about *Galway?*" JR said. "No, though he wants to talk to young Ross."

No real surprise there; it was one reason the Monahans had been invited aboard.

"What else did he say?"

"We talked about him mediating between the EC and Cyteen."

There was a general quiet around that answer. Mum folded her arms and looked grim, and Fletch just heaved a sigh and shook his head.

"He's earned the right to try, and fair's fair, I brought it up first," JR said. "The EC has always had a fondness for people who sit in offices. They'll try to deal with him, until they start to shove too hard. I think there'll be a period when it all works. Until it doesn't. And do him credit, Emilio knows it, too. The Konstantins have sat in that chair about as long as there's been a Pell Station. The Earth Company is going to come in here with their usual finesse, they're going to claim ownership of everything and complain about having to steal plans that, in their opinion, should have been added to the Stream—" Meaning, they all knew, *Finity's* plans. "And they're going to demand a complete update on the modifications, at which point he's going to tell them no, it's *not* theirs for any asking, to figure it out themselves—same as Pell's engees did—and they're not going to like it. They're going to have to get used to the word *no* on a lot of points. They'd be mortal fools to antagonize the Konstantins, they'd be absolute idiots to press Cyteen, and that's where the Alliance can make a difference: it may be up to us to convince them of that reality. Getting Pell and Cyteen both signatory and on the same page before Sol gets this far will be a major step."

"There's no love lost with the Cyteeners," John said, "but Earth's proprietary notions actually *might* bring the Carnaths and Konstantins to a wider agreement."

"Double-edged, that," Mum said. "If the EC has any sense, which I don't grant, they'll view the Konstantins as the best ally they could have. Raise Konstantin hackles, push Pell and *us* into alignment with Cyteen and against them, and I'm afraid it'll be the Carnath's vision for the future that prevails. Hopefully whoever the EC sends will be able to see it, too. Pell has proven it can hold its own against Cyteen, but if Sol pushes too hard, they'll come smack up against Cyteen politics, and that will not end anywhere comfortable for anyone." She shook her head. "Rampant expansionist territorialism is the plague of human history. Let Sol out of its pusher-bound bottle unchecked, and we get it running amok on both sides, with damned little consideration of what might be waiting on their own borders, maybe something a lot older than the hisa, and not near as welcoming."

Beta, everyone in the room made the connection. That station nobody named. Proxima Centauri. The pusher *Santa Maria* had docked there to find the station empty, intact, and no clue what had happened. Not being fools, nobody had ever gone back to try to find out . . . possibly to stir up whatever lurked there.

Would the Company be as restrained in exploration as the Hinder Stars had become? Cyteen's expansionism was a worry. Greed tended to make fools of the smartest people. So much depended on having rational people in charge. And the Company's history . . .

Wasn't *that* the elephant in the room?

"We do what we can," JR said. "It makes it all the more important to get the agreement into operation, and follow through on what we've promised. We take it we've got the agreement with Cyteen sewn up, at least before the EC makes it to Pell in any force. Quen has been informed and will carry a copy of the signed agreement to *Dublin*. We have to trust John Reilly on that one. And thanks to the agreements signed with the Hinder Stars stations, the only way the EC will move *beyond* Alpha is on one of our ships, and that's not happening in any hurry. I hope to God that Abrezio, with our backing, will be able to talk sense into them."

"Alpha and Pell both maintain the Stream," Mum said. "They still do talk."

"Across a massive lightbound gulf," John said. "And face it: we paint the picture we want Sol to see and Sol paints the picture they want us to see. We don't know each other. We *haven't* known each other since *Gaia* launched."

"That will change," Madison said, "the moment *Galway* drops in on them."

"Granted they get there," John said.

"Six years on, they'll still get the news," Madison said, meaning the trans-mission from Alpha, on the Stream. "And the numbers. Even if *Galway* doesn't make it, doesn't mean the numbers aren't sound."

"One way and another, it *will* happen," Mum said. "And when Earth goods do start flowing to us, Pell's lifestuffs are going to lose a little value, but not much. Might even improve as soon as the Sol market discovers them. Earth's always been touchy about what gets to it. They're understandably protective of the motherworld biology. Pell's equally protective of Downbe-low, and can teach Sol a lot about the topic. We've learned a few things out here. We can maintain the protections. And Earth proper's not the only market there."

"Exotics will still move best," John said. "Liquor, flavors, scents. Designs will flow both ways."

Mum raised a brow. "Once we have a path in, we *will* trade. That's a big and populated system of planets and satellites. Except for a few personal transactions, the pushers have always dealt directly with the EC. Who *knows* what we'll find?"

"It'll be a sort-out," Madison said. "Pell, more than Alpha, will be the heart of it. With most to lose if it goes sour, most to gain if it goes well."

"Not sure I agree with that," Mum said. "If Sol breaks all expectations and comes in with a renewed lot of trade, Alpha's too small to really take immediate advantage of the flow. But it *will* grow. If the EC plays fair, that whole region could flourish."

"The Hinder Stars," JR said, "are owed something in all of this. But it's going to be tough. They've got *Rights* hanging over their heads. The EC will blame Alpha engineers, they'll move in their own people, and they'll be continuing the project. I wouldn't put it past them to demand the revised plans as part of any deal they consider making with us. Does the EC ever give up an idea, once they launch it?"

"Stealing the plans and then demanding the updates is a little much," Mum said dryly. "Konstanstin's no fool. Sol will find that out. But they'll make a try, with *Rights*. If history is any indication, they'll be throwing ad-ministrators at the problem instead of engineers, and firing them one after the other, granted they haven't learned anything, as they probably haven't. They'll promise. They'll threaten. They'll deny they threatened. Then prom-ise again."

"Unless," Fletcher said, "*Rights* is only the tip of the iceberg and they have a fleet of sensible, proven FTLers waiting to head our way, bellies filled with Enforcers."

"They'll find they've no place to dock," JR said, "if we can back the

stations." It was how the Alliance was supposed to work, everybody supporting the one in trouble; and if the one in trouble happened to be larger than
a ship and inconvenient in distance, like Alpha, that was what still had to be.
"Now that we've got Pell's signature, with Cyteen to follow, there'll be no
trade and no supply if Sol wants to argue. That may have to happen once or
twice. They may have to run that reality past their eighty-odd governments
to figure it out. But we'll manage. That's all. We're taking on another full fuel
load right now . . . no knowing what kind of time we're going to need to
make. And counting on Emilio to come through with his council, we're
going to be loading for Venture, with goods all the stations down the line can
use, not a high profit margin for us, but a decent one."

"I do like the word profit," Mum said dryly.

"So do we all. Foodstuffs, metals. Small canister-loads, obviously. We'll
take the load to Venture and let local ships take it from there—unless, worst
case, the Monahans lose control of *Galway*, the points prove out, and the
EC is already back at Alpha, in which case, I think we have no choice but to
push through to Alpha and talk to them. With luck, *Little Bear* will be waiting at Venture with news. Min said he'd wait for us."

"We owe him," Fletch said.

"We certainly do. But we all benefit from Alpha being armored against
the EC when it arrives. Getting the plumbing fixed and plenty of food on the
table will definitely help Abrezio maintain his grip."

"*Firenze* herself might make that jump, once she's got her upgrade." That,
from Katrin D, *Finity*'s chief engineer. "She's a tough old lady."

Whatever patch-together she'd had for nav, whoever did her last engine
conversion had done a proper job. With a new nav system, she was due to
make the Venture route, which was the ultimate test for a First Stars ship.
Firenze was the Alliance's showcase project, their proof of concept—about to
be famous clear to Cyteen, for rising from the near-dead. Her successful rehab
would prove the Alliance could keep its promises: seal and stamp on the idea.

"Anyone else just the slightest bit queasy?" Fletch asked. "I want to count
the Alliance a success, but there's still too damn many unknowns."

"Getting *Firenze* back on schedule without Sol materials and without the
EC mandating anything is major," Madison said. "Everyone can look at her
and say: we can do this. I mean, *nobody* wants Sol back in the picture, real
time. Not really."

"Except the Hinder Stars," JR corrected quietly. The recent trip had been
more than a bit of an eye opener. Sol wasn't just the EC. Not to the Hinder
Stars. The First Stars, as they called themselves, both stations *and* ships,
wanted that route to Sol opened up. They didn't want EC interference any

more than the rest of the Families, but they wanted Sol trade. Their futures, their ability to become, in their own minds, viable members of the emerging Alliance, lay in getting that Sol trade and moving it out to the Beyond. They couldn't hope, under current circumstances, to compete in the Beyond, but with the exclusive rights to Sol trade goods, coming at FTL speeds, they had a chance, a real chance for the first time in living memory, to thrive.

"Except the Hinder Stars," Fletcher repeated. "I just hope, for their sakes, the EC doesn't try to drive them out with ships of their own making, with crews loyal only to the EC."

That . . . no one wanted to see happen. The Alliance existed specifically to *keep* it from happening, whether it was Sol or Cyteen or Pell herself. No one, *no one* was carrying cargo except the Family ships. At least . . . that was their starting position. He and Abrezio had talked at some length, and as the bridge to Sol, Alpha would have the unique clearance to accept non-Family cargo . . . but only from Sol. From Alpha to the rest of the Hinder Stars and to Pell herself . . . that cargo would go on Family ships. Period.

He hoped it wouldn't come to that. Hoped that the EC would see the value in letting merchanters handle the interface between stations, the value of leaving FTL to those inured to it from the womb.

Sol was going to remain a factor, wanted or unwanted, but she'd soon find out she was just one more star with planets—a lot of planets, and a living planet, yes, but that bounty made her equal with Pell or Cyteen, no more, no less. That was where it all was going, the EC's opinion notwithstanding. The Alliance was the solution to the problems of the Beyond, problems centuries in the making, problems that arose from the isolation of stations, and the imbalance in economic power. Sol as a whole could be a major player in the Alliance network, Sol and the trade Sol System provided. How much of that bounty the citizens of Sol system decided to hand over to the EC was their business, but the EC and EC notions of ownership had no place in the new order out here. Massive pusher-ships no longer ruled deep space. Sol-produced goods no longer kept the stations alive. The Beyond, and now the First Stars, had other interests. Their survival was far more dependent on the politics of Pell and Cyteen than maintaining any vital interest in Sol.

No EC. No complex Earth politics. No blessing from the mother-system required.

That was the answer they'd found, the concept they'd all signed onto. A universe of trade, in which what one did and how one fared affected every-body, short-term, long-term, and equally.

But Mum had said it: they all needed to quit spending money and get back on track to earning it.

"So small cans, foodstuffs, and materials for the Hinder Stars," Mum was saying, Fourth-shift captain, once Senior. "No risk. Fast trip. And then back to our own business. Take our Monahan guests on a tour of business as usual, hoping we can reunite them with their ship."

"That's the plan," JR said fervently.

Book II   Section ix

The rest of the Galways turned up at the first game shop, a huge room filled with vid screens and electronic equipment. They were sitting in strange chairs, with plastic hoods over their heads, below which their entire bodies were twitching in uncanny unison.

Ross and Jen walked in unnoticed, dropped their packages, and collapsed onto a small couch, footsore and exhausted. From across the room, Dot, one of their Finity watchdogs, glanced up from a shelf of displays and came over with a grin on her face.

"I think we've found a winner," she said. "But I'm not exactly sure what or how much, since we haven't been able to pull your cousins away. This is the newest VR—came out since *our* last call here . . ."

"*Ga-aa-aa-aa!*" Frustration filled the air. One of the hoods lifted, and Ian thrust himself up. "Where's the nearest loo?" he asked, looking a bit desperate, and Dot laughed and pointed.

"Take his seat," Twofer suggested. Nice guy . . . one of Jen's fellow security, who'd been sitting quietly nearby watching the players.

Ross looked in that direction, but Jen grabbed his arm. "I know you, spacer-lad. You get started and I won't see you for hours."

"Ten minutes. Set a timer. Word of honor."

"Go. Get yourself killed. See if I care." She gave a wave of her hand toward the gallery of chairs. "I'm going to check on tickets for the Garden."

He went. He sat, slid his hands and forearms into padded sleeves attached to chairarms. The hood lowered . . . and suddenly he was in the midst of sound and fury. Something came at him and he flung up his hand, which miraculously gripped a sword. He swung it wildly in self defense.

"Heads up!" Siobhan's voice rang in his ears as something came flying at his head. A dome materialized around him. Everything blurred as a force grabbed him and set him on a high rock, where he could actually view the chaos. Something shaggy and snarling rushed at him from the left and without thinking, he swung the over-large sword in a wide arc—and a shock reverberated through him as the sword met a body. Fur and teeth disappeared in a burst of fireworks—

—and *two* shaggy things came at him.

Ten minutes later, when Jen's voice hauled him out, and the hood raised, he told himself a batch of these chairs needed to be added to *Galway*'s overhaul, to hell with the gym. Not that it would happen—the promised refit was to bring *Galway* up to merchanter standards . . . not to provide a state of the art gameroom.

Still . . .

He looked wistfully at the deceptively simple chair as he pushed himself to his feet, and thought of Bryant's and Alpha, where just one of these units would revolutionize arcades . . . staggered as surprisingly fatigued muscles went to jelly. He welcomed Jen's hold on his arm as he turned and found Ian, whose hair was spiked with water from the lavatory. Or sweat.

"Did you get me killed?" Ian asked.

"Three times," he had to confess.

Ian heaved a huge sigh, and scrubbed his hair into submission. "Save us from this. We won't be able to walk tomorrow."

"Shush," Jen grunted, once more occupied with the Pell-network pocket com only she carried.

"Problems?" Ross asked.

"That new exhibit," she said, without looking up. "Booked solid for days." She was frowning. But a grin flashed up at him. "But I'll get us in. Don't you worry! Trees *will* happen!"

The other Galways had hoisted themselves free of the VR-chairs as well, and came over to find out what was going on. All agreed the game was a keeper, once they discovered there was a conversion unit that would let them play it on any legacy system, and that once the conversion unit was added to *Galway*'s system, even more games they'd never seen would come available. Like all copyrighted digital material, games transferred from station to station via the feed, but unless *Galway*'s systems met the minimum requirements of a game, they'd never even see it listed. That conversion unit itself was a real find, and as for the game, if they bought it here, so the flashy ads claimed, it came with extras . . . for a few creds more. But those few creds would get them a fancy light show and a pair of flashing toy swords emblazoned with PELL for the youngers.

So they ticked several more names off their list.

While Ian was negotiating with the sales clerk, Ross caught Jen looking quizzically at him.

"What?" he asked.

"It didn't bother you," she said, which left him still in the dark.

"What didn't?"

"The game. Total immersion VR, and you brush it off like any normal human being, but you're spooked by a few bouncing monkeys."

That stopped him cold. Made him wonder, until he suddenly realized: "Because there was never any doubt."

She looked smug. "Keep going."

"Because *I* put on the helmet and sat in the chair, and deliberately went into the game's reality. It wasn't just jumping at me in the real world."

She tilted her head a moment. Then nodded. "Interesting. Keep that on your backburner, Nav 1.5."

"Will."

His pocketcom beeped: a message from Maire telling them to hurry up, and he realized the others had escaped the store while he and Jen were talking. As they hurried toward the door, he grabbed Jen's hand, and said, "Thanks."

She glanced up at him and winked. "Anytime."

They found the others waiting in an adjacent bar. By the time they'd recovered from the game, exclaimed over the scarves and bits of fabric, and designed at least three improbable outfits for Winslow on Maire's handheld, they'd officially joined forces for the day, making a rather large and fairly riotous party. But since the Finitys were on strict orders, and the Galways were highly conscious of the impression *Galway* patches left on the locals, the rioting was polite and limited to a walk further down the row, where a toy store and a regular supply store with a sideline in patches turned up some gems, patches for Cyteen-side ships, no less, and the Viking iron pusher, *Edward Gorey.* Those were gold, back home. They *had* some *Galway* patches to trade, and those, as Alpha patches, produced a fair handful of change—it was a great and prideful temptation to say those were going to be worth a bit more, come a year or so—but the order was deep silence on dockside, where it regarded *Galway's* business, and they gave not a clue.

Jen continued checking her shore-com, hoping for news on the tour of the Garden. The party had grown steadily, until they had a total of twelve, including all the Galways and their two additional Finity guides. Getting two admissions on short notice was rarely a problem. Even four was sometimes, with good luck, granted within a few hours; but twelve? That needed special application, an assigned tour guide, and a stack of oaths of good behavior.

And no chance, none whatsoever, that they'd get a slot for the maindawn spectacle Jen had hoped for. Jen put on a face about that, and asked for the Pell Department of Guest Relations.

For a time, it appeared not even Jen's gift of persuasion would be enough to make an opening in the next few days. The two extra Finitys offered to bow out, willing to wait for the new stuff, but Jen insisted they not give up yet, a renewed resolve in her eyes. Ross suspected that Fletcher and possibly even JR had become involved, but, knowing Jen in pursuit-mode, he didn't venture to ask.

The call came while Jen and Ross were having a gelato at a certified-authentic Italian booth. The group had split up temporarily, unable to settle on a single treat with so many options available.

"Yes!" Jen said, and flipped her way through the message. The triumphant gleam faded as quickly as it had arrived.

"Problems?" Ross asked, swallowing a mouthful of goodness.

"Not really. They got us all in. It's just . . . short notice."

"How short?"

"*Really* short. Tonight. Maindark." Her eyes flashed up at him. "There goes our fancy dinner in the Jade Room and an early-to-bed evening." Her thumbs flew, sending a message to all the others. Within moments, she had answers from the entire group, and distributed the ticket downloads and the address. "I've told everybody to meet us beside the elephant. We barely have time to shower and change."

"How'd we get in?" Ross asked, as she set the com down and applied herself to her own balls of frozen dessert.

"Cancellation," she said. "A local party."

"That was convenient."

"Oh, cut the sarcasm, spacer-boy. Whatever deal *Finity* made is nothing more than she'd do for any of us, if occasion warranted. Us being on a short shore leave, sometimes we have to pay a little extra to accommodate our schedule, and stationers *will* budge. Chances are it cost no more than a bottle of Scotch. Okay? Time is short." She shoveled the last of her dessert in a single large bite and immediately pressed her fingers to her throat. "Ouch! Brain freeze!" She hopped to her feet and pulled him up. "We have got to shower, re-dress in casuals—there is water involved—and meet the transport. Move-move-move!"

A bottle of Scotch to get already-pricey tickets, and he had the feeling she was serious. A single shot of the real stuff was way beyond his Alpha imaginings. Ross licked the last taste off the ceramic spoon, dropped the spoon and the cup into the return at the exit, and headed out to find the elephant.

Their room in the Royal was extravagant, no end, but for all the overboard color and furnishings, there was, like the gilt elephant, a decidedly playful sense of fun to it all that didn't take its specialness seriously. And if the odd tassel cast weird shadows in the bath or an embroidered elephant-shaped pillow didn't quite tuck into any part of the human body, the bed itself was decadently comfortable, with a plethora of pillows that *did* tuck perfectly well into the odd crook of an elbow, or under the neck.

"Check this out." Jen turned off the ambient light and a moment later, the room was filled with tiny, glittering spots of lights, randomly floating.

Ross twisted around on the bed and watched, lifting his hand into the air to catch those glittering motes . . . only to have them flitter away as if they were alive, and found himself thinking about those motes highlighting a rather differently shaped body part.

That was inspiring.

"Fireflies," Jen said, and her finger slid down the list beside the dial. "We can have stars, rainbows, birds . . . anything you want tonight." She cast him a wicked look. "Even monkeys."

"I'm good," Ross said hastily, and Jen headed for the shower with a giggle. He lay there, watching fireflies, doing his damnedest not to think of monkeys and tigers, trying to sort all he'd seen, to imagine what more there could possibly be . . . besides trees . . . but the games and the shops and the day on the docks hazed rapidly down into the dark behind his eyelids. For a moment he was back on *Galway*, ready for an Alpha run. Going home. . . .

Fallan was at his post. On *Galway*, they were side by side. And Fallan went about business, cool as ever, while he felt a vague anxiety . . . he couldn't say why.

"Fal," he said. But Fallan kept checking and pushing buttons, and he couldn't remember what course they were setting. He'd been wrong. It wasn't Alpha they were going to. The numbers didn't look familiar.

"Fal," he said again, and he might as well not have been there. Fallan just went on doing what he'd done. Again. And again. Like a replay.

He was stuck in this—until he wasn't. He was back in the row behind Kate and Bucklin, behind Ty and Jim.

And Jen was trying to get his attention.

Damn. That was weird. Crazy real. He reached to turn his pillow over and burrow into it, but a tassel hit him in the face, as *somebody* pulled the pillow out from under him.

"Wake up, sluggabug. Shower! Now!"

God. He was anxious to shake *that* dream.

"You can join me." His hand found smooth skin beneath dripping hair.

She twisted her head and gave his palm a quick kiss before pulling away. "Not and make it to the elephant in time. Go! Up! Move!"

He sighed, forced muscles to move, missed the edge of the bed and re-covered himself, barely, with a foot on the floor. The motes still surrounded them, and the room had shapes and edges. It was light enough to wake by.

"No lingering." Jen's voice reached him from outside the shower. "Shower and out. The trolley is going to be here."

He showered, started with a cold blast to wake himself up, then hot as Hades to get his blood moving. He *didn't* linger, but by the time he came out, Jen was ready to go. She stood by the door theatrically tapping her toe while he dressed.

"Time," she said. "Time." He hurried.

As they were leaving the room, she slipped her hand inside his elbow and hugged his arm especially hard. "It's showtime, spacer-boy. I have so looked forward to this. And for sure, you're going to see trees."

Book II   Section xi

Jen kept it moving, and gathering members, but at the last moment the party boarding the trolley outside the Royal suddenly shrank, not in number, but in sheer mass. Sadly, Twofer had had to get off and bow out, apparently an onboard meeting, for which Jen was genuinely sorry and *so* afraid she was going to get her own call from Fletcher. But that call didn't come, and there'd been a waiting list of Neiharts anxious to step up to fill out the party: as Twofer left them, young Will, cook's helper, literally came running and jumped aboard, all scrubbed and polished and out of breath, excited to have won the lottery. Jen introduced William to the Monahans as they all piled onto the trolley. Ross responded with the polite words and a nod, but to her eyes . . . he still wasn't, quite, all there. . . . Hadn't been, since that phase-out' in the room.

Time, Jen thought, as the trolley rolled up-ring through the increased noise and bustle of the newly waked mainnight crowds, for some serious Ross-distraction. He'd been dreaming, there in the room, calling to Fallan— which he hadn't done in her hearing since the very first days after Alpha.

Somehow, she didn't think it was the monkeys this time; with luck, they'd put that weirdness to rest. Maybe it was the sheer size and noise and racket of Pell, but again, that had seemed settled. Maybe . . . maybe he *was* still hearing the star. That would be scary, and she wondered should she talk to Kate, find out if *she* understood what he was going through. Whatever had happened when they'd dropped into Pell had shaken him, she was sure of that, but she was not sure whether it was because of Pell itself, or because Pell meant the end and be-all of their trip, the point past which . . . The point past which decisions had to be made. If all went as Senior Captain hoped, they'd get loaded for Venture—cargo going back the way they'd come, des- tined to help the shortages at Alpha. At Venture, they would meet *Little Bear,* and discover what had happened behind them at Alpha. Depending on what they said there, the Galways would stay aboard, would join them for a normal round of Viking and Mariner . . . or return to Alpha.

So this was the turnaround point. Was that what had begun to affect him, in all the raucous silliness of the Royal?

He covered it well, but when he thought she wasn't looking, a shadow crossed his face.

The Winslow hunt had done him good, as had the VR game, but her ace in the hole, the promise she had made him clear back at Alpha, was *trees.* And *trees* he was about to get. If that didn't distract him from doubting him- self, if that didn't give him something to tell Fallan about, other than feeling stars . . . nothing would.

The trolley pulled up at a closed airlock, a small trolley-sized door within a much larger freight-sized pressure lock, which was in turn set into massive section doors—standard precaution against a breach in the ring's integrity. The small door opened automatically, and the trolley moved into the lock.

"Not there yet," Jen turned in her seat to say, raising her voice over the burr of the tires on the decking. "Most traffic goes on where the deck nar- rows. We're now in a restricted area that serves as a protection for the station and the Garden ecosystem—one of the containment protocols that keep both this small patch of Earth safe from us and safe from getting where it could reach Downbelow. The decon protocols for people going down *to* the planet are brutal, what I hear. Question: do the hisa go into the Garden? Answer: no. They come and go to the planet and decon would be a problem. Those section doors back there are matched on the other end of this stretch. Has there ever been a biological breakout? No. They're careful. *Real* careful."

They continued in a passage a fraction of the size of the docks they just left. Tiny, to her way of thinking, just big enough for two standard cargo movers to pass each other, but comparable, she suddenly realized, to the overhead free-space on Alpha's Strip, Alpha's version of Pell's docks.

"Weird," Maire said. "It's all signs . . . advertising stuff. No shops."

The walls, she meant, where the walls were covered with screens and constantly shifting images.

"We're actually traveling under the garden," Jen explained. "Above, to the sides . . . it's all plants."

Beside her, Ross just shook his head, staring around him at the visual cacophony, looking not particularly happy. Jen reached out and locked fingers with him, and with a blink, he smiled down at her and squeezed gently. "Soon," she whispered, as the trolley slowed, slowed further, and stopped, opening its passenger gate to let them off. Still holding Ross by the hand, she hopped off and led the way down the single step ahead of the rest of the Monahans. And young Will. The empty trolley simply reversed and headed back the way it had come, a diminishing whine in a comparative hush. She led her Monahans through that quiet, down a painted stripe in dim lighting. The only sounds other than their own footsteps were the soft thumps and wheezes. The only movement was a gentle cold airflow.

A second and then a third stripe joined the first, one on the ceiling, one on the floor, signs that, in a ship, would be orientation markers for zero-G. And as they approached the Garden entrance, the adverts stopped, a brown stripe joined the white, then a third, green. Finally, as they came to the lock on the inner wall—fancy letters painted in white on brown and green proclaimed:

Edmund Pell Garden.

And below, in smaller letters:

Experience the magic.

As they approached the Garden entrance, a large floating sign lit up, announcing scheduled events: a thunderstorm at 17:00, which it almost was, sunset at 17:45. And the current time and temperature: a comfortable 24C, humidity 40%—slightly soggy—and, notably, an experience in itself, a wind at 20 kph.

Wind? Ross wondered. Air moved in a station. Fans, air circulation, temperature differences, all such things caused mostly unpredictable air currents. In Alpha, there was a hellacious gale from the core lift when the doors opened, far greater than the promised 20 kph.

Ross rather looked forward to this *wind*.

"Thunderstorm?" Siobhan asked and Jen answered:

"Rain. Wind. Thunder. Lightning. All at once. Sims, mostly, but the water's real. You can get wet. Haven't experienced the storm, but I've been in the rain shower. Which is gentler. Did I say, Don't wear your best clothes?"

"Cool," Connor said. "Seriously cool."

"So," Jen waved them toward the door, flashing her com unit in the process. "Let's get in there before we miss it. Move, move, move, friends!"

Ross moved. At the side of the door, a square panel lit and began to blink:

Admission, it said. *Show code. For code, apply online at Pell Ticketing. Admission is restricted to persons over six years of age. No exceptions. Groups are restricted to twenty. All admissions require a guide.*

They didn't give a price.

Jen held her com over the blinking scanner and the painted door slid open, not on paradise, but on a glaring white chamber. A cheerful voice said: *"Each group must lock through together."*

They walked in. The outer door sealed behind them.

"For the protection of the specimens, there will be a decontamination. Please hold out your arms, stand quietly, close your eyes, and breathe normally. You will notice a slightly sweet odor and a rather bright light behind your eyelids. There is absolutely no danger. At the chime, you'll be safe to open your eyes, and enter the garden.

"Flash vid is strictly prohibited. Official photos and vid of the garden are available in the souvenir shop at the end of the tour.

"Thank you for your cooperation, and enjoy your visit."

Ross closed his eyes, the promised scent and light followed, and at the sound of the chime, the door opened . . . to a rather anticlimactic staging room lined with images and text describing the construction of the gardens. At a tug from Jen's hand, he stepped into the room, and then it hit him: scent and humidity on the promised wind. For a breath or so, he just stood there, basking in that weird and wonderful air that lifted his hair and tickled his nostrils.

The lock doors thumped shut behind them; the ambient light dimmed.

"Welcome to Pell Gardens!" A cheerful voice greeted them, and a young-ish man appeared in a door on their left, the source of that pungent breeze. "My name is Andrew Ridgeman. Please . . . call me Andy. I'll be your guide today."

Average-looking fellow, dark skin and eyes, a slightly over-energetic Pell accent, a dark green jumpsuit, and a name badge emblazoned with *Edmund Pell Garden Tour.*

"Are we all here?" their guide asked, and when Jen nodded, "Excellent. If you'll all move on to the veranda, we can get the fun started."

He stepped to the side, made a sweeping gesture toward the door, and a dimly lighted area, beyond which it was quite, quite dark. No walls, just a clear, waist-high barrier with a rope-blocked opening, and a nearly invisible ceiling that rose in a shallow peak above them.

As his eyes adjusted, the blackness began to gain shape and texture. Strangely shaped fronds moved in those air currents, and the floor was nei-ther metal nor rug, but something . . . granular. Smooth, but it moved and piled as he pushed at it with his toe. Gradually, in and around the group chatter, a distant pinging noise, like a cross between a condensation drip and the post-jump showers, teased his eardrums.

"You've arrived just in time—" their guide said, and suddenly light, blinding white, flashed as a sound like a six-way transport collision reverber-ated through every bone of Ross's body. He tensed, waiting for an alarm, fearing some major catastrophe, a breach of some seal . . .

But there was no alarm. Not even a hint from "Andy" to retreat to the safety of the staging room. Cautiously, he looked up, through the shield . . . to find nothing but roiling grey overhead. And when another assault on his hearing came, he felt the fool: the promised storm. But they all had flinched. Even Jen, who was checking her handheld again.

"Seventeen on the clock," she said, with a hint of relief in her voice. "And here comes the storm." As water began to pelt down on the transparent roof.

There was nervous laughter all around. Just . . . part of the show. Show, hell, Ross thought. It was damned unfair. *Scary* and unfair. No wonder they banned tiny children: kids would be traumatized. Hell, *he* was traumatized. Another blast and he still had to convince his nerves it wasn't the station coming apart at its seams.

The pattering sound became a steady drumbeat, as hundreds of tiny falling streaks came pelting down. Not a flood, as water would come out of a faucet, nor the pounding spray of a shower, but like millions of those condensation droplets that fell from high places. They hit the transparent plastic of the roof, making fractal patterns down that sloped shield, and sheeting off the edge to the ground just outside their shelter, where they formed real puddles of real water.

Another flash and this time, forewarned, they all just stared as the brilliant light streaked a jagged pattern on the far side of that clear barrier. With each flash, light momentarily filled the stormy murk beyond, where mysterious silhouettes appeared and vanished again, hints of the wonders to come. And after the foremost—Ross and Connor Dhu and Siobhan—had stuck their hands out into the downpour, declaring it pleasantly cool, and just as shock and awe turned into their Engees Connor Dhu and Netha speculating on the technology involved, the thunder and lightning receded off to the right and the darkness overhead began to break up into light-edged, puffy shapes . . . which led to further speculation as to whether the designers were just that clever, or if someone or something was actually listening to them and had triggered that end to the show.

"Oh, shut up, the lot of you, and just look!" Maire said, and pointed ahead, where shafts of light burst through the "clouds," bringing the mysterious shapes that had been shrouded in darkness into lush, green life: plants, banks of plants, like yet unlike anything hydroponics offered aboard ship. Those shafts of light caught water droplets on huge leaves and spikes of brightly colored flowers, making them sparkle with all the colors of the spectrum.

And above it all, a transparent arc of color against the dark clouds, bands of that same spectrum.

"Rainbow," Siobhan breathed. "Wow . . . just . . . wow . . ." Which pretty well summed up Ross's feelings.

Their guide, Andy, excused his way through their group to stand next to the chain-blocked opening. He turned to face them with a set smile, and his voice took on the practiced cadence of an oft-repeated spiel. "Welcome to the Edmond Pell Gardens, the pride and joy of the station. Opened to the public only nine years ago, it is the realization of a dream decades in the making. Its creation is a story in itself, a story memorialized, along with time-lapse 3D imaging, in a vid available at the end of the tour. For now, we encourage you simply to take in the magic of Mother Nature, as only the Garden can present it."

Weird, Ross thought, and caught Jen's eye, saw her stifle a giggle. Apparently this florid introduction was normal.

"As you move through the gardens," Andy continued, "you will notice a variety of new scents, some quite potent. We assure you it's perfectly safe to breathe here. We really have only three hard and fast rules. One: stick to the paths. However, you're free to take whatever path you wish. They all loop back to the main walkway, and I'll bring up the rear, to make certain we leave no one behind. Secondly, we request that you touch only those exhibits clearly marked for that purpose. Specimens you may not even notice are extremely fragile, many are irreplaceable, and some, which we have carefully placed out of reach, are poisonous."

Well, *that* was decidedly useful information.

"Finally, and most obviously, do not attempt to take any specimens. If you desire a piece of the Garden to take home as a souvenir, safe, duty free items are available in the gift shop. Violation of any one of these rules will result in a fine and immediate expulsion from the Garden—without refund—without exception. Fair warning: all areas of the gardens are video monitored. This is for your safety as well as the Garden's. —Any questions?"

Behind him, Ian murmured something under his breath, and Andy's eyes flicked briefly in that direction. *Not* an oblivious caretaker. But when Ian remained silent:

"Excellent. Feel free to ask, should anything come up during your stay." With another glance Ian's direction. Then: "As a final precaution, expect some condensation on the walkways and drips from overhead, and please watch your step. Biological substances and fallen leaves can be slick."

Andy reached into his coat pocket and passed among them, handing out small round discs about the size of poker chips.

"Carry these in your pockets, or otherwise about your person. It contains a locator, should you somehow wander off—yes, it has happened—and if you press and hold the button on the edge, it will give you a lighted pathway to the exit. Pressing the central dot will activate signs located throughout the exhibit. These will give you general information regarding individual plants and their origins. The holo signs are proximity and direction sensitive: one press of the button on the chit to activate, two to suppress."

Predictably, holo signs flashed about those tantalizing green mounds along the visible pathway. On, off, on, off. Andy laughed, and continued his spiel in a more normal, relaxed tone.

"Should you have additional questions, I'll be happy to try and answer them. I have a *very* large cheat sheet." He grinned and lifted his handheld. "You may turn in the chit at the gift shop for store credit. They are useless beyond this tour."

Still he didn't lift that chain. Ross, already tired from a day of too much and too rich and too new . . . began to drift. He looked at his disc, identified the dot in question, but he didn't press it. He wasn't really interested in the names of things, or what Andy had to tell them. He wanted trees, and Andy was standing in the way. Beyond their human roadblock, Ross could see three paths, all edged with rocks that were carpeted in something green and (one assumed) living. One path was of brown pebbly stuff, another was black, and one that branched off the black had larger reddish stones. The brown path to the right curved off and disappeared into shadow under an amorphous arch of green, growing plants. The air wafting from that retreat smelled wet, and rich, and strange. It was mainday bright out now, and the plants, glistening with wet from the rain, beckoned. The beams of light coming through the shifting, fluffy shapes above carried a warmth where they struck human flesh. He closed his eyes, basking in that heat. What spectrum was that light? Tau Ceti's? Or Sol's? How much difference was there between them?

He should know. Part of his training was in the energy given off by stars, and part of prep before jump was analyzing the star at the center of the well. He'd ridden the boards into the wild angry creature that was Tau Ceti. That was the problem: he knew Tau Ceti, but he didn't know Sol. No FTL Navigator knew Sol like that . . . unless Fallan and Ashlan were, even now, diving into a Tau Ceti-type angry well, one filled with millions of smaller objects spinning around that other brilliant sun—

Jen's elbow jabbed him in the ribs. "Wake up, spacer-boy!"

"And now, my friends, welcome to the Tropics," Andy said, and stepped aside at last, taking the chain with him.

Ross headed straight toward that brown pebbly path and its inviting shadows, but Jen caught his arm, pulled him back to a pedestal tucked in among the shrubbery at the branching of the paths. There was a plaque that read "In loving memory. Anna Konstantin. Mother of the Garden." And one of those holos hovered above, image of a pleasant-looking, elderly woman.

"Who's she?" Maire asked their guide.

"Anna Konstantin, grandmother of our current stationmaster. Anna maintained a bonsai museum, open to the public, which is still going strong, for the best of her collection. But this garden, a loving dedication to humanity's birthplace, was her dream. It wasn't until we added the docking ring that it became a possibility. Sadly, she didn't live to see it, but she's buried here."

"Buried?" Ross took a step back. That was just . . . creepy.

"Well, her ashes. Quite a lovely tribute, actually. The whole story is available in the gift shop."

Siobhan asked, breaking an awkward silence, "So why isn't it called *Anna's* Garden? Seems only fair."

And better than walking on her, Ross thought with a suppressed shudder.

Andy said, "I don't really know." He checked his electronic "cheat sheet" and shrugged. "Sorry."

"Branding," Nolan said. "Name recognition. *Marketing*. Just images of this place would be a trade gold mine. They want those goods linked to Pell, not some unknown individual."

"So why hadn't *we* ever heard of this place?" Ian asked, and with a wink at Jen: "Until Jen brought it up, of course."

"I suspect the prices in the gift store will answer that one," Siobhan said, a little sadly.

"Well, fellow merchanters," Jen grabbed Ross's arm and pulled him back over to the brown path, "We don't need no stinkin' pictures! We've got the real thing, and my spacer-lad and I are off. We've got trees to find!"

The others spread out, leaving that rather disturbing pedestal behind, and awed exclamations filled the air. Ross pressed Jen's hand to his side, and she glanced up at him.

"Thanks for breaking that up," he said softly, and she answered in the same tone:

"Heck. We've got our own Cargo. Let them get started, and they'll go on for hours."

"I meant—"

She cut him off with a boot of her hip. "I know what you meant, Galway, and with *any* luck, your First Stars will soon be flooded with goodies from Pell. That's the whole point, isn't it?"

Of the alliance of merchanters, she meant. Of independence from Sol economy.

"Yeah," he said, with an emphatic nod. "Yeah, it is."

A bend in the path isolated them from that plaque, and he relaxed, letting that deep green blanket that seemed to go on forever, draping itself over rock and gravel, become his momentary reality. That blanket was a substrate for taller plants, many of which even bloomed, in colors no living thing should be. He was surrounded by things you didn't see except in vids, and you would never ordinarily believe, since computers could make up anything.

He stopped short. His thoughts flashed queasily on monkey holos, and suddenly he had an almost overwhelming desire to touch all that green, to make sure his hand didn't just pass right through them.

"Problem?" Jen asked, looking at him with concerned eyes.

"Tell me they're real. Tell me they're not just more holos."

She relaxed and grinned. "They're real, spacer-lad. There are a bunch you can touch up ahead."

"There'd better be. I dunno, Jen, between monkeys and that game . . . it's a wonder anyone on Pell knows the difference."

"Trust me. This is all real. I mean, just imagine the lawsuits if it turned out not?"

"Good point. So . . . what did Andy mean, tropics?"

"He explained all that."

"Must have missed it."

She chuckled and let her hand slide into his, swung it gently as they began to move again. As they wandered past large flowering shrubs, she explained about zoning, about the need for a tropical wet area, a dry, desert section, and a section for plants that needed distinct seasons, all to accommodate plants that originated on the same planet. Hard to imagine a place where so many environments coexisted, where land masses were so large, these living things could spread kilometer after kilometer, where these paths that rose a few steps might be mountains. Hard to imagine a place where temperature wasn't regulated by machines, where dehumidifiers didn't pump 24/7 to pull out every bit of excess moisture for recycling.

Beyond the flowering shrubs, the ground rose, terraces of rocks, which were, according to Jen, fake, but looked real enough to him, and earthen mounds (real) where more plants grew. Beyond that wall of rocks and plants, of live water cascading in silver ribbons down through the crevasses to disappear into the green below—was the corridor they'd walked to get here, or so common sense insisted. Jen poked him and said *Quit thinking so hard*, but that was easier said than done, especially for someone whose life was figuring where a ship was relative to everything else in the universe. But as the path meandered among rock and plants, consciousness of the wall, or the station, or the size of things faded. Clever use of lighting and other visual tricks made it seem like that vista just went on and on. Smells came and went.

And it all made him more than a little uneasy. He stopped at the top of the next mound, where plants reached out and laced together overhead, obscuring the artificial, disturbingly endless sky with something that was real.

Real, but . . . wrong.

He stared back the way they'd come, where paths meandered aimlessly among mounds of things that . . . made no sense.

"Ross?"

He lifted his hand to stop her, trying to figure out why his skin crawled and why every shadow seemed to hold secrets. The breeze didn't reach here, and yet the air moved. Where there should be nothing but the constant *thrums* and *thumps* of a working station. A part of him responded to those sights and sounds . . . genetic memory, he'd heard someone say, back before they'd split up . . . but natural or not, his skin *still* crawled.

As he stood quietly, there were buzzing noises, and the air itself was filled with motes that, rather than drift aimlessly like dust, moved with seeming purpose from flower to flower. He swept his hand through the motes and like the lights in their Pagoda room, they scattered, disappearing into the shadows. The buzzing stopped.

"Bugs," Jen said softly, and he turned back to find her standing with one hand palm up and nestled in it, what looked for all the world like a butterfly. The lights played across her skin, as the motes returned and danced around her, and he reached slowly into his pocket for his handheld, hoping, *hoping* to catch her before she moved. He had a lot of pictures of her in his archives, but this was . . . special. Her eye flicked toward him, then back to her butterfly, and she waited until he'd snapped the picture. He checked it, and it was pretty good. He was getting better. But then, he hadn't had much practice. He'd never had much interest in taking photos . . . before Jen.

"More holos?" he asked, as he started to put the handheld back, but she caught his wrist to stop him and when she reached out and put the butterfly on his hand, he actually felt it. He jerked and it flitted off.

"They're bots," she said. "They're partly for show, but they pollinate the plants and do other things, like clearing out dead leaves."

"What? Like duct cleaner bots?"

She grinned, and he caught that look, too, just before she stuck her tongue out. "Something like."

"O . . . k . . ."

Bugs. Pollinating. Plant sex.

All around them.

He drew a breath. "Experience the magic?"

"Something like."

Ross kept the camera out, tried hard to get some shots, to remember everything—not the names of plants, or what part of Earth they came from, but what it smelled like, felt like. He tried to remember, not just for himself, but for absent Monahans who couldn't be here. An obligation that made it really hard to simply relax and . . . experience the magic.

And despite Jen's assurance, a part of him continued to want to reach out, to confirm that reality. Just as the urge became nearly insurmountable—their path crossed another, where they discovered Connor and Aidan, Cargo 1.2, stopped at a little pedestal of plants in pots, with the sign *Yes, it's real. Safe to touch. Do not take the leaves. Preserved specimens are available in the Gift Shop.*

They touched—Ross defied anyone to resist that temptation, and as they exclaimed over the sometimes velvety, sometimes prickly textures, their guide overtook them, with Nolan and Netha, who stopped for their own touch. They moved on as a group, taking a left-hand path, which disappeared behind them as it meandered among the plants. Huge numbers of them. Of different kinds. Hydroponics he was familiar with. Potted plants. These were just all over each other.

Crowding each other for space. Resources wars. Trying to crawl across the walkways.

"Does it bother you?" he heard Nolan ask, in a low voice, and Netha: "The paths?" And at Nolan's assent: "They curve all over the place. No rhyme nor reason. It's not *natural.*"

And suddenly Ross realized the source of his own underlying queasiness. Corridors were straight, or they curved with the radius of the station. Walls met at right angles. This eerie meandering, like that limitless sky, just . . . wasn't right somehow. He supposed in those light-years-away lands on Earth, paths did this, following natural contours, detouring around growing things and free-running water . . . paths created by his ancestors between points of interest, ancestors for whom this *was* . . . natural.

God. He couldn't imagine.

Something heavy landed on his shoulder and he nearly jumped out of his skin. Patrick's rich laughter identified the hand.

"Experience of a lifetime. —You, cousin, owe this young lady."

"And you owe me a pacemaker."

Laughter rang as others of their party joined them, pathways converging. Patrick triggered the labels and this time Ross paused to read them. Common name, scientific designation, initial propagation method—seed, cutting, bonsai—and, curiously, "donated by." Some were just names, but others . . . the vast majority of those visible . . .

"Those are merchanter names," he said, and their guide nodded.

"Absolutely. I assumed, being merchanters yourselves, that you knew. All of these plants, in one way or another, came from the old pusher ships."

"Pusher ships?" Netha looked skeptical. Bonsai were popular on stations. There were a few in shops along Alpha's Strip, not for sale, just as part of a display, some plastic. The fancy ones were mostly a stationer side thing, in areas and establishments where spacers didn't go.

"When Jen first brought up the Garden, I remember Fallan mentioning something about bonsai on the old pusher ships," Ross said. And for the sake of their guide. "One of our crew. Kind of a big thing, according to him. All the ships had them. Don't know why we don't."

"I think I can answer that," Andy said. "They can't survive FTL. The first FTL converts discovered the hard way that FTL doesn't play nicely with plants, particularly woody bonsai. In jump, they just failed. The older they were, the more vulnerable they were to what we now call jump-rot. And no one knew why. Still don't, though the garden's botanists have been working on the problem for years. Fortunately, while *Gaia* was here, her last call as a pusher, for reasons her crew never really explained, she offloaded a number of specimens—sold a few to private citizens, others they donated outright to Anna Konstantin for her collection. When word got out about the FTL effects, pushers began donating their best specimens before going in for conversion, until Anna had far more than the museum could hold. Then the ring-dock expansion came, and, well, this is the result."

"So . . . what?" Connor Dhu asked. "You just took these bonsai, stuck them in medium and they grew big?"

"Pretty much," Andy said. "They aren't changed genetically. Simply kept small mechanically, so-to-speak."

"How old are these?"

"Many are well over a century old, but their unfettered growth, if you will, is at most seventeen years, which is when the docking ring went operational. The flowering shrubs tend to be a bit more resilient, so they went into the Garden first. The trees took a little more time in the back rooms before they could be safely moved out here. Most of them have been free-growing ten years or less."

"Speaking of trees . . ." Jen's hold on his arm pulled Ross into motion, and their guide, with a glance at his watch, winced.

"Is there a time limit?" Ross asked.

"Not as such," Andy replied, as they began to walk again, "but there's another group coming in soon. I've asked staff to encourage them to take the right hand path."

"Wow," Aidan said, a little breathlessly, and stopped short. "Look up."

Overhead, against the translucent blue light "sky", the lumpish edges of the "clouds" were accented now with orange and pink.

"Ah—" Andy said. "Sunset."

In deference to his stomach, Ross had avoided looking up, but slowly deepening color, an amazing array of shades as the shadow-side went to deepest purple . . . made it impossible to look away. Jen's head pressed against his shoulder. He glanced down at her and beyond her upward gaze and dark hair . . .

He squeezed her arm, and when she met his eyes, he nodded to the flowers around them, flowers that seemed to glow with some color just at the edge of the sensitivity of his eyes. Jen exclaimed aloud and called the others' attention to the curious phenomenon.

"Interesting," their guide said, in an approving—and somewhat surprised—tone. "Not everyone can even see it. We have yet to determine if it's simply an idiosyncracy of the sunlight simulation or denotes some physical reaction of the plants. We began the sunsets as pure entertainment for the visitors, an attempt to recreate to the best of our ability an idyllic evening on Earth itself, but we soon noticed the plants were thriving under the change. Our botanists are still trying to determine exactly what effect these environmental factors have on the plants. Moonlight is another example."

"Moonlight?" Jen asked.

"Earth's Moon, simulation of course, will be rising shortly," Andy said. "The garden is open around the clock, but the day-night cycle is critical for the plants' respiration, so we added the moonlight for safety as well as ambiance. Again, certain plants responded positively—for whatever reason, and so now moonlight is a regular part of the schedule, whether visitors are here or not."

Silence surrounded them as the colors dimmed, and they walked on. Light diminished. The "clouds" parted and in the empty space, points of light winked into being: the night sky as it would appear at Earth's equator . . . or so Andy said, and friendly arguments arose over which of those points of lights was the home of what station. Finally Andy held up his chit and tapped the button in a complex pattern . . . and a handful of stars gleamed brighter and holo-signs proclaimed their names and associated stations, another tap and other lights and holo signs gleamed, ancient constellations they knew only through historical reference—gods in the sky.

Which was all well and good, but they were hardly here to see fake stars, and at the moment, the trees they'd come to see seemed farther away than ever, dark as it was getting. Then behind them, another light source grew, casting shadows and flooding the air with a dim, bluish light. The promised moon.

"Big," someone said in the dark. And, "Hell of a navigational hazard." That was Ian, Helm, which made everyone laugh, and broke the spell.

It was, in its way, more pleasant than the glaring yellow of the virtual sunlight, and in the areas where the shadows still reigned, a soft blue light illuminated the path and touched the undersides of the plants. Three taps, Andy said, would temporarily bring the local ambient lights up brighter, and show the true colors. The path led them to a section of familiar plants. They were, according to Andy, plants impervious to the dreaded jump-rot. Spider Plant spilled down a rocky face, and a massive Ostrich Fern sat at the base of it, all moving, wind-blown, ingeniously spotlighted. Lettuce and rosemary, ferns, cucumbers and peppers: such plants were familiar, yes, but never had they seen them in this vast, overwhelming size and quantity.

Still . . .

"Trees?" he whispered, and Jen's hand closed on his, gave it a squeeze as they entered a tunnel of sorts, some plant that rose on a twisted, woody network and closed overhead. Flowers and leafy tendrils, eerie in the ambient blue light, brushed their heads. The wind increased here. A rustling sound rose in the distance. It had texture, and moved about and over them with a sound powerful and alive. Unlike the core draft, it didn't howl or shriek. It whispered in a thousand voices at once.

"Wind in the leaves," Patrick murmured, and Siobhan laughed nervously. Ross felt it too: something . . . familiar. Something at once wondrous and unnerving. Just his mind making connections, a part of him insisted. Another part laughed at his determinedly rational self. His ancestors had known these sounds, had read them, *felt* them, as surely as he had felt that monster star. Instincts as ancient as humanity. Spooks in the dark.

Which rationalization didn't stop him from being relieved when someone tapped the button and the lights rose on the pathway. Another turn, and moonlight lay ahead. They exited the tunnel.

And there began at last to be trees.

Ross stopped short, looked straight at Jen. "I thought you said they were about your height."

She grinned. "Wasn't sure you'd believe the truth."

Holo signs flashed in every direction. Palm trees, thick as a man's arm, with, curiously, orchids—which Ross did recognize—growing right on their trunks. Crabapple, one sign read, of a tree with a network of contorted branches spreading from its trunk. A holo next to the sign showed a miniature version, covered in tiny pink flowers, and another covered this time with red berries.

The sign read: *Evolutionary response to seasonal temperature variation influences this tree's method of propagation. Details available in the museum at the end of the tour.*

"Seasons?" someone asked, sparking a debate over the word, until they reached a group of "willows", the tallest trees they'd yet seen. Monsters towering over their heads, with long, thin branches that hung nearly to the ground, moving green curtains that swept violently sideways in a sudden gust of wind, startling everyone into silence. Another gust; another rustling ripple.

"That was no chance breeze. They set that up on purpose," Connor said, and moved near the edge, craning his head to find the source of that gust. Andy frowned and reached for him, but Patrick grabbed Connor's arm and pulled him back from that barrier.

"These were some of the first trees planted here," Andy explained, relaxing. "They were mature bonsai when they were planted and they're nearing the end of their life cycle; some have already gone. Sadly, we failed to allow them enough space. We have seedlings started in the nursery to replace them. Those will be at least twice as tall when their cycle comes to an end, having spent their entire life free-growing."

Twice as tall. Maybe as much as much as ten meters. That . . . was impressive.

"What happens to the dead trees?" Ian asked. "That's a lot of biomass."

"There's a waiting list for segments of the trunks. Artists eager to try some of the old woodworking techniques like carving and turning. We've had no few disasters in the trial and error of getting the Garden to this state, and the word has gotten out. You'll find some beautiful items for sale in the gift shop. Rest assured, nothing goes to waste. Everything not sellable is recycled into the garden soil."

"Do you sell the raw pieces?" Nolan, Cargo 1.1, asked, in a tone designed to imply innocent curiosity, which didn't for a moment fool his cousins. The gift shop items were certain to be out of reach for profit, but, like the scraps for Winslow, these raw pieces, on Alpha, could be a windfall.

"Yes and no. We sell a piece along with the right to use our shop in the back. Nothing leaves this section that isn't processed and sealed. The risk of contamination is too great."

Well, that was one way to corner the market.

"Contamination?" Maire asked.

"Pell lies above a living world with a very different, but not different enough, biology. Wood is a living thing, and could harbor unseen things that could work their way to Downbelow, creating unknown havoc."

"What . . . things?" Patrick asked. "What *kind* of havoc?"

Andy's face went a little hard. "Frankly, we've no desire to find out."

"Sorry," Patrick said. "No offense intended."

Andy relaxed. "Sorry. It's a bit of a touchy topic, even for those who have grown up on Pell. We've had several locals who wanted to buy stock for their own personal garden, and even a few representatives of other stations who want create their own public gardens. Some have gotten quite . . . insistent. We've been forced to take an extremely hard line on the topic. All our stock dates back to the pusher-age, one way and another, obviously, and more than plants made their way out from Earth. Moss, grasses, even microbes, many of which seem to have a beneficial, symbiotic relationship with the plant itself, permeated every plant. Before Pell was established, when there was no worry that they could ever contaminate a living world, ships and stations traded specimens about, with very few records kept of any sort, and no concerns about the plants' microscopic passengers. Nowadays, orbiting the living world of Downbelow as we do, we are *extremely* careful. All donations are closely inspected, and any suspicious specimens are refused entry. Those accepted have their DNA recorded and spend at least a year in isolation before being put into the garden. Importantly, *all* traffic up from and down to the planet is meticulously decontaminated so that no fungi and no plant or bacterial matter can cross that line—for our own safety, as well as the planet itself."

"*Death* from Downbelow," Patrick intoned ominously, to counter the darkening mood, and everyone laughed obligingly, but in this setting, with plants marked "poisonous", the popular horror vid trope gained a bit more cred.

"I assure you," Andy said with a chuckle, "*nothing* gets past our safeguards. Nothing ever has and we don't intend to break our streak. On the other hand, here in the Garden, we're trying to get as balanced an ecosystem as possible, and that increases the risk of contamination exponentially. Hence the sealed section, and the decontamination going in and out."

None of which should stop them from selling the raw wood and shipping it in sealed, decontaminated containers, if they were so inclined. No, this was *ex-clu-sivity*. An enterprise aimed directly at what Ross was beginning to realize was a luxury market virtually unrecognizable to the First Stars' trade. People who used bottles of Scotch as thank you gifts.

On the other hand . . . should the route to Sol prove out . . . Sol had trees. Lots and lots of trees. And seeds might not get jump-rot, *or* carry contaminants. And talk about a massive profit to mass ratio . . .

He took a mental note.

"If there are no records," Aidan interjected, "how do you even know what they are?"

"Classification of some of the plants is tricky," Andy said, seemingly pleased at their interest. "We have some reference materials, and we requested, decades ago via the EC stream, a current reference for all Earth botanicals, complete with DNA sequencing, on which, sadly, we are still waiting. While the willow there is fairly obviously a willow, the moss around its base is somewhat a puzzle. It accompanied the oldest of the willows, which came to us from Viking, where it was grown from a cutting imported from Venture, and before that, Glory. Glory is . . . well, of course you know Glory, being merchanters. Anyway, the original came from Earth on the pusher-ship *Gloriana*."

Ancient history. Glory was part of *Galway*'s route, and while it was unlikely the guide had any idea who or what they were, beyond guests of *Finity* crew, those billowing trees were, suddenly, an eerie touch of home.

Living proof of how interconnected they all were, stations and ships. Crazy how *Finity* and Senior Captain's alliance had colored his thinking.

"Ready to move?" the guide asked. "We're climbing again, and there will be naturalized terrain, so watch your step."

The path led upward by steps and incline, large flat rocks surrounded by finely ground-up stone. There was a hand rail, and Ross was not the only one to make use of it. It had begun to be an effort—far more walking than a spacer was used to and the twists and turns, the uneven ground worked small muscles he didn't know he had.

His *toes* hurt, for God's sake.

As they went up, the ambient air became dryer. Warmer. There were cacti, which were popular on stations, but really large ones; another zone, their guide said, this one of plants that stored water, and that could suffer from too much of it. Not particularly interesting, but not a bad backdrop for . . . other subjects. Ross made use of his camera, even catching some of his cousins, who, realizing they were being immortalized, hammed it up rather embarrassingly. Not that Andy seemed to notice, and Jen and the other Finitys proved as bad.

As the winding steps led downward again, quite steeply, he pocketed the camera, ignoring the protests, to steady himself with the handrail.

Thankfully, the path soon leveled out to soft terrain, greater humidity, and more trees—apple trees, the sign said, two with fruit in progress, tiny globes that were, indeed, "apple-green" in color. They were not as impressive as the willows, but they might be younger, Ross thought. Apple was edible. They got it in synth, the flavor anyway; it was fairly popular, and combined with a lot of things. And next to the apples was an orange tree, laden with tiny round globes.

Oranges. *Real* oranges.

"But they're so tiny!" Siobhan said, "and *green!*" and Andy assured her the fruits were far from ready to harvest, that the orange color was the final indicator that a fruit was ripe. A basket atop one of the touching pedestals held samples of the full-sized fruits, irradiated and preserved for appearance. Fruits which practically glowed in the moonlight. Andy assured them the textures and colors and even smells were perfect . . . and there were samples available in the gift shop.

And with a push of a button, more holos appeared, again with the seasonal changes in the trees. Interesting, but . . . not real. He wondered what it looked like when all those branches were covered in tiny flowers, or heavy with "ripe" fruit.

"Someday," Jen murmured, and as if she'd read his mind: "I want to see it in bloom. I think that would be . . . really special."

He squeezed her hand. "Send me a picture?"

She stopped and looked up at him, her brow twisted with a sudden sad thought. Realization, he was sure, that sharing the real thing was never likely to happen.

"It's okay, Jen," he said, very softly. "We've got this."

Her eyes glimmered in the moonlight, before her mouth stretched into her just-between-them grin. "We sure do, spacer-lad."

They hurried to catch the others, who had disappeared into a growth of tall, deep green trees with strange leaves, if "leaves" was the right word for the shiny fronds. The trees grew close and thick, and towered above them, so for the first time they were surrounded by trees on both sides.

Red cedars, the holo sign proclaimed.

"You may touch this one, if you like," their guide said, of a tree closer than the others.

Those shiny fronds were—Ross discovered, running his fingers hesitantly through them—surprisingly soft. Delicate. Almost lacy. And the covering on the trunk, *bark*, the sign called it, was hard. Human hands had worn it smooth and shiny and strange, but above and below easy reach, it was rough and stringy. Ross, taller than average, could just reach it with his fingertips. A tiny bit of bark came back with his hand, and Andy let them all examine it before taking it into custody.

"It's like armor," Maire said, leaning her hand against the tree, then rapping it with her knuckles.

"Very much so," Andy said. "The bark protects the living cells that transport nutrients from the roots to the leaves. The cedars are prolific—they seem to *like* to be crowded—and we have to thin them as they grow. Fortunately, they are a very versatile plant. The local artists buy the culls and, using our safe rooms, make a wide variety of objects, even weaving the bark into baskets and clothing, which are—"

"Available in the gift shop," Patrick finished for him, and they all laughed, even Andy. They were all merchanters, in their different ways, and damned if merchanters couldn't appreciate a good pitch.

They moved deeper into the trees and the wind, which had subsided a while, gusted. Water droplets came down on them, and the foliage sighed softly. Again there was that visceral response, something both threatening and right about the envelopment of sound, atmosphere and smell, as if this was a place both remembered and surreal. Ross felt Jen's hand brush his arm, felt and heard cousins all around him, and still felt alone and, if he were honest, a little scared—as if this place was sinking into his mind, and saying *son*. . . .

It was not a feeling he could describe to anyone who hadn't been here, and he shied away from asking the others, chatting easily all around him, if they felt it. He *didn't* belong to this place, didn't *want* to belong. It was beautiful. Spectacular. Fascinating . . . but as far from his existence as the void of space. *Farther.* Space was always just a bulkhead away. Yet for some reason, his mind turned to that moment he'd stepped outside *Galway* into the void of space, into the greatest dark there was. . . .

That memory met *this*, another vastness he couldn't express, only feel, and he wished aunt Peg, more a mother to him than his birth mother, were here to . . . ground him. He wished Fallan were. And Niall. And all of his *Galway* family. *That* was where he belonged; not some . . . *virtual* Earth. No matter the plants were real. A part of him wanted to leave right now and go somewhere filled with noise and *station* smells, he wanted a beer and to get drunk enough to ask his cousins if they were as confused about this experience as he was. Jen picked that moment to ask him if he was enjoying it, and he couldn't find an answer. It wasn't enjoying. It was scarier than that. It was like that plunge through black, aiming for a pinprick of a hole on *Finity's* hull, for life, and safety.

For *familiar.*

It was breathing air that could have been inside the bubble of *Galway's* hydroponics, but was foreign, and scented, and far, far richer. It was too-soft light shining through layers of branches and foliage, plenty to see by, but filtered, and changed, like no light he'd ever known.

They moved on, past spiky pine, and trees with trunks so thick, he wasn't sure Jen could reach around them, living things—but that big.

"Ponderosa Pine," their guide said, "a North American species. These are our five oldest. They came in with the original Pell core, aboard the pusher *Valiant.* The original owner had some notion of planting them on Downbe-low, but the terraforming notion died an early and well-deserved death. The donor was Alberta Theiss. Impressive, yes? But come ahead . . ."

They were being rushed, now, no question, just when they'd gotten to the trees he'd come to see. But he wasn't sure he resented that fact. He was getting tired. Overwhelmed. He wanted to see it all, but—

The path took a deeper turn and the moonlight became markedly less. As the pathlights came up, they revealed vapor obscuring the tops of the trees. Droplets condensed and fell, and it was more than a little chill.

"Is it going to rain again?" Dot Neihart wondered.

"Mist," their guide said, as the path turned through a close screen of, according to the signs, *Hinoki Cypress.* Shorter than the cedars or the pines, they had twisted limbs and fan-shaped leaves. Twisted and a little confused . . . rather like he felt, dropping out of warp space.

He liked them. Really liked them.

"Mist is frequent here," Andy was saying, "especially in early evening. It's good for all the evergreens, but we're also entering a very special environ-ment, for a very special new addition to the garden."

And with that, they descended again into a clear space, a really wide clear space. Three very different trees stood in that open area, alone, widely-spaced. Taller than the surrounding Hinoki, with wide branches, ending in fronds, like the cedars, but not. "Prize of the garden," their guide said.

He liked the Hinoki better. Seemed like a whole lot of empty for just three trees.

"What are they?" Maire asked.

"These are *infant* Dawn Redwoods," Andy said, with more animation than he'd yet displayed. "The sole living species of the genus Metasequoia, and the most ancient tree species still in existence. In their long lifespans— human civilizations rise and fall. Their origin predates humankind—all the way back to the Jurassic. Their ancestors knew the dinosaurs."

Babies that towered over his Hinoki. And dinosaurs. The mind boggled.

"They grow very rapidly," Andy continued. "The young ones grow upward, in favorable conditions, more than a meter a year. Their initial growth spurt has slowed in the last year or so, but these trees were a meter tall, even as bonsai, when we received them, and they will challenge the overhead of the garden long before they reach their full growth. At that time, sadly, we'll have to replace them with their own seedlings. We're excited to have them because of their antiquity. In fact, they were long thought extinct, existing only in the fossil record, until a last stand was discovered deep in the Asian continent of Earth. According to our records, they were popular bonsai choices on Earth, but for some reason we hadn't been able to find any samples, though they've been at the top of the Anna Konstantin museum's published wish list since long before work began on the garden."

As he spoke, a subtle shift of the trees happened. A ghostly holo-image shimmered and grew. Up and up. They all stepped back to give the branches room, for all those branches had no real substance. And as that virtual Dawn Redwood reached for the virtual sky, it gained more and more substance and shimmered in the virtual moonlight.

A not-so-virtual shiver rippled down Ross's spine. It was just a bit too much theatrics for him, but many of the others exclaimed in wonder. Jen's hold on his hand tightened and he glanced down. She raised a brow; he shrugged; and she winked and turned back to the virtual damn tree. He was less and less enamored of these holos. It was yet one more assault on that grip on reality that was the foundation of Nav.

He wished their guide would turn it off. The real trees were wonderful enough.

"When these came in, we had a bit of a scramble to accommodate them," Andy continued. "We had to clear this area of several established trees and make preparations, belowground, to hold these future giants steady, and to supply their roots with water and nutrient apart from what the environment already provides. These will be, though you and I will not see it, spectacular."

"Speak for yourself, stationer," Jen said, in a whisper only Ross could hear. "Promise me, spacer-lad, that you'll get your tail back here for that, at the very least."

He just squeezed her hand.

"Quite the coup for whoever found them," Ian said, and the holo sign flashed, but it lacked donor information.

"So who *did* provide them?" Nolan asked. "What ship? Where'd they come from? When?"

"The provider wished to be anonymous, for reasons beyond my pay grade," Andy said, with a disarming grin.

Anonymous, Ross thought, looking up, and up, and for some reason that excuse sounded hollow. For a specimen that had been on Pell's "wish list" for decades? What ship wouldn't want *that* kind of PR? What local citizen? He glanced at Nolan, their cargo master, and caught a flash of dark suspicion before Nolan caught him looking, and the expression vanished.

"As I mentioned, *most* of our specimens were donated, but some were traded for, or outright purchased. And some providers, especially where credit is involved, choose to remain anonymous. It doesn't make us any less grateful."

"You said," Nolan spoke up, "that they were a meter high when they arrived. That they grow, what, a meter a year?"

Andy nodded. "They were designated as bonsai, but their entire trunk was still flexible, indicating they were little more than seedlings, and there's no obvious signs of growth stunting. Since we got them, they've been very carefully nurtured, first in the quarantine nursery, and then here. We closed this section to protect them until they were well established, and are thrilled to be able to open it to the public at last."

A meter a year. *Nolan* was tracking something interesting. This time Ross caught Nolan's eye and saw the same calculation going on. Andy had not answered the "when," but these were at least ten years old.

"Their lifespan is still a mystery. Some of the first trees planted since the original grove was discovered on Earth are, we understand, still living." Andy's enthusiasm for the garden's newest treat was on a roll, and while he went on about osmosis and its associated height limits, and the trees' unique system for getting water *above* that limit, Ross was thinking . . . these were odd in far more than their water-handling. They'd arrived a meter tall. *Maybe* they'd come to Pell as seed in someone's pocket, but why not just donate the seeds? What about all those rules about plants grown outside this protected area?

Except—major point—they hadn't *been* donated. They'd been *purchased*. Proof of product would add much to the asking price, which might not be worth risking the wrath of the local inspectors, but might well be worth the risk of starting seeds elsewhere and bringing them in. There'd be that risk of jump-rot, but who knew how many started that trip . . . from wherever they *had* been potted?

What *were* the odds for surviving jump? How many would have been started? How much room had someone some*where* needed for that tree nursery? But the trees were young when they arrived. Why did it take decades for them to make their way here? Especially if Pell was willing to pay for them? It didn't make sense, what the guide had said. It really didn't make sense.

Station trade boards had a rhythm. Things came from places that made them at a certain rate and ships arrived and left in patterns that became ingrained in a spacer's gut. And there were things about those three trees that just didn't fit in with those rhythms, didn't make real sense, and even as Andy called to them, and he and Jen hurried to catch up with the others, he kept turning the thoughts over and over, still coming up with unreasonable ideas.

They were nearing the end, so Andy said, with a hint of regret in his voice, but Ross smothered a sigh of relief. The Garden had been all Jen promised and more, but at the moment all he wanted was to sit down with his cousins and get their help in sorting out all those crazy thoughts he'd begun having, thanks to the Garden.

He kept turning the puzzle of that Redwood over in his mind as the path sloped down to visit more trees beyond, less exotic, a ginko, also given, the guide said, to be a prehistoric species, but not rare. There was a banyan, off in an isolated area, a monster in the moonlight, shrouded in curtains of its own roots and looking like some bizarre alien lifeform brought up from Downbelow.

Their guide was talking again, and Ross concentrated on the words, trying to ignore the questions spinning in his head.

"The way the redwood grows *up*," Andy said, "the banyan spreads out, which is why we give it so much room. It is of all the trees one of the oddest—an epiphyte, which is to say, it attaches to another tree and overgrows it. We sacrificed a willow to this one, well before the garden opened. Fifteen years ago, and the willow is gone."

Interesting. Yes, indeed. One tree eating another. Damned weird.

God, he wanted to sit down.

They were moving again. There came the thump of an airlock, which one hoped was ordinary.

"The main gate," their guide explained. "We're nearing the end of our tour. It's been a pleasure. This whole sector of the station is devoted to the Garden, and if you're interested in a behind-the-scenes look, we have another tour you can take of new areas under development, not yet open to the public. If you care to see the design process and the labs, that is still another, separate tour."

Beyond the ginko and the banyan, they met stands of bamboo, small and large, species they all knew from vids. The plants were very fast growing, and were, according to Andy, routinely harvested . . . the source of many of those fabric scraps they were taking back for Winslow. Bamboo fiber, their guide said, had proven so lucrative, it was being set up in an orbiting facility along with the fish and algae tanks that were essential to every station, and was also being established at Viking and Mariner and Cyteen.

No one brought up the obvious question: why bamboo and nothing else? He had to wonder if it was licensed . . . and if Pell got a cut from those facilities.

There was, yes, clothing made of it. Available in the gift shop, yes, which was next on the route.

Thank God.

Ross's legs burned. He had never walked so far or so long in his life. Treadmills didn't compare with the uneven surfaces and the standing and walking they had just done—not to mention Jen's shopping venture. He was ready to sit, definitely ready for a beer—and more than ready to discuss those trees that made no sense.

Nolan had been tracking something; he was certain of it.

Jen tipped their guide, evidently generously, by the man's reaction, and they all filed into decon, and from there, at last, into the gift shop, which smelled of flowers and tea. No way he'd get his sitdown without a tour of the shop, and they *did* owe the cousins souvenirs, if they could find anything they could afford, so he followed the others through the crowded aisles: popular place.

There were very small samples of wood which could be bought, but they were coated in some hard clear substance that masked both scent and texture. Not even a temptation, to his mind. And there were larger pieces, the promised boxes and figures and plaques—also coated and all as expensive as he'd suspected. There was no possible way resale in the First Stars would be profitable, though, like the scraps for Winslow, one of those inlaid boxes could be a communal treat, if added to Winslow's display case. There were seeds in vials with sealed packages of soil and small fancy pots. Provide the seeds water and light and it would sprout, the package said.

And not a tree seed among them. Oh, Pell had this monopoly thing down to an art.

There were bamboo cups, far more affordable than the other wood pieces, with a picture of the redwoods laser-etched into them, for whatever illogical reason. And there were pymglass plates that had real leaves embedded, green and forever unfading, with the legend *The Earth Garden, Pell Station. A Walk through Wonder.*

Those were flat, and fairly reasonably priced, and if he had to buy one for every Monahan stranded at Alpha, they were a good deal more compact than other options.

And there were the promised garments made of bamboo fiber—socks, underwear, and loungewear—even sheets. Most far too pricey for any self-respecting spacer to consider, but there was a sample to touch, soft and smooth.

And the socks were fairly reasonable, and *extremely* compact.

Ian called them all over to a display of holo-plates, flat tray-like objects of various shapes and sizes that projected slideshows of the various plants featured in the Garden, along with their bonsai predecessors. The largest was an overview of the entire Garden, with everything from the rhododendrons to the waterfalls to the towering Dawn Redwood. It could be set to show the shifting sunset, moonrise . . . even the storm. It was, they all agreed, the perfect souvenir to take home to the Family . . . and utterly beyond consideration, pricewise, although Ross noted Ian pausing to look back at the display.

And Jen, dammit, had been listening with a bit too much interest.

"Don't even think it," he said to her in a low tone, and her brows raised.

"Not a clue what you're talking about." And in a raised voice: "Anyone else hungry?"

God, yes. There was an attached cafeteria, and chairs, and Ian and Aidan and Nolan moved off to claim a small table in the corner—helm and cargo: looking to the future, bet on it; and maybe calculating a few things to tuck into their bags for resale back on Alpha, to targeted individuals.

Maybe discussing the mystery of those trees. Ross wanted to join them, but theirs was an obvious retreat from the group.

So the rest of them pulled two tables together—there *were* safety-tracks here, which was a nice comforting change—and collapsed, laughing at their own exhaustion, around. The place offered real tea, the sign said, product of the Garden, for a forbidding price. God, Ross thought, reading it twice.

A waiter arrived the moment they were all seated. "Tea all around?" Jen asked blithely, *Finity* to the core, and what was there to say? They all agreed to tea, that being, apparently, the strongest drink to be had, and since they had just spent the equivalent of dinner and drinks at Rosie's on the tea, Ross decided that, hell, Fallan *did* need a bamboo cup with a picture of the redwoods. It had looked durable and had a suction base: a good quality for anything shipboard. Maybe one for Niall.

Though coming back from Earth itself, they should have souvenirs to beat all.

Jen took his hand, there on the tabletop, lacing their fingers together. "Well? What do you think?"

"It's special," he said. "It's real special." He drew his mind away from

Galway and back to Pell docks and a fairly special pair of eyes. "Thanks for setting this up, Jen. Thanks to *Finity*. From all of us."

"You didn't look happy, just now."

"No," he said. "Not *un*happy. Just . . . thinking."

She grinned. "Don't strain anything."

"Too late."

Her brows lifted. "You're serious. Share?"

"Just . . . a puzzle that won't leave me alone." Funny how *that* puzzle had driven his disrupted sense of *place* into some mental recess. But it had and he'd far rather the trees. "It's those Redwoods. Where'd they come from? Did some Pell stationer grow them from seeds? I mean, he said they were a meter high when they arrived. Who'd grow three of those in the back room? Who has that kind of space? And if they came in on a ship, what about the jump-rot he mentioned? And if they were willing to buy them, why didn't somebody, whoever had them, sell them sooner? Just to get monsters like that out of their way?"

"Been wondering the same." Aidan, with Ian and Nolan close behind, swung a chair around and straddled it. "Timing's a puzzle. A meter high when they got here, and likely not that old, if they survived jump, and now, say, ten at most . . . which would make it after, what, nine years max? He said a meter a year, for young ones. You suppose that's right?"

"No reason to lie," Jen said, and pulled out her handheld, started punching buttons. "As for when, there's got to be records, maybe just not something he's at liberty to discuss. Part of the anonymity thing, maybe."

"Only if it came in on a ship," Ian said.

"Even if grown locally," Jen responded, still poking. "You heard him: they're crazy careful of any biologicals coming into or out of the station. And legally, according to—" She waved her handheld before poking some more. "—privately owned plants have to get inspected regularly. He said they register the DNA of every plant. And they're right about how tall they get," Jen said, holding up her handheld again. "Thirty meters in forty years, max of fifty meters."

"I believe how tall they get," Nolan said. "It's how tall they are *now* that I'm interested in. *Andy* rather pointedly skirted the question of how long they'd had them, don't you think? He said they'd cleared out *established* trees to accommodate them, so it was after the garden went into operation."

"I remember when it first opened," Jen said, "the tour was shorter. Some's added each time we dock. That whole last section from the fir trees on, that's new, this trip. Except the ginkos and the bamboo: the exit's the same. But there used to be a wall. Probably letting them grow to *impressive* before opening it up. —And don't assume age when it arrived. They grow slower in pots."

"But he said they were flexible," Ross said. "Little more than seedlings. Wouldn't that make them pretty young?"

"Something's not right," Nolan said. "Understand, cargo's my thing." That to Jen. "I *know* about that wish list. I've had feelers out for those very trees throughout the First Stars since I was a trainee. I guarantee no one's harboring a miniature version of them out there, not with Pell-grade credit being offered. If someone found seeds, I'd know. Damned if I wouldn't. Which is not to say they actually came from our side of things. But whoever found them, however they were donated or sold to the Garden, *someone* should have taken them off that wishlist, and I'm here to say, they're still there." He lifted *his* handheld.

"Are we sure these are legitimately this Dawn Redwood and not something, I don't know, manipulated genetically from some other tree, not some scam Cyteen's pulling on them?" Aidan asked, and Jen answered:

"The Garden wouldn't risk their reputation like that. It's got to be legit."

"Which means, bottom line, they came from Earth—at some point," Aidan said.

Heads dipped in agreement.

"Transfer of live biologicals at Alpha was banned when Pell was established, due to fears of contamination . . . in both directions," Nolan said. "Downbelow was a serious gamechanger in so many ways. By what I know—and I've studied trade boards and trends since the first FTL converts—those particular trees haven't been traded anywhere, on any list, even before they banned any plant that wasn't already in trade. So either the parent tree was already on a Beyond station . . . or it's the result of contraband trade from Sol. But *that* means taking one hell of a risk. The fines would ruin any First Stars ship."

"Even for seeds?" Jen asked. "And coming *from* Sol?"

Nolan nodded and began referencing notes on his handheld. "That list has been around for decades. More than enough time to get word out through the system, even enough to arrange a blackmarket trade from Sol with pusher crew. Those redwoods were at the top of the list. People *had* to know Pell wanted them badly."

"Wonder what they ended up paying for them?" Siobhan asked.

"Hell of a lot more than they'd pay for seeds, even if whoever had them could prove what those seeds were for. Not all seeds germinate."

"I want to know what ship they came in on." That, from Ian, which roused a universal:

"Hell, yes."

"If it were *just* the trees, I could buy a long lost packet of seeds being found," Nolan said. "Somebody could have started a bunch to prove what they were, and maybe only three made it through jump—but it's not just the trees." He nodded toward Ian and Aidan. "We've been talking. There's stuff in the shops, all along the strip, a piece here, another there. . . . All with the Sol origin stamp . . . And you *know* what it means to counterfeit that mark. *Station* will have your hide, let alone the EC."

God, Ross thought, and Jen asked, with a frown: "How much 'stuff' are we talking about?"

"A fair amount," Nolan said, "none of which I've ever seen on the lists at Alpha. Class F, according to the signs." Which was to say, personal items sold off by ship crews, immune from duty. "Again, that might explain it, if we were dealing with the odd, single item. But there was that model boat. You saw it, Aidan, in that shop next to the gaming store."

"Water-going boat," Aidan said. "And *not* printed. Built, plank by plank by someone there in the shop. Real wood, with metal fittings and fabric sails. Tiny cannons. The display wasn't for sale, but the *kits* were. They had four of them. *Four.* Sealed and stored on a shelf above. I didn't think to check the box for a manufacturing date—no real reason: was way beyond my price range—but I guarantee, there's been nothing like that come through from Sol in *my* lifetime. Where'd those boats come from? That's what I want to know. When? Sol stuff *sells*. The clerk said he'd just sold one the day before." Aidan being second to Nolan, cargo was his field, too. "I have this hobby of scanning the F-class for, you know, ancient pusher goods. Real good profit, if you can ever lay hands on it. And I never saw *one* of those kits, let alone, what, six total? Minimum? Never opened?"

"Granted they're legitimately from Sol," Nolan said, "it's possible they came in a long time ago—before our time—that they've been in storage waiting for better times, and somebody on Alpha decided to quit paying storage locally and to pay freight costs to send them to Pell instead . . . But why didn't *we* hear of it? If any of us Alpha ships could make that Venture-Pell hop, *Galway* could."

"Just doesn't make sense," Ian said. "Any way you look at it."

Ross, relieved to have his suspicions confirmed, and trade not being his field, just listened, but Jen asked, a little sharply: "What shop?"

"Spinward down the row from us," Aidan said. "You and Ross were at lunch. Trader John's, it was."

"Like the trees," Nolan said, "we should have at least heard about these. Nothing gets here from Earth without going through Alpha. And something like those boat kits? Bragging rights alone would warrant a free drink."

"Did you ask the store where they got them?" Jen persisted.

"Won't reveal their sources."

Protecting a resource? Or a ship's preference for anonymity . . . like the trees?

"They can demand anonymity all they want, there'll be a record somewhere," Jen said, so grimly Ross barely recognized her. This was *Jen Neihart,* with the ship's Security arm-band on her sleeve, right below that cold-black-space patch, that undefined, starless black patch that was *Finity's End,* with all its resources. "Order another tea. Anything you want. I'll be making some calls. —Nolan, can I borrow you a minute?"

As Jen and Nolan walked off, Ross frowned, and looked back at other frowning faces, suddenly aware they were sitting in the café neighboring the gift shop having this discussion, potentially detrimental to the Garden itself. They'd been keeping their voices low, but people had come in and sat down uncomfortably close.

"I think I'm going back to get one of those bamboo cups." Which would give him a chance to stop wondering what was going on with Jen. He supposed a ship bypassing the biological ban was something the newly formed Alliance might want to investigate, but that grim parting look continued to bother him.

"I'll go, too," Maire said, and together they ended up with five bamboo cups, a stack of pymglass plates, and a printable that could create a fairly endless set of souvenir images of the garden, all to be sent to the Royal.

For the crew. For the Monahans who couldn't be here. Who were waiting it out at Alpha, while *Galway* made the run of her life, and for those who might be at Earth by now, using their wits and their knowledge to keep the EC off their deck, and to tell the Earth Company the route they had to take—and maybe take back a few trainees, to give them the skills to make that run. It was a modest tab.

He signed the credit screen, *Ross Monahan, Finity's End,* which was for credit purchases. That, until he got back to *Galway.*

Jen didn't come back. She sent a message that said *Stay with the rest. I'll see you tonight.* That was all.

It wasn't comforting. Pell Station was a very big, very worrisome place to have things go flaring off sideways.

"I saw the trees," Ross said to Fallan, via the handheld—an internal file, which had him hoping the pictures he'd just fed in didn't run the device short of room. But he wanted to record the day, while it was all fresh. "Today was something, Fal, honestly. It really was. I'm exhausted from walking, but it was worth it. They don't let you take pictures in the Garden, it's a money-maker for them, but I bought you a cup made out of a bamboo stem. With a picture-thing they do sell. The newest display is baby trees the size of a utility pusher. Hard to wrap your mind around. They say they'll grow as high as the overhead, which is way up there—I think they could almost park *Qarib* on the Strip, dockside, as they call it. I guess I could get the exact numbers on it, but I'm lying down right now. Jen's due in later, but she's gone over to the ship on some business, something Aidan and Nolan saw in a shop. Nolan went with her. Somebody's selling a model boat, labeled Earth Origin. How weird is that? I mean, if you're going to counterfeit something as Earth-made, you'd do something like a souvenir or a patch or something, wouldn't you? I mean, something that's actually *likely* to turn up? Even as a rarity?

"But whoever could think of a boat? So that, and the fact some of the stuff in the Garden that shouldn't have been imported might have been, that's raised some questions. We don't know what ship, can't figure how these things got to Pell, not being a route any Alpha ship takes, nor anything Alpha's ever seen, for that matter. Hell, I better shut up. I don't want to say too much until I get me and this device back aboard."

Ross lay back into the pillows, staring up at random colors chasing across the ceiling, wondering when Jen was going to get back, trying hard not to worry, trying to get all the important stuff in without stepping over some line he couldn't even see. What had made Jen go all serious?

"Pell's gotten all of the trees, would you believe it, from bonsai pots— apparently the plants can take off and grow full size if they get the right conditions. And Pell provides the conditions, just like being on Earth, close as they can make it, even to mechanical bugs, some that light up and some that pollinate the plants. You should see it—hell with that, you will see it, when *Galway* gets that overhaul. You'll see it. And when you do, it'll be even more amazing than is it now. They say it's not all developed yet, but, God, it's beyond anything Alpha ever imagined. Our legs were aching before we ever got through the walk, which is a lot of up and down and sideways. We walked for hours.

"But a lot of what the guide said about these trees didn't make sense, even to me. Nolan and Aidan came up with a question as to who got these three trees here, and when, because of that model boat kit with Earth Origin markings. I'd credit Aidan and Nolan for knowing the price of everything that moves in the Alpha reach, and bonsais are restricted to the hilt. If you sell one, you have to prove provenance, Nolan says. Nolan says the ban on Earth biologics dates from when the EC knew they'd stolen the Pell core and taken it to Downbelow, and it was because we were suddenly dealing with another living planet. So Earth stuff shouldn't get to Downbelow nor vice versa. But FTL kills the bonsai and so, during the conversions of the pusher ships, Pell got their hands on all sorts of plants. When they started planning the new ring and realizing how much space they were going to have, they got the idea of creating the Garden as it is now. They are so rich, Pell is, you can't imagine what they can't do. I mean, the Garden has scientific interest, I suppose, and it's history, but it's a whole sector of the new main ring, for God's sake, and I do mean sector, of which there are twelve. The scale is just amazing. And I wish like hell they allowed pictures.

"I don't know what it cost to get us all in there, but a cup of tea in the gift shop would buy you dinner and everything at Rosie's. I see these prices and I think, hell, do I want to live like that? I really don't want to get where that kind of spending is an 'of course.'

"And, you know, it is for Jen. She just expects it. She's *Finity*. With all that means. And me, I really like her. I like her so much. But I want to get back to *Galway*. I want a beer at Rosie's. She's over on *Finity* about some sort of trouble that worries me, and I keep seeing those big trees. They were beautiful, but you know, their kind was alive before human beings ever existed. And that's scary, how old they are. And we aren't.

"I haven't seen a hisa. Probably won't, Jen says. But I know they're here, in the tunnels. Spooky feeling to know they're there, maybe not that far away.

"Anyway, don't think I didn't like the experience. I'm glad we did it. Really glad. I won't forget it. Maybe you have to spread out an expense over how long you'll be glad you did it. If that's the case, that's going to be forever. I see trees when I shut my eyes. And hear the sound they make in the wind. That was scary. But it got to be a good sound. God, I do wish you'd been there."

He thought maybe he drifted off. He opened his eyes to a ceiling gone to black. His handheld had auto-stopped recording. He tapped the button to start it back up.

"I'm sleepy now. Jen might just spend the rest of alterday over at *Finity's* office—which they can just walk to, at one *G* and warm. You can walk on and off the ship like you were going to a shop, here. The captain's got his office there and so does Security, where Jen's gone, so, well, I don't know what's stirred up, or what's going on with this question Nolan and Aidan stirred up. But I haven't got enough brain left to deal with it and for me, it's night. I just hope it all works out so *Finity* goes out of here in the right direction. I really don't want to try to find our own way back to Alpha from where we are."

Book II   Section xiv

There was a box in the middle of the table, when Jen followed Fletcher into the conference room: a large new-looking box emblazoned with an image of a sailing ship proudly plowing through white-topped waves under blue sky and grey clouds. No one asked, but everyone checked it out before taking their seat.

Jen kept her silence. Captain-Uncle had his reasons for putting that kit front and center, reasons she didn't begin to question. She had been included in this high-powered meeting for one reason, and one reason only.

Captain-Uncle, Captain John, and Captain Mum were there already, and Rennie Neihart, Research and Records, and Lucent, Technical Records, which was the black box system. Katrin D, Engineering 1.1 was there, too, which was interesting, and Kate, Nav 1.1. Captain Madison was the last to arrive. He stared at that box a really long moment, then met Uncle's carefully blank gaze, one eyebrow lifted, before taking his seat.

"So," Uncle said, when Madison had settled, "we had some information come through this evening, on which we did some fast research that raised several red flags. It all started when Jen came to me with a question on be-half of our *Galway* guests, about the current star attraction of the Pell Gar-dens. Jen?"

She swallowed hard. Thought she'd have a minute or two at least to settle in before all those curious eyes turned to her.

"Yes, sir," she said, relieved to discover her voice was steady, and at his nod, explained: "It's called a Dawn Redwood. The tour guide made a really big deal about it. Said they'd been looking for one since way back in the early planning stages of the Garden, back when it was just a bonsai museum, be-fore they got really ambitious with it—there was a Konstantin who was very instrumental in the planning, and those trees were on some wish-list that supposedly went out on the black box system. Those things are already large and will get downright huge. And they live forever. The new exhibit that made tickets so hard to get is all about them. They were very young when the garden got them. Probably only a year old. They've grown them in isolation and they've just recently opened that section to the public. What's weird is, the source is listed as 'anonymous.' Only one we noticed that didn't have someone's name as the source. Most are donations. The guide said these were purchased. Nolan, who is *Galway's* cargo master, has known about the list for decades, has been looking for these very trees and can't see how they could possibly have come from *their* side. We all got to talking and seriously wondering where they came from and what took the owners so long to re-spond to that list. Long lost seeds is a possibility. So is blackmarket straight from Earth. But Alpha's rules on the ban—I mean, who's risking that?"

Captain-Uncle interjected quietly. "Alpha being the gateway to the mother of all worlds, their rules *are* very tough. Both directions. Detectors are hair-triggered and the penalty for violation is the same as murder. Local court rules, and your ship can't protect you."

Nolan had told Uncle about that, which was pretty scary.

"Then there's the stuff in the shops." She thought of the unexplained box on the table, and glanced at Uncle for a cue. Uncle gave a brief nod and she continued: "Something else the Galways spotted. F-class items, so the shops claim, stuff supposedly of Earth origin—but stuff *they've* never seen before or even heard bragged about. Shops won't reveal sources, but it's multiples of fancy setabouts. Not like something you'd find buried in family storage, un-less you're a storeowner, and if that's the case, why not just say so? So did some Alpha stationer freight it all the way *here* rather than sell it at Alpha or Bryant's? And if they freighted it to Pell hoping for prices to offset the ship-ping, why wasn't *Galway*, the Alpha ship most likely to manage the Pell run, at least involved? That's what the Galways were saying, anyway, and they know Sol trade and Alpha ships a whole lot better than I do. None of it sounded right . . . so I called in."

And just that quick, her part in the meeting was done, and even that was kindness on Uncle's part. Mostly she suspected she was here in case someone had questions Uncle hadn't thought to ask her or Nolan earlier.

"You thought right," Uncle said. "For the record, Nolan Monahan, *Galway*'s cargomaster, who is available by com should we need him, gave us a list of the suspect F-class items, into which records is still looking. But first the trees. —Rennie?"

"Purchased nine years, eight months, and three days ago, station time," Rennie said. "First displayed to the public nine months ago. The seller of the specimens was one Connie Bellagio. Ship name—" Rennie paused, glanced around the table. "*Come Lately*, Bryant's registry."

A murmur traveled the table, and Jen pressed her lips on an exclamation. *Come Lately.* One of their missing ships. *Here?*

Rennie continued matter of factly: "Purchase price 130,000 VC, was actually a court settlement, whole case rushed through in five days; and that took a bit of finagling to discover. The freight office delved deeper at our request, and, credit where due, Emilio gave us a stationwide clearance, without which we might never have gotten answers."

130,000 VC? That was quite a price, for five practically no-mass items. And why in Venture *chits*? How weird was that? Why not just take Pell credit and do a black box transfer of the balance to Venture . . . or wherever they were headed . . . when they left, like everyone else did? And them being *here* was weird to begin with. Venture-Pell was an extremely hard pull for ships of that vintage, by what the Galways had said. By what they'd said, *Galway* herself couldn't make it fully loaded, and *Galway* was the newest and most powerful ship there was in the Hinder Stars.

"That was the first of the two visits Emilio told us about," Rennie said. "*Come Lately* took on low-mass dry goods, foods, and medicines on that particular trip. The whole cargo weight under 2 tonnes, incidental to a supposed contract for transport of iron ingots listed at 3 tonnes, destination listed as Bryant's, though no buyer's name is listed. However—as *our* touch at Bryant's tells us, and we in Research are very confident—Bryant's records do *not* show any corresponding ship-call at Bryant's, certainly nothing about that iron ore . . . which *was* paid for locally with Venture chits. Prior to, I might add, settlement on the payment for the trees. The next *recorded* appearance of *Come Lately* at Bryant's was almost three years after the sale of the trees . . . keeping in mind *Come Lately*'s black box is, as we've noted before to our frustration, old and likes to keep its secrets."

The virtue of *working* black boxes was records from everywhere the ship docked, updated at every station with every ship call. But *working* was the operative word there.

"Contract for transport," Mum said. "Would be somebody else's iron, somebody else's purchase, a freight-only haul, bulk, not cans. Unusual for Bryant's. They don't do a lot of manufacturing there."

"If it had gotten there," Uncle said, "we probably wouldn't think twice. A Bryant's local, seeing the ship's ultimate destination as Pell, might well have made a last minute request of the Bellagios, it being hard to get raw metal out of Venture. But the order didn't show on Bryant's or Venture's manifests. Neither did their other cargo. We have no clue where she dropped those goods. And there *is* that three-year gap until *Come Lately* turns up at Bryant's. What did they do? Carry the iron around all that time?"

Lucent lifted a finger for attention: "It should be noted that this is not an unusual dropout of records for *Come Lately*. Venture records do not have it docking with any regularity, and Glory—well, Glory has periods when the entire system is down, so no help there. But the point is, I'm not sure this *specific* silence should be considered significant . . . except in that it is part of a pattern of black box behavior, whether by design, simple negligence on the part of the Bellagios, or a faulty system, is hard to say without physically examining their box."

"Provenance of the specimens?" Mum asked, which was *Jen's* question, and Uncle answered.

"The Bellagios told Pell—paraphrasing from the transcript of the settlement hearing—it was a chance find at Bryant's, *supposedly* from a hobbyist who happened to have found unidentified seeds, started them, and found himself with these trees he thought might be the ones on that list. The Bellagios claimed they took a chance that these were the trees Pell wanted and made the jump to Pell primarily on spec, but supposedly only after that order for iron came through to cover the trip. Fiscally smart, but a curious bit of detail, to my thinking. For one thing, there's no evidence that they listed on the boards *anywhere* as bound for Pell—but I digress. In their statement, they claimed they knew nothing about the *Pell* ban on biologics, but curiously—and even more curiously, a question nowhere posed in the transcript—when they actually got to Pell, rather than declare their find to customs, which by that ban would have gotten the trees immediately destroyed, they just smuggled them directly to the Garden office, in, apparently, sealed containers inside crew duffles, and the seedlings so excited the chief botanist, the Garden got a court injunction against their destruction— and of course latched onto them. The white-coat folk examined them up and down, declared them the real deal and free of contaminants and were not about to give them up. It ended in court when the Bellagios sued to get compensation. They ultimately settled for 130,000 VC for the three that survived, which was, according to the transcript, far less than they'd wanted, but since they had tried to skirt the ban, far more than Pell legally had to give them. But here's the thing: there's no name given for the supposed Bryant's hobbyist, and no evidence of *Come Lately* docking at Bryant's in the time frame necessary. It's possible the Bryant's hobbyist is a cover story for an under the table trade with pusher crew, but that theory has its own problems. —Fletch?"

"Nolan Monahan said he had personally spoken with both pusher crews about the wishlist," Fletcher said. "He had *specifically* asked about these Dawn Redwoods, and did they have any, bonsai evidently still being a favorite pastime on pushers. Both said they did not, however one crewman did imply a little under the table was not out of the question. Nolan wasn't interested, however armed with the knowledge of that wishlist, some enterprising and mildly larcenous pusher crewman could have gotten their hands on the seeds—on Sol Station, who of course wouldn't give a damn: the only contamination they worry about is incoming from Pell—and done that under the table with some other ship. I looked up, and those seeds are damn small. You could outright palm 'em through customs real easy. Any ship could have done the transaction in any friendly bar restroom, and later traded them to *Come Lately* . . . or even that Bryant's hobbyist, to prove viability. If this *is* the actual scenario, that bathroom trade was not made with the Bellagios. According to Alpha's records—because we *are* thorough and checked every angle of this—in the last thirty years, station-time, *Come Lately*'s docking schedule has not corresponded to either pusher ship's presence at Alpha—nor, for that matter, has *Miriam B*'s."

"None of which explains that thing on the table," Mum said dryly. "Seeds can be slipped hand to hand, but not something that size."

Curious eyes turned to the box in the middle of the table. Jen pressed her lips tight. She really, *really* wanted to know what they'd found out about that model ship.

"We'll get back to that in a minute," Uncle said, with a glance her way. "So. We have these three trees Pell Gardens wanted so badly they didn't *want* to pursue the origins too carefully. They had what they wanted, to hell with the biologics ban. Cyteen might not be so forgiving if they caught wind of it, and the political fallout of Pell actively *violating* the biologics ban would be huge. Hypocritically, destruction of the specimens would be, I'm sure, unthinkable—to all sides. I'm including Cyteen in that. You can bet

Pell will get their 130,000 back just selling cells to the Carnaths. Likely already has, though I don't think records has checked that one."

"Not yet," Rennie muttered, and tapped the table's touch keyboard in front of him to bring the computer alive. "You might have said."

"Just thought of it myself. —So rather than try to sneak these trees into their collection, Pell waits ten years, then makes a big deal of it, too big to have anyone question the ancient transaction, marks its provider as *anonymous*, and gives it as vague a cover story as they could manage. Meanwhile *Come Lately* exits, if not flush with cash, at least full of fuel and with a small cargo. Not how you *prefer* to do business, but let's assume she broke even on the run, and her crew got a chance to see Pell firsthand. Again, there's an explanation, even for the subterfuge. The Hinder Stars are suffering, big time, ships and stations, and she's not the only ship who runs mostly dark, and likely runs some exotic contraband. If it were just the trees, just the iron, we might be inclined to write it off. But that . . . is a big if. —Fletch?"

If? It struck Jen suddenly what recent study of ship cargos in the security office might have been for.

"Throughout this trip," Fletcher explained, "we've been building a picture of what Hinder Stars finance looks like for repairs and other Alliance operations. Peripherally and not in any overwhelming urgency, we've been looking for the Mallorys' *Miriam B* and Bellagios' *Come Lately*, two ships that are off and on in the black box system and have been overall elusive. But here's the interesting part: in the record of goods-on-hand just ticking up and down mysteriously from time to time throughout all the system— there may be the heartbeat of our two ghosts running supply. We're not sure, but we've been working on that. Depletion can be a station draw on supply due to some local situation: people eat more than you plan. But a sudden *rise* in a commodity, without ship manifest corroboration, there you are. Ghost action. And now, thanks to all the stations', including Pell's, complete cooperation with records, we're beginning to see how that ghost might be operating. Simple cash deals. A tendency on the part of Hinder Stars ships, including here at Pell, to take payment in Venture chits, which are spendable anywhere in the Hinder Stars, and hard to track. Clever notion, and a massive *thank you* due to Research."

There was a murmur. Rennie nodded a balding head. "Numbers, numbers," Rennie said, all the while tapping his keys, his eyes fixed on a tabletop directional display visible only to him. "My division's *not* been enjoying life on the docks. Thanks to our guests' observations, we know we're chasing something more than seeds and trees. Once we plugged in the Venture data—and you know Venture chits are good clear to Glory—that uptick and downtick of supply began to look more obvious. And when we plugged in figures clear to Alpha, there was little doubt left. We believe those two ships on more than one occasion bought electronics and printing supplies at Venture that *don't* turn up down the line. Who's ever cared about little ships? Their records never get checked. And but for one extremely lucrative sale of one high-demand, unique product a decade back, with a claimed provenance at Bryant's—we might never have put the pieces together."

Uncle lifted a hand to stop Rennie, giving everyone time to process. When he lowered his hand, Rennie continued, no longer tapping.

"Brothers and sisters and cousins, once you look at the big picture, there's just a lot to worry us mathematicians. Ghost activity in the commodities. Supplies of various things turn up. Others just disappear. It's no wonder, really, that Emilio doubted Abrezio's claims of need—and there's the tragedy. Alpha asked for aid and was denied . . . because Pell *has* received Sol goods that did not come legitimately through Alpha—not in the last thirty years, at least—including Emilio's scotch. It's possible those were hoarded, waiting for the selling price to escalate, but the return numbers are even more worrisome. More consumables have been purchased, in the name of the Hinder Stars, than have ever made it to those stations . . . unless Glory is overflowing with flour. And it's not just the odd food lot. Massive lot of electronics that we know hasn't gone to refurb Alpha." He tapped the table in front of him again. "And here's the big tell: twenty years ago, ship parts and supplies desperately needed in the Hinder Stars disappear from Venture and *don't* show up in station inventory down the line. Parts that *could* account for two elderly ships suddenly able to reach Pell and other places that you wouldn't think they could."

Ears perked at that.

"Doing their *own* upgrades?" Katrin D asked. "Retrofitting, except the black box?"

"Is that even possible?" JR asked, and Katrin shrugged.

"No one's ever tried, that I know of. No reason to. The new systems, with the integrated boxes, are better than any retrofit. But this lot . . . looks like they've done everything possible to avoid the modern box, doesn't it? Pretty massive case of paranoia."

"Any evidence of any other big Pell paydays for *Come Lately*?" Mum asked, and Rennie shrugged.

"What we found confirms what Emilio told JR. Only two appearances on the Pell market for *Come Lately* in the last eighty years, the trees being part of the first, and the second one two years and change ago. Ship trade was similar to the first time: nothing much coming in, consignment going out, paid with VC. We're still checking into the whole category of F-class items which could be attributed to that last call, including those." He raised his chin in the direction of the boxed ship model. "Lot of stuff marked Sol. As Jen pointed out, sometimes in lots rather than individual second hands. Low mass stuff. And again, it's all stuff our Monahans haven't seen or even heard about—I sent a list to Nolan Monahan just before this meeting, and he confirmed. Records thus far indicate it all came from *Come Lately*, and landed them a nice little nest egg. Other F-class trickles in on other ships on the Venture-Pell route, but nothing like what showed up on *Come Lately*'s return visit. But it all indicates there *has* to be pusher trade involved somewhere, the question is, when. Were those items warehoused at Alpha and the owner just got tired of waiting and made a deal with *Come Lately*? Or is it . . . something else?"

"Maybe *Come Lately*'s making secret runs to Sol," Mum said dryly.

Clearly impossible, Jen thought . . . and then remembered *Galway* . . . and had to wonder.

"When did Abrezio say he got those coordinates for the Sol run?" Madison asked, and Uncle shook his head. "Since the last pusher left. Timing doesn't work."

Mum snorted. "Doesn't mean someone else didn't find them. —Redline it."

Which meant: don't just delete the possibility.

"Anything about *Miriam B*?" John asked, and Rennie nodded.

"Only one Pell docking for *Miriam B*, to and from Venture, some six years ago. The only particularly flag-worthy trades from the Mallorys were Scotch and coffee, and those only because of the quantity involved. They wouldn't be the first to keep a bit in reserve for emergency dock charges, but the quantity would suggest a fresh supply, an observation that had Nolan using highly colorful expletives. Some evidence of F-class cash trade with locals, but mostly standard ship credit transaction, more than enough of that to cover the round trip between here and Venture, and leave them with a nice little cash reserve."

Damn, Jen thought. Fresh supply? Those ship models? Had these two ships had some kind of sweetheart deal with the pushers coming into Alpha that left all the other ships . . . like *Galway* . . . struggling? And if she was thinking that, damn sure others were, maybe some not in this room. She bit her lips and looked from one to the other of her gathered family, wondering were they thinking the same?

"So," Uncle said, "thanks to our Monahan guests, mystery not solved, but a spotlight shone on our two missing ships, both on first-gen box systems, which they claimed here at Pell were broken, but no, and, no, they don't want to install a modern box, even if Pell offers it free, along with a nav system upgrade. They don't want one and there's no law saying they have to have one."

"They're right about that," Fletcher said. "There is no law. The original black box was an add-on. Information being a high commodity, no merchanter in his right mind ever thought of refusing it."

Lucent said: "For our non-technicals present, the modern black box is an integrated part of the modern FTL nav system: if your ship runs, if it comes into port, it's logged. The old box system is a separate unit—doesn't integrate with nav. The old boxes—and those are the last two left except for *Firenze*, which is currently getting replaced—also turn off and on at the discretion of the crew. That was part of the deal in getting the original boxes generally accepted. A handful of times forgetting to turn it back on and losing the data-flow revenue associated with it cured most Families of the obsession for that bit of privacy. However . . . it would explain the ghostly presence of these two dinosaurs in the records."

"Their systems may stay off during certain runs," Fletcher said. "But that doesn't explain some of the gaps in *station* records. They're going *somewhere*. Clearly."

Rennie frowned and tapped the table again, reactivating the computer.

"Overall, except for that clinging to the old black box, there's not that much difference between them and the other First Stars' ships," Uncle said, as Rennie's fingers flew on his tabletop keyboard. "The entire lot are clinging to existence by any means they can find. The nature of the Bellagios' official trade, within the Hinder Stars, is small stuff and random. How they've kept operating is not a question anyone ever seems to have asked. No *merchanter* has complained about their actions, and stationers don't much care. They're figures out of the old days. Among the very first purpose-builts. Marginal traders. Certainly no economic threat to the locals. Everyone just pats them on the head and lets them slide through the rules. One suspects their secret is that F-class trade. Merchants buy from them, under the table . . . everywhere but here. F-class is a hole you can put a planet through. But it's a sacred cow. And apparently it's been enough to keep them going."

Jen wondered how the Monahans were going to take this assessment, what they were going to think about being played this way.

"The Bellagio's dealings here are . . . curious. First trip really seemed to be all about the trees, which, incidentally, were also listed as F-class, until station got wind of the deal. Ten thousand of that 130,000 was exchanged at Pell for Pell chits, possibly for F-class trading with Beyonder ships' crews— stuff that could have real value in the Hinder Stars. Pell, as we can attest, requires a record on every damn thing that changes hands on the station, *including* F-class . . . except for where it's between ships without the knowledge of station. First time here, *Come Lately's* F-class logged trades were typical of their dealings in Hinder Stars stations: handcrafts, self-made stuff, and second hand curiosities. Their second trip was quite different. Sol goods . . . of a variety and number that hints at warehoused goods, including *that* very curious piece." With a nod to the ship-model box.

Rennie dipped his head. "They've gotten away with it, because nobody, until *we* set up the Alliance and asked the stations for the numbers, *nobody*, from Pell to Alpha, has ever seen the patterns and asked *why*—until a handful of Alpha spacers came to Pell and went through the shops, and saw things that shouldn't be there."

"This kit," Uncle said, indicating the box with the boat, "is a proverbial smoking gun. It is, according to the shop, one of nine, one assembled for display, four sold. That's the first red flag. Multiples, particularly expensive items, are usually forgeries, and that kit is fairly expensive. We bought that one for testing, to rule out the possibility that the kits were printer-created off an original—it wasn't. It's real wood. Cast metal. *Linen* sails. The instructions are printed on wood-pulp paper, and while the date on the box is scarred beyond reading—we believe deliberately—the date on the instructions sheet isn't. Any way you cut it, it's from Earth, and by the copyright date on the internal material, no matter how stretchy you make stationtime versus shiptime, it didn't come by way of Alpha. Not legitimately. And not from a warehouse. It's been almost thirty years since Alpha's gotten a pusher load that wasn't designated for the *Rights* build. Our Monahans say the pusher crew F-class has been virtually nonexistent. So the question is, where did these kits of tolerably recent date come from, if *not* from Earth, through Alpha?"

A very loud silence followed that question.

"Another thing that makes no sense, if those ships have been Pell capable for twenty years . . . why aren't they coming here?" Mum said. "It's both too many discrepancies for a one shot and too few for an ongoing arrangement. One has to ask: Is this one individual's stupidity or something higher up, and where's the rest of this exotic trade going?"

Not to Alpha. Or Bryant's or Glory or even Venture. That was pretty clear.

"The whole string of Hinder Stars," Mum said, "lies about the same direct distance from Sol, *if* the EC sent pushers straight out toward them. Longer push than to Alpha, add a decade to a round trip, but doable. When the Great Circle ran, even then, not all the pushers went on to the next star. Some went directly back to Sol."

"We damn well know Sol can build pushers," Fletcher said. "They've got unlimited resources. They could build as many as they want. *Send* them wherever they want, and not necessarily carrying cargo."

"It's been a decade since those trees sprouted." Madison snorted. "Twenty since those two ships, presumably, got upgraded. What's the EC waiting for? Hip replacements?"

"Well, they made a hard try at Alpha," Uncle said grimly and all eyes turned to him. "No saying that's all they've been up to. Earth is rich. It can afford more than one angle. But before we get carried away, all we've got at the moment is a ghostly trail of goods that might be leaking out of some covert EC operation, and a couple of merchanters that aren't easy to track. But one thing we know, nobody can communicate faster than a ship moves; and the EC at Sol can't communicate FTL."

Mum's chin lifted, and Uncle said, "All due, Mum, but if those ships were hopping, with what we saw at Pell . . . I can't believe the first thing they'd have brought back wasn't Enforcers."

Mum frowned . . . then shrugged. "Point. —So? Where'd those model ships come from?"

"It's definitely *not* Alpha—" Rennie, who had been silently tapping away on his keyboard, suddenly looked up and around the table. "Cash or credit, I can say those physical goods our target took on here at Pell never made it back to Venture, let alone Bryant's, Alpha, or Glory."

"You're certain of that?" Uncle asked, and Rennie nodded.

"Significant item, brand name. You know Billi's Breakfast Buns?" Rennie asked.

Who didn't? Jen's mouth watered at the thought.

"Well, an obscene number of those lovely things went aboard *Come Lately*. Remember the 10,000 they got in local cash? Went into ship's stores. If the Bellagios consumed all of those, I guarantee someone would have noticed and no retrofit could haul their mass through jump. Pell product. You can't get them on Venture. I asked. Second trip, they tripled the order."

Katrin D said, "Another thought: even if they did their own upgrades, they have to have had some support, somewhere to work. Which we know wasn't Venture shipyards, Pell's. Or Alpha."

"So I repeat," Mum said impatiently, "*where?*"

"If their objective is to take on Pell headon," John said, "Sol could send a pusher with Enforcers straight to Pell for not too much more effort."

"But a pusher . . ." Madison said. "The *people*. If they sent a force, they'd be Family with concerns for their kids by the time they got there, with different priorities, different attitudes."

"Happened once and a dozen times," Mum said, "but the EC *knows* that.

They didn't really care, back in the day. Pushers existed to move product. If Enforcer ships exist, the young ones, supposing the EC didn't neuter the lot, could be more fanatically EC than their parents, given enough lies and indoctrination en route. They *could* send us a live cargo of Enforcers, straight from Sol."

"But move in on Pell, cold . . . no," Fletcher said slowly, "not straight off a pusher ship, with no experience of stations, no *real* idea what kind of resistance to expect. For all they know, the entire population of Pell is armed militia. If I were planning any kind of takeover, I'd want a stable point of operation where I could control the traffic. I'd want a substantial force and a stable base *within* the proven FTL routes, ideally maintained with minimal noise. And it's harder to maintain security the farther you go, the farther you stretch your supply lines. We've worried that Sol could be building FTLs in hope of finding jump-points to use them, but if they just built more pushers, which they obviously know how to manage, and sent them one after the other to revitalize a mothballed station, man it with recruits from the Hinder Stars, labor at first, then Enforcers in the next-gen . . . they could have an organized, systematically supplied base of operations a hell of a lot closer to Pell than Alpha, and make themselves a relevant force again."

"Question is," Mum said, sounding really annoyed now, "where?"

Which made Jen think *Mum* already had a damned good notion, and was waiting for the rest of them to catch up with her.

"There's the whole Galileo Reach," Uncle said. "Not forgetting El Dorado. All abandoned. All built for handling pushers. All within ten lights of Sol. Well, excepting Galileo."

Madison said: "El Dorado's fried, Galileo's toast, Olympus' star, Groombridge, is a hell hole for FTL, but there *is* Thule."

Thule, Jen knew from Fletcher, was on their own short list as a possible point the Alliance could stash supplies and use as a layover, if they had to stage a general withdrawal of service. And *it* was only one convenient hop out of Venture. No wonder Madison sounded a bit disappointed.

Damn. This was getting . . . scary.

"Nasty tempered little star," Kate spoke up for the first time, "but viable. Easy jump. Better than the others in the Reach."

"*If* the EC's building a base, they've kept damned quiet about it, which is suspicious in itself," John said.

"What they do openly is build a megaship at Alpha." Jen hadn't realized she'd said that aloud until they all looked at her. She ducked her head, embarrassed, but:

"*While* recruiting a large number of Enforcers," Fletcher added. "Hundreds of Enforcers."

"Decoy?" Uncle asked.

"Possibly," Captain John said. "Possibly a dual action. If they *have* been maintaining pusher-routes we don't know about, maybe more than one, they're invisible to us when we're in transit, no way we could even spot their trail if we crossed it."

"Give or take Thule's star has bad habits," Fletcher said. "Where else do we have?"

"Well, directly next to it, also mothballed, conspicuously, Olympus," Kate said. "But Olympus is a damn horror show. Early FTLers found that out the hard way and word spread, after a couple of disasters." She was silent a minute, frowning at nothing, then said slowly . . . "There was Galileo-to-Olympus-to-Thule-to-Venture. . . . that was all right. But after Galileo died, it was just not a very profitable run, and Thule was small. Very small. Most pushers bypassed it, went straight to Olympus. The FTLers used it, but only to get to Olympus, which, with those accidents, just faded. Not worth the effort, ultimately, just to get to Olympus and have to backtrack."

"Olympus is *not*, however," Mum said firmly, "a horror show for a pusher. I never handled *Gaia* there personally, but I heard from senior crew. Olympus was *the* place in their reckoning. Even above Alpha. She did get a few pushers direct from Sol, but only early on, when the Great Circle was operating. Venture's always been what it is, Thule was mostly an underfunded scientific station, and El Dorado was the same. Galileo was where the research money went—until it blew. But Olympus . . ." Mum's voice trailed off, and her eyes were looking at something none of the rest of them could see, and Jen listened. Hard. Captain Mum didn't often talk about the deep past, didn't often go there, old as Mum was, and those stories were what she'd heard from others' memories, that far back. "Pushers in the Great Circle Trade, Glory to Alpha to Bryant's, to Thule, Olympus, and Galileo, then Venture and on to Pell and back again. *Gaia, Polaris, Golden Hind,* and *Argo*: Earth launched us, each with a station core, but of them all, only *Gaia* ever returned to Sol, the once, and twice, before we pushed the Beta core to Proxima Cent. What we found at Sol that last time . . . we never wanted to go back. Other ships took on the Sol to Alpha run, but of those . . . only *Santa Maria* and *Atlantis* managed to stay with it."

Jen longed to ask what she meant by that, longed to ask what *Gaia* had found second time back at Sol, but she knew better. Maybe she'd ask Uncle later . . . and maybe she'd just let the past go. There were dark, dark places in that remembrance, and the silence fell on everybody . . . until Mum, with a shake of her head, broke the spell.

"Well, we were not constrained by jump-points. So routes were possible that aren't, now. Back then, everything took time. Until Cyteen and Pell started breaking the pushers down and converting them to FTL," Mum said. "Earth stopped building more pushers. Pointedly stopped building them. They weren't about to feed steel and parts to Alpha just to be junked. They saw conversions as destroying everything they'd built. So routes died that would still make sense. Olympus, who *needed* pushers to survive, was a case in point."

"Hell if. Sol sat on their hands meanwhile and sulked when they *could* have built a whole string of pushers to supply Alpha and make an economic killing," John said.

"Maybe," Jen ventured again, "the EC doesn't really care about profit. I mean, *we* do, but . . ." She let her voice trail off, not certain where the thought was going, not wanting to make a fool of herself with the seniors.

"Maybe," Uncle said, with a quick nod to her, "that's the first question we should have asked. Why *didn't* they build just one more pusher for Alpha, or go slower with *Rights*, and keep Alpha supplied? Was it a thoroughly stupid project, doomed to failure? Granted it wouldn't be the first such. Did they think starving out the Alpha merchanters was going to give them some desperate Family crew they could recruit? Or maybe Alpha isn't their first concern any longer. Maybe it hasn't been for a long time. *Decoy* makes a lot of sense. A rather scary lot of sense."

There was a small unhappy silence.

"We all were working for the EC," Lucent said, "back in the days of the Great Circle. Families seeing to their own best interests, following the rules as they were given, and staying alive. Sure there are routes FTLers couldn't and still can't take; doesn't mean there are dark pushers running to some resurrected station. Nothing to say our two ghost ships aren't just doing their own business the way we all did, dealing directly with the Alpha pusher crews and just happening to make a windfall trade for F-class stuff. The cash dealing could be to keep questions of origin to a minimum. Maybe they were just trading goods for goods, under the table, at Bryant's and Alpha, skirting the laws and not thinking twice about it. Who they're dealing with at the stations could be another story."

"No, no, and . . . no. They've *got to have* another damn port," Rennie muttered, turned off his keyboard with a hard jab, and slumped back in his chair.

"I agree with Rennie," Mum said. "And chances are those two ghost ships have already carried news of the current status of Alpha and *Rights of Man* to the EC at some ghost port. Which will be, I'm increasingly thinking, in the Galileo Reach, and I'd lay odds it's at Olympus. Some folks loved that station. A few of the oldest refused to leave when one of the last pushers made the run to evacuate, headed for Venture. Wanted to die there rather than on the pusher—because it wouldn't make port for a decade and more." She looked around the room. "That from the Gallis. Their pusher made that last run, got *Firenze,* the first purpose-built in the Hinder Stars, as a reward. Had some hair-raising stories about Olympus. But viable? Depends on what the junkers did to it. And courts stopped them."

"We *need* to talk to those two ships," Uncle said "*Galway* put us on a deadline which may already be reality out at Alpha. At absolute worst case, Sol already has an FTL route to Alpha, proved out by these two ships. But if the EC is operating closer than that to Pell, if they've established an independent and well-armed base, and have our two FTLers of unknown ability running errands in *our* time frame . . . we need to know about it. Yesterday."

"It's possible *Little Bear*'s run into at least one of our ghosts," Fletcher said.

"Maybe," Uncle said. "But it's become far more than a signature on a line we need from them at this point. —Rennie."

"Sir."

"You say our two ghosts have an off-the-record port—so what location would *you* bet on, of Olympus and Thule?"

Rennie folded his arms, ducked his chin. "Until I noticed those missing ship parts, I'd've said Thule, with some long layovers, but Mum makes a good case for Olympus, and if Kate's right, if Olympus is, in fact, doable for a ship out of Venture, going through Thule . . . some of the gaps in the ghost appearances could well account for runs that long. As Mum pointed out, the amount of Sol goods we've located doesn't indicate a regular source, unless it's *really* under the table. Personal bet, those ships are using luxuries as bribes for contacts and information. I'm betting there are some interesting artifacts in certain Pell stationers' sitting rooms, not to mention in the living quarters of our two ghosts. With the marked exception of the trees and suspicious F-class stuff in the shops, the rest of their trading has been pretty standard: lifesupport stuff. Food. Medicines, and printer materials, which makes sense if they're trying not to be noticed—or helping supply some mothballed stations. It's possible the toy ships were legitimate F-class, just a private trade. Pocket chits. Merchanters being merchanters and financing their entertainment, but I'd bet a bit more than that. If we're reading this right, if they're running errands for the EC, the ships themselves need a bit more than fuel money. The EC might have said sell whatever you don't need for bribes, just don't do it in the Hinder Stars. The trees—that was high finance. Sorry I missed the tour. They sound like a real sight."

"Just for the record," Kate said, and tapped the tabletop. "Been running the numbers, such as we have, for real. Groombridge Point's going to be a beast even from Thule."

"Noted," Uncle said. "Nonetheless, we have to go check this out. Rennie, latest data on Thule and Olympus, stations and stars. ASAP."

"Sir," Rennie said, beaming.

"Copy the pertinent data to Kate when you get it. Sorry about the leave-time. Major sorry. We're not even going to unpack here."

"Aye, sir." Rennie reacquired his keyboard.

"How's the loading?" Uncle asked, and Rennie, without even looking up said:

"Five hundred sixty-seven cans an hour ago. Sir."

"Out of five thousand promised." Uncle frowned. "I'll talk to Konstantin. —Continue the fueling. Offload what we loaded, and get it to some holding area on a backup carrier. Madison, we won't be doing a long runout. I want to contact *Little Bear* at Venture if we possibly can, but we might beat her back and we won't wait. We'll be running light. Rennie, I'll need those work-ups as fast as you can manage."

"Funds," Madison said. "We're dipping into scarce territory, here. We've used up almost all our reserve."

There were frowns, all around the table. They'd run all the charity work they could afford, emptying their reserves, assisting three other ships out to Alpha and back, with major complications. There were, as yet, no contributions to the Alliance, at least on the Pell side of space.

Good deeds didn't pay the bills.

"I'm headed to Blue," Uncle said, meaning station admin. "Madison, I want Konstantin in his office for at least an hour, and I want a trolley at the gate in fifteen minutes. Fletch."

"Escort?" Fletcher asked.

"Witness," Captain-Uncle said. "In case he shoots me."

"How much will you pay me to save your life?" Kate asked, her eyes to the directional screen.

"What have you found?" Uncle asked.

"There might be another doable route out of Olympus."

"To?"

Kate's eyebrows raised. "Pell."

Silence, then:

"How certain?"

"The points are there. Never tried. Never mapped. Not remotely viable for converts, and by the time purposebuilts came along, Olympus was out of the picture."

"Run the numbers," Uncle said. "And let me know. Everybody else, we've got a board-call warning coming in about two hours. We'll part dock as soon as we finish filling, which is about . . ." He looked at his handheld. "Fifteen hours forty-five . . . call it sixteen. Rennie, a major thank you. Thank you to all your staff. Kate." He dipped his head. "Now let's break up and get to it."

Book II   Section xv

The cousins could move fast when the need arose. JR and Fletch were among the last to leave, and Jen was waiting for them just outside the door.

"Sir," Jen said, in a quiet, steady voice. Jen, who otherwise called him Uncle Robert or Uncle, sir. Jen . . . who had recognized the significance of the Galways' observations and had brought them this bombshell information. "What can I say?"

Meaning to the Galways.

"They'll get the same explanation the rest of the Family gets," JR said. "We're heading back to Venture, and we're not discussing it on dockside. But in their case—if they want to stay on Pell, finish with the sights on our tab, and catch a courtesy ride to Venture and on to Alpha, we'll arrange it, but they'll need to come and pick up their stuff and get a ride through station offices. They *don't* discuss our business on dockside, not any piece of it."

"I'll relay that," Jen said, and only an uncle who knew her well would detect the strain in her voice. "Can I ask—at least are we still going to get them back to Alpha if they stay on? They'll ask."

JR exchanged a look with Fletch, who had finessed the Jen-Monahan situation, and Fletch said:

"Can't promise our own cousins a destination right now, Jen. But we'll drop them off at Venture if they choose. That much we can do. Understand, we don't *know* what we're going to find out there, but we're investigating the undercover doings of a company that built a military personnel ship the size of *Finity*, and beggared the Monahans' home port to do it. We can't promise anything past Venture. Tell them that. Tell them come aboard to get the real story, and pick up their stuff if they decide to stay here at Pell. Make it clear it's their decision, with no judgment attached either way. This has just gone way beyond anything they signed on for. They'll have until the board-call to consider their options, and that will go out about mainday noon."

"Understood," Jen said, as sober as ever he'd seen her.

"Sorry," he said sincerely. "For what it's worth, we'll *all* miss them."

She nodded. "Uncle, sir. Thanks. I'll say so."

She left, behind Madison and John B.

"We could lose her here, JR," Fletch said quietly. "Or at Venture. She's seriously attached to that young man, and I suspect the feeling is mutual."

Not something he hadn't considered before, but JR steeled himself against a sense of personal loss. "Her choice entirely."

"I'll tell you, *I* don't want her to go. I've spent three years training that kid, she was good on Alpha, good on Pell, and damn it, JR, I love that kid. I don't like dumping her off headed for Alpha with a Family that's going to go at loggerheads with the Company. I *really* don't like what I'm feeling about these latest developments."

"Neither do I, Fletch," JR said quietly. "Neither do I. Frankly, I've been wondering if I ought to order all the kids, their mothers, and their minders ashore here along with Jen and the Monahans. Even if it will put holes in Third- and Fourth-shift."

"I forecast the Monahans will want a piece of this if it turns into what it could. At least *Rights of Man* won't be a factor any time soon, and if the EC comes in at Alpha, they'll be a while sorting the loss not only of the mega-ship, but the hundreds of trained thugs they were counting on to help them take back the stations."

"Granted Emilio comes through and gets that cargo through to them to have the Alpha locals employed and happy. *We* can't take it."

Fletch grinned. "We're counting on *Captain James Robert's* golden tongue to convince him, *and* make him happy to cover the bill."

JR pointedly ignored that. "Emilio will come through—it's in his own interest. I'm *really* not looking forward to that meeting with Xiao Min."

They had been at the point of dismissing their three allies, still helping in the Hinder Stars. *Nomad* and *Mumtaz* were likely done with Glory and headed back even now to Pell. The Xiao ship, *Little Bear,* had agreed to delay their return trip at Venture until a certain date—hoping to intercept *Finity* for a final debrief—before moving on to Pell and bidding farewell to the whole set-up operation. As it turned out *Finity* could win the race back to Venture. He hoped that wasn't the case. Xiao Min needed to know what was going on.

Fletch said: "We sure could use their backup. If nothing else, as an alternate means for getting word back to Pell about . . . whatever we find out there."

Whatever we find out there.

On the bridge, there was a plaque. A bronze medallion of Earth, worn bright by generations of Neihart fingertips. It was the only recognizable part of *Gaia* left. He'd never imagined he might be forced one day to risk that medallion—and all it represented. He felt a flash of empathy for Niall Monahan, Senior captain of *Galway*, who'd made the decision to risk everything that mattered to him . . . and his Family . . . for the future of everyone.

Niall had made a decision, then found himself attacked aboard his own ship in an act of piracy unimaginable to anyone outside of EC offices.

That aggression—that piracy—could not stand. Not at Alpha . . . and not at some secret base in the Galileo Reach.

Time had become essential. They'd made inquiries at Pell that might have let information slip. And that simple, ridiculous issue of three trees and an ancient, insignificant ship could have set rumors in motion at Pell that could warn a far more serious problem, namely some shadow EC operation, that the jig was up.

God . . . one had to wonder if the local EC office was a part of . . . whatever was going on.

Timing. Timing had become essential. There was a ship scheduled to undock, en route to Venture, in the next twelve hours, that would be carrying information about *Finity* and *Neihart* business in its immutable black box. Not all of it, because Emilio still had some things on hold. But there would be other ships; ships that would dock, exchange data, and leave, *after* Emilio was forced to release everything; ships that would travel both to the Beyond and the Hinder Stars. *Finity* needed to get ahead of that wave front, that was all, before those two ghost ships disappeared altogether, along with their answers.

Book II   **Section xvi**

The door opened. Ross set an elbow against the mattress and lifted his head, seeing it was Jen, back again and being quiet. "Everything all right?"

Jen shook her head, and came and stood by the bed, in the dark, hands thrust deep into her pockets. "Board call's going out. Senior Captain says

Galways don't have to go. You can stay here, on *Finity's* tab, see stuff, and we'll leave instructions with admin to arrange another ride back to Alpha for you when you're ready to leave. But you would have to go now and get your stuff off the ship. We need to tell the others."

Her body language said reserve. Worry. Definitely no prank.

"What in hell?" He waved a hand over the bedside light switch, winced at the sudden general glare, and tried to make out her face, which was, yes, upset. Had she been crying? "Go? Go where? And why would he want to leave us here? Did one of us create a problem? Jen, did *I*?"

"No. No, nothing like that." She chewed her lip, then: "Just don't want to ruin your chance at Pell, y'know? And . . . we just have to move out. Life's like that."

No, he didn't know. She was hiding something. Something big. But, damn, could someone be listening?

He sat up, indicated the space beside him, and she sat. For a moment, she just stared off across the room, hands clenched in her lap, then suddenly she twisted and put her arms tight around him.

"I can't leave them," she said, her shaky voice barely audible. "Love you. A lot. But I can't leave them."

"*Leave* them? Who? *Finity*? Of course you can't. Jen, what's going on? *Where* are they going? Is it something about *Galway* or—" If something had happened at Alpha . . . or *to* Alpha . . . where his family was . . .

But if it was about *Galway*, however bad, why would *Finity* want to leave them behind?

Damn it, he was still half asleep.

Fingers on his lips warned him to silence, and she brought her lips right against his ear. "Got a lead on those two ships we're hunting. Could take us off the Alpha route. Way off. And we have to go."

His heart was beating hard. It made a sort of sense.

"We just need to get everybody to the ship," Jen said, "Now."

To the ship. Where they could talk safely, and didn't *need* to come back onto Pell's deck. He got that much, and worried all over again about that too-public discussion about trees and Earth imports. The conversation had sent Jen racing off to *Finity*, with Nolan in tow. He'd been puzzled by her leaving. A little worried. Just a little.

Just how stupid had they been?

Whatever the reason, though, it was nothing directly to do with *Galway*. That, at least.

Jen pushed herself to her feet and began stuffing things in her carry-bag. Ross, fully awake now, collected his clothes and pulled them on.

"The stuff we sent to the ship," Jen said in a low voice. "I can get that sent here if you decide to stay. But best you pack. In case. Got to tell the others pack and come. Either way, stay aboard or leave, *Finity* will settle all the charges."

He took up his handheld and keyed up a group message to his cousins: "Meet me at *Finity*. Board call. Now. Bring luggage. Questions later," and sent it before he snatched up his own carry-bag and swept his own toiletries into the safety bag.

Jen meanwhile went into the bath and came out with all the little bottles and samples the Royal provided. She dumped those into his carry-bag.

"You *can* go on using this room," she said. "If you come back. But in case."

Ross tried to arrange things, using a Royal courtesy bag to contain Jen's raid on toiletries.

Come back. Hell. Nine of them staying here, nine of them trying to get a ride to Venture with some other ship, with some unknown crew that the Monahans—he supposed—couldn't tell everything they knew, while curiosity about where they'd come from and why would be running wild?

Space for *one* free rider was hard to ask for. Even with help from Station Admin, it would be a piecemeal nightmare getting them all home.

And God, yes, there'd be questions. He and his cousins knew too much without knowing how it all connected, and that could make their slips of the tongue dangerous. He knew that. They all knew. And they tried to be careful, but like that discussion in the Garden bistro, there were things they might let slip, one loose remark, one lover's idle conversation, and rumors could spiral way out of control. They were Alpha spacers. Strangers. Noticeable. They understood that, dammit, and yet, first night on the strip, they'd gotten too relaxed, too careless . . .

But Jen said it *wasn't* the Monahans that had triggered this sudden board call. Something else had happened. *Those two ships* and *take us off the Alpha route* . . .

They were old First Stars ships that *Finity* was hunting. They shouldn't be able to make it to Pell—let alone Viking. How far off the path could they go?

"Where's *Finity* headed?" Surely she could tell him that much.

"Venture," she said, then put a finger to her lips, caution against further questions.

He took a deep breath and worked the toiletries bag into a pocket in his black duffle. Damned if he was coming back alone, not with *Finity* headed in the right direction.

Even if they went with *Finity* only as far as Venture, at least if they were set out there dockside, to find a way home . . . Venture had ships headed the right direction. Ships they knew. Families fully up to speed on the situation at Alpha.

But . . . *damn it all!* He wasn't ready to leave *Finity* . . . not when *everything* was—

Flash of dark and a blazing red sun, naked furnace, blinding and terrible. A glowing red shape in the dark, and the sound of his own breaths. Pain in his forehead . . .

He twitched. Damn it all. Every time he got stressed.

"Ross? You all right?"

Stinging acid breath, blood-spattered light of the star, *Finity's* pale shape far below, and above . . . That was the last time he'd been close to *Galway*. Fallan had shoved him out the emergency lock, then gone to save *Galway* from those EC pirates. He'd been cheated of being part of that fight. Necessary, yes, to alert the Family and all the rest of the Alliance what had happened, but if those same pirates, or at least their corporate cousins, were operating at *this* end of space, they, the Galways at Pell, had to survive. Had to find out what was happening *here* and carry that message to Alpha. For Fallan. For all of them. The EC was fighting dirty, and *Galway* was literally in a fight for her life.

All he'd had to show for that battle for *Galway* was a blow to the head that left him with that bloody, shattered memory . . . and guilt that he'd left his shift behind.

He'd left Family behind again, when he'd gone with *Finity*. Left them behind to suffer the sheer boredom and inescapable aging of station life, left them to carry the burden of worrying about Niall and Fallan and all the rest in real time, years, when all he'd suffer was months. Sure, he'd gone to learn everything he could. To do his part for Fallan and all the Monahans. To be ready when *Galway* returned triumphant—and ready for the upgrades *Finity* had promised . . .

But to leave *Finity* here or even at Venture, and find some other way to get home . . .

Give up the connection? *Run* away again?

And what was Jen saying? Did they really have a choice? He couldn't believe they'd be forced off, not without some better explanation. The Neiharts had played fair with them, more than fair. The Neiharts had shown them modern systems, taught them things, shown them things they'd only imagined. And he wasn't finished learning, dammit. He'd known they might part company at Venture, depending on what they heard from *Little Bear*. But that was an expected part of leaving Alpha in the first place. He wasn't ready for a call in the dark. He wasn't in territory he remotely knew, and everything was suddenly going sideways—

But the ship called.

He froze, his world suddenly snapping into focus.

If the ship called, he didn't know *how* to stay. He didn't have a question what was right or wrong, smart or not. He *knew* one thing and one thing only: he didn't belong on Pell, or Venture or any other station. Not if he had a choice.

And if he truly did have a choice, damned if he wasn't in on whatever this was. Being left behind *again* . . . watching *Finity* and all her promises leave them stranded at station, was just not an option.

With new purpose, he started packing his living-on-station clothes, rolled them all back into a fairly wrinkle-free bundle. He made a reckless try at the new coat, Jen's gift, which wasn't designed for the kind of packing he knew.

"Give me that," Jen said. Jen took it and folded it. Same with the new pants. She stowed them both, neatly.

"Thanks," he said, embarrassed.

"Here," Jen said, and handed him his duffle.

Book II   Section xvii

"Maindark," Emilio said, sinking into his chair. "God, you come in at maindark, you do business in maindark. What in hell's going on? Something to do with that special clearance you requested? Something about the Garden, for God's sake?"

"Short version," JR said, "that special exhibit put us on the track of something big. At least it could be. That's what we have to find out. Basically, we have, thanks to your local record keeping, a whole lot of numbers that don't add up involving the only two ships that haven't signed on to the Alliance. *Earth* imports that, by all the numbers, and according to our Monahan guests, *didn't* come through Alpha."

Emilio held up a hand to stop him.

"Give me a moment." Emilio swung his chair around, reached into the cabinet, extracted the Scotch and three glasses, onto the bare desktop. "One finger or two?"

"Make it light for me. I'm in ops. You'll want two."

Emilio gave him a worried look that shifted to Fletch, standing silently beside the door, then uncorked the bottle and poured . . . two glasses. He shoved the lesser glass to mid-desk, and JR half-rose and took it, settling back with it warming in his hands.

"So," Emilio said. "Come again?"

"Nothing's proven, mind you. Yet. We *think* those two are trafficking recent imports from Earth via some route that doesn't involve Alpha."

"You're bloody kidding."

"I wish I were. We've no reason to believe they've independently discovered an FTL route to Sol, but *something* out there has Sol contact *somehow*. We suspect we've got at very least a pusher base that's been operating for years, and trying to hide the fact. Remembering what they were doing at Alpha, recruiting and training Enforcers and building personnel transport, it's forming a picture we don't like."

"A pusher base *where?*"

"That's what we hope to find out, and why we're leaving as soon as we get everyone back on board. We're *guessing* the Galileo Reach. But here's what we know: our Monahan guests found F-class items in local shops that they've never seen or heard of at Alpha, one of which contains copyright info that dates *manufacture* to twenty-one years ago, max, which precludes some stationer selling off their warehoused hoard. Then there are your mega-trees. The seller, *Come Lately*, claims they were grown from seeds found on Bryant's. Not an impossibility, but where grown and when purchased and from whom was pointedly left off the paperwork. They took the payment, converted it to Venture chits, only ten thousand of which they spent locally. Those F-class sales were also chip transactions rather than station credit. Venture chits are used everywhere in the Hinder Stars. But very little of that chit windfall shows up on Alpha or Bryant's or even Venture. Neither is there any sign of the ten thousand breakfast meals they bought here. Wholesale. That's what you call a long-term supply, for a single ship."

"No question I remember the trees. It was a minor hassle. The ship demanded some insane amount. Committee said no deal. The Garden fought to keep them. It got to the court system. The Garden got their trees, and we ended up paying the ship—bargained down, I guarantee. —A pusher route *where?*"

"Possibly Thule. More likely Olympus. We think there's a safe FTL route from Thule. We don't *know*. We're going hunting."

"God. How did you figure—?"

"The pattern of *Come Lately's* movements and her intersection with commodities' rise and fall, the fact that she shouldn't be able to make it from Venture to Pell . . . but does. A cash buy of ship parts at Venture some twenty years ago that never made it to another station, parts that *could* account for our two ships being able to visit here. The question of where those upgrades might have been done. The question of where other apparent purchases ended up . . . Maybe she spends a lot of time at Glory, from which *Finity* has no records as yet. But that's no great attraction. Maybe that's where she got her suspected upgrade, but Glory's not the place for that. If she trades a lot at Glory, she'd have to go via Bryant's, where she's rare, even by the commodities ticks. Same story with *Miriam B*. Known at Alpha and Bryant's, but mostly Venture, and sometimes here. Slippery. Very. Two ships with that pattern, that buy electronics and manufacturing machinery at Venture, and trade Scotch by multiple cases on a schedule never intersecting any pusher at Alpha. —Yes, we're suspicious. And disturbed enough to risk the ship going after the truth."

Emilio's expression had grown more and more guarded. All the way over to troubled. "On the trail of a pusher route we don't know about." He looked up. "You're sure it couldn't have come in at Alpha."

"The last two Alpha pushers were exclusively moving stuff for *Rights of Man*. Practically no station goods."

"So Alpha's said."

"And our Monahans concur. They say even F-class from the pusher crews was cherry-picked by Cruz, the head of the *Rights* project. Caused quite a controversy, to say the least."

"And yet we have this relative abundance of Sol goods floating around the market, not to mention the total food *sales* for the Hinder Stars. There are reasons I always thought Abrezio was exaggerating his problem. —Thule, you say. You think some of those food sales are headed there?"

"Maybe. Maybe Olympus. Thule's an easy jump from Venture, and from there, at least by the numbers, a relatively easy in and out of Olympus. Olympus is *not* easy to or from Venture direct."

"Those records you wanted . . ." Emilio rubbed his forehead. "They gave you all this?"

"Only when combined with similar from here to Alpha. Just a matter of putting a lot of dissimilar but intimately related pieces together. Looking at who's moving where, and the commercial data, it's been there. Just not a puzzle that mattered to anybody—until we began looking for a specific ship's movements over decades." Time, JR decided, to up the ante. "Point is, there's no reason Sol couldn't build more pushers, couldn't use them to set up a base nearer to Pell than Alpha, and man it with loyal EC personnel."

"A base nearer Pell. To do what?" Emilio asked sharply—not that Emilio, always suspicious of the EC, would be short of ideas, none of them pleasant.

"I think we got a taste of that at Alpha. It's a good bet they want to reclaim what they feel they lost. I suspect we're dealing with a goal that predates even FTL, but which FTL certainly brought to a head. The Galileo Reach is a string of hard-luck operations, from the EC's point of view. The mutiny at Venture, the theft of the Pell core—Galileo blowing, Thule being ignored by the pushers . . . then Cyteen and FTL happened, and when FTL ships realized Groombridge Point at Olympus was a disaster waiting to happen, putting Olympus out of business . . . Basically, once Pell opened up, nothing ever went right for Olympus and Thule."

"The Olympus situation affected all of us," Emilio said. "Companies ferried their people and operations to Venture, which couldn't handle the numbers, and so eventually to Pell. Several of our major companies had their start on Olympus. Protocorp set up at Venture. FTL certainly tipped our power structure. We still had an office here, but quit listening to them altogether. It didn't take FTL for the Beyond to collectively boot Sol interests back to the Hinder Stars. —So now you think they're coming to take it all back?" Emilio looked a bit in shock, and JR couldn't blame him. *He'd* had time to get past the initial realization. Emilio hadn't.

"At the moment," JR said, "if we're right, all they have on this side is two FTL Family ships servicing them. Old ships, purportedly with ancient nav and engines, which shouldn't be able to make the run to Pell economically, but are doing that, which leads one to suspect those systems aren't as old as our records show. That power upgrade and unique Earth goods, luxury goods, and some odd food purchases explains what *Come Lately* is getting out of it, but one has to wonder what they're giving the EC in exchange. Somehow, one suspects pusher-loads from Earth are supplying this hypothetical station with all its physical needs—if 10,000 VC in breakfast buns and some flour is all the freight she's hauling."

"Except information," Emilio said. "Money in, information out. Bribes. God help me, I'm going to have every negotiable chit in this station marked and tracked!"

"A little late now, if our suspicions are correct."

"Who knows how long this has been going on? For all we know, they're *at* someplace like Thule building a fleet of FTL ships, filling them with Enforcers, arming them with who knows what kind of weapons to blow a hatch and board the station whether we like it or not!" Emilio took a swallow of the Scotch and stared at something infinite, and not, by his expression, pleasant. Then at JR. "Please tell me this is some move of your Alliance to panic us shore-dwellers. I've *signed* your damn agreement. You really don't need a sales pitch."

"I swear to you it's possible. We hadn't put it together, either. Now we have."

"Those two over in the EC office." Emilio's lip lifted in a snarl. "If they've known about this, and kept it silent, playing some *game* with us while feeding information . . . damned if I won't have them locked up until we have an answer out of them."

"I doubt they'll admit to anything. Only way to know is to go see for ourselves . . . and hope to God that it's not *Beta* they've been reviving."

"They wouldn't dare. Not even the EC could be that downright stupid."

"Never underestimate the EC," JR said grimly. "But we don't think so. We've found the Earth products here at Pell, and Beta to Pell would take them all the way through the Hinder Stars. Our money is on something closer to Pell."

"Lovely."

"We suspect Thule or Olympus. We're heading down the Reach to find out if we're right. Whatever's going on, you need to know. Stationmasters clear to Alpha need to know exactly what's going on."

Emilio drew a deep, shaky breath, leaned back, staring into his glass until he regained control, then said slowly, "You scare them, you know."

"Scare them? Me? The Merchanter's Alliance? That can't be a factor. Earth doesn't even know about it yet."

"Not you, personally. *Finity.* I know what I'd be thinking, if I were sitting inside Sol Station, in a system with infinite wealth, and got those plans and specs for *Finity* dropped in my lap."

"What? That we're going to one-hop from Alpha to crash their party and raid the coffers? We can't do that. *Finity's* good, but she's not that good."

"Isn't she?" Emilio raised his eyebrows skeptically. "We built her and in all this time, I've still never seen her true specs. Keep those close, you do. You and John Reilly, both."

"Even if we could top 6 lights, *which we can't,* have you any idea the havoc we'd pull in with us, running that hot? First V-dump at Sol, we'd be sprayed with our own gravitational shrapnel."

"You might know that. You might even believe it. Not sure I do, and I'm damned certain the EC CEOs don't know or believe it. For them, interstellar trade is a habit, not a way of life. The stations slipping out of their control was a loss of face, not a financial blow."

"Oh, I'm sure they noticed."

"Historically, the stations were sources of information, not wealth. The fact they've started making money, and lots of it, and none of that wealth to this day is making its way back to the EC coffers has their shorts in a majorly painful bunch, but doesn't affect their bottom line that much. For generations they've hidden behind that pusher-time barrier, able to pretend to their constituents that they were in charge of it all. Pell, Cyteen . . . how real are they to the population of Earth? Who knows what bullshit the EC has passed on to their own population about us? Hell, you've seen those crazy vids they send out in the name of entertainment. It's possible they started . . . whatever you believe they're doing, the day they got the news of Olympus' shutdown; but I have this inevitable thought that whatever those plans are, they went into high gear when they saw those blueprints for *Finity*. When did you last look at the production notes the EC stole? Those who designed her sincerely believed she could do Alpha-to-Earth."

"She can't."

"But that's what the EC has to go on, and that means their generational buffer is gone. The unnamed threat from the traitorous stars *could* be on their real-time doorstep." Emilio's face hardened. "So . . . what now?"

"No choice, really. We've *got* to find those ships, and we've got to find where they're based. We're set to rendezvous with *Little Bear* at Venture, and if our ships haven't run across the ghosts yet, we'll head to Thule and, if we don't find anything there, on to Olympus. We've got to know."

"And you're going to take your ship, and your people, and tell this EC station . . . if it exists . . . we've twigged to their secret, that FTL is coming to Sol via Alpha, and, oh, by the way, if you want to join the system, you're welcome, but here are the rules."

"That's one outcome."

"And if they don't want to play by those rules?"

"Clause thirteen of the agreement you signed. *If Alliance merchant trade is in any wise restrained or denied at a station, signatory stations will support the Merchanter Alliance in settling the dispute, such support to include finance and logistics, diplomatic efforts, and if necessary, embargo of the non-compliant station.*"

"Meaning that if . . . let's assume Olympus . . . doesn't play nice, you'll cut off trade they aren't currently admitting to."

"First we talk to them."

"How? If you're right, *Come Lately* and *Miriam B* are running goods, and, one assumes, carrying information to them already."

"We'll meet the ships, hear them out, give them the option to join. If they join, by the terms of the agreement, they cease trading with the EC until the station signs the agreement. If no one signs, no other station will do business with the ships as long as they're doing business with Olympus, effectively freezing them, trees or no trees."

Emilio heaved a breath. "About all we can do, until we know. So.... is this after hours visit just a 'for the record,' or is there something *else* you want from me?"

"One more favor."

"*What* favor?"

"That load of foodstuffs, medicines, and technical items you authorized, to be parceled out to Bryant's, Alpha, and Glory, of which I've only loaded a fraction. I've bought the goods, but I need them to be transported and I haven't time to work out the details. Can you make that happen? We'll off-load most of it. We're fueling full up. You can use the Alliance agreement, explain the situation to whatever extent you feel necessary."

"Arrange a shipment at whose expense?"

"Here's where it gets tight. Sir."

"I thought so."

"You *know* we've used our own account hard. Very hard. We've hoped to make that back once things level out, but that return to normal keeps slipping away from us. We're not looking for repayment for what we've already outlaid, just some help, here—in the *stations'* interest."

"Credit."

"We need that supply to get to Alpha."

"To prop up the station that's due to become the EC's gateway."

"Only if you want this plan to succeed. Only if you want that gateway to be a viable, *happy* buffer between you and the EC. And only supposing *Galway* makes it through and those jump-points test out. If it does, it could actually help in negotiations if the EC finds a string of healthy small stations to do business with on the FTL route—and Pell, of course. Proper business. Not business backed by a clandestine build of a mega-ship military transport, which right now is not going to be finding any military to transport. By now, the Alpha young folk should have gone back to regular work in antici-pation of *goods* arriving from up the line. It's the hope of the stationmaster to do repairs and rebuilding, to meet whatever *Galway* brings back with a healthy, potentially profitable, situation. If they look good to the EC, the EC *may* listen to them. The EC has never, historically, wanted complicated an-swers."

"Like a clandestine pusher-route? What do we suppose they're doing?"

"Here's where *our* arrangement comes in. We go have a look. We may take a close look. We may let them know we know. We may even talk to them. Depends. But our Alliance depends on a principle, too, which is that cargo moves on Alliance ships to Alliance stations, who may *not* deal with non-Alliance ships except on humanitarian grounds."

"That's a hard push, Captain. A provocation."

"It's the essence of what we must have from them, with Alpha the only possible exception. And I doubt the EC at Olympus, if our guess is right, has carte blanche to make war or peace. They'll have to consult. At lightspeed. Which is a two decade round trip for them, and then some. In the meanwhile, if the gods of space smile on us, *Galway* has been there and given them a way to get to Alpha and join the FTL universe by that route, and that means we'll have a higher authority on tap, and them *wanting* the wealth that's out here. Which we can offer enough of to tempt any board of directors. What we know of Earth and Sol—it has too many pieces ever to agree, but pieces of it can agree, particularly if they get goods as a result."

"If it works, you'll be a hero. That base, if it exists, would put EC FTL ships uncomfortably close to Pell. Your Alliance could prove itself. However, if the EC takes exception, if that truly is a military base . . . you could be in trouble, Captain. Very big trouble."

"It's a risk we need to take, but obviously, we will be careful. In the meantime, we've spent deep into our reserve, to *your* benefit. And this EC operation, if we're right, is near enough to Pell and Venture to involve you both, should anything go amiss—so consider it to your benefit."

"It's the amiss part that worries me."

"Whatever can go wrong is short-term out here, and it'll take Earth a decade to hear it. Whatever might go wrong, we have more time than they do, and time is options."

"You just sent a messenger to Cyteen-space. He hasn't left yet."

"Not with *this* information, sir. And he won't get it. Last thing we need is years for misinformation to proliferate based on a rumor. All he has is what we got on the last trip: the signatures on the Alliance contract, the jumppoints to Sol and what happened aboard *Galway*. This pending operation is a chance for Pell-space and the Hinder Stars to settle this illicit trade situation on their own, before Cyteen even hears there's a problem—a problem they assuredly *won't* like. Cyteen involvement can only complicate negotiations with Sol. Cyteen's *existence,* however, gives you leverage with the EC once it does come in."

"You warned Cyteen about *Galway*. On an imminently departing ship. *That's* going to spread its own rumors."

"That I did, sir. It would have been bad faith not to. But just remember, when I deal with the Alliance on Cyteen-side, I'm not speaking to the Carnaths and the Emorys. I'm speaking to *Dublin*, to John Reilly, merchanter, with merchanter interests, *and* with the ear of the Carnaths and the Emorys when he needs it. As I have yours. Things will get explained out there, directly, and one of the things I will definitely have to account for eventually is *not* sending *Dublin* word about this possible pusher-route. The simple answer is, we simply don't yet know, and we're trying to find out. We *will* be messaging John Reilly as soon as we have solid information, but I hope to be able to tell him that our newborn Alliance settled the problem with Pell's full and energetic cooperation."

"You owe us, Captain, you owe us for your ship-build, our support against the EC, and your freedom to do what you damn well please!"

"Mutual, sir. We've organized the Alliance on your own theory, that makes merchanters the *third* power in the Beyond, so stations can maintain a glorious isolation, with us as the go-betweens. I'm telling you, the *Alliance* is officially telling you that, if I'm right, we've got a problem shaping up at the aforenamed stars and we're headed out there to address that problem and isolate it, while *they* take the necessary twenty-plus years to talk to Sol authority and get an answer. Let's get this operation settled before *Galway* gets back to Alpha with whatever shakes out from that."

"JR," Emilio said. "Level, here. If you don't level with me, at this ungodly hour, in this situation . . . I need to know *specifically* what you're going to do about an EC operation if you find it."

"Frankly, I don't know there's anything I can do but shine a light on it and tell them that if Alpha's about to become an FTL port for Sol—as it may— then a new pusher-port close to Pell is not entirely a waste. There are items Sol could inject into the system that only pushers could conveniently deliver, if that's what they want. But *Galway* may not have gotten through. The jump-points could be foul. We may not *have* Sol coming in here FTL after all. And if that's the case, then we still have twenty years to figure this out, and *maybe* to convert *Rights of Man* into an honest merchanter with a Family crew. It's all to work out. But I need your backing . . . and your trust. I will try very hard to calm the situation, not inflame it."

Emilio gave a heavy sigh. "I've got a council to convince."

JR drew a breath and gave his final, most potent, argument. "Tell them this: if they *are* at Olympus, if they have modern, purpose-built FTLers . . . there's a direct-to-Pell route they can use."

Emilio just stared at him.

"It's there. It exists. We've had the points, but the converts couldn't do it. By the numbers, it's pretty hellish. But it's there. *Finity* could manage it. Anything less . . . depends on how desperate they are."

He let that sink in. Then:

"So, my old friend, you get on your council and let's solve this before Cyteen comes back with questions. *I've* got to get out of here before some research intern says the wrong thing, and someone else asks a question. What gets asked after we leave can't get ahead of us. Do we have backing?"

"Damn you, JR."

"All you like."

"Hell," Emilio muttered, then: "Go. Get out of here. I'll transfer it as a loan. If you survive, if the outcome's good, I'll forgive it, good of the station. If it isn't, I may have to hang you and *Finity* out on a long, long tether. I can't be drawn into this. Pell can't be. Understand?"

"No question," JR said, drank his Scotch, rose, and set the glass on Emilio's desk. "Thanks, old friend. Wish us luck."

Book III   Venture   Section i

Reality re-shaped itself.
Two faint voices, one soft, one a little uneasy, a little unstable: Bella and the Beast.
Old, familiar friends. Why had he never heard them before?

Book III   Section ii

Dark gave way to blurry vision.

JR blinked, fought to clear his eyes and see the schematics. There were lights, green and steady for Helm, Nav, and Longscan, well hyped up out of trank and responding. Com and Engee were green but blinking. Scan was steady yellow, but soon to follow.

Lines moved. Nav tracks converged.

Period of black.

Second V-dump.

Heart raced. Space-time smoothed out.

They were in. But not in the ordinary way. *Finity* wasn't hauling on this run, little more than fuel and ship's stores. Ship's chrono said they were dead on estimate—Kate didn't miss—and they were tracking exactly where they'd intended to be, in Venture's zenith jump range, six minutes light out from the station. It would be six realtime minutes before Com heard direct communication from Venture Station, but they were meeting station's ongoing datastream. Their system maps were filling in and longscan was starting to project current positions.

"We look good," JR said to those awake to hear him. "Is Com up?"

"*Com's working,*" Com 1.1 said, and cleared his throat.

"Scan?"

"*Getting a position,*" Scan said. "*Yes!* Little Bear *is here, coordinates lit.* Helm."

"She's standing off midway to the station," Helm said.

"*Projecting as stationary,*" Longscan said, meaning relative to the station and *Finity's* incoming vector.

"Com, hail *Little Bear,*" JR said.

"*Hailing now,*" Com said, and their signal went out, saying *Finity, Finity, Finity.* Station hadn't yet ID'ed *Finity* on its own map, would mark their incoming position in about two minutes and posit a likely course for them. It would take another six minutes for *Finity* to see Venture's version of the system map with their position and trend added to it.

"*Standing by for* V-*dump,*" Helm 1.1 said. "*Park with* Little Bear *in two?*"

"Com, advise *Little Bear,* advise station. We're dumping V to match *Little Bear's* position. Helm, that's a go for one of two."

Book III   Section iii

V-dump blurred vision, felt like weight, then weightlessness. Not-here and here again. Ross blinked rapidly, fighting for vision, keyed again, confident but not being a fool. His stomach objected. The universe tilted, righted itself again—it was the inner ear that didn't like what it was getting, but that happened, and hype helped. Ross squeezed to get more juice, and felt warmth shooting through his arm.

He wasn't dead-on course this time. He saw Kate's line, and Bucklin's, and his line was out, too, too conservative, off by three. He'd never dreamed of coming in this close, this hot and dumping V this fast. Power. *Finity* was power incarnate, at the moment, and in a hurry as she'd not been before.

Meanwhile, the map reformed itself. The system's data now began to populate the screen. They were within a .04 second lag of the position they wanted, which was sitting just outside the inbound jump range, inertia fast narrowing the local scale, and he'd just been lessoned in the extreme finesse a ship of *Finity's* power could apply.

Finity's power and Kate Neihart's skill. His line matched Ty and Jim. He'd thought he could shave it fine. He had. But not as fine as Kate.

They would pose no danger to *Little Bear*—no problem there. Both Venture's suns, Bella and the Beast, were astern. Ross couldn't swear he'd ever really *felt* a star, before Tau Ceti, but it was as if, now his gut knew what to expect, he'd always felt it here: two faint voices, one soft, one a little uneasy, a little unstable, both a little startled at *Finity's* unusual shockwave. Venture anchored around a piece of Bella's realm, an ill-formed lump of a planetoid called Austen. It outgassed, but couldn't hold an atmosphere. The Beast, Krueger 60 B, had a temper. He had a decided distrust of it in the wake of that shockwave, but it *felt* quiet.

Mentally drifting. But Nav's job was essentially done, just down now to being aware and watching as the system map that Venture output actively refined itself and showed *Finity* and *Little Bear* in their current and projected relationship.

"Well done," Kate said to her crew. No praise was due the trainee, however. Ross felt that. He hadn't earned it this time. He wanted to talk to Kate when the chance arose, he wanted a walk-through of the whole process, and likely she would oblige, Kate being the generous soul she was.

But right now his mind had to be on their options. *Finity,* with one V-dump yet to go, was still carrying considerable way, and, as the system numbers refined the schematic, *Little Bear* was now reading as carrying a little stationward momentum in a slightly different vector. *Little Bear* ought not to be lying where she was, right at the edge of the entry zone, unless she was just arrived—which was possible, but a hell of a coincidence if that was the case.

Except it wasn't coincidence, at least not the fact she was here. According to the brief they'd all gotten, *Little Bear* had agreed to wait for them at Venture with the most current information from Alpha, waiting for the go-ahead from Senior Captain to return to their regular routes. Maybe she'd finished her business with Venture and was sitting out here to avoid racking up dock charges, eager to get back to those routes the minute her business with *Finity* was done.

And maybe—his ears buzzed as his heart raced—maybe they had news from Alpha. News they didn't want to give dockside.

He willed that heart rate down with mediocre success. All he really knew was that *Little Bear* was back from a crazy-fast run to Alpha—carrying a repair component desperately needed back at Alpha—along a direct Venture-to-Alpha route he'd never imagined . . . until Kate had set her trainees to calcing it for *Finity*. Practice, she'd said, but one thing was certain: plugging in *Galway* numbers would leave her drifting, unable to come down. He knew. He'd tried it in sims.

On the other hand, *Little Bear*, hoping to meet *Finity* here, might be carrying mail from the rest of the Monahans, a *hello, how are you*, the way he and the rest of the Galways with *Finity* had left messages at Bryant's.

Still . . . and his heart sped up again . . . enough station-time had elapsed that there was a possibility of it—time enough that, if everything had gone at max speed, *Galway* could have come back to Alpha. That would not be good news. Not good at all. Niall had promised to take all the time he possibly could, hoping to give the Alliance time to stabilize Alpha . . . but Alpha's stationmaster having already transmitted the coordinates for the jump-points on the light-speed Stream meant *Galway* had no more than six years to make the trip.

Niall's plan was to get ahead of that information front, to time the route not as slow as light-speed, but not as fast as *Galway* could do it, using the need to carefully map those two points as a legitimate delay, hoping to give *Finity* plenty of time to get to Pell and seal the Alliance before Sol got into the act . . . and giving them time to sort Alpha out. Which they had done before they left.

But if *Galway* had already returned . . .

If that had happened—everything had gone wrong. Fallan would never surrender the coordinates. Fallan could destroy *Galway*. Just change a decimal. Nav 1 could do that. And Fallan would, if Fallan was the only one aboard with the numbers and if they couldn't regain control from the EC.

But if—worst case scenario—the EC had won the battle for control, and *if* they had the numbers before they ever boarded, and if *somehow* those sim-trained newbies who had caused *The Rights of Man* to abort her first jump had managed to navigate those unproven jump-points and arrive at Sol—

If all that had happened, then, running as fast and hard as *Galway* could, the EC *could* be back at Alpha right now, in control of Alpha *and Galway*.

If all that had happened, and *Little Bear* was waiting here to warn them . . .

Couldn't happen. Couldn't happen. Of all possibilities—no. Fallan wouldn't buckle. No matter what. And that EC crew couldn't navigate. Either way, Ross just wished he'd gone with them, with Niall and Fallan and all the rest of the First-shift crew. As he'd tried to do. One more Monahan might have made a difference.

"*Go to* V-*dump*," the captain said, General Hail that came over their ear-pieces. "*Second* V-*dump. Prepare to execute.*"

Ross punched the final variables into his calc . . .

"V-*dump in thirty seconds*," Helm said. "*Twenty-nine.*"

. . . and sent it to the Nav comp, and braced himself for another jolt.

They were all tired, hell, they were a *mess*, after that fast turnaround at Pell, but for this entry, given they were not planning a station approach, they had a whole new problem. First-shift Nav needed to be mentally adjusted to ensure a safe rendezvous with *Little Bear*. They did not get a lengthy period to rest. Reality was about to adjust itself. He needed to be sharp, coming out.

Countdown ticked to a zero. Ross kept his eyes on the screen and concentrated on the numbers as they arrived. They were—Ross ran the math determinedly in his head—going down hard, really hard. The schematic kept redrawing itself in a mad overlay.

They were, to a nicety, where they expected to be.

Close approach to another ship. Nav was not going to get a shift-change until that was plotted.

Book III   Section iv

Little Bear was a blip on scan, a distant blackness against the star-studded black on visual. JR, having showered, having taken down several nutrient packs and with his stomach moderately settled, watched from his bridge-side office, sipping a cup of coffee and ticking through Venture's output on trade and local news. Their own arrival had gone on Venture's boards with the footnote, *in transit, not expected to dock*.

That would probably upset some people expecting shipments. That first message was Com 1 doing her job on entry.

But he had personally sent a second and more reassuring message: *Shipments anticipated to arrive on* Finity's End *have been consigned to other ships at Pell and are expected to be in transit to Venture at this moment.* Finity's End *has arrived at Venture for a brief conference on Alliance business and will be departing shortly after.*

Beyond that, he intended to let Com do the official talking, and not to answer inevitable questions. Their time here *was* measured in hours, mostly the finesses necessary to get *Finity* and *Little Bear* in proximity for face to face contact, because seeing Xiao Min was sometimes very necessary in dealing with Xiao Min.

A narrow zone was marked in red between *Little Bear*'s position and their own, not that station traffic routinely extended that far, but it was there for the record: a ship was obliged to report when in operation and show its path, and *Little Bear* had duly reported itself as *outbound but delayed*. On *Venture*'s display, number three display on the row across the wall, *Finity*'s location and *Little Bear*'s were two red dots in a yellow box, indicating that they were traffic not threatening each other but moving as a unit and declaring that nobody should invade that space.

Stability was not *precisely* true: there was relative motion; but it was small enough for a pod to handle, and a pod was indeed already in transit, had *been* launched even before *Finity*'s official invitation had gone out. Min was wasting no time.

Little Bear had been in dock, had fueled and offloaded cargo. *Venture*'s records showed that. *Venture* had all the content of *Little Bear*'s black box, and that would have included news of *Galway* had *Galway* arrived back at Alpha, but there were other things that could have gone wrong, things that might not have made it into the record. By those same records, *Little Bear* had ferried the vital parts for *Firenze* to Alpha as needed, and had come back here, giving Pell as her next registered port, and beyond that, via Mariner Station, a return to Cyteen space and her own business. If Min was intending to leave them here, one certainly couldn't blame him. That had, after all, been the plan when they'd parted company at Alpha.

So JR waited. First-shift had gone off to shower, eat, and rest, in whatever order. Second-shift had come on, meaning if they were working with *Little Bear* or the pod in transit, Madison was watching over the technicals, but Min would expect to deal directly with the Senior Captain.

A glance at the uppermost screen said *Little Bear*'s pod was three quarters of its way across a gap that *Finity* and *Little Bear* were lazily closing at 14.2 meters a minute, but would miss each other entirely by 982.51 meters— not counting the broad expanse of *Finity*'s as-yet unfolded vanes. It was one of those 'take a visual' moments, when junior-juniors were going to be crowding the video center to see it magnified to the max on the big screen. He'd been one of those junior-juniors himself once. He could still remember his first time in the center, seeing Pell, seeing other ships, in the crazy patchwork of sunlight and dark.

He could have that feed here in his office, but while the ships passed each other at their closest, he hoped to be in productive conference with Min—not necessarily guaranteed, but he had, he hoped, managed a certain understanding of Min, of the Xiaos in general. He *trusted* Min to a degree he would not have predicted at first meeting. And the Xiaos were inclined to take to a task with dedication. Finding *Little Bear* camped out here, waiting for them, which could have dragged into ten, twenty days of sitting—

But hadn't. That was beyond expectation. *Finity* was here well ahead of schedule, without the promised cargo. So Min knew something was up on *Finity*'s side. And *Finity* exec could think the same about *Little Bear*, who appeared not at the moment anxious to hold discussions on Venture dockside.

The Xiaos were not the easiest to deal with, of merchanter Families. They either saw something as in their interest, or they did not, and there were times the language gap got in the way—but they were staunch allies if your purpose agreed with theirs. *Little Bear*'s ship-speak was absolutely impenetrable by outsiders, Min had a crew that obeyed him with a prideful snap-to that made people nervous, and, shortly put, Xiao Min left station-folk a little glad he wasn't staying but not overall sorry he'd been there.

The Xiaos operated more on the Cyteen side of space than on Pell's—it was likely the Reillys of *Dublin* who had talked them into joining *Finity* on the run to the Hinder Stars—and their presence had made a very important point, that Cyteen merchanters were fully committed partners in this alliance they were forming. By the time they left Alpha, JR had been very glad to have the Xiaos in the company.

Nervy? Extremely. Nervy, self-contained, and touchy in the matter of their own independence—apt to do any damn thing, Madison had said of them. Apt to do any damn thing, indeed. Min himself had *probably* been behind the incident that had blown up the situation at Alpha.

Chair reclined. A cat-nap, intermittent with a glance at the screens. He hazarded a nutrient bar and when that stayed down, a second. Another cup of coffee. JR put in a call to Madison. And Fletch.

And fastened the final few buttons on his dress uniform. His smallest. The one made for him when he officially took his position as Senior Captain . . . and it was still somewhat loose. One more run, then damned if the Family wasn't getting *three* weeks dockside at Pell.

The pod reached them, braked, accelerated slightly, and linked on with little fuss.

It was zero-G back there. There was the mate-up to be made, gear to shed. It all took time. The snatches of nap hadn't helped that much. Their visitors were going to be sharper. It was not the way to go into conference with the Xiaos. JR ordered the galley into action, and a choice of coffee or tea in the conference room.

Black coffee. Bitter and black. With sugar on the side. He didn't like it, but there were times it helped. Tea. Min's preference. The good stuff.

Files. Datasticks. He had made several copies. Best that more than one ship carry them.

Thump from the airlock, up from the core.

"*A visitor has come aboard,*" *Finity's* voice said, and JR headed for the conference room.

Book III   Section v

Xiao Min arrived, small man, steel-spring bearing, smartly-uniformed as if it were a station-offices outing; and with him, cousin and brother-captain, Xiao Ma, not a small man in any dimension. There were courtesies, needful under the circumstances, the hot tea definitely welcome, considering the outer-frame chill.

JR, with Madison and Fletch on either side, took coffee—loaded in sugar—and waited patiently. He, along with Madison and Fletch, was markedly younger than the two Xiao captains. *Finity's* new systems had caused a generational shakeup unique to her crew, and respect for age, part of every Family crew, was carried to an extreme in the Xiaos. While he was the unquestioned leader in this Alliance operation, JR nonetheless waited until a flicker of Min's eye indicated he was ready to proceed.

"Any word on *Galway's* return?" JR asked, by way of opening.

Min took a sip, unadulterated, at his own pace. "No."

"I'm glad to hear it."

"And Konstantin?" Min asked.

"Has signed."

Min nodded slightly. "I am glad to hear that."

Two major issues down.

"Glory?" JR asked.

"Has signed," Min said.

"Good. *Nomad* and *Mumtaz?*"

"Likely on their way here," Min said. "They will ply the Venture to Bryant's route for the next while, and *Santiago* and *Qarib* will run Bryant's to Alpha and Glory."

"How goes the repatriation of the *Rights* crew?"

"Nearly complete. Those unwilling few have been isolated in a secured area along with Hewitt. Their only contact with each other is through monitored vid. *Rights* is being maintained by Alpha engineering. They're going through records looking for possible mechanical reasons for the failed jump. Monahan engineers are involved. They've sent a file to their seniors aboard your ship. Test results, specs, everything they have, sent with Abrezio's blessing. *Give Connor something to keep him out of trouble*, they said."

That was interesting. If Abrezio could get that ship operational, the entire station would have additional bargaining power. It would be a hell of a step up for *Galway* crew, would it not? But the Monahans had a ship, and due to be a famous one, if it made it—would the Monahans want to surrender that? As for *Rights*, given those files, *Finity* systems techs might be able to figure it out in much shorter order, but he wasn't about to dispense that information by com to a station the EC could potentially lay hands on, and not about to leave *Finity* crew stranded there for whatever time it took, for a ship that might have other problems.

Besides, *Rights* could sit, so far as he was concerned, a monument to EC mismanagement, until *all* her problems were resolved.

"No sign of *Come Lately* or *Miriam B?*"

"Not there. But *Miriam B did* show at Alpha while we were en route. They left no word with Stationmaster Abrezio about signing, although the stationmaster did bring the matter up with her captain. Noncommittal, was his word. By her registered route, she went to Bryant's from there, and from Bryant's to Venture."

"She is *not* on the record here," JR said.

"No," Min said. "She is not, nor has she been, according to local records, within the span of our mission. Neither have they seen *Come Lately*. Nor has Glory. We have that from *Mumtaz* and *Nomad*."

"Do you have the records?" JR asked. "Such as they are?"

"We have them." Ma's deep voice reverberated off the walls. He patted his jacket, then took out two datasticks and laid them on the table, and a third, from a different pocket, set slightly apart. "The trade records as well as the docking records, for Bryant's, for Alpha, for Glory, as complete and as current as *Mumtaz* had them. The third is personal, for your guests, from the Monahan Family, including the files on *Rights*. We met with them, in courtesy. They appeared to be doing well and they are resolute and optimistic."

"Thank you," JR said, putting the Monahans' letters in his left pocket, handing the other sticks to Fletch, who immediately disappeared out the door, taking them to Rennie, who was waiting anxiously. "Profound thanks, from our Monahans. For our part, we have the records from Pell, up to date, and reaching back three decades." He took out his own set of datasticks and laid those on the table. Ma's hand engulfed them and slipped them into a pocket. It was a fair guess—but not a certainty—that they would go to Cyteen's databanks. Min's points of honor were at times obscure and finely delineated, but he had asked for the data current at Pell.

"You arrived early," Min said. "And without promised cargo."

"The cargo is on its way. At Pell, we received information on our missing ships that required us to leave immediately."

"So . . . you continue to bleed money for this mission."

"I believe it to be necessary. I have backing from Pell. I hope, when you have the facts, you'll agree with me."

"We are listening."

"Regarding those files I just gave you," JR said, "it's best we all have this set of records, to disperse it wherever it needs to go. In addition to the official records from Pell, it contains certain files in which our own analysts have extracted information, calculations, and speculations regarding the totality of what we've learned."

"Speculations from Pell? Regarding those two ships?"

"Investigations from *Finity* regarding *Come Lately*. Pell was not aware of a problem. The Hinder Stars have shared official station data with Pell, but trade records in the Hinder Stars do not record anything but cargo officers' statements for ships outside the black box reckoning—including those two very little ships; and of course pushers. This means neither Hinder Stars nor Pell ask enough questions when it comes to docking our two problems who aren't on the box."

Min blinked, as much surprise as he was likely to show. "Our targets have been trading at Pell?"

JR nodded. "Notably *Come Lately*, dealing in a lot of cash, in the form of Venture chits."

"A far run for that ship." A blank-faced pause then: "Has she been to Pell since we left?"

"No. And calculating the numbers indicates either very slow transits, or unlogged side trips. Slow transits would *not* get them to Pell, and we have reason to suspect their systems are more modern than they've let on."

"How would they do that?"

"It would take a station to do those modifications. Or something like it.

They haven't gone beyond Pell. Unless there's a back door to Cyteen space no one's told us about."

Min drew in a long breath as if he would say something, and picked up his tea cup instead. JR waited while Min looked at something not present.

Min was not saying everything.

And JR waited in the half-hope Min had another answer, one that Cyteen might solve. But he didn't want to spill everything *he* knew at once, didn't want to unwittingly taint Min's reasoning with their own conclusions, and didn't want to dissuade Min from a suggestion of his own. Trust the man wholly? On some things. There was relief even in knowing Min was not dismissing the problem or heading for Pell and beyond. Another very keen mind, another set of opinions, a view from clear across the Pell-Cyteen universe, might show up possibilities they'd overlooked.

And one hoped the meeting continued Min's support. The upcoming action was *not* something JR wanted to undertake alone, and there were no ships Pellside as agile as *Little Bear.*

"Side trips," Min said. "Thule?"

"Thule or Olympus, or both. We thought at first—running supply. I am less convinced of that. The supply is minor."

"Information, then."

"Information. Possibly movement of persons. We've been trying to piece together their movement and trade from those fluctuations. —The details and reports are all on the sticks."

"So," Min said. "Side trips to mothballed stations. What are we dealing with?"

"Pushers."

That—neither Min nor Ma might have expected.

"Olympus is a nasty hole for FTL," Min said. "Salvage there ended after several near disasters. Early converteds, back then. Maybe easier for newer ships."

"Maybe. The trouble is going Venture direct. Thule to Olympus vector is safe—we think."

"Olympus poses no hazard to a pusher," Ma observed slowly, "and the very fact that Olympus *is* inconvenient for FTL would be of value to an operation bent on secrecy."

Thule had never been much. But, as Mum had said, Olympus had been the biggest thing going, in the days of the Great Circle trade, when pushers alone had connected the star-stations. But Olympus proved a problem for FTLers. And a coronal mass ejection from EV Lacertae took out Galileo,

Olympus' next-over star station. Bryant's trade shifted immediately to the Venture-Pell route, an immense boost to Pell, impoverishing Thule, the first star in what had been the Galileo Reach, and creating chaos in the Great Circle. Thule and Olympus were mothballed over loud EC protests, and Bryant's-Venture-Pell, a longer jump for FTLers, became the route not all could take—effectively defining the Hinder Stars and the Beyond.

"Olympus does seem increasingly the better answer for a covert pusher-fed operation," JR said. "And that sort of operation could explain a lot. The EC has been investing heavily in *The Rights of Man*, while simultaneously starving out Alpha's people and the merchanters that serve them. They've created poverty and desperation, when all they really needed to do was build another pusher for the type of goods that have kept Alpha and the rest of the Hinder Stars viable for centuries. It's as if they *wanted* Alpha to fail."

Madison said, "If our two ghosts have been deliberately seeding the Beyond with Earth luxury to stop the rumors of deprivation in the Hinder Stars, it would serve to hasten that failure. The Hinder Stars have had to depend on Pell just for food, let alone everything else that makes life worth living."

JR nodded. "That obsession with *Rights* never has made sense . . . until this. It's not saying that EC actions have to make sense to us—they never have. But sacrificing a station increasingly out of their control, to create a massive personnel carrier filled with troops farmed from the station, a ship that could then be moved to a different, completely loyal, well-equipped station several jumps closer to Pell, combined with a ship with the capacity to scare hell out of every struggling station in the Hinder Stars . . . that makes a scary lot of sense. The expense of such a dual operation is mind-boggling, but they have huge population, effectively infinite resources. They're possessive, greedy . . . and Cyteen scares hell out of them, to be honest, friends. Particularly if they think the megaships are capable of making the Alpha-Sol jump, which Cruz, the EC flunky in question, definitely believed and *we* are not about to try. The whole of Sol system is constantly bombarded with the notion that Cyteen is building an army of clones to take control of the home planet."

"Ridiculous," Min said. "All the Emorys *really* want from Sol is coffee, artwork, and booze."

"Sorry to say, a Cyteen invasion has been the number one trope in Sol's action and suspense vids for two generations," Madison said. "We laugh at it, but—it's dangerous. And up close, with FTL from Sol an increasing possibility—it's damned dangerous. We're worried. We've happened across something—we can't leave unexplained."

Min pushed back from the table a little, frowning. Ma sat motionless, massive hands laced on the tabletop: according to Madison's notes on *Little Bear*, Ma was a master calligrapher and watercolor painter.

JR let the silence run. Had, he hoped, said enough to convince them.

Min was much more a Cyteener than a near-sider. Cyteen was fully capable of slamming down an embargo and concentrating on its own colonies, letting the EC do as it pleased with all of the old Circle trade. As Min pointed out, there was nothing on this end of space they actually needed.

But a paranoid, FTL-capable EC on Pell's doorstep was not something even Cyteen dared ignore. He hoped Min would see that.

"What is *Pell's* part in this new operation?" Min asked, in that tone that said "this operation" had already gone long and cost his ship heavily.

JR said, "Pell is funding us to go take a look at the situation and see where these questionable goods might be coming from. That's all."

"We *took a look* at Alpha. And now, if those points prove out, Sol will be on us in at most ten years, which we may have accelerated. We have yet to advise Cyteen."

"Word of what we know from Alpha *has* gone to Cyteen. I was able to make contact with the Quens. But nothing about these newest suspicions. We may have something going on a lot closer to Pell than Alpha. Something Cyteen will also want to know about."

"Something onto which you wish to shine a light. To open talks."

"*Finity* will go in at Thule and at Olympus and shine that light. If we have a pusher operation going on in either system, it will be fairly evident. What I want from you, my respected friend and ally, is for you to follow us in, and stay safely out of reach. I seek advice. A wise head on whatever problem we find out there. And if things do go wrong, I want you—fully funded, mind, by Pell—to get out of there without engaging the problem and warn Emilio Konstantin. *Then* go on and get word to Cyteen, whatever it is we've stirred up—with the hope that if we can expose it, we can get ahead of it and get Cyteen and Pell to talk to it. We're running with max fuel, no cargo. Drop whatever cargo you've got, with *Alliance* orders for it to be carried on to Pell via the ships that are bringing our cargo in from Pell. Pell is paying for it. Come after us. Observe. And then get out of there in good order. Tell Konstantin and the Carnaths to work it out."

"Are *you* going in if you find something?"

"If we find something, yes. I do have questions for them. And an invitation to talk about it and sign the agreement."

"Of *course* they will sign. Just like the EC pirates at Alpha jumped at the chance."

"Of course they *won't*. Which may trigger an embargo, regarding their operations, but who knows if that threat will carry any weight with the station, assuming they're getting all they need on a direct line from Earth. One suspects their main interest in Pell would lie in information. But again, it's talk. If they'll talk, we can reason. If they won't—we will find that out, and wisp out on them fairly quickly, with more than enough to convince everyone that the Sol threat is far beyond one wildcat pirate named Cruz and the vague possibility that Sol is about to break out. You, meanwhile, will be well away, so the EC will be quite sure they're no longer secret, which means either the local stationmaster has to make a unilateral decision . . . or wait years for orders from Sol."

"*If* they're there," Min said. "Your arguments are assuming a great deal."

"And I may be wrong, which will cost *Finity*, but not *Little Bear*, that much I promise you. A fast departure is all I'm asking of you."

"Except staying with this operation another year."

"For which you will be compensated. By Pell."

God, he hoped that was true.

Min heaved a heavy sigh. And another. "You know Grandfather will make the decision."

"I know. We understand. Respects to Grandfather Jun. We have our alliance. We have done everything we set out to do. There is no disgrace in stopping now. But we also have Alpha and our experience to advise us we need to know if Sol is already moving. I'm very sure you *want* to know and so will Cyteen."

Min lifted brows. "You are the devil, JR. We are *merchants*."

"*And you want to know*." JR allowed a hint of a smile to show. "Bottom line, Captain, you like to gamble. You also like to stir pots. This may be a discovery that will save us. Or it may be nothing. But . . . in the end, would it not be a shame to be outmaneuvered by the EC, after all we have done?"

"The *devil*, I say." Min took up his cup again, frowning.

"It would be an advantage to the Xiao Family," JR said, "beyond the personal satisfaction, of course. The mission we undertook, securing agreement to our Alliance from every ship on Pell-side, lacks two ships. But I'm very remiss not to have said immediately—I received word from *Estelle* that agreement among the Beyonder merchanters is a hundred percent. And Pell *has* signed."

"Signed. Physically."

"*Signed,* as I witnessed. *Estelle* says that Cyteen will sign if Pell will. So our Alliance is real, pending the first arrival of word at Cyteen, and the Cyteen stationmasters setting their signature on it, which will happen with the full knowledge of the situation at Alpha. A credit and an honor for our ships, individually, for the Xiao Family, the Druvs, the Patels, and us Neiharts. Merchanters in particular will hold us in good favor. But less so, *less so,* if we lose everything we have gained by failing to make one last run—"

"We are *Xiao Xióng Zuò,*" Min cut in harshly. *"Little* is our name, but *Little Bear* is not an endlessly patient bear, brother captain. We have used up our capital. We are *ready* to return to our own affairs. Now Pell, finding Sol much closer than when we began this, is running scared. —Is this your idea? Or Konstantin's? Are we being used?"

"I went to him with the information and request for aid. He'd already signed and was compelled to acknowledge this matter falls within the scope of mutual benefit. I asked for aid with getting the cargo to Venture. I hoped at very least for a very long term loan. He *offered* to forgive the loan, if this pans out."

"Which means, if it's nothing, all this cost falls on *Finity.*"

He nodded. Min's eyes narrowed, but he didn't pursue that. The fact *Finity* was willing to take that risk was probably the most powerful argument JR could make for how real they believed the threat to be.

On the other hand, *Finity* going bankrupt was not something Pell wanted either, and Emilio would not let that happen. In the end, it was to everyone's advantage to find the truth.

"Is that all he's offering?" Min asked. "Sol's looming arrival affects him far more than us."

"I would argue that what affects one part affects the whole, which is the essence of the Alliance agreement, but in point of fact, I have nothing in writing, and there was no time to bargain specifics. We needed to get ahead of the information wave, the rumor of the questions we'd been asking at Pell. We didn't want to scare off our ghosts. But Emilio is sensitive to the problem. Grateful that we're taking this on. That will translate to substantive gratitude. Favor-points from Pell is not a minor advantage for the future."

Down went the cup toward the table, but very gently placed at the last moment. Min looked up from under his brows. "Younger brother, you credit this slow wit with so much imagination. May we beg specifics before this becomes more entangled?"

"Emilio Konstantin has gone out on a long tether in signing our documents, but as of our departure, he had yet to convince his council even of that, let alone the associated cost of funding this mission. However, that signature is binding. By contract, Pell will be henceforth a safe port for an Alliance ship. By the agreement, Pell will give us fuel and repairs on promise of repayment from the Alliance. A safe port should one ever be needed—in uncertain times. A Cyteen-based Family can call on the Konstantins of Pell and expect to be heard on a matter of policy and trade, and since our agreement is reciprocal, he may call on us. As part of an Alliance decision, he is obligated to help with the costs."

"This much has been a part of the agreement since we signed it. Specifically, in this case. We invest time, money, and risk. What does Pell offer?"

"Compensation," JR said. "And a united opposition to EC demands on us, in a season in which the EC will be far weaker to make demands than it will be if we let it run unchecked."

"Sound arguments. However, *you* made this arrangement with Pell. Unilaterally decided to act on this information you got at Pell. Three ships are needed to make decisions for the Alliance. Where are your three ships, younger brother?"

"At this point, *Finity* and *Galway* and Pell are in agreement."

"The contract is for three ships. Three *Families*."

"And every station has signed as a partner. Interests are intertwined more than we anticipated when we wrote that document. At the time, we believed only trade was at issue. If Sol plans to turn their ships into personnel carriers, into some sort of policing force, the stakes have changed. Our power lies in keeping the issues economic. Which means, in part, laying to rest fears over phantom invasions. Once Sol enters into the FTL time frame, once their representatives experience what we've created out here real time, we stand a chance of convincing them of seeing the value in joining us. That's always been the plan. But we might just be meeting the problem a bit sooner than anticipated. We will undertake this run on our own if we have to, or maybe ask one of the Pell merchanters coming in with our cargo to back us, but I had rather have *you* for the third ship. I had rather have the power of *Little Bear*. I had rather have your experience and steadiness. I had rather have the participation of a Cyteen-based merchanter, should we encounter an active EC operation, to have it clear to them that this is not the doing of one station or one ship. Sol needs to see *from the beginning* that we are organized, and that we will trade, but we will not be ordered."

Another of those silences then: "And if Pell is part of the decision to make this venture, Pell is automatically involved in *paying* for it, and since we are the ones risking ships and lives, they can foot the bill for the operational costs."

"Something like."

A low chuckle. "Clever, younger brother. But I suggest you get that officially added to the contract."

JR dipped his head in acknowledgment of the mixed compliment. He only hoped he was clever enough to convince Emilio of that obligation.

"And should the EC arrive with shiploads of luxury goods? Can you guarantee Pell will not succumb?"

"Not if we all stand by the contract. Mutual cooperation is what makes it all work. If Pell will not, then Viking and Mariner will not. Alpha, as the waypoint, may be forced to compromise, but if she gets support from us, she compromises from a position of strength, from the ability to tell the EC to go to hell."

"And if the EC arrives with ships full of Enforcers?"

"Considering what happened at Alpha, what they were trying to pull with *The Rights of Man*, I would hope all the stations have begun fortifying their masts and docking stations against such a move. If we have any such EC operation underway, particularly something aimed at Pell, that would not be a good development for the Beyond—including Cyteen. Cyteen will be very grateful to be advised by the Xiao Family as to what happened at Alpha, what *is* the source of Earth goods at Pell, and what Pell's attitude is now regarding the EC."

Min spoke to Ma for a moment in *Little Bear's* ship-speak, in which JR only caught the words *captain, ships,* and *Olympus*. Ma nodded soberly.

"We will present the question to Grandfather," Min said, and added: "We will recommend your argument."

"It's all I can ask. The Xiao Family is the best backup I could ask for."

"Will you dock here?"

"No. We will be straight on for Thule, then to Olympus. We *can* do it and get back here easily: the most massive thing we're carrying is fuel. We have current charts we will most gladly share."

Min gave a nod of agreement. "We are most grateful."

"Can I offer you hospitality? A drink stronger than tea, if you will, before you brave the cold?"

"A bottle for Grandfather," Min said, "and a drink for the two of us. Our ship is lessening the gap as we speak, but it is, indeed, cold and dark out there. Grandfather may order our most precious and vulnerable ashore at Venture if he approves this. In that case, five days delay. Be advised. We stand empty of all but fuel, expecting some redefinition of plans; and I shall remind Grandfather no ship can keep up with *Finity's End*, so we should not be laggard. We assume the bill for our run will be paid."

"Konstantin will definitely honor that," JR said. "As for us, we will be heading out, with about time to have two decent meals. We will maintain current heading until you reach *Little Bear* safely, then reorient and do a hard burn. We would be very grateful for a message, either yes or no. We have been running hard, and need real sleep and real food before another jump. Two days. We need tell Venture nothing else of our business, except that Pell has signed, and we will send that news to the stationmaster. In either case, the Neiharts, the Monahans, and I'm sure the Konstantins of Pell send deepest respect to the Xiao Family, and especially to Grandfather, of course."

Min bowed. Ma did.

"And you," Min spoke past him to Madison. "Make certain your Senior Captain follows his own orders. *Skeletons* do not negotiate well."

Madison threw him a glance. "I'll do that."

Book III   Section vi

They shared a round of drinks before Fletch returned to escort Min and Ma back to their pod. Not one, but—Madison's order—*six* bottles of Scotch arrived in a pressure-sealed container, and there was a second round of bows.

"What are the odds?" Madison asked when they'd gone.

"On Grandfather Jun agreeing?" JR said. "Grandfather will weigh the risks and benefits . . . but I think Min believes they'll be there."

"Lonely if they aren't," Madison said. "Damned lonely if they aren't."

"We can only *hope* it's lonely out there," JR said, and: "It would be really nice, if there is anything, that it's all new, but I don't hold out much hope on that score. Pell's trees aren't from just yesterday, and *Come Lately*'s ghost upgrade came ten years before that. We see Sol goods trickling into Pell on other ships for the last twenty years that we *assume* came from *Come Lately*, but those goods could have been coming for two hundred years, for all we know, just masked by the legitimate Alpha cargo. But wherever they've been getting their suspect cargo, it's been at least a couple of decades. If they're telling the truth about mystery seeds found at Bryant's . . . I guess seeds can live a lengthy while. But there's sniffers and bioscans and hell to pay if you transport biologicals, with the EC doing shipboard inspections at Alpha *and* Bryant's. So how'd they get the trees aboard? And, if the EC *is* the source, and granted them some kind of special dispensation at Alpha . . . they *still* had to get past Pell customs. The amount of trouble you could get into carrying actual recent Earth biologicals could *break* a ship. I mean, if we're right about where they got them, they were only *lucky* Pell wanted those trees badly enough to accept whatever story they gave."

"One wonders who they dealt with. I mean, the trees are a completely separate problem, but I'd love to know what ships actually traded with them at Venture to create the constant trickle into Pell."

"At this point, I don't really care," JR said, stifling a groan as he stretched his shoulders up and around. "I doubt any Pell ship even questioned provenance, just took it for legitimate F-class and counted themselves lucky. But you know what's shadier than the trade? The fact that *Come Lately* didn't spend that mega-profit on its own supposedly decrepit systems, there at Pell. Why not take advantage of the best engees this side of Cyteen? Why trust them to EC engees?"

"Because they didn't want the modern black box."

"Obviously. And damned if they didn't get away with it for at least two decades."

"Possible they did their own upgrades," Madison said. "No knowing how capable an EC set-up there might be—wherever it is."

"If the Stream's still operational from Olympus *or* Thule," JR said, out of that thought. "It's possible the station's just being used as a message and cargo drop. It's possible, granted the reactor's still keeping the systems up. Maybe our ghosts are just using the station's Stream capability to get messages out. Slow as it is. Maybe those Sol goods are just salvage."

"Copyright."

"Oh. Of course." He drew a deep breath. "God, I'm tired."

"Can't imagine why," Madison said. "I'm pretty sure if it's what we think it's not just a drop point. A pusher-load's a fearsome lot of stuff. One damned load could bring far more *stuff* than all the F-class we tracked in Pell in the last twenty years. I think how one pusher-load, prior to the *Rights* build hijacking them, and as infrequent as they are at Alpha, supplied every Hinder Star station, not to mention clear to Pell and beyond, with a burst of luxury goods we don't see for another number of years. And that was in addition to the basic upkeep items for the entire Hinder Stars operation. Leads you to wonder—"

"Even if most of its load is going into reviving Olympus or Thule . . . cases of Scotch and coffee would pay a lot of a small ship's bills. And as bribes—very effective."

There was a hollow, distant sound, as the ring let their guests and escort out into the frame, on their freefall way toward *Little Bear*'s pod.

"God." Madison stretched. "You . . . go. Eat. Sleep. Min's right, can't have you fading in the stretch, and you've been running yourself hard. Kate's going to call Nav and Helm together to plot our course with as many variables as she can come up with. She wants numbers to cover every contingency. She also wants us both there for conference. Awake."

"I'm going to ask you take this next leg," JR said. "And I want First-shift to be next-up when we get to Thule. I want a look at it. I want Research to have a look, and get all the data they can. But I'm not expecting to linger there."

Book III   Section vii

Ross waited. They all waited, a knot of Monahans gathered near the drink dispensary in the post-jump lounge. Ian and the twins were there, First-shift. Patrick had come in, with Aidan, Netha, Connor, and Nolan, no questions asked beyond an initial shrug from one and the other of them.

They sat. They waited. They'd long since had enough of the juice and started on the coffee. Food was available in the cafeteria, but no one made a move to go after it. The ship was moving, if slightly, and under ship's rules there was no alcohol to fortify their nerves, much as they could have wished it, stupid as it would be under the circumstances.

No word. Nothing. They talked about the recent jump, talked about their arrival, speculated on their next course. Whether *Little Bear* had brought anything that would divert *Finity* from Thule. Venture was where they all might have left *Finity*. And wouldn't. They'd decided that, all together, back at Pell. Whatever was happening that involved the EC expanding out of Alpha, the Monahans would be part of it.

Now there was word on the screen that the Xiaos were leaving, conference done. A few minutes more, and non-ops, juniors, and off-shift Neiharts were happening by the cleanup room to ask if there was news.

"No," was the general answer, and being Neiharts, and their accessible knot of anxiety being all Monahans, the questioners, even the juniors, left without discussion. Someone came back with a plateful of sandwiches. The Monahans all just stared at it. Waiting.

Suddenly, Ian stood up, staring at the door, and they all glanced around and, as one, stood up as Captain Mum came in, official and businesslike, and ordinarily in her sleep cycle at this hour. Very quietly, Jen appeared behind her and stood silently by the entry.

"*Little Bear*'s report from Alpha," Mum said. "No sign of *Galway* yet."

"Thank God," Patrick said, as all of them breathed.

"So *something*'s gone on," Maire said.

"Likely," Ian said, "but."

But was the other possibility, that the point of mass hadn't been enough to pull *Galway* in, or that the gravitational point they thought existed was a multibody rockpile, almost as bad.

"Likewise," Mum said, "Stationmaster Abrezio has retained control of Alpha Station, the station as a whole has concentrated on reactivating its industry as supply begins to improve. Employment is improving. Locals in training as Enforcers are being shifted to station defense or moved to repair and refurbishment of mothballed businesses and industry."

"Isn't the worst news," Aidan said. "Isn't the worst at all."

That summed it up.

"Senior captain sends word," Mum said, "regarding *Little Bear*. They met with the Monahans and found them well and optimistic. Their words. There is a datastick with letters from them."

That brought silent excitement, desperate excitement. But Mum was not through, and the next news was its own kind of dire. "From here, you know where we're headed, and it could be a nothing—or it could be major. And if it's a nothing, we'll get you back to Alpha ourselves—there's business we could do. But if it's *something*—we'll choose a course based on what we find, and it may take us straight back to Pell. We fully expect, at this point, that *Little Bear* is going to follow us to Olympus as backup; we have appreciated the hell out of the help you've given us, but we will gratefully bid you farewell here if that's your choice. I hear you want to stay with us and find out what you largely turned up for us. But this is the decision point. No long wait here for a way to Alpha. So if all or any of you have second thoughts about getting involved in chasing this willy-wisp into that much uncertainty, we can still take the time to set you ashore here. *Galway*'s done far and away enough in this business. We'd thank you and see you off."

"No, ma'am," Ross said, quick as breathing. He didn't want to read any letters before declaring.

Others all said the same, a respectful *no*. They'd settled that on the runout from Pell. They'd hoped there would be letters when they met *Little Bear*.

And evidently there were, and they'd share those and probably cry tears. But if Andrew Bloody Cruz or his spiritual clone had another part of an operation going on . . . bloody hell, they had to know, that was it.

"No, ma'am," the lot of them repeated, quietly. Solemnly.

Mum nodded. "So, well. The Neiharts will be glad of your company. Since we're not diverting to pod range, we're going to be entering another takehold in about forty-five minutes. It'll be a long one. Best go where you want to be for a while. We'll be doing a series of burns making time toward jump, and having no traffic ahead of us, we won't linger once we get there. We'll be having two good meals in the interval, given time for the galley to put it together. That will come one hour after start of Third-shift, whenever that falls. Second-shift will do the long burn. First will take over at Thule. Stock up on extra jump packets. We don't know what we're getting into at Thule, but we'll probably just skate it. Questions?"

There was a general shaking of heads.

"Thank you, Captain," Ian said, and with a nod, Mum left.

Jen didn't. Jen stood by the door a moment, then came in quietly, as businesslike in her way as Mum. She held a datastick out to Ian.

"From your Family," she said. "Security comp scanned it and copied it to all your handhelds, and you can send it where you like, but I thought you might want to keep the stick itself."

"Thank you, Jen," Ian said, for them all.

She waited a moment, wanting, Ross was sure, a signal from him. He shook his head; she dipped her chin and left, as quietly as she'd come.

He ought to go find her and talk. But there was, in fact, the matter of Family, and a decision. She'd understand that, when he got a chance to explain.

"Last chance, cousins," Ian said loudly, and reached for a sandwich. "You can still change your minds. You heard it. Rides to Alpha from here, no question."

"And never know if those bastards are up to something up at Olympus?" Maire said, and snagged her own sandwich. "Hell if!"

Ross looked at that stick Ian had laid on the table, next to the plate of sandwiches. Thought of those waiting at Alpha who had sent it. Thought of all they'd experienced, while the rest of their Family waited, living like stationers—with maybe *only* that prospect ahead of them.

But no, dammit. Senior Captain had promised. *Galway* would be back, one way or another. Always presupposing *Finity* made it back from this highly questionable mission to authorize that replacement ship.

He really didn't much want that sandwich. He didn't even want a letter from Peg and his cousins.

Except . . . he did. So much it hurt.

"Well," Siobhan said, around her own bite. "We've got time. We get this settled, whatever else is going on, and *Finity* will see us right. No question they will. Whatever mess things are at Alpha, we stay with *Finity* and *Finity* will sort it out. Personally, I'm not leaving this ship until she takes us all the way back to *Galway*."

"I'll tell you what else," Aidan said. "I'm pissed. I'm *seriously* pissed at *Come Lately* and *Miriam B.* No matter what, they're playing some kind of game that's making them freakin' rich. If they've been living high off Pell trade that should, by rights, be supporting all of us and all of the First Stars, while we've all been struggling to stay afloat with shit-all to trade . . . hell . . . I want an explanation or I want a piece of them."

"I want to know," Ross said. He took a plain sandwich, trying to convince his stomach it was a good idea. "I want to know exactly what they're up to. For Niall and Fallan and all those making the run to Sol. For our cousins. Hell, for the Alpha folk, Rosie and the rest. We own a part of this. Damn right we've *contributed*. I want—"

"*All Helm, all Nav,*" the general address said, "*meet in Bridge 2 eight hours after the takehold. Eat. Sleep and be ready for a long session. We will be reviewing data and running sims on multiple courses to and through the Galileo Reach.*"

All Helm, all Nav, Ross thought, exchanging a glance with Ian. They'd not done that before.

And the Galileo Reach. Words he thought he'd never hear in orders. Thule. Olympus. And a little research station that had met a spectacular end. Captain Mum was wearing a piece of that station, a little lump of green glass, a gift from Fallan, who'd gotten it from someone who'd been there in the aftermath of the disaster, looking for survivors, back in convert days, before modern FTLers. Star-cooked, that piece of glass. Lost lives. Lost dreams. Lost, the way a whole arm of what had been the First Stars had been lost.

So now, urgently, they were being called to do a work-up on the course, drawing recent data from Venture in passing, but the next destination would be a new star, at least new in the sense *Finity* had no recent data. It was nothing near what Fallan had done, doing the calc on a wisp of a theoretical jump-point, but it was still a serious business, going off the edge of recent charts, depending on light-bound astronomy. Two stars' relative motion, and only a statistical hope of a clear entry, in a system where there might be no robot sweepers or designated safe zones. And he and Ian *were* included, or they would have said *seated* Helm and *seated* Nav. It was a dead serious thing, and a courtesy to them. He cast a glance at Ian's sober face, and figured Ian was thinking about it, too.

Interesting session. It was bound to be. He looked forward to it and dreaded it.

But Ian dismissed the meeting, there being a takehold imminent, and they exited the room and straggled down-ring toward the lift.

Jen was waiting for him at section-end. She tipped her head in question, and he linked arms with her before moving toward the lift, welcoming her presence and support. It was easy to get the shivers in the drafts of the main corridor, post-jump and still wobbly, and with the prospect of doing it all again. Second-shift was going to have that honor, after they all, under Kate's guidance, figured out the old route to Thule, which, in the way of stars, was not quite where Thule used to be, by a number which in human terms stacked up rather huge.

Fallan, he was going to add to the record—he had it halfway composed in his head—*Fallan, they're giving me one hell of an education on this run. Not what I expected. Nothing new to you, for damn sure nothing to what you're doing* . . .

Headed down the old Galileo Reach on this one. Going to see sights you've seen, be where you've been. It's an adventure, isn't it?

"Ross?" Jen said. "You all right?"

The lift between levels had come, and Jen was holding it. That was how fogged he was. For a moment he saw Fallan, as he had been at *Galway's* e-hatch, telling him to go. Hurry.

He saw the black, and the red light of Barnard's, that was Alpha on the human list of stars. The beginning-place. The start of everything. Where they'd lost touch with *Galway* and split up the Family.

Black.

"Ross," Jen said again.

He was just that shaky. He'd been that afraid, sitting in that side room, waiting for a report from the captains' conference, that *Galway* might have lost the battle and that *Little Bear* brought definitive news of it. He'd sat there with Ian and Siobhan and the others, holding it together.

"Ross!" A third time and sharply, calling him back.

"Yeah," he said. "Sorry. I'm fine. Lot on what passes for my mind right now."

Jen hugged his arm tightly. "Can't say I know," she said, "but we're going. For all of them. We're going to find out what's what."

Find out what's what.

The thoughts came flooding through. *We can't leave* Finity *here. If Galway's met trouble with the EC, where else do we find allies for the lot of us, but where we are?*

Got to stay.

Got to know.

"Ross?" Jen knew he was tripping.

He pulled himself back, made himself steady. "Yeah," he said. "Find out what's what. For sure."

Book III   Section viii

End-of-shift and Jen didn't stay for the takehold. She needed to talk to Fletcher, which meant she had to get topside again before the warning sounded.

Ross didn't question, just quick-hugged her, closed his door, and collapsed onto his bunk with his handheld. He anchored the webbing in case he fell asleep, and viewed the messages . . . a group message from the lot of them, which, God knew where they'd found that picture of all of them; and one picture on the strip, and one in Rosie's, all happy, all enjoying themselves, all swearing they were fine and not wanting for anything. Alpha was taking care of them . . . well it should. It was for Alpha that *Galway* was in trouble. But at least it *was* happening, and bills were paid, and the Family was staying in their usual hotel for layovers. Then there were the messages each of them had—messages from everyone, even the kids, by the look of it, and there would be time to go through those in order. He searched *his* messages— looking for one from Aunt Peg.

And he found it. She looked, well, like Peg, a little smartened up for the vid, but Peg. *"Thinkin' of you all often, Ross. Hoping you're seeing the sights and enjoying the trip. We're all in good shape, best of care, all that. They've been taking care of us, first rate.*

"So, Ross me lad, you just relax and enjoy your ride. Stationmaster and his wife have been grand to us—in person, no less. And so we're now well past the worst case return date. That's the bright spot. We're sincerely hopin' not to hear anything for at least another couple of years and we're refusin' to worry until it's been six.

"It's beyond strange, sittin' still for so long, but we're all findin' new ways to spend time. Jill's taken up fencin', can you believe it? I'm in a gamin' team and Padriac's takin' courses. Meanwhile we've been studyin' Pell and Mariner, for when our precious Galway *gets all shiny an' so will we. Just the options we're seeing are blowin' our minds. Did you know there's a hotel with a lifesize elephant?*

"Anyway, me dear, darlin' boy, I know you. You're all worried you can't be nine places at once and takin' care of everyone, but you can't. You just concentrate on what you're doing, have fun with that pretty little lassie, Jen—get her pregnant, if she's a mind to! I'd like to boast a grandniece or nephew on the great Finity's End *. . . and come back to us even smarter than you were.*

"Love you, my dear boy,

"Aunt Peg."

God, he missed her, Ross thought, and brushed the damp from his eyes. He missed them all, but Peg, next to Fallan, was the one he most wanted to share this adventure with.

He could be there. He could go there, from here. It wasn't too late.

But he knew there wasn't a one of the nine aboard that was going to take that option.

Book III   Section ix

"Got a minute?" Jen found Fletcher alone in the security office, last chance to talk with him before jump.

He gestured to the chair beside him, and she settled gingerly into it.

"Problem?" he asked.

"Worried about Ross," she said. "I've been doing my best, but I don't think it's working."

"Heroic efforts, indeed," he said, straight-faced. "I'm surprised the lad can still walk. We're all just a bit jealous."

But after a lifetime under his tutelage—and discipline—she knew what lay behind that face, and it wasn't humor. He *was* listening.

"He says he's going with us. They all do. I think . . . I think he's going with *them.* They have their reasons. I'm not sure of his. Seriously. I'm not saying

it well. I'm not sure he's not going with *me*. And that worries me. I think . . .
I'm not sure he should go. Not sure he should sit the boards with so much
else on his mind. —I'm *worried* where he goes in jump. And why. It sounds
crazy when I say it. But—"

His brow tightened. "He's still having nightmares from that EVA? Pretty
traumatic. That was a nasty concussion he operated past."

"I don't think that's all of it. Mostly from what he doesn't say . . . I think
the nightmare behind the nightmare is being forced off his ship—Fallan
and his senior captain and the rest of his shift going without him. He thinks
he should be with them. That he ran, somehow, even though he knows
someone had to carry the message. And even though he doesn't say much,
this *feeling the stars* thing has had him pretty spooked—like he's marked, in
some way."

"Kate mentioned that. He's not unique, but it's a gift. Makes him a top
navigator. Thought he understood that."

"I think it's putting him in a corner. Or maybe just one stress too many.
As for staying with *Finity* . . . I think that's maybe linked to his being forced
to leave *Galway*. He won't go twice out that airlock, so to speak. Won't leave
the ship or the mission. I'm not sure he had a choice about staying with us,
and conversely, I'm not sure they did, *because* of him. This *feeling the stars*
thing has marked him for them, too. How they regard him—maybe that
hasn't changed, but he has this added status, now, and it's a damn circle. —Is
that crazy of me? Maybe. I'm not sure I'm explaining it right. But I'm worried."

"He hasn't been to medical about it."

Which meant Fletcher was tracking such things. She shook her head.

He looked at her a moment, thoughtfully sipping an off-duty beer. "Well,
I'm not altogether surprised. Nav handles the interface between real- and
hyperspace. Most stressful job on the ship, if you want my opinion. Considering the rest he's been through . . ."

"So I'm not crazy."

"Not about this. —Paradoxically, we can't throw him into a pod and shove
him off. Well, we could, but it might well do more harm than good. And
would it be fair to put the lot of them ashore, given what we're still chasing?
The answers they wouldn't have for years if at all? If he doesn't want medical
to help him sort it out, we can't force him. Do you think he's unfit? There's
that question."

"No." That came before she thought. Then: "Kate oversees him, doesn't
she? She'd know best, wouldn't she? God, Fletcher, I don't want to screw
things up for him. I just—"

"—worry about the lad?"

"Where we're going now, it's not in his direction. Nothing they signed on for."

"Tell me this," Fletcher asked. "Do *you* want to go with him? You could. Your privilege, sorry as we'd all be to have you go. Are you thinking you could lure him off, and the rest of them follow?"

"No." Shaky no, but it was true, even after she thought about it.

"Do you *want* to go?"

There it was, the question that had haunted her subconscious since he'd been dropped, bloodied and more than half-dead, in her lap. Deep breath. Major try at a rational answer, because *going* wasn't just flit-here, flit-there. Leaving was—forever, as ships moved. And dealing with that put a knot in her throat. "No. I don't—I couldn't. Now, especially. Scary as this is. *Finity* needs me. I need her. I need the Family."

Fletcher's hand pressed her shoulder, and her whole self steadied. "So does he, Jen, and *he* hasn't got a ship to anchor him at the moment . . . just Family in trouble and scattered across light years. Don't you think that's rather dominating his thinking? This is the ship his family *can* reach, a ship from which they had a chance to do something proactive before there's another round of hell at his home port. The Galways were the first to spot the problem, have been participant with us in working through the evidence. They also have other issues, back at Alpha, which involve sitting and waiting. They have a legitimate choice now, and I frankly think his hindbrain is in better order than you think it is. You're worried about influencing his decision. I don't think you can do that. You wouldn't take a pod with him—and he won't take one with you. You're not why he's staying. And you know that. Figured it correctly. What you can't be is responsible for his choices. Understand? He has a lot of other reasons. Not the same as yours. But definite reasons. Does that make sense to you?"

Took a moment. Damn it, the room was watery. She tried not to blink, and one eye spilled anyway. A traitor track coursed down her cheek and she refused to wipe it. "Does," she said.

"Shipboard relationships," Fletcher said. "Damned hard, Jen. Give him room. Give yourself room. Your instinct's right. He's going with us for his reasons. You have your own. What we all need, more than anything else, is answers. With luck, we're going to get them."

"Got it," she said. The knot in her throat wouldn't untangle. It's not your fault, was what Fletcher was saying. And the answer to that question that haunted her own sleep—she wouldn't leave. She was fairly sure of that, now. She could leave—she wouldn't. Leave his kin? He wouldn't. Clear as an oncoming rock. She was already embarrassed by the track on her face. She refused to wipe it, rising to leave. "Knew it. Knew I knew it. Thanks for the listen."

Book III   Section x

Jump prep. JR shed clothes, tossed them in the laundry bag, and sealed it. God, he felt as if he'd just come out of the *last* jump . . . which was fairly well the truth. He *had* eaten . . . in fact it seemed every time he turned around someone had shoved something into his hands and stared at him until it disappeared. But sleep . . . well, he'd gone horizontal once. Did that count?

JR swallowed the dregs of his coffee, the last of it for a realspace couple of months, rinsed it in the sink and shut the cleaned cup in the fragiles-locker. It was an heirloom, a treasure that said *Ann's Cup, Dammit*. Great-gran's. From old *Gaia*. He didn't risk it on the bridge.

Stupid, to take a stimulant before trank. But he had since his teens. Wasn't going to reform at this late date.

He sat down, pulled the connection tubes from the bunkside dispenser into comfortable reach, pulled off the seal, and inserted into the soft-gel patch at his elbow, a negligible sting. Seated crew and trainees all had the special rigs in quarters, on the same system as the bridge, because the shift had to come up on cue, and accelerate recovery if there was a problem.

He lay down. There were—Services had already set them out—abundant nutrient packs, in the slotted shelf right under the dispenser unit alongside his bunk. Where they always were. Even a jump-fogged brain could find them.

If anything went wrong. If Madison needed him—a short move down the executive corridor. If anything surprised them . . .

God, he thought, as his eyes drifted shut, he hoped there were no surprises. Hoped if they found anything it was a half-assed operation, a couple of marginal merchants and an EC operation trying to set up . . . doing the work, creating a living space. That might take some time. Salvage had had decades to work before the EC tied everything up in court. Word was the junkers had stripped Thule of most everything worth having, right down to the radioactives and the exotics—those first, actually, with a couple of armed standoffs as the junkers fought it out with illicit lethals and machetes—then moved on to Olympus. Long in the past, those days. A few Venture-registry merchanters had gotten their start in that quasi-legal trade.

But they wouldn't know until they saw and they had to see. Had to be sure. He hoped it all went smoothly, and they would be back here in short and good order with a much better idea what sort of problem might be out there.

Min would catch them up either at Thule or at Olympus, wherever they stopped . . . a final confirmation had come through only a few hours ago, with a caveat from Grandfather Jun: the Xiao Family was going to confront the ghost ships with fraud. The Scotch was not as old as the label claimed. It was, so Grandfather insisted, much too dark. They'd tested the bottle and label and found traces of another label. This, Grandfather Jun insisted, was not acceptable merchanter behavior.

Grandfather Jun was, so Min declared, extremely good at finding personal reasons for cooperation. Nor had the color stopped him from drinking it.

Whatever it took. It was worth a smile. JR was just relieved that whatever they found, it would not be on *Finity* alone to get the news back to the Alliance . . . *if* they needed to make a fast run to Alpha to advise *them* there was a problem.

And problems upon problems . . . Jen had talked to Fletch, who'd come to him with her worry that Ross Monahan was on a survivor's guilt trip, and wouldn't talk to medical about it. Insisted he was all right, but she was afraid it would affect his performance on the bridge, maybe affect him permanently. Jen was now all upset and possibly, Fletch reported, the relationship was entering its final phase even if Ross stayed. Ross's choice, certainly. He'd be welcome on *Finity*—so would any of the Galways. But it certainly was a hell of a time for that relationship to go critical, for Ross's sake.

Ross's board wasn't live. That made his input no threat to *Finity*. Equally important, however, was that *Finity* avoid hurting him. He had grit. He was a hero by any standard, but he didn't try to trade on it.

So far, his performance had impressed them all. Inconsistent, but that was to be expected: *Finity* was an entirely different kind of ship than his *Galway*. What Fletch reported had to be factored in; but Kate, bless her, with a master Navigator's sense, had promised to handle whatever glitched in him . . . and thus far, that had been near zero.

A subtle vibration reached into his gut: the vanes powering up, prepping for jump—the shortest jump in the whole of space. In the black behind his eyelids, he saw the system, saw the star, the station, the line the ship was taking. Their heading wasn't where ordinary traffic went, not where JR or *Finity* had ever gone—a vector toward a patch of dark and a moody red dwarf that no ships came from and no ships went to, these days.

Or—no ships *should* come from or go to, these days . . .

And beyond that, Olympus, which historically had it in for FTLs. Groombridge 34 was a highly volatile binary, but it was in a quiet phase—at least as observed from Venture. Which meant five years ago. Up close, you got newer news. They wouldn't truly know what they were up against until they dropped into the system.

They'd kept contact with Venture Station minimal. They'd picked up the observational reports on all the local stars, everything within ten lights, then told Venture Station just *All well aboard. Thanks, Venture.*

Their heading going out would raise curious questions among Venture technicians who observed their course, but it would take a wasteful lot of time and effort to pretend to go other than where they were going.

As for hypothetical curious techs . . . if they *hadn't* asked yet why two ships, neither of them ordinary at Venture and one of them extraordinary anywhere past Pell—were back again and gone again, without stopping at Venture for so much as a drink, their curiosity was bone dead.

And if *Come Lately* and *Miriam B* and every stationer this side of Pell didn't know *Finity* was on the hunt for them, they were deaf to rumor, since first *Finity* and now every other ship had asked after them up and down the line.

The Venture stationmaster, her staff, most of the residents, and certainly every ship at dock, knew what *Finity* and *Little Bear* were actively promoting, having signed the Alliance document. They also knew that *Finity* had returned early and without the promised cargo for stations further down the line.

And if *Finity* had rendezvoused with *Little Bear,* and not even come into dock, Venture could well guess it was because *Little Bear* had told them something significant. *Little Bear* had just come in from Alpha. If *Nomad* and *Mumtaz,* as part of *Finity's* mission, had gone to Glory (*Little Bear's* black box would have fed Venture that information) then maybe those two were back at Alpha or Bryant's . . . but why in hell was *Finity* now chasing off to Thule?

Thule? *Nobody* went to Thule.

Or nobody bent on trade would go to Thule.

That was the talk likeliest to circulate among the three ships in dock at Venture the moment *Finity's* departure heading hit the docks. Everybody this side of Pell *knew* by now what had become of Alpha's megaship, and where *Galway* had gone.

Was there more trouble at Alpha?

Had *Galway* returned?

Was *Pell* taking action?

But why Thule?

There were bound to be whispers: until there was a result from *Galway's* mission, every station and every ship was going to have ears up for every rumor that came in. But setting the rumor mill in operation was better than docking, losing days, and having questions flung at them from station offices and random people in bars.

They were prepped for jump, now. They were in count, and building V steadily for the button-push that would bring the jump engines live and form the bubble. Youngers were all snug abed, babies in the Loft were secure. First-, Third-, and Fourth-shifts were snug in their bunks.

Madison was in charge.

JR tried to turn it all loose. He *wanted* to turn it all over to Madison, and generally he was good at doing exactly that.

But it wasn't the typical run in any sense. He asked himself to this minute whether he *should* have left all the youngers and a group of minders at Pell, where they would assuredly be safe, whatever happened. But they'd never forgive him and it would have outlined their departure in glowing neon, as far as rumors went. Difficult questions had been starting to circulate on Pell when they were there, awareness that something significant had happened at Alpha, and by now, the hold on the data feed would be over and the news would have broken even on citizen level, first that there was an Alpha ship headed for Sol, and second, that *Finity's End* had come from Alpha and was headed that direction again.

By now it was likely clear to everybody at Venture that there was an agreement being circulated and mostly signed—an agreement declaring a new order, agreement of Pell and other stations to merchanter sovereignty in opposition to the EC and its rules—and that Alpha, awash in EC business, had just sent a merchanter to bring Sol and the EC in, even as Alpha and all the Hinder Stars were signing with the Alliance, to which even Cyteen was agreeing to agree.

So what in hell, people would be asking now at Pell and all along that string of stars, what in merry hell was going on back at Alpha with Sol and shipbuilding and all? And what was the EC going to do?

People were always nervous whenever Alpha came into question—nervous because Alpha was the only remaining contact-point for Sol, and anxious because Alpha sat next to Proxima Centari, Beta, the lost station, the one the mere mention of which could force a spacer to leave their bar of choice and come in again for a retry at manners. Beta. The vanished colony. The impossible-to-solve mystery.

And of all the worries everybody had about the future, the one that everyone shared was the fear that Sol, unable to find any other way, stupidly ignoring the threat, might build itself a megahaul FTLer and try to one-hop it the significantly shorter distance to Beta Station.

Sol could technically do that. Sol had the knowledge, it had the design, stolen though it was, and it had the resources. Sol could afford to waste ships, waste crews trying that route—its resources were immense. Nobody on this side of space could ever forget that. Konstantin could reassure Pell that Alpha would eventually be able to handle its own problems now, but did even Alpha believe it?

"Stations report." Madison's voice, over general address. They were starting the countdown.

Same start, same words, every voyage. JR and Madison and John had been kids together. They had grown up in the routines. Youngers learned them now, kids who would inherit their posts. He saw, eyes shut, the readouts, the boards, heard the exchanges of the sections talking to sections. Madison would hear from the Section officers, from the Loft, first, and the Care unit; then from the officers in charge of zones, and the nether deck, in a set order, down to the junior-junior monitors, reporting all accounted for in their sections, all doors secure, all locked things locked and nothing rattling loose.

"Any exceptions?" Madison asked, not a routine question. *"Juniors, this is life-and-death serious. Does anybody have an exception? No punishment for a yes,* hell *to pay for a lie."*

Meaning: was there anybody for any reason not in his officially listed place?

God, *should* he have left the non-essentials and part of the Family ashore at Pell? Gone on this voyage with two shifts, not four?

But no merchanter ever opted for that. Never taught fear to the youngers, either.

Except *Galway* had made that choice, put its Family ashore with far, far more reason than any ship had ever had in all the history of FTL.

No, he'd done right. Making a commotion about their voyage and raising questions at Pell and Venture was not the way to deal with their problem. Get in, observe, get out, running only a little more risk than *Little Bear* had agreed to. Pell and Venture would want to ask questions when they got back, but, if they found anything, it *still* was not going to blow up quickly.

Even if they had to advise Venture and Pell, behind closed doors, that they were both sitting next to a very *big* problem. Slow problem. But big. FTL linking them to Sol was not going to do anything on a massive scale— yet.

They entered pre-jump burn. The bunk compensated. It was time to trank down. JR pulled the tab, clenched his fist slowly, several times, sending the juice into his system.

Do it right, Madison, he thought. *Wake us early. I want to see this place. Thule. Mum remembers it.*

Mum. Fallan Monahan. And a fading number of Hinder Stars merchanters.

Not all that much even in its day. A waystop on the route to Olympus, but the need for it's gone, gone when Galileo blew, and Olympus faded.

Com was saying something familiar. The pre-jump warning, he thought. But trank was taking hold, faster than usual, deep and dark.

A small star. Old. Tired. Startled out of its torpor by the monster so rudely invading its isolation . . .

"Wake up," the automated voice said. *"Wake up. Wake up. Wake up. First-shift to the bridge. Wake up. Wake up. Wake . . ."*

"I hear you," Ross muttered, and closed his fist, hard, repeatedly, feeling that dislocation of mind and acceleration of his heartbeat that attended the wake-up. Eyes were blurred. Mouth was foul. "Status."

"System arrival. Status normal. Time is . . ."

"Cancel, cancel, cancel." He drew breaths, assuring himself he was in his bunk, *not* on the bridge. Contractions of his fist pumped more of the wake-up juice into his system, but no more hype than the machine would give him at max. He couldn't hurry the juice in a status-normal condition: the system wouldn't let him. He was sunnyside up in his bunk and trying to move, *could* move. Rotation was coming up fast, but he shouldn't disconnect from the machine. He took in all the machine had to give at its set rate, and slowly managed to sit up without disconnecting until it beeped *done.*

Then he could disconnect, strip, and grab the towel pack, shortcut substitute for a shower, sopping wet, warm as blood, and quick-dry.

Are we alone here? he desperately wanted to know, but the system couldn't tell him that and the bridge was busy. He tossed the wet towel into the midst of the bedclothes, per custom on *Finity,* and not his problem. He staggered two steps to the loo, dealt with that necessity, and worked his face into some sensitivity . . . beard didn't grow much in jump. It could wait. Everything could wait, because it wasn't a case of next-shift moving routinely into place at a routine station. Everything here was chancy, First-shift was prepping to go up, but Second-shift on a cautioned entry was tasked with having the ship movement-capable before they turned the boards over. First-shift would be on a hold until Second called them.

The wobbles cut in, nature's own reminder that humans weren't built for what humans had chosen to do. He ripped the tab off a room-temperature nutrient pack and gulped it down as fast as experience told him he could get away with, meanwhile hearing others on the deck stirring, little echoes and plumbing operating elsewhere in the section.

The nutrient hit bottom. Or his stomach did. It was all right, all right: he wasn't going to heave it. He needed water. He got that, ice cold, from the dispenser, and slugged it back—

Instant regret as the chill caused spasms. He held on to the counter-top, because that was stable, clamping his mouth shut and repeatedly swallowing to reverse the heaves.

Stupid, rookie move. *Never* put cold in a post-jump stomach.

Are we alone out there? Come on, bridge, give us a clue . . .

"*We are in arrival at Thule,*" came Madison's voice finally, calm and clear over the general address. "*We are two hours light from Thule Station and picking up nothing but a ping. We'll be carrying V into the next shift to see if anything reacts to our entry, so redlight caution remains in effect for all but First-shift and Second. We are now ready for shift change. First-shift to the bridge at your convenience. We'll be getting up optics in the meanwhile.*"

Good, Ross thought. So far, good, granted his stomach would accept another nutrient pack. He wasn't thirsty. That was a bad sign. Usually it was nerves. Novice nerves. He wasn't going to give way to that, damned if he was.

He went after more water. Room temp. Sipped determinedly, and when that was gone, opened the second pack. It went down easier than the first. And, yes, wanted more water. Good.

Something was nagging at his senses, like a forgotten mission or a promise unkept, something that wanted to be remembered, and dimly, then, very dimly, he knew it was the star talking, a muted, self-absorbed kind of presence. A little star with his own name—he had used to think he was named after the Ross stars, but he wasn't. When he was a child he had thought that. Being a child, he'd taken a good deal of the universe personally, before he knew it wasn't that way.

Before he'd known suns came in white and yellow as well as red.

Before he'd known about flare stars and other treacherous creatures.

Before he'd taken up with Fallan, and heard Fallan's stories.

Fallan, who had seen Ross 248 in operation.

One of your old ports-of-call, Fallan, back in pusher days.

He wasn't going to throw up. He held it. He was broken out in a cold sweat, and chilling in the breeze from the vent, but he had blinked his vision clear.

Pushing hype too high too fast, was what. The body was kicking back.

And that faint subskin prickle, that *was* Ross 248 talking to him. He was fairly sure that was it. Not his fear. The star—that star, combined with the wobbles, just felt like fear. He could shake it. Once he figured it, he could zero it out. Background noise. Not significant. Bring up the other sounds instead, the air in the vent, the occasional thump of Ian, next door, in the same process of rushed wake-up.

He wet his hands at the sink, swiped his hair back, then shook his jump-suit out of the elastic that held it and climbed into it, quick and simple tabs, needing only a sweep of the hand to seal the closures—then a feel of the breast pocket to know, yes, his keycard was in there, where he'd put it, knowing he was going to be dim as a rock during wake-up.

He had two more nutrient packets in the right leg pouch, had his ID—that never left him, and he was hearing doors working in the corridor. He handed his way to his own door, a matter of five steps, and out, into clean, cold air, grey panels, and the intermittent glow of guide lights.

Ian was just exiting his quarters, on the same timetable. Siobhan and Maire were ahead of them, getting onto the conveyor lift. They went up one after the other and Ross took the step onto the plate, arriving topside at its deliberate pace, and stepping off, conscious of unsteadiness in his gait and doing his best to walk straight. He was still a little light-headed, still putting a hand out to the wall just for reference as he walked. Takeholds were always in sight, but forget that, he said to himself: at their speed there was no avoidance, just deflection. A vector change now wasn't remotely possible.

And First-shift was going to take charge under these conditions, a projectile hurtling through the system at a scary percent of C.

Didn't do this hellride in any inhabited system, no, no, no. Except at Alpha. It struck him he'd seen *exactly* the same at Alpha. He'd been in Rosie's Bar, watching the vid as *Finity* scared hell out of the station. Damn them, he'd thought then, while everybody on Alpha had sat there helpless, imagining everything from a malfunctioning ship to an arrival of God-knew-what out of unmentionable Beta Station, something alien and lethal.

He hadn't been on the other side of JR's mindset back then. Hadn't remotely imagined that JR had been keeping *Finity's* speed for far more than impressing the locals in the bar.

JR had been reading the system all the way, deciding when and whether to approach the station.

JR had been finding out where *Rights of Man* was, damned sure that was the case. Calculating where she was and, most importantly, what she was capable of.

And determining whether *Little Bear, Nomad,* and *Mumtaz* were in dock as they were promised to be. All those things.

They were doing the same thing now, proceeding near exit velocity, using the sun's mass to actually increase their velocity, while Ross 248, as red as Alpha's sun and complaining steadily in that low, prickly whisper, was hauling hard at them, bending their course as it bent space itself. He was sure of it without seeing the course plot. On the bridge, Nav 2.1, Tuck—Tucker Neihart—was monitoring that curve, while Science was keeping a close eye on the sun.

The curve—he'd been in the conference when they'd set course—was not uncommon for skimming jump-points, but it was a move he'd never seen run this close, and never with a live star. He had it in his head, what they were doing, what they intended—a power and an accelerated mass that could do this fool thing, tug on a star and *use* a star's distortion of space this way, but his gut objected mightily. He was anxious to take his seat. He made it to the bridge, back among the stations: Tuck, at Nav 2.1, and on back. "Early," Nav 2.3 said. "Good."

"Yessir, thanks." He passed 2.4 carefully, and displaced Nav 2.5, a honey-skinned, spiral-curled kid of about fifteen if she was that. "Pat," he recalled as the girl edged out of her place, as wobbly as he was. "Thanks, Two-five. Good job. We're in one piece."

"Yeah," Pat said, heaving a deep and shuddery breath. "Yeah, all yours, 1.5. Sir. Scary bit!"

Pat stuffed two drink-packs into her jacket and eased out, white-knuckling the takeholds, as if that could help much. Ross eased into the body-warm seat, let it shape around him, watching the screens the while. He saw the curve, saw the projection. They were letting the star carry them where they wanted to go, around the bend of space, and that line, that white line, which was Tuck Neihart's plot, was going to deliver them to the vicinity of the station, but nearer the star itself than the station and its planetoid anchor.

Bucklin came in, displaced Nav 2.2. Jim and Ty arrived. Ross adjusted his headset, fussed with the volume, then pulled out a drink pack and took that down in slow sips while *Finity* hurtled on her trajectory.

Kate arrived, gave them a: "Well, we made it."

Ian had settled in at Helm 1.5 and Caplin, Helm 2.1, had given way to Jim B. The bulk of First-shift was in, transitions all through the rows, as exhausted Second-shift found their way to the lounge and a deserved rest.

Time to concentrate now. They weren't called on to *do* anything. The course-plot was in front of them, and they were where they were supposed to be. The region near the sun was not guaranteed to be junk-free, but they were still playing the odds of relative size and the system ecliptic, not a highly populated ecliptic at that, and one they were going to stay out of until they came to a lower V.

Last-arrived at their posts, Science came up—a post *Finity* had, and maybe other ships in the Beyond had, with all sorts of equipment and sensors regular ships didn't have—just stations did. And if ever there was a time aboard *Finity* when Ross was personally glad to see that section lit up and multiple people in those seats over beyond Scan, this was it. They were probably getting stuff from scan and longscan just for starters, looking for whatever was out there.

JR came in—a bit dark around the eyes, but walking arrow straight—displaced Madison with a quick exchange not on general com, and settled into place, invisible now to Nav 1.5, in the back rows, who ought not to have his eyes off his screen.

Nav's job was to watch that screen, on which Ross 248 was an actual presence, with their trajectory distinctly bending. Nav's job was to constantly track the options, should Helm decide to change that course. They were lucky: the star-station, or what was left of it, was going to be in view as they passed.

Needing to dump V now, Ross kept thinking. Any time now, Captain, sir, we would be very happy to dump V. If we go much further we are going to be down on that slope. This is going to be too damn close, *sir.* . . .

Kate was talking directly with Science 1.1, who for this operation was Antonia, that was the name, Antonia, and with Pete, Science 2.1, who had stayed past shift. Ross supposed they'd be *Doctor* this and that on stationside—there was gray hair enough. He'd met them in common mess, in the run-ins along their route, friendly enough, and curious about him and Ian, but tending to their own company, and using way too many words of three and more syllables for him to follow.

Right now he wanted all the three-syllable words to add up to observations and plain orders from the Senior Captain telling Helm and Nav to get them a little breathing room before they drifted the hell down. Their shielding was just fine, he was sure of that, but, *damn*, he was not comfortable. The sun was whispering now, just whispering, but red suns were unpredictable, and for his money, it was a lot better to be spotted by some lurker, with all the political mess that would entail, than to be just a little too snuggly with a muttering, unstable star.

"Presence negative," Science said: Ross was fairly sure that was Pete reporting, physics, Ross remembered. "No trace of passage here within our recept zone. No output from the station. Their reactor's still live, but that's expected. We're getting hellish interference from the sun. Are we good on that closer look?"

"We have it," Senior Captain said, to Ross's relief. "Good enough. Helm, your call."

There was no hesitation. "Nav," Helm 1 said, "Engineering, stand by for jump when we hit this point on the far side. We'll be taking it down to 83%. Say when ready."

Dumping V. All right.

"Ready," the answer came, and Ross keyed in the code he'd been composing, wanting only a handful of variables that came with the 83%. His course flashed on the screen along with four others, five lines lying so close together the colors merged, all in agreement. First dump.

Down, then, bubble half-formed, still deformed by the sun's steady push, overcoming its inward pull. Vision blurred. The deck and console, crew and all, wavered in vision, until that pit of the stomach drop settled smooth as silk. Sensors reacted, reestimated reality, and showed them out, considerably out, comfortably out, from their prior position. Still traveling scary fast, but nothing to intercept or intersect—if they were lucky.

"Optics on the station," Senior Captain said. "Center screen." He received an acknowledgment from Scan 1, recorded image coming up.

Took a moment. In peripheral vision, the central screen, which had been displaying their course schematic, showed a hazy grey and orange object and kept focusing in and in, extreme magnification. It was hard not to look.

"We are stable for the moment," Senior Captain said. "First and third seats may have a look."

That continued a moment. Then: "Second, fourth and trainee seats, take a look."

Ross looked up, and sucked in his breath. It filled the large screen, a toroid, touched by a ruddy sun, red-stained grey surfaces pasted on absolute black, where no sun touched. It still rotated, but barely, gravity-anchored to a sun-blasted rock of a planetoid, partly in view. There were still green lights here and there, not as many as should have been, and a panel, a panel as large as a cargo runner, hung ajar, trailing hose like entrails.

"Eyes down," Senior Captain said, meaning back to business, prepared to take action.

"Bit of a mess," Helm 1 commented. "Hell of a mess."

Neglect. The bots that should automatically do the external housekeeping were lost, or at least not functioning. The visible mast had taken serious damage.

"There's an automated output," Com 1 said, "but it's just an ID, Thule Station, and a request for ID. I gave it, but it's not had time to respond."

"Surprise if it did," Senior Captain said. "Scan?"

"Not picking up anything," Scan 1 said. "A few small objects, attracted in or shed from the station, not sure which."

"Science?"

"No temperature anomaly, no output, nothing within range."

"We'll continue," Senior Captain said. "Save the scans and vid. I don't say we won't be back here, or someone will. It's a wreck, it's not going to maintain forever, but it's a convenient point of mass. We've talked about sites for a supply dump, for us, for whoever. Could be, for the future, and I want those records. Nav, lay a new line for Olympus, and Helm, stand ready."

Book IV   Section ii

Thule was grey, and aged, and . . . spooky . . . as any place Jen had seen. The images that came out to Security revealed wreckage from some impact nothing had stopped. Ships all departed. Bots likely damaged, decayed, or just strayed off into irrelevance.

Fletcher had called everybody into Ops 2 for this one: Parton, Twofer, aides Paul and Josh, Lewes and Marcy D, who mostly handled the minders' issues. And her. She'd debriefed with just Fletcher and debriefed twice at Pell with the team, but it was her first time being called to entry duty with the team, and there was a seat for her at the end of the console, beside grey-haired Marcy D. It wasn't a good time to say a thing, just to absorb what she saw, and to sip the nutrient stuff—she wished she hadn't opted for strawberry: she'd had the real thing, and this wasn't. Not near. Her stomach was upset. Her brain full of what she was seeing, a place where people had lived, and kids had been born and grown old and died, generations of them, back when pushers ruled and the Circle Trade was still anchored at Alpha.

It was something to see it abandoned and decayed like this, shedding bits and parts. And that large, gaping hole . . . some monster sunbound rock had done that since the shutdown.

"We're going to be through here in quick order," Fletcher said, by way of opening. "We've seen what there is to see, nothing active, or if it is, it's deep-hidden and *we* don't have the resources or time to go stirring it up. Only thing we know for certain is, the station is not currently habitable."

"Any sign of a pusher just parked in the dark here?" Marcy D asked.

"Not so far, but damned hard to spot in shutdown. Whole lot of room to search, but no track showing. Maybe worth a return look and a bot setup, but barring some indication around Thule station itself, we'll be moving on to Olympus—taking a good scan of the station, in the process. Senior Captain's been talking about sites where we could stockpile supply, and for the Hinder Stars, this is a definite possibility."

"Damn near at Bryant's door, too," Paul said. "Which is good, supposing we ever have trouble at Alpha."

"Supposing we had trouble anywhere this side of Pell," Fletcher said. "Thule's in easy reach from Venture, nice place to sit and wait, pick up supply and trade in the cold. If you're clear of the junk field."

That possibility of safe refueling and dark ports for the Merchanters' Alliance took a sudden scary bump toward reality. Fletcher was right: Thule would be ideal, as close to Venture as it was.

"But we might not have that option," Fletcher said, "if the station becomes active."

"Active?" Twofer asked.

"Olympus died because its Venture-side exit's a death trap, and lack of traffic down the Reach took this place down as well. But if Olympus, somehow, is alive again and willing to become part of the system, using Thule as *the* route, as a safe vector for entry into Olympus—it could see a fair amount of traffic again."

"Unless they try to open UV Ceti again," Paul said with a grimace. "Positionally, that would be Earth's best gateway to Pell itself."

UV Ceti. Definitely scary.

"Nobody in their right mind," Parton said.

"The EC did it once," Fletcher said. "Big set-up, special shielding." Slight shrug. "Nobody ever accused them of being in their right minds. The end was fast, at least."

"Still nasty," Jen said.

"Very."

"Just hope Sol uses sense when they get FTL," Josh said, "and that a boycott never even has to happen. No matter *which* direction they come from. UV Ceti. Groombridge 34." That was Olympus. "Either one as a bridge to Venture and Pell—is not going to be that convenient. Or safe. Alpha's far from Venture. But it doesn't have near the problems."

"Hoping that route proves out. Hoping *Galway* makes it," Lewes said. "Honestly."

"Hoping they do," Jen added in a low tone.

"Know you do," Marcy D said. "Know you do, Jenniebug."

"We *all* do," Fletcher said. "Lewes is right. No matter what we find out here, we want that Sol supply line and all its politics to route aboveboard through Alpha—and far away from Pell. I mean, we think of those jump-points out of Alpha as bad news, but look at the good side of it. If they *do* route through Alpha, it leaves the Hinder Stars a role in the future. We're thinking of the safety of *Galway*, yes, but also the future of the Hinder Stars, and if that route works, the EC gets a slower, saner entry into the Beyond. We really don't want to be negotiating with the EC on two fronts at the same time, one at FTL speed, the other decades behind reality. The fact *Galway* hasn't returned to Alpha yet doesn't really tell us anything other than that *either* Cruz and some novice navigator managed to take control and *Galway* is now subatomic particles—or that the Monahans won and Cruz and crew took a cold dark walk. The one thing we know that *didn't* happen is that some novice EC navigator got them through three messy, unknown jumps. So the best thing we can do for the Galways, and *all* the Hinder Stars, is to find out what these two ghost ships have been up to, and try to get whatever-is-going-on at least partially dealt with before a Sol-based FTL shows up at Alpha."

As much as four years just to get to Sol, Jen said to herself. That was how long the Monahans had hoped to give them. *Galway* just needed to prove the coordinates sent out on the Stream and needed to tell their version of events to the EC before whatever Cruz might have fed into the Stream, six years in lightspeed transit, muddied the truth in Sol System. A three-hop series of jumps, taken conservatively, could account for the better part of one year station-time. Thoroughly mapping the jump-points could add as much time as *Galway* dared take. Once they got to Sol, negotiations with the EC were also bound to take a while. Five years total wasn't out of reasonable possibility. They'd for sure like to have it all sewn up by the time Alpha's lightspeed message got there.

And getting back again, shorter by reason of having the map they'd made: that would go fast, if Captain Niall and Nav 1 Fallan were in charge. *Finity*'s own course was turning out to be jump after jump, taking up that time in gulps. Getting to Alpha had been . . . crazy. Meeting Ross, and all the associated chaos at Alpha had been a bewildering series of changes in her life. Ross's presence on *Finity* and the anticipation of showing him Pell had energized them both on the hellbent trip back to Pell . . .

Then, just as they were ready to relax and enjoy themselves and their still-new relationship . . . the Garden, the trees, and the discoveries in the gift shop had happened. Suddenly everything had shifted, radically, and set them on an accelerating new course toward suspicions and unknowns and the very real possibility that stopping the EC operation at Alpha wasn't enough. Multiple questions loomed, all on the far side of space. Thule. The EC. . . .

Olympus and its notorious jump-point.

Ross wasn't the only one who had nightmares this trip.

"Suppose the station tanks are anything like intact?" Paul was saying, and Jen, with a mental kick, forced her attention back to the screen.

"The place has taken a beating, but if the pile's still going, possibly interior bots are still maintaining, and the sectors may have sealed. If we've got the bones of the place still sound, it wouldn't take that much to set up a depot here, and some of the trash becomes a resource. Set bot miners at it. Let them work it."

"A fuel dump and a message drop's dead easy," Josh said. "Whatever the condition of its guts."

"Meeting in the dark. Direct trading," Lewes said. "As if *that's* never been done in the short history of the Beyond."

"One step at a time," Fletcher said, and keyed up a rapid series of shots from the cameras, showing the entry ports, closeups of the accumulated small fragments, one after the other, and at the site of the worst damage, a gaping wound in the ring, probably penetrating clear to the personnel spaces. A strand of conduit still connected a massive panel that had come free in that area.

"That one looks like it blew from inside," Jen said. She'd done her own research on Thule's structure, read everything she could find about the trade that had used to be there. And the outdated systems. "Maybe it was left pressurized."

"Possible, that," Josh said. "Or maybe a salvage operation that didn't give a damn about anything other than grabbing whatever they could get. I looked it up. There was a company formed on Bryant's and another on Venture to salvage the station. Word was they'd already started when the EC's order arrived—fifteen station years late—for the stations to be mothballed instead—and then the operations got stalled in the courts. Court ruled the companies didn't have a legal claim. There was a considerable to-do about EC influence on the judges, then Pell got into the act. Apparently it dragged on in lawsuits and threats of lawsuits, seconded by a court on Bryant's—it was a mess. The companies folded, the EC won, and there it sits."

"Unless our ghost ships have been looting it," Fletcher said.

"Don't you think they'd clean up the access points first?" Paul asked. "Those metal bits floating all over would be hazardous . . . and damned if they'd find any of that high quality Sol merch here. This is all a waste."

A waste, Jen thought. What a sad term for a sad, dust-spattered wreck. It hung in the red light of its sun, its masts still blinking come-ahead lights to the unanswering void, three of the four lights at the cardinal points of its ring, and debris following it around. Spooky sight, a station so badly used, half-stripped, violated and left. Its slow rotation was mesmerizing, another loose set of panels trailing what seemed to be ducting of some sort—a wound that would only get worse, with the exposure of inner parts that never were rated for deep cold and UV.

People had lived here once. Had called it home. Those people were long gone, now. Their descendants had become citizens of Venture, mostly. So could it revive as a supply dump, serve the Alliance? Maybe the supply Uncle talked about leaving here could be gravitationally associated with the station, maybe even fixed to the mast. But then—if it became any kind of mapped waystop and traffic began coming through here, who knew? Ships might do a bit of profitable scavenging along the way, particularly for higher value stuff that might be left inside. It would be hell to police a free-for-all prospecting site. An honor system wasn't likely to hold.

Mostly, now, passing rapidly by them, Thule was a point of mass, its red sun itself a jump-point, a gravitational foothold in political games she'd never imagined.

Thule, Galileo, and Olympus. All EC property in the old days. All bypassed by an FTL universe. Never much more than a fuel stop. As for Galileo, the terminal station on this reach, it had gotten a station because some science types pushed for it, assuring everybody there wasn't a present threat and of course there would be warning signs.

Galileo's star, EV Lacertae, had flared off with a really spectacular UV flare, taking the station with it—the source for Mum's pretty piece of glass. The EC would be complete fools to go back there, that was the general consensus.

Scary place. She had no interest in cruising past Galileo, and she hoped no one suggested it as a follow-up, even if Olympus looked like this.

"Cousins and friends." That was Uncle James Robert, Senior Captain, on the horn. *"We've had a physically hard run getting this far. For what we can tell, we're unobserved here, but we are not comfortable in that assumption. We're going to continue as we bear with no V-dump through this watch and the next, which will be Fourth-shift, mark that. Repeat: next watch will be Fourth-shift. Third-shift will take us into jump in very short order, and First-shift will again be next up on arrival at Olympus. That is the current schedule. Sleep, relax. If you feel any abnormal effects of our schedule, report it to Medical. That is a firm order. Our entry at Olympus Point may*

give us a few days to rest and recover, but a medical crisis will not help us if we have other issues there, as we could, cousins, so do not have one.

"Matt is going to order us up one good feed before jump, and our schedule will let us get at least four hours natural sleep, so drop by mess and take it as you can. It'll be buffet-style, starting in one hour fifteen minutes. Jump is scheduled for 2330 hours, which may be delayed, but don't count on it.

"Olympus arrival will be, we hope, to a quiet star, but we cannot guarantee that. The Xiaos are going to join us there, if that word hasn't gotten to your shift. We will have backup. But we can't take safety for granted, including the fact that finding nothing here heightens the likelihood of finding something there. Be prepared for anything, including a rough entry or a quick jump out. I don't plan either, but the best we can do is see to our health and the ship's order right now, assuring that we arrive at Olympus fit to perform.

"Junior-juniors, no hijinks on this next one, either. This is life and death serious. Get yourselves where you're assigned to be, restock your kits, and report to your section chiefs once you're ready to shut the door on your cabins. I will personally interview anyone who wants to be the exception and you will explain to me at length why you thought you were the exception. Have that clear. Olympus Point is a rough entry under any circumstances. I will not be in a forgiving mood.

"All aboard, eat and sleep as a matter of duty, get your jump kit in order, and keep in mind we may have to leave Olympus itself on an emergency basis. Think ahead, restock, don't leave anything to chance, report any situation that could become a problem, and let's do this in good order, all of us."

Captain-sir meant it, Jen had no question about that. It was not time for anybody to flout the rules or be where he or she wasn't assigned to be, which included double-bunking. She and Ross had a little time. It was a good idea to take food at the earliest possible, and give the gut a chance to process it before time got all weird with the body.

"You heard it," Fletcher said. "Senior Captain's got us on the clock, now. Josh, take the feed, talk to Science, and get us whatever might possibly be useful. History, observations, readouts, everything in one package, file under *Thule.*"

"Got it," Josh said. "Everybody hit the buffet. I'll pass this to Mark when he comes in, and we won't see each other again until Olympus, barring something bleeping up in the interval."

That was it for their shift. They were free. Or she was. Lewes was staying on with Josh; and Marcy and Dave would take their handoff as Fourth-shift took over. Security wasn't always active during approach, but they weren't exactly approaching, either. They were reconnoitering, taking notes and collecting data—in this case, getting the best shots they could in case they had to cut and run. Science was doing a work-up, and Scan was, all in the theory they might even have their *own* use for the place, if things with the EC went way sideways.

Which everyone hoped they didn't, and nobody counted on.

She gathered herself up, pocketed her handheld, still linked to SecOps, and headed off to do things that needed doing, arranging her quarters being one of them. Food, nutrient packs, and whatever jump-juice Medical was handing out on this one.

When she was still woozy from the last jump.

She threw herself down on her bunk and stared at the ceiling, worried about Ross and that battered station in equal turns, and wondering whether she should go to him or leave him alone.

Damn, when had their rather magical relationship gotten so damned delicate?

If she were honest with herself, she wished on some level she'd never taken the Galways into the Garden tour, that they'd never found what they'd found in that gift shop. If they hadn't, if they'd all just let go of the *Miriam B* and *Come Lately* puzzle, they'd have just settled down to supplying Alpha and having more free time on Pell, and they wouldn't be here asking questions and running risks no merchanter should ever have to run. They wouldn't be involved, and things might have just worked themselves out the way stations and ships always solved things—messily. Over time.

And they might, if worst speculations proved true, have EC enforcers on Pell's doorstep within the decade. No, it was good to have found it out. She was glad she reported it. Proud she'd recognized the necessity. But, damn, she hoped they all survived. The image of the gutted station was going to haunt her a good long while.

As for the Galways . . . she realized now they'd taken a wound that hadn't near healed. She began to understand, on a visceral level, *why* the Galways had chosen to stick with *Finity*. You said "EC" and "underhanded dealing" and they couldn't *unhear* it. *She* couldn't have gotten Ross to turn down a ride back to Alpha, back to his family, but he and all his cousins had done exactly that, not for *Finity*, but for another go at whatever had the stamp of the EC in the Hinder Stars. The EC had threatened their Family, and they just couldn't turn their backs on it, not a one of them.

Could she have?

She couldn't even imagine the situation.

She did know *she* couldn't leave *Finity,* any more than *he* would ever have his mind free of *Galway.* That was reality . . . for a merchanter. She wasn't sure she'd ever truly understood that, until now.

It was pre-jump jitters. She didn't want to be here, doubted, really, that anyone on the ship *wanted* to be here. The whole operation *Finity* was involved in began to look huge and enveloping. She wanted to say to hell with all the Hinder Stars. Let the EC have them. She wanted Ross and she wanted him and all of them, the whole Monahan Family, safe at Pell. Safe and together and with her—which wasn't going to happen. Damn it.

Galway had seriously screwed things up, making the deal with Alpha. But she understood why they had. She also understood that *Pell* couldn't do what *Finity* was doing. Some ship had to do it, had to go physically and find out what was happening at Olympus, and they were the best and the ablest Pell had . . . same as *Galway* was Alpha's best. But—damn. Just damn.

Ross *would* be going back to Alpha after all this. But would he be happy? His family were aging there. His shift-mates were aging at still another rate on *Galway.* Lives once in sync had more and more trouble matching up and finding connections intact. It was one reason people *needed* to be with their own. Uncle-sir had warned her. He had told her she could end up sorry.

Uncle hadn't warned her that *Finity* herself wasn't veering back to normal. That they were still involved with the Galways, that the Galways were veering off into *this*—whatever it was, in these lonely, wrecked places—she hadn't seen that ahead. But it was. It was one thing for *Finity*: they were defending their territory and they had to do it, part of that deal they'd always had with Pell.

But this EC business had grabbed hold of Ross and all the Galways in a very personal way, edge of a gravity well that just didn't let them go.

Go back, she should have said, much more forcefully, at Venture. Go, goodbye, have a nice life, remember me, get off our deck and go home. We'll send you word. We'll keep our promises . . .

But it wasn't the promises that kept them aboard. It might have been that on the way to Pell, but not now. They were hunting the other half of what the EC had been doing. They were in it. Same as *Finity* was . . . but not. They were *part* of this, in a way she wasn't.

She'd ignored every warning Uncle Jim had given her. She'd gotten herself involved with a Hinder Stars man, one of the left-behinds, that had never had a reason to be in her world. She, dammit, loved him. But he wasn't looking to her, now, not for reasons. Feelings hadn't changed, at least she didn't think so, but motivations had. It was answers that the Monahans were chasing. And even if they found nothing at Olympus, and left the chase and simply went back to Venture, to go on as before . . .

It wouldn't *be* as before. They'd gotten into this gravity well, spiraling into it, her and Ross.

She loved him. She needed to stop loving him. She was scared as hell for him. And for herself. And for all of them. Because *Finity* was caught in that same well.

Stupid mistake to have gone this far. Stupid mistake to have committed so much—to someone whose life was stuck in that nightmare he kept having— drifting freefall between ships. With the damn EC wrapped around his heart, squeezing it, insulating it from life itself.

How did I get so tangled in this? Why isn't it simple? Why can't it *be* simple? Why can't I even talk to him?

Learn from it, Uncle had said when she'd broken her arm, stupid reach after a lever she couldn't hold. What's it worth, otherwise?

I'd like it not to hurt, she'd said, then, ten years old.

She'd learned that much, at least. She really would like it not to hurt.

Book IV   Section iii

The ship ran. And ran. And ran that course that carried them away from the star and the station—a closer brush with both, in Ross's estimation, than he liked, but that was what Senior Captain wanted, and it was where Helm had them, shielded, vanes folded, and traveling like the proverbial bat. It was Nav's job to set up for Third-shift, running the exit sim and running it, a mundane operation attending a course that skated the rim of sanity. Kate was sure of their course. Bucklin was sure of it. Ty and Jim wore worried expressions and Ross just tried not to imagine failure.

They tested the calculations in the computer's reality. It was Third-shift that got to verify and tell Helm they were accurately aimed at Groombridge 34, which was the second stomach-wrenching prospect.

Time had a perverse way of standing still when the brain kept spinning through possibilities and checks and doubts, and it was a challenge to focus and focus and focus and not scatter. It was sim and sim and sim in an increasingly textured model, and Kate allowed no distractions in the process. If they failed the button-push by seconds, they'd blow the schedule by days and do a tamer exit, but doing it the way Senior Captain intended was their job, mad as it was.

Do you know, sir? Do you feel *it yourself? You're a damned fool if you're doing this blind. I can feel it. I think it's right. But I'm not sure.*

God, I don't like where we're going.

Are you sure, sir? You can't like it, either.

"That's it," Kate said. Wound-tight nerves and an upset stomach said there was a resolution, eighth time same result. Sweat was running down Ross's neck despite the chill normal in ops.

God, let us go . . . let us just go. Let us do this . . .

But their calc was prep. Third-shift got to re-run it. Not the top of Nav. Not Kate. Kate's calc would be hours back.

But truth was truth and physics was physics unless their destination itself wobbled. And it had no external reason to wobble. It was the best they could do.

"We will go with it," Senior Captain said. "Thank you, First-shift. Take care of yourselves, now. You'll have a full shift plus half an hour to prepare for jump."

Shower was not quite the first thing on Ross's mind, but it was close. He locked down his board, unclipped, and levered himself up and out.

He wasn't the only one to head straight through to the showers. Ian came behind him, tossed him a cold pack of juice. And breathing in a deluge of hot fog, while sucking down an icy tart limeade, was a fair head-clearer. He was shaking. Muscles twitched without his willing them.

They'd make it, he told himself. They'd done things with this ship they'd never contemplate with *Galway*. Kate didn't miss. Bucklin didn't. And Senior Captain wasn't going to pop this ship into the sun. They were waiting for a solid fix on Groombridge 34, as of about four hours ago. It should be turning up in another fifty-odd minutes, Third-shift's problem, Third-shift's turn to sweat. The graphic kept playing behind his eyes whenever he shut them and soaked up the mist.

Going to be all right. We did it right. . . . Third-shift is going to take our numbers and their fix and it's going to match or we'll abort . . .

"Anybody scared?" Ian asked.

"Honestly," Ross asked. "Hell, yeah. But we signed on, didn't we? We can't head back to Alpha not knowing what's what, can we?"

"Hell, no," Ian said. "Owen would ask us, so what's going on that had both *Finity* and Pell spooked? And we'd have to say, 'Damn-it-all, Cap'n, sir, sounded kinda scary so we just decided we didn't need to know.' Wouldn't we?" The last he said in *Galway*'s ship-speak, a waft of home and all they knew. Not shutting the Finitys out. Just thinking of Family, and people, and home, and being there.

"Damn straight," Ross said. "Can you imagine telling the cousins we've had a nice trip to the golden elephant and all, and a lovely walk in the trees, but no, sorry, we don't know a thing. —As Fallan would say, if those benighted bastards think they're puttin' one over on us, they've got another think comin'."

Ian grinned at him. "And that's the truth."

He held up a thumb, leaned back against the shower wall and let the water hammer an overheated brain. He shut his eyes, and saw the star burning in memory. Surely it was memory. He felt it, felt it continually, grumbling along, surly creature that it was. Underestimated. Little humans in little ships left their debris here. But it wasn't eternal. It was push-pull between gravity and the tides that washed out from the star, a short-term contest, as humans reckoned time . . .

"Ross?" A hand touched his bare shoulder. He opened his eyes under the battering of water.

"Asleep, man?" Ian asked. "You all right?"

"Yeah," he said. What else was he to say? Nav 3 had the calc now. Confirm or reject.

Not his job. They could all die. They could all end up in his namesake's belly.

At the end, his line had deviated from Kate's the width of the line itself. They all had been that close.

If they were wrong, they were dead wrong together.

Book IV   Section iv

The jump to Olympus was a tricky bit of navigation, and Ross 248, Thule, was not a stable object in terms of output. Came time, and Third Captain, John, was in charge. JR, in the sanctity of his office, had already changed into his heat-managing blues, pockets stuffed with requisite items and console amply supplied with juice packs. Now it was the sheer worried boredom of waiting for the move—a steady, wish-I-were-doing-it anxiety, because it was *not* a routine maneuver John was handling.

But the close pass saved an immense amount of time and fuel. It was a maneuver they had done uncounted times in sim and four times in reality.

Just . . . John hadn't done the reality part. Nor had Mum. But sooner or later John had to, if the universe kept going in increasingly unpleasant patterns, and if the future kept handing them responsibility for questions like this. *Finity's End* was a merchanter, and she counted her change, she conserved her resources, and she outbid her competition. That was who the Family was and all they had ever wanted to be, since shiptime had divorced itself from Earthtime and stationtime alike. But here they were again, doing what had to be done, because without the power and the speed *Finity* had, it didn't get done, and the Family, even with Pell's backing, didn't have the resources to take endless time about it—*or* the inclination to ignore the threat and hope for benevolence from the EC.

They'd taken a Family vote at the outset of their leaving regular trade. They hadn't taken one since. The drive to get the job done had become all one thing, chasing down those last two marginal ships in the great dark of the Hinder Stars, with one simple focus, until those ships had become a puzzle unto themselves, and until the Alpha stationmaster had made a dreadful gamble and played hob with everyone's plans.

To ease the tension between Cyteen and Pell, merchanters had long been playing go-between and keeping supply up, but with all that was coming down on them, the role of negotiators and deal-makers had acquired a this-decade urgency and needed some teeth. Cyteen insisted on Emilio's signature: if he'd sign, they would; if Pell and Cyteen agreed, other stations would comply. Everything they'd done and won so far insisted on Emilio's signature, and Emilio and this whole end of human space had an accelerated problem . . . because Sol might not stay in its bottle.

Finity had gotten sucked into Emilio's problem, which led to Alpha's problem, and now bid fair to become everybody's problem. The Beyond hadn't had time or physical togetherness enough to plan. They just did as they could. Time someone found out the EC's intentions. Not just merchanter business, but what had plainly become, collectively, everybody's business.

The situation on the monitor ticked away. *Finity* followed the course they'd planned. JR half expected John to call before pushing the button. But what could John ask him? If he saw anything amiss he'd call John. He didn't. John could conclude he saw nothing. The line was where it needed to be and Olympus was steadily moving into the box.

Olympus. Which was to say—Groombridge 34, a binary like Venture's

Bella and the Beast, only less friendly, as one came in from Venture. Thule-origin was inherently a much safer approach than launching out of another binary—one of several factors that had killed Olympus as a station. A binary star had its tricks in a jump, bad enough when your charts were fresh. They'd been renewing their own information on Thule's red sun as they went, and were steadily updating what they could gather about the binary ahead of them, several light years up the observational timeline from Venture . . . you always updated; but the information gap on Groombridge 34 was deep and wide by reason of years of neglect—and it was a complex system, not only two stars, but planets and planetoids involved. Double reason to be conservative, which John always was, and ask Third-shift to handle the jump.

John had made a face at the request, and John had hesitated, but that wasn't John ducking responsibility, that was John thinking through the problems involved and asking himself whether he was up to it. When John thirty minutes later said yes, that was a considered yes.

There was Beth, Nav 3.1, backing that, a senior Navigator who wasn't the Family's most scintillating conversationalist: Beth didn't talk much, but a lot of Nav weirdness went on in that curly grey head. Garry, Helm 3.1, was dead calm no matter what was going on, absolutely business-only, and fast enough to decide when he needed to. No questions, there, either. Garry might have stood for a captaincy, if he'd had the inclination. He didn't want it. Wanted what he did, and did it well. Every shift needed an anchor, and the way Kate anchored First-shift, Garry was that personality on Third, stolid and outspoken. John had confidence in him. And Garry had confidence in John.

The one hour warning sounded. Madison came in, likewise in work blues, and sat down at the adjacent console. They'd ridden out together as kids, aboard old *Gaia*, in her convert days.

"You talk to John?"

"He's checking everything, driving the watch bat-crazy. You know John."

"Yeah. Nothing's coming loose on his shift. Count on that."

"Saw Mum leaving as I came in. She's heading down, no problems. Says she's going to sleep in unless she's needed. Checked with Tommy." That was the chief medic. "All clear on drug pickups. Nobody's waiting til the last minute on this one."

"Good for that," JR said.

"Nervous on this one," Madison said. "I won't say not."

"Got to go in," JR said. "We committed Min."

"Second thoughts?"

JR hesitated. With two individuals alive he'd give the true answer: Mum and Madison. "Plenty. But we're in this."

"So's Pell," Madison said, which was true. "We're not alone on this one."

"There's that. But damn little they can do for us if Olympus is fully staffed and not interested in being found. Maybe they've been preparing for their cover to be blown. Maybe they've got a few mass-drivers ready to aim at unwanted visitors."

"So we take a few readings and get the hell out."

"Doesn't get us many answers."

"If they fire at us, especially unprovoked, we have all the answers we really need."

"Hate to put the cousins through one more no-rest jump. Not to mention the baby. We can park us out of reach."

"We'll survive. Just concentrate on your job. We'll concentrate on making it happen. That's our job."

They sat in companionable silence, watching the screen where JR had the images of Thule displayed. Sad little place, Thule. It had been a little station even in its heyday. Mostly it had been a science post, supplied by a couple of tiny ships that had died with the shutdown of Thule, one of the small but tragic stories of little Families that had tried their best with barely capable FTLs, and had had the luck run against them. The Lily-Youngs had settled down on Venture, JR had learned that. They had had a particularly close call. The Jacksons had found berths on the Viking cargo-pusher *Mistress Mary*, and merged with the Buellers.

The lives and names reeled past, the ones they had come across when they started out with their list of spacer Families, the converts, and then the purpose-builts; the whole of the Alpha Reach, the Hinder Stars, the way the Beyond saw them; the First Stars, as the people who lived out there wanted them to be called . . .

It was Pell that had kept the Hinder Stars alive, though the Hinder Stars might insist it was Earth. In fact it was Pell's rivalry with Cyteen that had played into that situation. So long as the Hinder Stars were viable in the least, Pell had kept them going, or kept Venture going, and Venture had kept the ones down the line alive—barely, which possibly caused the EC to decide it had an excuse to devote all its pusher-loads to *The Rights of Man*.

Cause and effect: it was all speculation where the EC was concerned. He knew Emilio. Understood Emilio in most ways. He didn't know the faceless EC at all, could only speculate based on their choices. Either way, the old status quo was changing.

"*Five minutes warning,*" Com said.

"Time," Madison said.

"Time," JR agreed. He opened the console beside his seat, saw the green light blinking, indicating the system was ready. The office systems always were, both seats. He applied the patch to his inner elbow and half reclined his seat. Madison did the same. The only captain opting for a sleep-through on this jump was Mum.

Minutes ticked down. Neither of them spoke.

"*We are one minute and counting,*" Lanie said: Com 3.1. "*One minute and counting. Is there any problem anywhere? Speak now or don't. All coms are open.*"

Memories of being a kid. Of pranks played, and you caught merry hell next time if the victim figured you out. Or if it got the attention of the seniors. Innocent times, aboard *Gaia,* in her day.

"*Thirty,*" came from Com. "*Twenty-nine . . .*"

Stomach was upset. All the feeds had cut in with the patch.

The chemicals were flowing. Senses would go soon.

Fear would go fairly soon. Doubt. That would go, too.

His leadership. His decisions, ultimately, that had put the Family here. They'd run hard, this far, hard enough to impact their senior-seniors, and the baby. And he worried. Mum and Vickie monitored each other—no junior aide for them, thank you. They could take it. So they assured him this time. The senior-seniors damned sure didn't *want* to ride it out in Medical, with the baby.

Fear wasn't leaving soon enough, dammit. It was his job to worry—about them, about the rest of the Neiharts, who hadn't exactly signed on for this, but if not *Finity* . . . who?

Drug haze came on.

"*Five,*" Com 3 said. "*Four . . .*"

"*Clear for jump,*" John said. "*Nav?*"

"*Center of the window,*" Nav said. "*Go for jump.*"

"*Helm,*" John said. "*Execute.*"

Raging storm. Nuclear hell shedding heat and light, arcing power and prominences . . .

Two stars objecting mightily to their intrusion.

Two stars pushing back . . . hard.

One path, only one safe passage.

Oh, my God, was the dim first thought, and Ross moved his arm. It floated uselessly over in zero-*G* and the patch stung.

"We are in arrival. First-shift to the bridge. First-shift to the bridge. Put it together and move it, cousins and crewmates. We are in arrival at Groombridge Point and we have immediate indications we are not alone here."

Third Captain's voice overlay lines of code flashing behind his eyelids.

He was in quarters, not on the bridge. No controls to reach.

"We are at the system barycenter," the same voice said. John Neihart. *"We are still remote from Groombridge A. But move it, people. Do move it. We need more brains on this one. Shift-3 will not dump V. Shift-1 will make that decision."*

No! A voice inside him screamed. *Don't wait! Do not fucking wait!*

"Yeah," Ross said aloud, in case anybody was receiving. His voice croaked. He cleared his throat. "Ross Monahan, awake and moving."

Or trying to move. It was like a dream where you tried to move and your arms wouldn't work. Worst time he'd ever had waking from trank.

And still that desperate voice vibrated in his head.

Damn it. He *had* to get to the bridge. Their heading was *not* optimal. He worked his fingers, used a thumb to punch the release on the belts holding him to the cot, got one, but couldn't reach the second. The med-tube was still feeding him wakeup juice, and he had to be careful, moving, not to jostle that connection.

Groombridge A and B.

Foucault and Fizeau. Points of mass. The barycenter was the jump-point, but Foucault was the destination.

Fine. Nav had a problem. That vector was his concern. His job was to wake up his fingers and toes and get his brain online. He needed specific numbers. Location. For those equations spinning in his head.

He was awake enough now to open the first of the nutrient packs he had on him, body-warm and disgusting as it was going to be. He pulled the tab and took it in gulps, salty as sweat. The taste said his electrolytes were off.

V-dump. Hard one. He lay there and breathed a while, not envying Third-shift Nav at the moment, with a rough entry and a quick dump-down.

Thank—

Second one. Hard after the first.

Shit, that was scary. Engines scarcely had time to cycle.

But it felt better. But it was still *wrong.* There was still . . . pushback.

"Sorry, cousins," that was Senior Captain, on the bridge and now assuming command. *"No time for a warning. A little adjustment there. Welcome to Groombridge Hell. Should be inertial for a bit now."*

Ross reached after another packet from the shelf beside him, fumbled after the tear-strip, hands shaking, cursing the schedule that had him down-side, in his bunk. Damn strip wouldn't tear, then did. The nutrient goo flooded out in globules dancing in the dim light, going to get sticky all over stuff. He got most of it to his mouth, which activity provided him something other than the pull of two stars to concentrate on. He swallowed, and heard the engagement of the ring, deep and distant. Yellow globules adrift in the air circulation began to react to another force, and now he felt the sugges-tion of *down,* which, with rehydration, was going to have another effect in a few minutes. He hadn't heard the clearance to unbuckle, but the green light had come on in the overhead, so he ejected the feed-patch for a fresh one and rearmed the system—that was a thing he did like breathing. In case they had to get the hell away.

Which right now, given the second immediate V-dump, given the mad dash to get here, and the shape they were all in, physically, was an unsettling thought.

Couldn't. Wouldn't. Shouldn't need it . . .

But—

The larger mass, Foucault, was increasingly unstable. Fizeau wasn't happy, either. Damn . . . was that *Fizeau's* Ardaman? Clear out here? What the hell?

Couldn't be. Could not possibly be. This *feeling stars* was twisting his brain. Wake up. Get to the bridge. Get to the numbers. *Those* would tell him what was going on.

The globules were sinking now, toward the shelf, the floor, the sheets. He had that peculiar prickle of *down* beginning to settle his hair, his clothes, his body. He moved a hand to push a button to free all the latches, nice little convenience *Finity* had, when the body was beginning to want relief fairly desperately.

Had there been a 'clear to move?' Time slipped on him. Had-happened and would-happen married and merged and had triplets.

Hell. He swung a leg off, still in marginal *G*, and took a little help from the bunkside console in getting vertical. His arms could span from there to the far wall, and he staggered to the little water closet, as *Finity* so quaintly named it. Stripping clothes, relieving himself, breaking into the sodden disinfectant-smelling towel-packs, and rubbing down after a bath in free-floating electrolyte spillage—that was all autopilot. Getting the coveralls seam neat was a—oh, hell, fix it later.

"We are needing you up here, First-shift cousins, soon as you can . . . move!"

Book V   Section ii

"We are picking up electromagnetic presence." That was the word from Com 3 on general address, and Jen did a low *G* run down the corridor, moving fast, but not in good order. So sensors had picked up something at their entry point. Since that jolting double dump, they were in the grip of Groombridge 34 A, aka Foucault, a planeted system with occasional significant rocks on their entry path. Optics were being brought to bear. Antennae would deploy. That went without question. Third-shift Science had only a two-deep senior crew with trainees in all the other seats—but Antonia, First-shift, would be hauling herself up to debrief and displace them all, no question, with her team close behind her.

Security was already scheduled to go into immediate function on arrival, in case of internal emergencies from the rough entry, but the call Jen had flashing on her handheld was no incident call, it was an emergency summons *to* the security office, which had never happened like this. Wobbly and blurry as she was, she made it to the office and inside, grabbed the nearest seat-back—it was Parton's———to check her momentum, then swung into

her own place, hand-over-hand, dropping into her seat at near normal G.
Fletcher had his back to her, eyes glued to readout. It wasn't a time to ask.
The info was up. Parton was flashing through inputs at his console. Jen
shoved her earpiece in and keyed into Nav, so as not to badger Fletcher with
questions. It was arrival on plan, course as planned, all the lines in agreement, corner symbol showing shift-change in progress.

It was A, it was Foucault. Nothing wrong with their position or their
course. No crew emergency. She caught a glance at Fletcher's display, which
had a schematic of Foucault System—including Olympus.

"We've got a live presence-buoy here," Parton said. Twofer had arrived,
and took his seat, number three console. Input from the buoy flashed on the
side of Jen's screen and she took it.

Live didn't mean everything was actually up-to-date functional, Jen
thought. Logical to have had a presence detector on the Thule-Olympus
approach. The buoy could be something as old as Olympus and still live, like
the lights at ravaged Thule. They were, however, taking nothing as safe.

"We're also getting noise from Olympus," Fletcher said. "Active output,
nothing so far that doesn't say bot."

"Zombie bots could still be sweeping the lanes if they wanted to be help-
ful," Twofer muttered. "They'd be too poor and too far for salvage, maybe
still going."

"Stream buoy might also be functioning," Fletcher said, "same condition.
Even some parts of station."

"Optics is working on the visuals," Parton said.

"Have a cup of coffee," Fletcher said. "Whatever. Fridge is stocked."
Meaning it was going to be awhile. Go easy.

Then Senior Captain's voice came over the horn:

"Prepare for V-*dump.* V-*dump. Two minutes."*

Fletcher frowned at the schematic, which seemed to show them on
course. Shook his head and shrugged.

"What we don't know . . . hang on."

JR strapped into his seat on the bridge. Shift change had happened in record time. Those two abrupt V-dumps had them all shaken, and another was coming up fast. Their bow wave had triggered a crazed feedback from the Ardaman limit . . . unlike anything they'd encountered elsewhere. Foucault . . . well, Foucault gave back. With interest. Third-shift had punted, but refinement, so Helm insisted, was necessary.

"Dump in one minute," Helm said, and Nav's lines flashed up on the screen, not in agreement.

"What the hell, 5!" Kate's voice snapped over com, unusually wrought, and as young Monahan stuttered something: "Fuck! You're *right!*" Kate's own line for the V-dump changed.

Unprecedented.

JR squelched his instinctive objection. Kate wouldn't have changed her input if Kate weren't certain.

Which didn't stop him from clenching the seat arms as the countdown to dump began.

"*Our heading is now confirmed,*" Senior Captain's voice said over the security office com. "*We'll be inertial for several hours at least.*"

"Well," Parton said, "that was fun. So . . . where were we before we were so rudely interrupted?"

Jen took a swig of sugar-laden coffee, not her favorite under any other circumstances, but any other option just turned her stomach. Weird. But at the moment, she'd consume whatever gave her caffeine and calories.

Fletcher's body stiffened, then Fletcher said to someone, "Yeah." And to them, half turning. "Optics has them."

Fletcher keyed and several of the screens showed a cluster of fuzzy stars that lost fuzz at every blink of revision.

Is that Olympus? Jen wondered. Is that it?

It jumped nearer. Re-resolved. That was structure. Those were lights. That was definitely Olympus Station.

"Well," Parton said, "*somebody* left the lights on."

"*Could* persist," Twofer muttered. "But you'd think not that many."

The image adjusted again, fuzzier but larger.

It didn't look right. Even to a novice. Maybe they were looking down on its axis.

Should be a ring with a top and bottom mast. Like every Hinder Stars station. It was weird and there was a flare of sunlight either distorting the view or . . .

Something very large was attached to it.

What in hell? Jen asked herself. And then it made sense what she was seeing, what she'd only seen in histories, and in vids. Not just a hard-to-track merchanter limpeted to Olympus mast.

Pusher.

That was a pusher-ship in dock.

Book V   Section v

JR stood next to John on the bridge, as the first optics came clearer and clearer. John had opted to stay after shift-change. Now Madison had come on com. Consultation. Madison was in his quarters.

"*Accounts for the EM all on its own.*" John's voice came through on exec-com. It was policy, when the captains consulted on the bridge, not to distract crew with com chatter. "*What are the chances we've found exactly what we came here looking for?*"

"Station's live," JR said. "Can't imagine that pusher's just dead and abandoned here." Another, clearer image replaced it. But not clear enough. "What pusher could that be? Mum, are you seeing this? *Could* it have been abandoned here with the station? Were there any assigned here not accounted for?"

"I'm seeing it," Mum said, likewise from her cabin, with a little sign of strain in her voice. Then a long breath. *"And no. No unaccounteds. That's a pusher, no question, looks like one of the later ones. Hard to tell from this angle."*

They were certainly looking at *something* pusher-sized. And properly attached to Olympus Station's A-mast.

"Didn't come from Pell," JR said, endeavoring not to jump to the obvious. "Emilio would have said. Cyteen could have built it, but that makes even less sense."

"Trying too hard, JR," John said. *"Beyond a doubt, direct from Sol."*

"Got to wonder how long that's *been going on,"* Madison said.

"Could still be left over from when we officially mothballed Olympus," John said.

"Hell of a spendy thing to just leave out here at shutdown," Madison said.

"Olympus was *a hell of a spendy thing to leave out here at shutdown,"* John said.

"That's no leftover," Mum said emphatically. *"Get a fix on Sol. Look for a trail; pushers leave them. And there's going to be an active Stream and a receiver to go with that pusher, seeing it got here. Might even be the original buoy. Coordinates should be in records. We don't want to wander into it, but dipping in with a probe for a read on it could be useful. Hearing what they say about us might be interesting."*

"Very," JR said. "Nav 1.1. Get the zenith buoy data from records and plot us buoy to Olympus Station, current date."

The acknowledgment came. Easy to figure where the Stream might be flowing, simply by where the buoy was relative to the station. Easy to rig a pickup. They hadn't done it at Alpha, since they'd intended a direct approach to the station, and didn't want to engender a fuss if Alpha wanted to call it spying. But here—

Here? Whatever was going on at Olympus was hell and away touchier. One was very interested to discover if there was any communication between that pusher and Sol, maybe even with another pusher on the same track.

"One way and another, in a couple of hours anybody live on that pusher or on the station is going to know we're here, but it will be twelve *years* for whoever's here to get word to Sol once that information hits the Stream. So we do have time."

"So," Mum said, *"what's the plan, James?"*

"Not a lot of choice. We can't sneak out of here. If they're not dead or asleep, they'll see us, absent or present. Besides, we have to wait for Min to get here. Can't desert him."

"Hell, no," Madison said, with a muted laugh. "*Left to his own devices, he'd shake it just to see what falls out, and Grandfather Jun took that Scotch issue personally, he did.*"

"I think fake Scotch is the least of what we're looking at here," JR said. "We promised Min we'd handle it. And if we *don't* want Min calling the shots on this situation, we pretty well have to."

"*Question is,*" Mum said, "*what constitutes handling it. Is this a new operation, or does it go way back? What are we looking at?*"

"*New or old, the damn EC is what we're looking at, is my take,*" John said. "*And if we ask for the officer in charge, they're going to refer us to some office on Earth.*"

"*Up to no good,*" Mum said. "*Tell you what I'd do . . .*"

She stopped short, and for once, JR wasn't certain where she was headed. "What would that be, Mum?"

"*I'd suggest we attach a nice little EMP disrupter to another probe and zap the Stream relay quietly. Let's just leave no records here.*"

"God," JR said. "Madison? John?"

He didn't know whether he felt supported or deserted in the delay in their responses. It was a major crime Mum suggested, and Mum wasn't the one who usually offered wild suggestions. She was serious.

And the ramifications—blowing the Stream was a, illegal; b, unprecedented, and c, an act Sol could use to label the Alliance and them specifically as lawbreakers of a particularly shocking nature. Not that that charge would carry all that much weight Cyteenside, not even at Venture, Mariner or Viking, where the EC was not in the least popular. Pell, which maintained its own Stream, would not take it too badly—but it would send a massive shiver through the Hinder Stars, where the Stream from Alpha was a sacred, sacred remnant.

Never mind the EC had committed an act of outright piracy against a merchanter at Alpha . . . horrific and illegal. But the Stream was the legendary thread that bound the Hinder Stars to humanity.

"John?"

"Hell, yes." Short. Succinct. But then John—their firebrand—was dead on his feet and burning a little less hot at the moment. "*I vote with Mum. Blow the damn thing and tell them listen up, we have news for them.*"

"Madison?"

"*Anything they send is twelve years out from being heard at Sol.*"

Madison's answer came slowly. *"And any pusher in transit's got its own Stream and is still connected to Sol, plus their star fix, so shutdown of the Stream would just make them lonely, not stop them. But shutting down communication as an opening gesture? After what happened at Alpha, I think we need all the favor with locals we can get—even if they're EC. Mind, I'm not taking EC sanity for granted. But whatever we do here, we're way past business as usual. If things go sour, if the locals aren't sane, we can take out of here and Stream our own message to Sol from Alpha, just a 6 year lag, beating any story they come up with. What disabling it* could *achieve is upset and delay at this end, and forcing them to think for themselves, which could prove useful. So I think Mum's right, but not yet. We send a little device out to the relay. If all goes smoothly, we just send our little gift into the sun when we leave and never mention it was out there. If we do run into a Cruz situation and decide there is a need to make the station focus real suddenly on local business and their choices, it's there. They can cry foul, but proving we're responsible is another matter: EMPs happen. And by the time they could get it fixed, let alone send a message to Sol, there's a good chance that all issues will be settled by whatever falls out—or doesn't—at Alpha."*

So . . . two yes to one go-slow and one hell-if-I-know.

"Delayed action I can accept," JR said. "We can send something out there. Just let it sit. It doesn't have to move fast, just get there, unless we decide to take it out. We can put *Little Bear* wise to its existence. Min won't argue."

"Here's another, related thought," Madison's voice said. *"While we're talking about the Stream—what if our two ghost ships have an EC contact at Alpha, who's been slipping encrypted reports into the Alpha Stream for years without being noticed? This place is at a real long time lag on the Stream from Sol. But if our ghost ships have been running courier between Olympus and Alpha, just to use the Alpha Stream, they could cut Olympus' reporting time in half. And get orders here faster."*

"Good point," JR said. "First chance, we have to give Alpha a heads-up. Abrezio could dig into all the transmission records from, what, a couple of hundred years? It would be a nightmare, but not our nightmare, thank God. And maybe *Galway* will make it all irrelevant."

"As for them noticing us," Madison said. *"I'd be surprised if they kept too close a watch on arrivals—but that wavefront will get to them in . . . 2 hours 16.3 minutes. Just saying."*

"We'll see," JR said. "That should draw some sign of life, if it exists." And to Optics: "Keep fining down the image, Patty. Good as you can get it. See if you can spot any EVAs. Lights are still burning, but they were still burning at Thule, and it was blown to hell."

"*I do want to see that enhanced image when it comes,*" John said, his voice gone thready. "*And their reaction when it comes.*" He clearly was needing to go lie flat, if not call for an assist.

"I'll keep you briefed," JR said. "Go, John. Now. I've got it. Good job, cuz."

"*Yeah,*" was all John managed beyond that. John left, steering a little amiss, the hype running out fast; but he didn't have too long a walk to reach a bed.

"*Need me to keep an antenna up?*" Mum asked. "*I'm able if I'm needed. Otherwise I'm going to get some rest.*"

"Hell, sleep," JR said. "First-shift will plot us a continually-modifying exit course and have it active in the system. You sleep, snack, and stay in reserve, Mum. We're going to do that with both you and John. Two of us to scope this out, two of us ready to get the hell out of here real fast. Which two of us depends on what hour. Go get a muffin. Go to bed."

"*Behave yourselves. Lie quiet and don't stir things up for Min's arrival. He'll be highly exercised when he gets a view of the station. Think how we're going to restrain him from kiting out of here hellbent for Cyteen. I'm dead serious.*"

"I know you are. We need a plan. We need it to be underway when he does arrive, and he'll have his own take on what his best move is. This is where there's Pellside—and there's Cyteenside. And Cyteenside doesn't care all that much what they threaten. Can we work with Min? Here's where we really find out."

Book V   Section vi

The two stars had settled at last. Ross still couldn't believe he'd had the nerve to key that vector shift, reflecting the tides of disruption he'd felt from the time he'd come up from trank, the difference being in the fluctuation. But his timing had been right. Kate had said so. Had *changed* her input to match his. Taken the ship in on *his* calc.

Or maybe felt it herself . . . once she saw his numbers.

Wasn't sure how he felt about that. He wanted to be good at his job.

Wasn't sure he wanted to be that . . . far out there when he operated. Tracking reality was hard enough for Nav without having to factor his drug-hyped gut sense into the equation. In his insulated disconnect from reality, trusting his board was display-only, he'd input something he'd have been terrified to do if it were live.

And Kate had been right.

But he'd been right-er.

God. *Had* he? They were in. Where they wanted to be. Precisely. He was still shaking, and very glad of the separation of individual seats when his first attempts to bring up revised data resulted in five typos . . .

Forcing his fingers under control, he got the proper input on the number two and three windows. They were inertial at the moment, all positional changes predictable and easily handled by the computer. He sorted through the data from their entry, seeking the source of what he'd *felt,* saw the dance of Foucault with Fizeau as he'd envisioned it to be, let that data of where they were and how they were moving settle into brain and bone.

Then Kate put up a clip for the whole team and it almost undid his hard work. Almost. He controlled the shakes and took it in. The Ardaman limits of the system as a whole were flat out crazy. The output of two cranky stars and the gravity wells of the three super-planets churned the interplanetary medium into knots. Fizeau's Ardaman had a resonance that reached *past* the barycenter, all the way to Foucault's. Wildly distorted, it fluxed in a rhythm he absolutely could not account for, but *damn* if it didn't explain his shakes. Possibly it was still ringing from their entry . . . or perhaps their last V-dump. Foucault, in *conjunction* with its companion star Fizeau, together as Groombridge 34, were fully as bad as the reports. Neither was flaring. That was good. But decidedly uneasy . . . and at odds with what he was feeling now—but not with what he'd felt several minutes ago.

Damn. That couldn't be right.

A message appeared on his screen from Kate: *Good call. Debrief with me after shift.*

God, he was going to have to explain himself.

He *really* wanted to get off-duty, get a dose of sugar, get something to settle his stomach and dim the stars' voices in his brain . . . But he couldn't. He *had* to stay here, and dammit, he *could* stay here, he *could* deal with the voices—

—but the peak of hype right now was hell.

On the massive central screen, the hazy image of Olympus Station began to re-resolve. Olympus Station with a massive lump on A-mast—what his eyes tried to reconstruct into a classic pusher-shape. Alpha FTLers didn't see pushers but a few times in their lives. He could remember the last, and there'd been another when he was very, very young, but he was never sure that he had really seen it. Fallan and Peg had said he had—but it was like that in his memory, a pic on a screen, a little shimmery. Up close, aboard station, you'd never see it at all, except as a shadow on the whole ring.

"Damn," Ty said on the Nav-team channel. "Do you see it?"

"It's not *Atlantis* and it's not *Santa Maria*," Ross said. "Us Galways know where *they* are."

"Not a Viking pusher," Ty said. "They're different. Robotic. Don't need a crew ring. This is one of the old ones. Big. God, that's big."

"Can't be. All converted now," Ross said, and felt foolish for having said that here, amid old *Gaia's* offspring.

"All but Polaris," Jim said, and that left a chill.

"Don't even suggest it," Ty said, as if *that* door needed closing. Fast. *Polaris* would have been the last pusher to convert, except she'd failed her next port and never braked. For all anyone knew she was *still* going, and would go forever, unalterable, three-quarters of light, and only chance brushes with gravity to affect her.

No, it wouldn't be *Polaris*. Couldn't be.

And then he wondered . . . why did they all keep fighting the *obvious* answer? This was a new pusher, relatively speaking. Earth origin. Source of those trees and model ships. Source of a hell of a lot of luxury goods that should have been paying the bills of half a dozen spacer Families—not just two.

The image refreshed. Again. And anger—all the festering resentment of the First Stars—focused on that creature.

The station and the massive shape of the pusher were top-view, at a thirty degree angle. Whatever cargo it had brought was not visible, being on the far side of the mast. There was a, relatively speaking, minuscule crew compartment, which would be in lockdown at dock, the edge of which was barely visible beyond the shields. Their view from this angle was nearly all engine.

And there was a little sparkle of what might be utility vehicles, moving every which way around engines, like those mechanical glow bugs in the Garden.

"That's a new pusher," he said, because no one else had. "Current. Got to be. What I know, if those utilities are messing around the engines, they're servicing, which means she's offloaded."

"All right," Kate said sharply. "Stop gawking and get us some options. One line for Thule, one for Venture, then one line for Pell on the high route. Remember to factor in that wacked-out Ardaman limit. We're gathering data on that as fast as we can—permanent feature or happenstance, we're not sure, but we'll take it into account."

Are we leaving? Ross wondered. By what Senior Captain had said, they couldn't move out before *Little Bear* arrived. And *Pell?* What . . . ?

The numbers appeared on his screen. A route he hadn't known existed. A completely untested route. Scary, given what they'd discovered here. He hoped to *God* they didn't have to take it.

But Nav 1.5 wasn't here to ask questions of Nav 1.1. Nav 1.5 kept his mouth shut and keyed up for Thule, on which he had best data, before tackling that scary route to Pell. Scary, yes. But he'd do it, and damn right he'd take that *wacked-out Ardaman limit* into consideration.

"*We're going to be sending out a probe to intercept the Stream*," Kate said some unknown time later. "*Engee wants a fix on the path of the local Stream. Zenith relay buoy: coordinates in records. Calc for post upcoming V-dump. Coordinates incoming.*"

Numbers appeared on his screen: Sol's current position in the galaxy and the target for the local Stream, an EM signal going between an orbiting station to a—relatively—stationary zenith buoy to a string of relay buoys all along the path to Sol. His job was to calc the track of that first leg of the signal, including the degree of uncertainty regarding the position of the zenith buoy. Easiest and quickest of Kate's assignments, but lowest in priority. They were sending a probe? He wondered if the intent was to tap the beam. A good notion, to his thinking, particularly where it came to tracking station's awareness of *Finity*, and their reaction to it.

Their insertion into the system might have gone unnoticed, lost against the output of the star—except for that presence-buoy. While it wouldn't tell the station who they were, or even precisely *what* they were, it would alert the station to the bow wave they'd created on entry . . . which only a fool would take for anything *but* an FTLer.

He began to work the options for optimal departure from the system. Thule first. Skate Foucault more carefully than they had Thule—hell *if* they wanted to run risks with that insane Ardaman limit. Use Foucault's gravity well to accelerate back to jump speed. They could do that. Even after the upcoming V-dump, they'd still be hours out from Olympus, and nothing starting from the station would ever catch them.

If that was the Senior Captain's decision.

Either way, by that time Olympus would have to figure they posed a problem.

Olympus would have a lot more to worry about when *Little Bear* showed up, two ships being beyond coincidence.

So were they waiting for *Little Bear?*

Were they leaving?

Even as he considered the variables, even as he sent the Thule data to Kate and his fingers began calling up that scary Pell data on a route he hadn't imagined, one small recess of his mind realized that, going as they were, they had to drop V to reorient, and they had a ship promised to meet them, that *might* already be inbound, in that same narrow safe corridor they'd encountered on entry.

Intersecting tracks was not something that ever had happened, space being wide and ships, even *Finity*, being very small.

Ships were small. Reentry shock waves were enough to rile a star. And one or both of this binary were already unstable as hell, after encountering *Finity's.*

And they had another sizable ship due to come in.

Their departure would stir up similar chaos . . .

All of which he needed to consider in plotting those departures. And then there were all the variables in this that had nothing to do with the double star and its intricately warped space, or incoming and outgoing ships—most having to do with whoever, or whatever AI, was manning that station.

Zero chance of the pusher doing anything to them. Pushers did nothing in a hurry, especially not from sitting at dock. But that one . . . and the station it was attached to . . . certainly wouldn't be happy with them being here, not considering the lengths they'd gone to to remain secret.

Had they found what they were looking for? No question they had, and it was trouble—trouble, with a new-built pusher, trouble to match Sol's power grab at Alpha. Trouble that sat a *lot* closer to Pell—a single, complicated jump string from Pell.

What he'd never have anticipated—and surely the captains scarcely had—was a pusher actually in dock. Was this station receiving pushers so often that their unscheduled visit had just happened to encounter one? Just how much *under the table* trade had those two ships been doing?

Damn them, if *Galway* had risked everything to give the EC a fair shot at the modern age, while the EC had been lying to everybody . . . sinking everything into this station . . . so that everything *Galway* had done, everything they'd risked . . . came to nothing . . .

Just . . . damn them!

He made an outrageous mistake. He missed a decimal. He was rattled, no question, and he corrected it, embarrassed and angry at once.

Kate's voice sounded in his ears, forgiving and rational. *"Are you all right, 5?"*

"Yes," he said, feeling his face flush hot. "Yes, Nav 1, sorry about that. I'm on it. Head's clear now. Just having a little trouble with that pusher."

"Useful thing, adrenaline," Kate said. *"That's why there are four of us. All right. We've done the hard stuff. Simple calc now. Give us position on the Stream. Light it up, team."*

Ross windowed the Pell data and called up the buoy, shoved the anger out of his mind and concentrated on the numbers, figuring the most probable position of the zenith buoy, and the constantly shifting vector of the beam linking it to the station . . .

. . . and went back to the Pell window.

"What are you doing, 5? Get on that buoy."

"Permission to test alt option for Pell."

A pause then: *"Granted."*

He began working feverishly, fingers trying to keep up with the figures running through his head. He finished, checked and checked again.

"That it?" Kate asked.

"I . . . yes."

"Thule first, 5?"

"Yes. That Ardaman will play hob going direct."

"I agree. You think she can still make that next leg in one?"

"It's long, but . . ."

"She can. Good job, 5. First to notice. —Now get on that buoy."

First to notice. Was that why she'd had them run the numbers so many times? Waiting for one of them to see that you could take the safer route to Thule out of Groombridge, *then* pick up the high line to Pell, no time lost?

As he ran the numbers a third time, just to be certain:

"Unit in prep," Engee said. And not all that long afterward, from Senior Captain:

"Prepare for V-dump."

So they were not going out again. They were digging in. Waiting for *Little Bear.* Nav talked to Helm and numbers flowed. Ross read them and the lines began to come into his head, like that, while the star whispered to them and the numbers reeled past.

Nav did its job. Lines matched.

Helm activated. Ross leaned his head back against the rest and waited for the universe to spit them halfway out and suck them back in an altered reference. It was a gut-dropping feeling, a moment of intense disorientation, while the star's whisper became a distracting rejection, an angry, fearsome scream.

It was Nav's job to get their bearings, as troubled Foucault snatched them *down* again. Distance from star established; reference points established. They had an accurate system map in the computer's gut now, and calculations were nearly instant, so far as that went.

First thing was to double check the calculated Stream vector with their actual position. He tweaked his calc accordingly and waited for Kate to call for it.

They were significantly closer to the station—only 1.59 hours light, now, and their velocity, relative to the station, was cut by half. They had no need to slow further. Still moving, but tiny, on the scale of the system. It was possible the flare of their bubble had been spotted . . . or would be 1.59 hours from now, if Station had a station's normal awareness of its solar system, but Olympus might or might not be devoting resources to incoming traffic. Possibly not even setting a robotic watch, if they believed their operation to be cloaked in absolute secrecy. Olympus and that ship *would* hear the presence-buoy's alert—eventually, everything arriving in its own packet of reality, but they might think it one of their own—granted other FTL ships came here.

And it was a distinct probability one or two did that.

In any case, whatever the situation, there was damn-all a station or a pusher or two aged merchanters could do to *Finity*.

The image on vid resolved again, at their new vantage. And looked more and more like the pushers from memory. Like, but not. Subtle differences. Changes made in a design centuries old, for a run twice as long as any the first pushers had ever made.

Cook's mates, kids, came around to deliver a coffee and roll-ups, one size fitting all, and actually pretty good. Consume it fast, two bites, no crumbs; and the cups went back to the kids, who traded them for a water-pack for the hours to come.

The fact that they were feeding them on the bridge, even modestly, was an indication that Senior Captain was feeling more and more confident that they weren't going to bolt out of here on any emergency basis. They hadn't gotten a look at B-mast yet, to have any idea what other resources Olympus might have. But they had a better angle now. Image kept resolving periodically, and Optics should have B-mast soon.

Captain wanted a contingency exit plotted from various points along their path, both back to Thule and the far scarier direct-to-Pell route. Both would get them to Pell via the high route, but with their current vector, a return to Thule would be complicated, requiring an almost 180 degree turnaround, while a shift to the direct-to-Pell route would be minimal. All that was a computer problem, once they set up the initial reckoning. Ross finished his calc, gratified to see both in line with Kate and Bucklin, Ty and Jim. And took the chance to glance at the big forward screen, sensing a stir of some interest at the last image revision.

B-mast *was* slightly visible now, and, when one took into account the difference in size between Olympus and Alpha, those masts were huge. Twice the length of Alpha's.

"Shit," Kate said "Just how many ships are they planning on docking here? Suppose that's original? Or a refurbish modification?"

"Good question," Bucklin said. "And . . . speaking of . . . what have we here?"

Another refinement of image showed something docked in the absolute shadow of the station—black of space itself alternate with the red glare of Foucault on a once-white metalline skin. The shape that the imagination could construct of it didn't make immediate sense, relative to a station structure.

Another structure, maybe, that, like the pusher, didn't belong to Station. Part of the skin was stained with organics and other substances, evidence of time and travel. The other, unexposed, was pristine white, or what passed for it in Foucault's reddish light.

Senior Captain hadn't commented, but he was looking at it. He might be speaking on another channel. Ross stared at the large screen, trying to resolve the imperfect image.

If there was some sort of operation at Olympus Station, it could be temporary, concentrating on refueling and resupplying the pusher, something operated by pusher crew.

The image resolved again.

And suddenly made sense, a gridwork, a flat, canted surface, patches of absolute light and absolute shadow and jumbled angles.

It was the retracted top vane assembly of a smallish FTLer . . . in dock on B-mast.

"Well," JR said, over the private executive com in his ear, speaking only to Madison, who stood beside him on the bridge, and to Mum, who was still in quarters. Whether John was receiving or not was a question, but the bridge and the lounge were definitely receiving. "The pusher actually in dock is a major surprise. Could be massive coincidence, or they've got more than one supplying the station and they're a little less rare. But we may also just have found one of our missing merchanters in the mast shadow. Which answers some questions and suggests others. Scale is a problem here. Can we get that matched with a schematic of either of our ghosts?"

"At least we know now it's an EC operation," Madison's voice said, barely audible realtime in one ear, clear echo from his earpiece in the other. "There's no way a couple of Hinder Stars ships are all that's at issue here."

"*As if there was any question,*" Mum said. "*Considering what they were up to at Alpha, I think we can safely assume* Rights *was meant to come here—if* Rights *could move. Those monster masts are not that long on the old schematic, and the old masts were handling pushers.*"

"*Galway* may be dealing with Sol even as we speak," JR said somberly, "but Sol won't be telling them all the truth, now, will they? No more than *Galway* will want to explain everything to the EC. But Niall Monahan's no fool. He'll play it cautiously."

"*Whatever's going on here,*" Mum said, "*a pusher isn't exactly state of the art.*"

"Which is not to say Earth tech has sat still all these years," Madison said. "Plenty of activity around the pusher, some of which does *not* look like offloading."

"*Could be mining the pusher,*" Mum said. "*Stripping her down for materials. Can't conceive of what they could send back from here, worth her effort, that wouldn't have shown on Pell's reports, and her parts might be being used in the refurb of the station. They might even be planning to convert her.*"

"She wouldn't be competitive as a convert," Madison said.

"*Competitive, hell,*" Mum said. "*These are the people that damn near starved Alpha building* Rights, *when they could have sent this pusher there instead and kept Alpha fed and supplied and loyal. What a convert can haul is people. Maybe not as fast as* Rights, *if that egoboo doorstop were operational, but still, lots of people with lots of guns. More I think about this whole thing, the less appetizing it gets."*

"They *could* convert it," JR said. The possibility made a painful and scary lot of sense. "Established, proven, somewhat resource-hungry tech that could manage the Thule route to Venture, and from there to Pell . . . if they didn't care about profit. This is closer to Pell than Alpha. And if they take control of Venture, they can cut Alpha, Glory, and Bryant's off from Pell, forcing them back into EC control. You want food, Alpha? Get on your knees and beg. *Damn* them."

"Reconstructing Sol's empire," Madison said. "Maybe we're surmising too much, but the connection makes a zigzag sort of sense."

"Makes sense if you're the EC," John said muzzily, via com. *"Excuse me. I've taken a pill. But I'm following you. It's a hell of a construction. But it makes sense, in a way* Rights *alone never did. Risking* Rights *on a one-shot jump to Sol never made sense. People-moving does. Challenging us as a Pellside power—does.* Rights *didn't need to run for Sol. Damn right Cruz knew about this venture. They wanted to get* here. *When the chance of that happening fizzled, and* Galway *became his chance at glory, he deserted* Rights *and went for* Galway *without a second thought."*

"Maybe they wanted us watching the *Rights* build at Alpha," Madison said, "so we wouldn't look here. Who ever cared about *Come Lately* or *Miriam B* until we wanted to find them? Who'd ever come here looking, until the Monahans raised a question on Alpha trade? Everybody at Pell and beyond just assumed what arrived from Sol came through Alpha. Nobody asked."

"They're not going to like us here," Mum said. *"They're going to be as inflexible as the EC always is when it has to make decisions and it takes them ten, twenty years to consult."*

"We're here," JR said. "Their cover is blown, they may be fully aware they have a problem at Alpha, and that FTL to Sol may be possible and on its way. Given that FTLer is either *Come Lately* or *Miriam B,* there is a strong chance they know. And they know it'll take them twenty years to consult, via the Stream. Intractable isn't the only possibility. Maybe they'll listen to common sense."

"You're still considering talking to them," John said.

"I'm not set on any course, yet," JR said. "We have to wait for Min. We can't leave this, unexplained, in his lap. Min's thinking is from Cyteen's perspective: it's important to us to influence that. And Olympus is going to know we're here. We could leave them and Min to worry about it together, but that's not friendly to Cyteen, or Min, and we don't want to give Olympus that much time to form a plan, where right now I doubt they really have one that covers more than a junker operation straying over from Thule."

"If any has," Mum said, *"they've never been heard from again. And station is sure as hell not going to mistake us for a Hinder Stars FTLer, not considering the splash we made coming in."*

"Hostile action is definitely a possibility," JR said. "But *Finity* can evade or withstand anything they throw at her, at least long enough for us to accelerate out of here. And there's a whimsical off chance they *might* mistake us for *Rights*."

Madison gave him a disquieted look. There was a moment of silence from Mum and John.

"Bottom line, we can't leave Min here unsupported," JR said. "We did give our word."

"Station is able to signal us, likely able to send someone out to us," Madison said, *"if the mood takes them. But a second ship arriving in system is really going to spook them."*

"Likely," JR said.

"You have a plan?" Mum asked.

"I'm inclined to hold at this V for a time. It gives us maneuverability. I'd like to know what Station's saying to Sol right now, but Sol won't hear it for another twelve years, so we do have time to think about it. We'll have our bug in position, and it's likely they'll be telling Sol when Min arrives, which may be even more interesting." JR looked at the chrono—elapsed time from entry, standard time, ship's time, and Venture time, as the regional station most recently active. There was an entirely mundane consideration, that of whether they were going to go off Emergency status and down two steps to Caution, which would let some fairly useful housekeeping get done. "Com. Put us over to Channel B."

"Aye, sir. Channel B," Com 1.1 said, and JR spoke, hearing his own voice over the speakers. *"Cousins and friends, this is Senior Captain. We'll go to a Caution at this point. Olympus will be noticing us soon. We'll do one more V-dump in the next watch just because we need to, which will also make them a little less certain where we are. So up and about with due caution, restock as a priority, and, junior-juniors—"* Under a Caution, junior-juniors were still restricted to quarters. *"I know you've been under lockdown a long time, but just bear with us a little longer and I'll be remembering that when we get back to Pell. There will be a glorious pass to as*

many game-hours as you can possibly imagine. Your minders will be look-ing in on you and taking orders for food. Everybody else, hop to whatever it is. Com, back to channel A."

"So," Madison said, "*are* you going to talk to them?"

"I'll put some thought into it. Anybody with any observations is welcome. I'm going to be thinking on it. I'm *not* going to pretend we're *Rights*. I don't think that's a good idea, politically, and there are bound to be recognition codes. But I am wondering who they think we are." He pushed a slider on the shoulder mic. "Com, all com."

"*Aye, sir.*"

"If they hail us as *Rights of Man,* don't contradict them. Just pass me the contact."

"*Aye, sir, understood.*"

Book V   Section viii

In a Caution, it was just a case of waiting. Notes passed from station to sta-tion, speculation on Olympus and the pusher, *and* the FTLer on B-mast. JR had his own seat, and stayed there, communicating with various depart-ment heads via coms, particularly with medical, which was a continuing concern . . . another reason to delay here a few days, whether or not it made Olympus happy. The pusher was not a threat. *Finity* was still moving rapidly toward the ecliptic and toward Olympus, which used Foucault's largest rocky planet as an anchor.

It was a case of waiting—waiting for the station to take some action. Sta-tion, not expecting any ship, might not notice the presence-bot signal. But one would think it would still have a bot tending to business, a bot to notify humans long before this that they had a problem hurtling toward them.

Hard to imagine routine life on a station so desolate. Possibly nobody was paying attention at all. Granted communication with Alpha or anywhere else was measured in visits from ships like that FTLer and ships from Sol like that pusher, the station-keepers might themselves be bots. Possibly no-tifying ships at dock of an intruder was at the bottom of the list of actions to take.

But someone, be it the pusher, or Olympus management, would wake up and do something. Eventually. The activity of utility craft servicing the pusher argued it was not all bots.

More than ninety minutes passed. Then:

"*We have signal,*" Com said. "*We have voice.*"

"Put it on," JR said. It was the standard policy. The bridge had no secrets. The executive quarters had none, when it came to events immediately affecting ship status. It was the spookiest communication *Finity* had ever gotten, but all of them aboard had access if they were minded to use it.

"*Visitor,*" Olympus said. "*Please state your identity and your clearance.*"

Well, well, JR thought, at least they weren't assuming *Finity* was her lookalike on first guess. And clearance? Apparently there was to be an exchange of code words which they obviously didn't have. One wondered what Olympus actually expected in answer, which might depend on which FTLer was at dock—Min had reported the arrival of *Miriam B* at Alpha . . . who would have informed Olympus there was trouble, and that the name of that trouble was, indeed, *Finity's End* and her allies.

"We will not respond, Com," JR said.

Which set them for another lengthy wait—while the station waited for an answer, didn't get one, and decided how to respond.

Meanwhile station optics would be searching a vast lot of space to get a clear image. They'd made electromagnetic noise coming in. They'd disturbed the star, and the presence-buoy. The station's bots would have started looking, and checking the possibility it was the star's spontaneous action . . . assuming the station's faculties were all in operation. But knowing they had a ship incoming and getting a clear view of it were two different things.

Periodically, the station repeated its requests. It might be a robot: it had an identical inflection. *Something* was surely going on.

"Everybody," JR said, on channel B, "prepare for final V-dump."

"*Aye,*" the acknowledgment from bridge stations came in, followed by, in the following minutes, the acknowledgments from general security, on whose boards lights would have gone to green. "*We are go for the probe,*" Engineering reported. "*Area is clear and secure. We need coordination with Nav.*"

That took a moment, as Nav double-checked.

"We will eject the probe on Engineer's command," JR said. "Ready yet, Katrin?"

"*Ready,*" Engineering said. "*Affirmative.*"

"*Helm stands ready,*" Helm said.

"*Launch,*" Engineering said. There was a distant, dim thump, carried through the frame. "Clear."

JR took his seat, belted in. "Helm, Engineering, go for dump."

That was one more adjustment to their position. And now they were at a lazy rate of progress, comparatively, while station had one more ghostly energy bubble and evidently the problem of relocating them, since they had ceased transmitting.

Station had to be getting the idea, by now, that their inbound problem—which could, for all station knew, be headed out of Groombridge system again to report to Venture at this point—had noticed the outlandishly large object on A-mast.

Were the authorities in charge of Olympus nervous now? Unquestionably. *"Captain."* Optics 1.

An image arrived on JR's console screen. Another pale glint of reflective surface was showing beyond the station-shadow on B-mast.

That was undeniably a second ship at dock down there.

Come Lately? Had they found *both* of their missing and complicit merchanters?

JR stood up and turned to get the benefit of the larger image. Third- and Fourth-seat crew were seeing it, and a few senior crew cast glances up, and stared longer than usual.

The image refined again.

Call from Madison, elsewhere.

"Have we got them both?" Madison asked.

"Looks like it. If both our elusive merchanters are here, they know what's happened at Alpha and so does Olympus. They've hailed us as an unknown. We can't trick them. So I'm minded to give them our ID and just wait-see."

"Your problem, Senior Captain," Madison said. *"I'll play it wherever you set it down."*

At times there was leisure for a policy discussion. Finding an operation at Olympus had been such a discussion. Finding one of their missing ships at dock had been a contingency of that discussion. Finding a pusher parked on A-mast hadn't been: a glaring oversight, it seemed now, but a pusher hardly posed a threat of action, only more questions to be answered.

Letting Olympus think they could dictate terms, that, no. But letting

Olympus react in panic, also no. It was not time to make friendly overtures, but not time to scare hell out of them either.

"Com," JR said to the bridge, "give them an ordinary hail, no request for approach."

"*Aye,*" Com 1.1 said. "*Ordinary hail, no approach.*"

And that would run, in Len's crisp tones: "*Merchanter* Finity's End *in arrival. Salutations, Olympus Station.*"

That would give station a quicker fix on *Finity's* position and course, which might calm their nerves.

And then they would see whether station wanted to play the same no-information game and delay a response from their end.

That was all right. *Finity* could sit out here indefinitely, or more to the point, sit waiting for *Little Bear* to show up and give station more to worry about.

The call went out.

JR unbelted, got up, crossed the bridge and looked out over First-shift, contemplating not just the ones visible but a whole shipful of Family, from tiniest, newest infant up to Mum, who'd had just about all the stress and strain she could bear over the last couple of years. He *wanted* to get them back to safe territory. He wanted not to have to make a hurried run for it, and he didn't see, from present position, any likelihood of having to do that, at least. *Finity* could out-run or fend off anything physical a station could throw at her. Even powered warheads couldn't approach them unseen, and as long as her vanes were deployed, *Finity* could pull a protective relocation all on her own—if she didn't care about close objects.

No. They were in fact safe at this remove.

"Shipwide, Com, if you please."

"Aye," Len said, and the system beeped.

"*All right, cousins and guests,*" he said, hearing his own voice echolike from overhead, "*we have slowed and hailed station. Station knows who we are and they'll have to think about it. We will not be seeking to dock here yet, if at all, and we do not intend to come within spitting range of station at this point. We have possibly found both of our missing merchanters at dock here, but if Olympus is like Alpha was, EC rules apply and no one's aboard either of them to be able to talk to us. We're just going to need time for the situation to resolve.*

"*Meanwhile, apologies for the lengthy hold in quarters. Permission to move about under Caution. No further ship move is planned at this time. But since we do not credit local EC management with immaculate judgment, do not treat this as a holiday on dockside.*

"We are now waiting for Little Bear, *who will help us make clear our position as we suggest Olympus open formal talks with Pell and Venture, and cease any operations which might disturb the peace. In the meantime, we'll gather as much information as possible. The likely presence of our two missing merchanters and what we know of their prior travels indicates they know what went on at Alpha and they know Galway is on its way to Sol from Alpha, which will have some profound impact on them, and on that pusher crew. So they have a lot to think about and some decisions to make. Station has hailed us. We have now hailed them back. This is likely to go on at intervals while we feel each other out. Take this chance to secure your premises and restock for jump if you missed the chance before. Second-shift will come on at shiptime oh-three-hundred, which will put us back on normal shift rotation. Third-shift, Fourth-shift, kick back and relax. We're going to hold this path for a while and we're in no hurry."*

They were at slightly over 20 minutes lag, now, well outward of *Little Bear's* projected arrival, whenever *Little Bear* did put in an appearance. They would be communicating with the station, in fact, on a shorter lag than *Little Bear* would have with *Finity* when they came in. Which was fine.

A message from station did arrive.

"This is an EC restricted area. Merchanter Finity's End, *please state your business."*

JR tossed an empty cup into the sealed bin. "No response."

Forty-eight minutes on, as JR studied the system input, the likely location of mining activity:

"Repeat: this is an EC restricted area. You are in violation of EC regulations, merchanter Finity's End. *State your business."*

JR flipped to channel A. "Give me contact, Com 1. Scan, both levels, stay extremely alert."

"Aye," response came back from all three first seats.

"Olympus Station," he said, "this is JR Neihart, Senior Captain, *Finity's End*, Pell registry, out of Pell and Venture. We are conducting a station-requested inspection of unusual activity in this area. We note the presence of a pusher craft which may be engaged in transport of unexamined bio-stuffs, based on evidence at Pell. We ask proof of your identity and your right to operate at an EC property and to mine or alter scrap in this area."

There was no anticipation of an immediate reply. There would be lag, and there would very likely be a meeting of authorities involved. A ship at residual V from system entry and a station with only what the star gave it were not equal threats. A ball bearing launched from a higher V was a problem. And they could achieve that. Fast. A station couldn't. Even the pusher couldn't.

There were mining craft that could pose a threat with an old-fashioned rail-gun, but *Finity* also had one, all ships did, and station really, truly didn't want to pick that fight. JR bet on it. As for the two FTLers at dock, they would take time to undock and gain velocity, by which time, *Finity* could be long gone.

There was silence from Olympus, well past the reply lag. Silence continued as Second-shift began to move in, and Madison came onto the bridge.

"Anything interesting?" Madison asked.

"It's all yours," JR said. "Scan's on them non-stop, and all around; but no action."

"Want me to talk to them?"

"Only if the mood takes you," JR said, "or the situation arises. We're just moment-to-moment on what happens here. We are drifting into a better view of B-mast. If you can get a firm ID on the two ships, that would be a good thing to have on record."

"Wonder if *they've* been informed."

An enhanced image replaced the last one.

"Station's looking well-kept," Madison observed. "Extremely. No scrapping here."

"We've counted thirty utilities around that pusher. Probably everything station has. Quite a respectable number of utilities."

"Sol to Olympus. Twice the distance to Alpha. The pusher's come a long, long haul, even if they have upgraded systems."

"Different mindsets aboard, station and ship," JR said. "Granted there's crew. No way of anticipating how EC they are. EC knows what happened to pusher crews before. Might have taken steps to make it not happen. They might not have any of the ship loyalty we're used to."

"Shipfolk may be in charge of Olympus. Or may have brought those who will be, now."

"They certainly won't be *our* culture, likely not any stations we know, and damned sure not like any Hinder Stars merchanter crew. Cruz and Hewitt mentality. Earth-born. Or close to it."

"Nor inclined to listen to the merchanters," Madison said, "if the EC at Alpha is any predictor."

"They'll have their orders, ultimately from people in a gravity well. Chances are, the officers all grew up in a gravity well, with blue sky and ground that bends the wrong way."

"Wonder what else that pusher brought," Madison said.

"Foodstuffs. Metals. Machinery. *Trees.* God knows."

"There was a big to-do once," Madison said, "about patching up the Pell situation by running a pusher direct from Sol to Pell. This one could have done it—and *wouldn't* the universe be different for it? Damn, that thing's surreal, sitting there. Those engines are huge. Bigger than pusher images I've seen."

"If Pell was going to have a pusher going direct, Venture wanted one, and Sol wanted to preserve the Great Circle Trade as was, back when it was a proposal. Pell didn't want it, Venture didn't want Pell getting it, and then when Pell persuaded old *Mercury* to push a new core to Mariner, *Cyteen* happened, way out of the EC's control, and *that* fried it. El Dorado blew, and Galileo blew, and thanks to FTL, Olympus and Thule shut down over the EC's objections. So here's a pusher pumping life into Olympus, anyway, just saving the old Circle Trade, do we remotely think?"

"Hell no. I'm thinking they could have saved Alpha a lot of misery if they'd just put this baby on the Alpha route."

"That they could have done," JR said. "That they definitely could have. And if they wanted to trade, they could have set up here and sent Pell a 'hello, let's deal!' but they haven't, have they?"

"Just sent out a couple of merchanters," Madison said, "just two merchanters being secretive and dodging in and out of the Hinder Stars, still running, gathering news. They're *not* crazy. Port authorities aren't after them. Nobody's coerced them to do a damn thing, and they're clearly dodging customs, but on such a small scale no station from Alpha to Pell has ever really cared. Meanwhile Alpha and Pell weren't comparing notes on their biggest payout. It took the Monahans to figure it. Credit to them for *that*."

"Credit indeed. Meantime, that sometime trade of luxury goods at Pell was feeding the myth that Sol was still sending out basics as well as luxe goods to Alpha and reinforcing the belief that Alpha was crying wolf to get better deals from Pell. All the while gathering information for their EC handlers in *this* little nest of mischief. Maybe sending the EC their reports *through* Alpha whenever they docked. One suspects that messenger-service in itself brought one of our ghosts some fancy trade goods."

"Wouldn't you like to get a look inside those two ships? See how they compare to the struggling Family ships back on Alpha? Bet they have the best stocked galleys on both sides of Pell."

"Scotch as a regular go-to. I wouldn't like to be in their shoes once word gets around on Alpha Strip."

"One has to wonder when that was scheduled to happen," Madison said. "This place looks fully operational . . . unlike *Rights of Man*. Wonder what would have happened if her shakedown cruise had been successful? All those shiny Enforcer recruits from Alpha would have found themselves relocated to a new home here, right on Pell's doorstep. And one big head-ache for the rest of us."

It was only what they'd speculated.

But considering their own arrival . . . and the behavior of Foucault, JR drew in a long breath, thinking of the problems Olympus posed for an FTLer. "They might have hoped they had a FTL port with no problem going to or from Thule, and from Thule to Venture. But that's Earth for you. It's not that easy. *Finity* caused quite a bump here. Our exit will do the same."

"Little ship might have a much easier entry."

"Might," JR said. "You know, if *Rights* had gotten here on her first run, it might have solved our problem. Nasty as the thought is."

"Gah. This is an ugly place to go. Why in hell can't the E damn C just be satisfied with a big fat profit from shit their pocket books won't even notice?"

"Well, Olympus can't have gotten all good news from our two spooks. They'll have told Olympus everything that Alpha knows, that *Rights* is no longer in the plan, but *Galway* is. But it doesn't entirely solve our problem. If Alpha becomes Sol's FTL port, all aboveboard and nice, Olympus, as a base close to Pell, but navigationally inadvisable from Venture straight to here, is as fortified as a castle, and all but useless for anything *but* Enforcers. The EC doesn't need *Rights*, just one port that draws from Sol System and a lot of smaller ships dedicated to moving people in and out of here—a lot of people with troublesome intentions and professionally faked ID ending up at Venture and Pell. Not a flood but a slow leak. You still end up swimming."

"It would really be a good thing if Min could somehow make contact with *Mumtaz* or *Nomad* before he comes. I'd really like to know what they know right now."

Operating, as those two had been, in the vicinity of Glory and Alpha and Bryant's, with the constantly imminent chance, now, of word about *Galway*'s fate. God. JR closed his eyes and breathed deeply. In some ways, it felt as if *Galway* had just left. In others . . . it seemed a lifetime ago.

"What Olympus doesn't know," Madison said, "what *we* don't know—both major. Are we *going* to talk to Olympus and try to level out that infor-mational gradient?"

"Right now I'm thinking the more questions they ask us, the more we learn about them. I'm brain-tired at the moment, not fit for give and take with them. I'd really like to know whether they have any aggressive capabil-ity, or not."

Madison frowned. "That is a question. I'd like to know *when* resurrection of this station began: before or after the *Finity* plans were stolen. Our two ghost ships' visits to Pell began after, but that doesn't mean this station wasn't already up and running again. The theft of those plans, and the *Rights* project starting, both made a pretty splashy news story for a while. The problems caused by the build remain a huge issue in the Hinder Stars. But overall, the *Rights* project has been a loud declaration of their own ineptitude, rather than a threat to us. One wonders . . . did the EC engees back on Earth anticipate the problems? Were they *counting* on those problems to draw attention away from what was going on here, which is, potentially, a much bigger threat? There must be some urgent and interesting discussions going on in the station offices, now they know that their cover is blown. Probably also trying to figure what to do about Alpha without instructions from Sol. I'd sure like to talk to those two ships, find out, among other things, how long they've been in dock."

"Wish we *could* reach them. We could try. But I very much doubt they've got anybody aboard, if Alpha's docking rules apply here. And any attempt to reach them would be noticed by station."

"I'm going to follow your lead," Madison said, "keep communication to a minimum with the station and stall, stall, stall. Observe, gather data, refine the optics, and just let them simmer til Min shows. Three things we know *they* know: who we are, that we're associated with Pell, and that there's a massive upheaval at Alpha."

"Four:" JR said, "they know that somehow, one way and another, their ghost ships led us here. That can't be sitting well. Who's participating in those discussions and with what authority might be interesting to know. However, at this point, it's all yours, brother. I'm no good if I don't get some rest. But waking or sleeping, I do want to know if we get a constructive communication out of them."

Book V   Section x

There was food, served in wrapped packets, but hot, of which Ross was glad, and the mess was packed, sensible people taking any opportunity to rest, eat, gather, and exchange guesses.

Jen was there, seated at table with a foot atop the opposite seat. She pulled her foot off as he approached, and glared off one attempt to appropriate it before he could settle in.

"Any news?" he asked, as he popped the lid stopper on his coffee.

"Was about to ask you," Jen said. "But I think we're just parking here and waiting for *Little Bear*. We don't have to go anywhere. We know why we're here. We know the situation at Alpha and the status of the Alliance and what we're capable of. Station knows squat. Station's the one with reason to be nervous."

"So long as they don't get too nervous. I'd *really* like to sleep the clock around. I don't know about you. This is the tightest set of jumps I've ever run, and I'm feeling it."

"Everybody is. And not to compare, especially as you, being First-shift Nav, have a special pressure, but mind, we strung jumps and skated jumps on the way to Alpha. Not like this last run, but still . . . Only so many pills you can take. The body just can't."

"I hate to tell you, we're prepping to go again."

"He won't," Jen said, meaning, Ross took it, the Senior Captain.

"No reason to. We're out of range of anything dangerous," Ross said. "Nothing station can really do about us."

"Unlikely they'd try. And we're into the Stream, now, picking up chatter, nothing significant, either direction. So if they're telling Sol everything about us—we'll know what they know. Hella long time before Sol does."

"I kind of hope," Ross said, "*hope* Sol is saying something like, *We just had an Alpha ship come calling. They're giving us FTL and all that. And we're bloody grateful to the Monahans, aren't we?* But if *Galway* is there, we won't know it for another twelve years sittin' here, will we, and meanwhile we have to use common sense and assume the EC's been asses about it all and intend to be going on that way for all time, damn 'em. Seeing all this, I'm no longer believing it's just at Alpha they're up to no good. Dammit . . . if we lose *Galway* for no damn reason . . ."

Jen leaned over and reached her hand, palm up. Ross, after a moment's hesitation, put his in it and squeezed.

"We did what we had to do, didn't we?" Jen said. "We all did. We were in a hard place. If *Galway* hadn't agreed to go, Alpha wouldn't feel half so obligated to you; and once Alpha transmitted the route to Sol, we were all in the game. Sol is going to get the route to reach us, and all we could control was when, and who got the glory. It was *well* done. It was the best thing to do."

He flashed on that final view of *Galway*'s bridge, where Monahan fists were trying to hold off EC guns, a view he'd had to leave behind as Fallan shoved him out the emergency lock to warn Alpha. Those EC pirates had commandeered *Galway*, had held Fallan, and Niall, and half of *Galway*'s

First-shift at gunpoint, to serve an EC crew that couldn't get *Rights* out of her own berth.

Jen's hand tightened. "I'm betting *Galway* got rid of the EC at the first jump. I'm betting your Fallan calc'ed it so those stationbred bastards were puking their guts out on the other side. I'm betting your cousins took them down with *no* trouble, and *Galway's* at Sol right now, safe and sound and making the deal of a lifetime. I'm betting what Sol sends back is going to be officials and scientists, cuz your Captain Niall damn sure won't let any *Enforcers* on his ship, not after Cruz did what he did. And your cousins are going to bend their ears with the facts of life all the way back, *while* Fallan scares hell out of them and makes them respect us spacer-types. They'll make it back. I believe it."

There were moments even before Pell when Ross didn't believe it. There were dark moments when he knew what a thin hope it was—that even Fallan's skill could steer them through untried jump-points. Fallan had said—if they couldn't overpower the hijackers—he'd wreck them. That was the other promise. A never-ending jump or a ball of plasma, the one a forever ride, the other at least quick, for ship and crew.

Most times he tried not to think about it. Seeing what sat at Olympus, the threat it posed, just brought it all back.

"If they're already *here*," he said, "what's the point, then? What's the point of anything we did? That any of us did? How can *Galway* cut any kind of deal—when *Galway* doesn't know that Sol's already here, within a couple of jumps of Pell, with two tame Families to do their bidding, and them feeling smug about it?"

Jen's grip tightened down on his hand. Hard.

"Sorry," he said. "Sorry. I try not to think in that direction. Gets the better of me sometimes."

"They're using *pushers*," Jen said. "It's not saying they've got any other way. It's not saying what *Galway's* doing doesn't matter. It does. The FTL route still has to come through Alpha. Through the Hinder Stars. The First Stars. This at Olympus is something new. This *maybe* is what *Rights of Man* was actually *for*, that's one guess Security is making now, and *we* know *Rights* isn't going to do what the EC wants. Being bigger doesn't make it safer coming into Olympus, it makes it worse. So we're still ahead of the EC. They're not going to like it, but we're still ahead, and damned *right* what *Galway's* doing at Sol matters!"

It was basic sense. Everything Jen was saying made sense. If there was another FTL route to Sol, that pusher wouldn't be sitting out there. That part made absolute sense. They might have FTL, they might have built

FTLers, but they didn't have crews to run them. And nobody had a safe route to Sol at least, because Sol System was complicated and hedged about with all sorts of unmapped mass. A nightmare entry, Fallan had anticipated, even with all his experience. Jen's hand clenched so urgently on his was an anchor to common sense, when he was slightly strung out, and tired, and negatives seemed to pile up.

"Yeah," he said. "Yeah."

But what the hell were they going to do now, at this end of things, not knowing the fate of *Galway?*

So they'd caught the EC operating in the dark, so it was a reasonable guess that what was happening here was connected to what had been happening at Alpha for decades, and maybe happening anywhere else there was an EC office, even including Pell, but—

"Seems to me," he said, "that we may be looking at an operation here that could go way, way back."

"That's Fletcher's current favorite theory," Jen said. "We're inertial right now, just improving our line of sight. We're not talking . . ." Two Neiharts changed seats and settled at their table in the other pair of seats, not saying a word. But it wasn't Alpha, wasn't a bar on the Strip, where information was secret.

"Both our mystery ships," one of the new arrivals said in conclusion to something. And, "Ohana," the woman said, offering a dainty and dusky hand. "Cargo. Haven't met you, yet."

"Ross." He released Jen's hand, took the offered one, and the other from a grey-haired woman who identified herself as Sarah James, Maintenance.

"Pleased to meet you," Sarah James said. "Pleased at you sticking with us, Ross Monahan. Whole team was saying. You folk could have been sitting with your feet up at Venture."

"Wanted to see it through," he said. "Thanks."

"So we were saying," Jen went on, "just what we can observe right now. But it's shadows on the mast from the angle we're at. We think we're seeing two ships. Maybe our spooks. Last I heard, we aren't talking, they aren't talking, nobody's talking. And that's apt to go on."

"Do they know about Alpha, do we think?" Ohana asked.

"We think they do," Jen said. "Those ships likely gave them the whole story. And are no friends of ours at the moment."

"Pusher looks to have offloaded," Ohana said. "The utilities are still running back and forth. Lots of activity. Repair, do we think?"

"Nothing definitive yet," Jen said. "Until *Little Bear* shows up, or they do something, we're just going to be sitting and watching and listening. They've got to know they're deep in the soup already. All we have to do is leave with what we know. And if anything happened to us, in remotest imagination, whoever we talked to before we came is going to know something happened and come looking. Either way, they've got to accept that their cover is blown. If we leave without talking, they're really going to have to worry about what's going to come back. *Come Lately* and *Miriam B* have got to be sweating bullets, if that's them."

"If we've got another Cruz and another Hewitt," Ross said—those being the troublesome EC officers at Alpha. "If those types are in charge, it's not going to be sense we get from them. And what nobody's saying . . . a pusher could bring in a lot of people. A whole lot of people."

"Limited by the need to feed them for a few decades or so," Ohana said. "There is that."

"Decades station-time," Sarah James said, "and everything they know out of phase."

"One pusher-load can supply four Alpha-sized stations for ten years," Ross said, "until the next pusher comes in. That's how it used to be. There is the question here—what *is* it bringing, and how often is that? Did we just get lucky, to find this one at dock? I've served Alpha all my life, and I've seen a pusher twice—and that by design. Alpha *has* only two of them in service, and *Galway* makes a point to intercept."

"That *is* a point," Jen said. "What *are* the odds of it, do you think?"

"Higher if this isn't the only pusher to serve this place," Ross said. "Sol's got endless resources. They could launch one a year, for what we know. There could be an incoming chain of them out there."

Jen looked at him with a frown on her face.

"They could," Ross said. "Sol's that rich. That's a *huge* system, rich, and cluttered with all sorts of stuff far as a light year out. It's why they've had hell's own time finding an FTL path through."

"A pusher a year," Ohana said. "God. Can you imagine the bar food they must have?"

"Going to bed," Ross said abruptly. The last shift came down on him suddenly, full force, along with the thought that just *one* of the pushers servicing this station being directed to Alpha could have affected his entire life. It was the news. It was the discovery that all their worst fears had been realized. It was the exhaustion of all of it at once. "'Scuse me. Got about enough brain left to get there."

He didn't delay for courtesies. He didn't say anything personal to Jen. He just left, while he had the strength. And Jen, reading him right, maybe, didn't follow.

Silence. Silence. And silence, from Olympus Station.

There were discussions going on, no question. JR, off-shift, tried to relax, office chair reclined.

Then the desk com said, Madison's voice, *"JR, need you."*

Something was up that Madison wasn't broadcasting to the whole ship.

JR snapped the chair forward, grabbed his jacket on the way, and had it on by the time he'd walked the short corridor to the bridge. Madison beckoned him across the line at the entry bulkhead.

"Screen." A new optics workup was on the main screen. It had tags now, one, two, tagged *Miriam B* and *Come Lately.*

But there was something wrong below *Come Lately*'s engine section and her folded vanes.

Something a little larger, jutting out from below, a rounded surface resolved out of reflected light.

That was—possibly—yet another ship.

There was not a sound out of the bridge. Senior heads were strictly down on business. A few trainees were staring at the magnified image. And at them, with worry evident.

"That *could* be a cargo collector," JR said.

"It's definitely not part of the adjacent ship," Madison said. "Imaging's working on it. Looks like it's standing off a little but we don't think so, which would make it about thirty meters longer than *Come Lately* or *Miriam B.*"

They had all the other merchanters on Pell's side of space accounted for. Signed. Sealed. Part of the Alliance. *Estelle* had said *Dublin* had signed up everybody else from Mariner onward. If there was some already-signed Cyteen ship trading with a clandestine EC operation, that was upsetting; and if it was one of the ships *they* had signed on the Pell side of space—

It was, JR supposed, possible that they'd been lied to by one of the Families that had signed on, but he hadn't felt that, in any of the people he'd dealt with. And he could name every ship operating in the Hinder Stars with a fair idea where they were at the moment, which was not here.

Besides, if that *was* a ship tethered and grappled, that curve and length argued for the size of *Firenze,* currently being overhauled at Alpha, the largest Hinder Stars ship other than *Galway* herself, who most definitely hadn't headed this direction.

"Well, that's a problem," he said to Madison, in front of all Second-shift. "We need an ID. We do need an ID."

"Working on it," Madison said. "I'm about to put us underway for a better view of B-mast. It'll take a while, but—"

"This is Olympus Station, office of the Director. We again request you state your business, visitor."

JR looked at Com, said nothing. It was Madison's shift.

"Well," Madison said. "I think they've figured our position and don't like our angle of view. I'm going to answer this one. They're getting testy."

"Your call, brother. We'll leave Mum the outcome."

Madison pushed a button on his earpiece and with a lifted hand signaled Com that he was answering. "This is merchanter *Finity's End,* Olympus. Surprised at the extent of your traffic here."

There was going to be a time-lag for an answer.

"Com," Madison said, "if and when they answer, go ahead and put it on speaker. Working stations only, however. People need their sleep."

"That ship at the top is pretty surely *Miriam B,*" JR remarked. "I read a 17 on the hull. *Come Lately* is also a definite ID, in my opinion."

"Third object could still be a cargo collector."

"Could be."

"Could even be just a cargo container," Madison said. "Something weird that the pusher brought."

"Could be," JR repeated, but his gut said no. His gut was certain that was a ship, which put a whole new twist on the situation. The takehold sounded, one beep, gentle move. JR, like Madison, took a grip on the console's takehold. The sense of motion was brief, directional jets only. Over the next few hours, they'd move to a better vantage, but sunlight was only going to shine where sunlight could shine, and the masts didn't rotate.

"Shall we see if we can raise *Miriam B?*"

"Hell, why not?"

"Com, standard ship to ship, *Miriam B.*"

"Com ready."

"*Finity's End to* Miriam B. *If you're receiving, give us a hail back. We've got a message for you.*"

That was going to be another wait. Til hell froze over, likely.

"Cup of coffee?" Madison offered.

"Sure," JR said. Madison made a gesture to summon the junior runner, said, "Two coffees," and the boy scurried about it.

There was a resting-rail between the captain's seat and the runner's post, below the master screen. Madison took advantage of it. JR did the same, leaned back, ankles crossed. The runner brought back the two coffees, to standing specs. JR took a sip, watching the bridge rather than the screen.

"They should have answered," Madison said.

"It is what it is," he said. "Still your show, brother."

"I'll be happy to share this one," Madison said. "All comers welcome. Really."

"Pretty sure John and Mum are asleep now. Should be. Especially John."

The chrono ran on.

"I even ask myself," Madison said, "if that's possibly a Cyteener down there."

"I can't think so. The EC and Cyteen colluding? No. I'd think of aliens out of Vega before I'd think of that pairing."

"Who's not going to be happy," Madison said, "is Cyteen—when they hear Sol's been running pushers this close to Pell."

"Pell's not going to be delighted, either," JR said. "What I don't want is any EC blowback on Alpha for our entry here. I don't want Sol concluding anybody at Alpha had the knowledge to tip us off about this, and I don't want it obvious to Olympus yet that we've got *Galway* crew aboard. Though if *Miriam B's* here, they likely know. Whatever we've happened across here, I'm fairly damned sure the Alpha stationmaster wasn't ever clued in."

"The only ones who might have been would be Cruz and Hewitt."

Those being the two officers sent out from Sol.

"I hope Cruz is swimming in deep space by now," JR said. "And I hope Hewitt's gotten damned bored with life. I'm not sure even Alpha's EC office had a thorough knowledge what this end of the line was doing. But then, whoever's sitting here at Olympus is probably not that knowledgeable about them, either. The EC's whole history is limiting its agents to mission-at-hand and close control."

"I just wonder which pusher that is out there. It has to be a new one, one the Hinder Stars have never seen."

"You know," JR said, "there was talk, just after Pell was set up, about a Sol to El Dorado pusher-route, wasn't there? They were looking to get face to face with Pell, curb that independence, demand space on that station. El Dorado being as close to Tau Ceti as they could get."

"Then El Dorado, being El Dorado, blew," Madison said. "Galileo blew, the same way, when *its* star kicked up; and after that, Thule and Olympus and the whole Galileo Reach were pretty well fading . . . with supply coming from Pell. It was like the cosmos was having a local snit about then."

"With Cyteen setting up, and no way to deal with them. The EC was upset with Pell and terrified of Cyteen. Knew things were slipping their control. So they dispatched a pusher maybe built for El Dorado, shunted it over to Olympus when they heard about the shutdown, and conceived of this for a base to monitor the Beyond. How's that for a scenario?"

"It's the EC. It's insane. What's unusual?"

"If—"

"Captain." From Optics. Another image went up on the big screen—the third object only, and its shadow on the mast, a massive zoom without the distraction of the much brighter ships.

And no commentary, until Madison said, *"Shit."*

What resolved was definitely an FTLer, travel-stained, but it didn't look old. No bright patches, just one general coating, mono-directional streaks, like the pusher's.

The crew ring wasn't visible from their vantage. There was no apparent hold, just a thicker spine than might be expected.

And there were *three* folded vanes, not just two—unlike any merchanter ship. Ever.

A murmur slowly went through the various posts.

JR said to Madison:

"That's a problem."

"Yeah," Madison said. "That's a grade one problem."

Book V   Section xii

Ross waked with the notion someone had opened the door. Thought it might be Jen, and it was. He expected a touch, an embrace, likely. And, eyes closed and still muzzy with a very short sleep, felt a hand on the shoulder, instead.

"Ross." It *was* Jen. It wasn't the usual approach. "Ross, got to talk."

"Yeah." He rubbed his eyes and turned over. "Yeah?"

"All the way, Ross. Got to talk to you."

Something was the matter. Seriously the matter. He raked his wits together—he'd been somewhere slightly troublesome in his sleep, bothered by something he couldn't quite remember, but now there was real worry on Jen's face, and Jen didn't worry lightly.

"What?" he said, and when sitting up failed, shoved another pillow under his head so he could see her.

"We've definitely found *Miriam B*," Jen said. "That's the ship that's docked on B-mast. *Come Lately* we're pretty sure is also there. But there's another one lower down. We haven't got a name on it. It's bigger than *Miriam B* or *Come Lately*, it's bigger than that whole class of merchanter, and it's not one we know. We can account for every single Family ship on this side and the other of Viking, we've got signatures from all but two, and whatever it is, it's FTL, and it's no ship we know."

Ice settled in his chest. "FTL. You're sure."

"Yeah. And that's not all. For one . . . it's got three vanes."

"*Three?*" He'd never heard of such a thing. Couldn't *imagine* the difficulty of balancing *three* fields at once. It would be magnitudes crazier than two. He tried to force his brain to work.

She nodded. "It's possible it's something they've built right here at Olympus, but there's nothing like a shipyard or anything. It's also all over dust, like a pusher. It's more likely the pusher brought it in, same as it would a station core, but we're just not real sure what's going on with it. Ross, I'm sorry to wake you up with this, but I didn't want you hearing it over general com."

His heart was pounding. Thoughts wanted to scatter in a dozen directions, the Monahans waiting on Alpha, Fallan, Niall, and the hopes they had of talking sense to the EC at Sol . . . all vaporizing in what they *didn't* know. Niall couldn't negotiate blind.

He made another try at sitting up. Made it and steadied himself with a hand to either side. "I appreciate that. What about my cousins?"

"I think we better tell them, Ross, but it's your call. I don't know any more than what I've told you, but something's off here, and I don't think the captains have much more idea what's up with this ship than we do. Fletcher woke us all up, and they're all saying it's an FTLer, but there's nobody it could be."

It was something that it made sense to his sleep-hazed brain. "Not Cyteener."

"Not Cyteener. I mean, there's Cyteeners we've never met, but we've got a list. *Dublin* gave it to us when we started out to get signatures on the Alliance agreement. And *Dublin* sent word by *Estelle* and that man Uncle James met, who stayed on Pell just to say *Dublin* had gotten everybody on the line, and, more's the thing, you just can't get *here* from Cyteen space. Not from Mariner or Viking either, and that three-vaned ship coming through Pell would have caused a massive stir. We'd have heard something when we were there. So where does this ship come from, unless there's some back-route from Cyteen itself, which nobody's ever said, jump-points nobody knows about, and what would a Cyteen merchanter be doing at a supposedly aban- doned station with a pusher-ship we don't know either? Cyteen, by all we know about them, doesn't make sense. Our go-to assumption is still Earth. Sol System. The EC. Who else would set up on an abandoned station and trade trees to Pell?"

"And who else would be crazy enough to put *three vanes* on a ship? *Pushed* here, I'd lay odds to it—because there's no way it's been operating with a sim-trained crew. Damn them. I hope they blow themselves to hell the first time they power her up!" *Pushed* in made sense. But what if it *had* run on its own? What if Earth had already found its own FTL route out, and everything—*everything* was a washout?

Anger rose up, a black wave that wiped out everything, conjured images of Fallan, Niall, all those that had taken *Galway* and risked their lives *and* the ship in a desperate move. His head hurt, where a scar was, a gash that had been pouring blood when Fallan had grabbed him by the shoulder and somehow gotten him to go to *Finity* . . . too late, too damned late to do any- thing about *Galway* and Andrew J. Cruz and the hijacking of their ship.

Fallan and Niall could *not* have lost. They could *not* have thrown away their lives and risked what they had risked for something Sol had already won, and sent *here*, to make everything they had done and tried to do abso- lutely meaningless. No.

"Ross." Jen's hand on his arm was a feather, her voice a waft of air, so fragile, when what was pent up in him was violence and more hate than he had ever tried to contain in all his life. "Ross, darlin', we don't know how it got here. We don't know what the deal is. We're *going* to find out."

We're going to find out. That was the thing. Find out. They *had* to do that.

Breath. And breath. One after the other. Jen settled beside him, tried to put her arm around him and instead he took her hand ever so carefully and held onto it, fragile, something to protect, some*one* to protect, who only meant good to all of them. He put his arm around her, closed his fist in her hair, rested his cheek against hers, and just held onto her, breathing.

"Ross, I'm so sorry."

For what? For telling me? Surely that's all of it. No secrets, Jen.

"Just hold on," Jen said, quiet voiced. Calm, but resolute. "We aren't done here. We're in this, too. All of us. If ever we find out how much the Alliance is good for, this is where it starts, isn't it? We've got the Xiaos coming in. Pell's with us. We're just not going to do anything crazy. But I don't think we're going to back off, either."

Back off from what? Asking questions the EC won't answer?

Sleek, modern, rich Family, used to having their own way . . .

Risking everything? Hell, the Neiharts don't know the meaning of the word.

Not fair, Ross Monahan. Not fair to them.

But . . . dammitall!

"We're not going to quit this," Jen said. "Whatever we do next, Ross. We're not. I know my uncle. And John. And Madison and Mum, for all that. We won't quit."

"What side do we have left to be on, for God's sake? There's Cyteen, which we're not. There's Pell, which is right next to whatever's going on here. There's Alpha, which is fairly well left out in the dark, if Sol has chosen an alternate way to Pell . . ."

"We don't know. Maybe *this place* built an FTLer. It isn't saying they can run it. That's still a pusher out there, still, we assume, the way they're getting supply. Maybe *they* pushed it in. The travel-scum looks like it. The dirt's all organized, like it faced one direction."

Pushed it in. A whole ship?

But a pusher could do that. Pushers moved station cores. Sol *had* FTL knowledge, and it was never in doubt that they might use it.

"What—whatever it is, Jen . . . Fallan, Niall . . . they don't know anything about this. What if the EC plays along, gets onboard under false pretenses, and . . ." He took a gasping breath. "God. I've got to talk with the others, Jen. They've got to hear this."

"Absolutely. But, Ross, keep in mind we don't have the answers yet. Don't panic. Help keep *them* calm. We're not done here."

Don't panic. That, no. He couldn't do that. He hadn't, when he'd come to *Finity* the hard way. He'd held together—being Nav. Being one of the two posts that didn't have that luxury. Ever. You gave up that right when you signed onto Nav.

He knew that. He knew he wasn't handling this well, and he deserved to be ashamed.

It was being waked out of sleep, after that close call, incoming.

It was too much history of losing.

It was the whole run-down mess at Alpha. A way of life he'd taken for ordinary . . . until he saw Pell, resplendent, luxury so thick you could step in it . . .

Maybe Alpha was out of time. Maybe *Galway* was, and they'd always been. But *Galway* had allies, now. Notably *Finity*, and *Little Bear*. *Mumtaz* and *Nomad*. *Firenze, Santiago*, even little *Qarib*. And Pell.

Pell wasn't a small thing, was it? Neither was *Finity's End*.

"Jen. If there's a say to be had, I think *Galway* deserves to have it, don't we? And I'm not the voice of us. Ian is. He's senior. We all need to be in on this. They need to hear this. No, I won't panic them. We'll talk about it. We deserve to talk about it. Us. Who have a bit of a stake here."

"Take Training-B. There's the boards and there's vid there and talkback. I'll get to Security. Fletcher needs to be in on it, not to interfere, understand, but to see you communicate with JR, and I'm pretty sure he'll be up, or if not Fletcher, I'll get Parton, and get the Galways set up there to see everything the bridge can see. All right? You're Alliance. *Galway* has a voice here. JR's going to listen. Right?"

"Dunno what we can do."

"You can not lie here and wonder what's going on. You have *Galway's* right to know. We may go under a takehold alert before this is done, so you all should move soon as you can. You never know when something you know could matter. Get dressed. I'm gone. Things to look up for Fletcher."

She squeezed his hand and started to leave. He pulled her back, kissed her gently before letting her go . . . not that convinced the private room wasn't charity.

But they'd been some use from time to time. They had *some* operational perspective, distant as it was from this dimple in the universe.

He got on com, punched in on quick-call.

"Ian. Training-B. ASAP. We're going to get a briefing. At least what they know. Maybe some input on this. Call the others. Jen's gone to get somebody, maybe Fletcher. Whoever's free. With a pipeline to what's going on. Hurry it."

"Yeah," Ian said. "Training-B. Calling Siobhan."

Siobhan to Maire to Connor and Nolan, and Aidan and Patrick and Netha. Nine of them.

Galway. Whatever happened elsewhere . . . *they* also were *Galway*.

Ross stripped off, reached for the gray patchless jumpsuit hung on the locker door, jammed his feet into deck boots, and left, still sealing the jumpsuit, headed for Training-B at a good pace, consciously aware of the takeholds along the corridor. It was far from sure what distance there was between *Finity* and trouble at the moment, or whether anything out there threatened them imminently—nothing an unsecured body was guaranteed to survive if *Finity* had to save herself. Even if their path was clean, there were likely mining craft loose in the system, and a mass-driver bot could hurl rock, if the station took exception to their silence. Their vanes were folded. But damage was still possible.

The lights were up full in the sector. Training-B's door stood open, lit inside, but vacant. He entered what could be a backup bridge, one of two redundancies, and the big screen—here it was the whole end of the compartment—was lit with a close view of Olympus' B-mast and a portion of the station hull and the pusher's. Consoles were dark. But *that* was there, just as Jen said, one of three ships on that mast, farthest away from the station, deep in shadow, the bottom-most ship a third again the merchanters' size . . . and unmistakably an FTLer.

It had no discernable markings, at least from this vantage. Part stained with travel, as the pusher was stained. Part not . . . in a way that had nothing to do with normal operation.

Ian arrived after him and stopped cold, staring at the screen, frowning. Then his eyes swept the rest of the room and he came in without a word, just a lift of his chin to Ross in greeting. There were duplicates of their own First-shift seats among the others, and not just mock-ups. Training-B could go live and function as main, if the bridge or any section of it were damaged. Emergency seals that could protect just this area in a hull failure—not the only such, and a serious back-up, such as *Galway* did not have.

Ross automatically slipped into his regular Nav 1.5 station, and Ian settled into the number 5 seat across the dividing aisle next to him, silently studying the screen.

Someone else entered. He expected Siobhan or Maire, or one of the others, but it was Fletcher Neihart himself, Security, ship's authority right under the four captains.

"Sir," Ross said, and stood up.

"No formalities, Ross," Fletcher said, and nodded to Ian who had also started out of his seat. Ian settled back. Fletcher folded his arms and leaned against the exec takehold rail. "The captains are asking the same questions you are. So go draw a coffee and have a sit til the others show."

Coffee wasn't allowed in the rows, but Fletcher said do it, and indicated the exec area forward, off-limits to general crew on the main bridge. Ross went and took a cup from the dispenser; and Ian did. Fletcher simply waited. They all waited, and now was the sound of footsteps in the corridor, several, coming fast, and the door was still open. Aidan came in with Connor and Nolan. The twins were not far behind.

"Netha and Patrick are coming," Aidan said, and then fixed on the screen image, staring at it.

"Coffee's being handed out," Ian said. "Forward. Settle."

Patrick and Netha arrived, and took cups. Paid a nod of deference to Fletcher.

Everybody settled, the bridge trainees in their usual places, quietly, and Nolan and the others in adjacent places. There was minimal talk—eyes fixed on the display.

"Is that current?" Netha asked.

"Yes," Fletcher said. "Top two we think are *Miriam B* and *Come Lately*, in that order. Third . . . is a question."

"Vanes don't look right," Netha said, frowning.

"Understatement," Ross said.

"Is that *three?*" Aidan asked.

"That is three," Fletcher said quietly, drained his cup, then walked over to drop it in the collection bin. Silence attended his walk back to his former place. He leaned there, arms folded. "Can't see all of it, but there are three. It's been proposed, theoretically, but nobody's got it to work. If this rig has gotten through testing—and this is a hell of a long spendy trip if it hasn't—it might even be capable of the high routes. Maybe not a match for *Finity*. Or maybe it is. A system to control it has been the hangup. So maybe they've solved the problems. Maybe it can go where the megaships go. But it didn't originate between Alpha and here. The bubble usually spits us out fairly clean. This has been traveling in realspace, on the bow of that pusher. It also seems to have a fairly small hold—maybe heated-hold, which would make it more profitable. And if that tri-vane rig works, it might have more speed than most. Which also is profit. *Maybe,* in contrast to the fiasco of the *Rights* build, the EC intends to make a statement of their own, at the other end of the scale. Go for speed. Take on a black box and get ahead particularly in the information market, which is no small thing. Speed could make it very competitive. There are also, when you look at their other ship-building and recruiting, and when you consider all this silence and secrecy—some more worrisome questions about their re-entry into our affairs, and how friendly they're not being. Olympus does not suit regular merchanters. It's like a castle set on a hill—hard to get to. One safe way in. Not real friendly to Pell. Definitely not friendly to Cyteen. We're not sure how the Xiao Family is going to view what's here. Maybe the Company is setting up to test that trivane, simply to get out of their bottle by piggy-backing a competitive ship into the routes that exist. But what, we have to ask, is *Rights of Man* about, at the other end of this operation?"

There was a cold little silence.

"You think this whole operation is connected to Alpha," Ian said. And all sorts of thoughts of *Galway*'s welcome at Sol came with it.

"What it's connected to," Fletcher said, "at least seems to be a resurgence of Sol's interest in operating out here. What connection that has with motherworld politics, we don't know. Information hasn't flowed freely in a long time, even where the Stream still exists. Pell kicked them temporarily off their deck, then let them back in. Supposedly relations are fairly cordial between the EC office and the Konstantins, but the EC also has never regained any real power on Pell. Probably their superiors would like to change that."

They'd certainly been all-powerful for years on Alpha, Ross thought, remembering Rosie's, and a knock-down drag-out with the Enforcers. The same on *Galway*'s bridge, before Fallan shoved him out the emergency exit. He had no forgiveness for the Company. None of them did.

"As far as our own intentions," Fletcher said, "we're just looking them over. We're mobile, and we want to maintain that: we'll be continuing the Caution indefinitely. We're somewhat constrained by the fact *Little Bear* is an undefined step behind us, so while we may move out of station's convenient range, we'll not be leaving the system, no matter what happens, until the Xiaos arrive and until we agree on next steps. One thing is certain, we don't want Min dealing with station on his own. Speaking entirely my own opinion here, nothing official, we do communicate with the Xiaos fairly well, even pleasantly, but we are two different ships, two different approaches to a tense situation, and the Xiaos *are* Cyteeners, with a Cyteener set of laws and regulations—which are not wholly congruent with ours. The Xiaos have backed us to the hilt—but they do not regard the EC as an authority or have the history with them that we do, collectively. So it's prudent to stay here and try to prevent misunderstandings. And we will try, still, to contact the merchanters involved . . . supposedly *our* people. We'd like to hope so. That, in sum, is our plan here."

Fletcher paused as there were nods all around, then continued: "One more important note: in the Merchanters' Alliance, in the documents we have all signed onto—there is a requirement for three Alliance ships agreeing to expenditures and actions, three ships constituting a court of record, or an official meeting. When *Little Bear* gets here, there will *be* three Alliance ships involved. *Galway* is, we hold, that third ship. Your voice, your agreement, your opinions—matter. This, from the captains."

Fletcher stood upright then, and looked somberly at all of them. "So that's where we are. No secrets on the bridge, none from Family, except we try not to worry the youngest, and we're trying to preserve a little quiet aboard so shifts one, three, and four can rest. You'll get your briefings with your shifts and don't be shy about asking questions. We will have a Caution in effect for the foreseeable future in this place, so we will minimize unnecessary moving about—but Galways are welcome to use Training-B as a hangout at any hour, and welcome to all its functions, except that switch over there on the wall, which would bring this room on line as the functioning bridge and upset all four captains. Don't touch that."

"No, sir." Fervently. From several voices.

"Training-B and Training-C are offlimits to all but seated crew. No scut service here. Pocket all debris and take it with you. No drinks, no food in here as a general rule. Coffee's an exception. Just drop all the cups into the return."

"Yes, sir."

"That's the information I have. As for current plans, we can rest as long as we need to, til *Little Bear* arrives and stirs the pot. If right now all the other side is doing is predicated on us being solo, they'll start to worry, then, and if things start to heat up, a quick exit will be a possibility."

"Thank you, sir," Ian said. "For all of us."

They all stood as Fletcher left.

There was quiet a moment.

"It's not the worst, maybe," Maire said.

Ian said: "Taken as two separate things, *Rights* and this creature, there's dimensions of this that go way far afield, way back in time. But pushing a whole ship—"

"No different than moving a station core," Connor said. "Less. Who knows how many they've got, all stacked up and waiting, with no jump-point to use. And now we're lookin' at giving them one. They've had the how-to on FTL forever. It's the where-to that's stymied them. And with that—and this fancy tri-vane thing—"

"Provided the EC is even interested in trade anymore," Ross said, fighting the bitterness. "Remember *Rights* wasn't meant to haul cargo. And this creature is supposed to have speed *and* distance."

"Those two merchanters at dock," Maire said. "You think the EC'd trust them to crew it?"

"Maybe the way they trusted us to go to Sol," Ross said, "with guns to our heads."

"Hell," Connor said, "if they were offered a ship, sure, take the offer. Then dump the bastards in deep space."

"Unless the EC has hostages," Ross said. "Been thinking about that. One way to explain what they've been up to. Maybe tricked them into coming here on the QT, then took a few kids and said, 'Guess what? You're ours now.'—If they'd been able to pull that maneuver on Alpha, they might not have had to take *Galway* by force."

"That is a question," Ian said. "Here, though . . . they've got a port and they've obviously been dealing with these two ships for years. Maybe these Families don't see the EC the same way we do. Maybe for them it's a sweetheart situation, and a brand new ship is the payoff. Maybe the final one. They couldn't take that thing into Venture without blowing the whole setup here. Maybe they were prepping to reveal it as soon as that design is fully tested . . . which they could do, here to Thule and back, none to witness, and maybe they've been promised an exclusive on Sol imports, once the operation here does go public."

And selling out. Dealing dirty with every other merchanter operating. Damn. He wanted to be generous, didn't want to think the worst of other merchanters, but unless they had hostages . . .

Or maybe this had all started back before *Rights*. Maybe they hadn't realized what was going to happen to every other merchanter this side of Pell, but damn. *Rights* taking every pusher-load for itself had sent Alpha into near collapse. Ships without resources to maintain standards, and getting worse. Couldn't they see that?

And those two ships *had* heard about the Alliance before returning here. No way not. *Little Bear* said at least one of them had called at Alpha since *Galway* left. So how did they justify coming back here, dodging all attempt to contact them?

And if the EC *was* holding Family as hostages, there were dozens of ways, during all those years of station hopping and selling expensive trees, that the Mallorys and Bellagios could have gotten a message to *Finity*. Hell, they could damned well have asked *Galway* for help.

"I think they're willing partners," he said slowly, out of darkest thoughts. "And I think Thule's the next development. While Foucault's tricky, and Groombridge Point to Venture is suicidal in either direction, there may be no real problem from Thule, for any ship smaller than *Finity*. So the EC has exclusive access to Olympus. They've got three FTLers. And a safe access to Thule, which is the universe's easiest hop to Venture. Which puts the whole of the First Stars in reach. If that ship tests out, the logical next step for the EC would be to revive Thule—hell, it might already have pushers destined for it as well. Fletcher said it: if they hold Olympus, they've got a virtual fortress . . . and if they hold Thule, they've got a platform they can use for *Rights*, without risking a not-so-experienced crew coming in here and upsetting Foucault. They could use this place to raise and train perfect little Enforcers, hell, they could bring them in from Sol System. And if there's a jump-point proved to Alpha, they could build a hundred super-fast FTLers and move in on every station in the First Stars. Even Pell itself."

A silence followed. Frowns.

Then Connor said: "You have a *wicked* mind, Ross."

"*Navigator*," Ian said. "And he could be right. Olympus *was* a disaster for early FTL converts. Big ships. That's what killed it and Thule. If you don't mind Olympus being accessible only through Thule, if you use it as a castle, and Thule as the drawbridge, it's a sweet place to defend against all comers. Ross is right."

It wasn't entirely his way of thinking, he wanted to object. He wasn't reconciled to it happening. It was him trying to understand what good the EC could possibly get out of this. It was too much time spent staring into the dark trying to figure why this had all happened to Alpha, and why two merchanter ships worked against all the others. Why anyone back at Earth couldn't see that they finally had a chance to make their investment pay off if they just stopped trying to strip it bare. Why this pusher, one of a breed the First Stars had fed and housed like princes, had come secretly to this place, rather than feeding Alpha and enjoying the ready market of a dozen and more stations. . . .

Except . . . had Sol ever had reason to think of them as a source of real trade profit? He had to think about that one. He tried to think what actually went back to Sol, back to the EC, and the answer was damned little. The fuel to get their pusher back. That was a big one. Rare elements. Science. The Beyond was starting to thrive. There *was* wealth to be had. Sol might have heard about it and believed it was theirs.

They might also have heard about things that scared them. Humankind, the Cyteeners, making human computers. And founding more colonies. It scared the First Stars. It was bound to scare Sol.

And Pell, glorious as it was—had been a flashpoint from the start, for all of the stations as well as Earth. In the EC's book, Pell never should have launched. The First Stars had used to hold that opinion themselves . . . until the EC failed them, and threw Alpha and all the First Stars entirely onto Pell's supply, via Venture. Now the First Stars were utterly reliant on what came from Pell, while the EC used Alpha pusher-runs to build themselves a copy of *Finity* herself.

Not a happy circumstance. Not a happy population. The EC built a ship that, it turned out, couldn't jump, and Alpha realized they'd starved for years for no damned reason . . .

"No matter how you look at it," Nolan said, "it's shady as hell. Why no word to the rest of us? Why not bring that FTLer to Alpha, if they were going to push it in? Why not bring the pusher cargo to all of us . . . unless you know damn good and well you're up to no good?"

There was a little quiet after that question, which was *the* question of all questions. Why deal with just two ships? Why the secrecy?

"If we needed evidence Sol doesn't trust anybody out here," Maire said, "I guess we have it, sitting right out there with those ships attached."

"Nobody *but* those two ships," Ian said sourly.

"So . . ." Ross said quietly. "Who do *we* trust? *Finity?* I do. But we aren't *Finity.* Where are *we* in all this? Niall, Fallan . . . all of First-shift are, please God, on their own at Sol Station, trying to find a future for us. Where the hell are *we*, now, if *Galway* makes the Monahans heroes to Sol, while we sit here waiting for a Cyteener ship to join us? The damn EC took *Galway* at gunpoint, and First-shift may have killed the lot of them. —And now we're supposed to be part of . . . what? Negotiations with the EC?"

"It's no pleasant array of choices we've had," Ian said. "None that they've given us. They're wanting crew for that fancy ship. You suppose they'll respect a Family's claim on it? Or you think they'll give it orders and then think they've got the rights to it?"

"Do we know they're Family?" Netha spoke up for the first time. "The Bellagios and the Mallorys? Seems to me these two ships have worked closely with the EC, who's upgraded their systems, and kept them running and maybe given them all sorts of bennies. Their goals might be more merged than we can truly understand, knowing what we know, and having made the decisions we had to make."

Silence ruled for several minutes after that, then Ian said:

"The Mallorys and the Bellagios. *Miriam B* and *Come Lately*. Among the first of the purpose-builts. And now the last. Creaking old."

"There's things Engineering can't fix," Connor said. "They've likely retrofitted themselves into a situation there's no ready fix for, upgraded their engines as far as their spine will take. They *won't* take the modern nav system, because it's black-box connected, they don't have the connectors for ring-docking, and even with their retrofit, they're underpowered for the distances in the Beyond, no question. They're in a box with no exit."

"Yet they've managed to stay solvent," Netha said.

"Running booze, biologicals, and pharma-ceuticals," Siobhan said, and Ross added:

"And three honking big trees."

"Ever wonder how they've passed EC inspections?" Netha said. "I don't. Not any more."

"Suppose they want out of the trap they're in?" Maire said.

"If we get a chance to talk to them," Aidan said. "Peeling two resources away from the EC might be worth it to Pell *and* to Cyteen."

"Maybe," Netha said. "But that shiny new ship . . ."

"Hell if I'd want it," Siobhan said. "They have to know *Rights* is a mess."

"Listen," Connor said. "One of them docked at Alpha, since. I've heard it was the Mallorys, but don't quote me. Either way, can't tell me they don't know damn good and well what Cruz did, and how our Ross came back with only half his blood still in his body. They could have sent word down the line. Could have gotten in contact with *Finity* or *Little Bear*. Any way you cut it, they knew and they still *chose* to come back here. They chose to come and inform their handlers here about what happened at Pell, and about the Alpha-Sol jump-points. Fast as they could scamper."

"We know what kind of pressure the EC can put on a ship," Ross said. "If we should go into dock—"

"I don't want any of us to go in there," Ian said slowly. "Damn, I don't."

Finity rested, station-keeping, with a constant eye to Olympus. She listened. The station listened. Neither communicated. JR reclined his office chair, shut his eyes, listened. And waited.

Not to say there wasn't activity at either end, and more of it, JR was sure, on Olympus' side of the equation, as the stationmasters and likely the captains of the docked pusher, the two elusive merchanters, and whatever authority surrounded that unidentified ship all did some furious speculation as to what *Finity* intended.

The obvious action, and *Finity* was indeed active about it, was data-gathering on everything visible and perceptible. The logical action over on Olympus was trying to minimize what *Finity* could detect, decide what they could do about it, and decide whether and what they should say.

Possibly the Mallorys and Bellagios were in the local bar trying to figure next moves, *or*—JR's most favorable speculation—the Mallorys and Bellagios had sent out a board call, meaning to get *Miriam B* and *Come Lately* mobile, either to make closer and independent contact with *Finity,* or to avoid encounter entirely and get the hell out of Olympus. They were merchanters. Good of the Family had to outrank EC priorities.

Madison was about to surrender the bridge to John and head for supper: it had been that long a wait; and JR had been on general duty longer and with less solid result than he wanted, when a communication did come through, a simple query from station as to whether they had a mechanical issue.

Well, that was a reasonable inquiry of a ship that had taken relative position and not come closer. It was even polite. Even friendly. JR sat up and took a sip of cooling coffee.

"So do we answer?" Madison asked, via com. *"They very likely know everything that happened at Alpha, they know we're looking for* Miriam B *and* Come Lately, *they know about the Alliance, and they know we're not good news for the purpose of their operation, whatever that might actually be. They know that they're found out, that they have some reason to worry about*

the loyalty of the merchanters at dock—and that their years of secrecy in their operation are done, once we leave here. They can assume we're listening and collecting data, and they just can't be overall too happy right now."

"I think that's a good summation," JR said. "Thank them nicely and tell them we're just fine, is my inclination. Let them go on worrying. Unless they ask the second question."

"Agreed," Madison said. *"Go get supper and get some honest sleep, brother. We two are about to go off and give it to John. No longer our circus."*

"Probably a good idea," JR said. He set the cup down, disengaged the earpiece and put it in his jacket pocket . . . he was never out of reach of that at any hour. Neither Madison nor Mum would trouble him with details unless things started to happen. Station, without his sympathy, could go on wondering—and trying to lay plans.

He went to his adjacent quarters, ate half a nutrient bar, bedded down and slept. He waked only briefly with the change to Mum's shift, shut his eyes again and resisted any impulse to know whether Olympus had been talking with Madison *or* Mum in any constructive sense.

Not his watch.

Book V   Section xv

Time passed, the gap was narrower, and the improved angle on B-mast only reinforced their previous conclusions. Ross was on duty when the engines gave another nudge to their vector, still on course toward the station.

Nav had different objectives when *Finity* was lazing along—*Finity's* definition of lazing along being still damned fast, letting Foucault do some of the work on her current heading. Nav on *Galway* mostly plotted place to place with well-known stats, routes, and schedules. Nav on *Finity* not infrequently winged it, as Kate quaintly put it, and as Ross scrambled to adapt, he realized he'd become addicted to the adrenaline rush, leaving him less time to be terrified. *Finity's* Nav was used to working with Helm and with seats *Galway* didn't formally have one of, let alone several of, like Records and several specialties in Science. For Ross, it meant learning things—important things—until the brain ached and charts danced through vivid dreams at night, taking on personalities and voices and arguing with each other.

And Kate had all Nav working on that wacky Ardaman switchback problem, testing to see what speculated behaviors could account for the historical problems of FTLers here, and seeking optimal paths in and out for
various ships, not just *Finity*.

It all blended somewhat with vid games and dragons. There was a lot of
that, too, between shifts, and sleep in the off hours became irregular, too
much rest coupled with hard mental work in a haunted neighborhood with
possible enemies watching them—the behavior of the station being nothing
that the captains chose to comment on, despite the free and easy guesses of
crew with crew.

Periodically station, bot-like, repeated its demand to know *Finity*'s business.

Finity didn't answer.

And Ross could say he now knew a lot more about Foucault and its companion star Fizeau than he had, both the historical figures and the local
system. So did the junior-juniors, who found themselves handed the problems of Groombridge Point in the daily lesson: as First-shift Nav, even in a
trainee seat, he had been ambushed by two deputations of teens trying to
win a week of no-scrub. It taxed his math skills, trying to teach, and it frus-
trated the juniors trying to learn. But it kept everyone's mind off the central
problem.

That was the way of it. At first, all the conversation in mess had been
"Have you heard anything?" but after two and then four days it was down to
anything *but* mention of Olympus or the pusher sitting at dock. A whole
generation of young Finitys had now actually seen a pusher at dock, which
was something to remember for a lifetime, but even that novelty wore thin.
Nobody hurried. Nobody was in a rush.

Until in the dark of mainnight, late in Captain John's watch, a notice
blared out from the com system. *"Fourth-shift to stations. We are calling
shift-change. Now."*

A dark space. Then the speaker called from overhead and the com beeped on the bedside console. JR reached for the com, thumbed it, saw *Min's here*, and the time. It was three hours and thirteen minutes into John's watch, with Mum's shift yet to go before his wakeup.

He keyed receipt and fell face-down into bed, adjusting the pillow, trying to shut down the concomitant thoughts and all curiosity what Min might have to say . . . all the time planning what he would say if Min took the position he thought Min would take.

He had perfect confidence Mum was going to deal with whatever response needed to be sent Min's direction when she came on. Perfect confidence that *Little Bear's* arrival would begin to get station's attention, and equal confidence that Olympus—if it was paying sharper attention since their arrival, and granted they were not dealing with bots—was going to notice *Little Bear* coming in on the same track and draw the obvious conclusion: that the second ship was *not* a coincidence and that their visitor problem had just multiplied.

He had an informational packet ready for Min, giving their refined images to *Little Bear*, with a little commentary and a polite salutation in Xiao ship-speak. Fourth-shift would be sending that on.

Yes, Min, that is a pusher. *And what you can't see yet, or will see when you get your wits about you, we've got a potentially larger problem on B-mast.*

Probably Grandfather Jun would be involved soon as the images got to *Little Bear*, whether or not it was his watch. Mum and Grandfather Jun knew something about pushers, and they were both an asset in that matter.

There was no knowing which shift was in command of *Little Bear* at the moment. What *Finity* had just detected was the hours-ago splash of a starship positioning firmly in Foucault's grip . . . and nicely done. *Little Bear* had come generally down *Finity's* track, but, after her first V-dump, seemed to be headed, long-range, for a slightly different observational angle. The packet would bring them up to speed, but Min deserved time to get his head together and *he* deserved the rest of his sleep while Min sorted out the initial packet.

Not early but not late, either. Clearly *Little Bear* had not wasted much time settling business at Venture. For *Little Bear's* smaller size, and given that Min had necessarily taken a more cautious passage through Thule, not having *Finity's* sheer power to skim the star's well, that arrival was still a damned impressive display from Cyteen shipbuilding and Min's crew. Worth dropping that word to Konstantin, as he was sure Min would have a deal to say about *Finity*, back at Cyteen.

So they now had backup, with another and frequently divergent viewpoint on the problem. They did *not* think the same, not he and Min, not Grandfather and Mum. But their differences gave them a second thought and in their debate on executive decisions, they worked out both sets of interests. Fairness? Pell and Cyteen and Alpha, for that matter, were equally represented here, as were the three requisite ships for the Alliance to make an official decision . . . not that that provision of the agreement they had signed was going to carry huge weight with Pell and Cyteen, untested.

But it was about to be tested.

Being in possession of disturbing information, ships of all three regions, operating together, were going to insist to the dual powers of the Beyond that Olympus' reawakening and the safety of the Hinder Stars stations in general was a problem for all three authorities—not just Pell and Cyteen, but the merchanters that knit them into a thriving economy—because without those stations as buffers, Sol was right up against them.

Then Cyteen had to think that it really needed Pell between itself and the buffer-stations.

Each region—including the Hinder Stars—had a separate and vital interest in what was going on here—and for their part, *Finity* and *Little Bear* had to get the temperature of this operation so close to Pell space, and not raise the heat any higher in the process. The EC *was* coming, one way or another, since *Galway's* run and Abrezio's message; and that was a certainty. Their part, now, apart from the effort *Galway* was making, and the upheaval against the EC at Alpha, was to report the local situation to their various authorities—and to do it as rigorously and accurately as possible—including the inescapable reality that the EC itself, the motherworld and all, would continue to exist and operate.

So let Olympus think it through: Cruz had messed up at Alpha, and the EC presence here had just lost its cover. Pell knew. Cyteen knew.

And merchanters, for one very widely-distributed interest in this, if they refused to move—as they could—a lot else couldn't move as it wanted to.

Finity and *Little Bear* had a choice. Dive out of here and start that process, or give it one try. Establish contact with the station—granted there was a live presence; and particularly talk to the merchanter component of the operation.

Sleep was a hard slog from there. Half an hour or more, trying. But he made it.

Book V   Section xvii

Mum was still in charge on the bridge, along with the senior-senior crew, usually a relaxed operation. Fourth-shift had worked so long together that ops could look like outright inattention if one didn't watch the hands and the screens. Things got done. Expertly done, with flair and finesse.

But at this shift-end, there was none of that casual attitude—just a precise, somewhat grim attention to business. The main display was, as it had been, the station. The pusher.

As JR entered the bridge from the port side exec corridor, First-shift crew was stacking up in the lounge, downing last cups of coffee, waiting to move onto the bridge from the rear. He waited at the yellow line, respectful of the last four minutes thirty-one seconds of Fourth-shift's watch, observing the master screen and gathering what was going on with *Little Bear* and with Olympus.

Nothing spectacular. Same positions they'd held since he'd waked and looked over the situation, forty-two unwilling minutes early.

Mum left her station and walked over to the last file of seats for a quick word with Science, picking up a data-stick in the process, then came over to JR where he waited and dropped it into his hand.

"That's the read so far. The Xiaos are within five minutes light, and closing fast. They did some very flashy braking—getting station's notice, if anyone's alive in there. There's really nothing that needs your touch at the moment. No pressure. You're looking done before the day starts. Have you had breakfast?"

"Wafer and a cuppa. I'm fine, Mum."

"Good God, go get a sandwich. I can shepherd the handover."

"Maybe after we hear from Min. If he's awake."

"If you—" Mum started to say conversationally, but Com's Active light flashed on the overhead.

Min, was JR's immediate thought. But Com 1 said,

"Captain, station's responding, I think live, wanting to talk to you."

"It's your baby," Mum said with a deep breath, and that was so, ultimately. JR bit his lip and went over the line, not to take Mum's seat—which was still hers for the next forty-odd seconds—but to cross the bridge and loom over Com 4.1.

"Stay put til we settle this, Sophie," he said. First-shift was in the aisle, ready to move in and JR gave space to Len, 1.1, to be sure he heard Sophie. "Fourth-shift com, all hold. Who, precisely, is calling?"

"IDs as stationmaster, sir," Sophie said. "Querying us, querying *Little Bear,* demanding in the name of the EC to know our business, same as a bot's been doing every hour less five, but this is a new voice reacting to *Little Bear's* wavefront, station signal now getting to us at about . . . two minutes fifty-two seconds."

"Message from *Little Bear,*" Com 4.2 said, Lowell, behind Sophie. "Sir. Also reporting a message, lagged three minutes forty-one seconds from us. Reacting to station query. *Little Bear's* wanting to keep one minute thirty second separation. Says he'll dump to handle position."

Translation software, such as station would have, might or might not get it straight. Com 4.2, however, was their number one linguist. And *V*-dump at this range? Flashy didn't begin to cover it.

"That should excite the station," JR said. "Possibly we should warn them."

It was truly a question how far to carry Min's brand of disrespect.

On the other hand, it would make an impression, and they didn't want to appear easy, should station think they were dealing with EC crews. There was no stopping Min. Not now. And a perverse impulse got the better of him.

JR said, "4.1, message for the stationmaster, assuming he bleeds blood. Tell him first, in my name, quote: 'Ship to station civil alert: *Little Bear* is repositioning and well under control.' Then tell him I want to talk to Captain Tom Mallory, of *Miriam B.*"

That should stir somebody out of bed, if there was a body.

That direct reference to Mallory also told station they had deciphered the situation on B-mast, and were gathering data.

"Done," Com 1 said, and then it was a matter of waiting for station's reaction.

It was *remotely* possible station might actually grant his request and give him a direct conversation with *Miriam B.* In the long history of *Gaia's* operation, the Neiharts and the Mallorys had never talked, never been in the same vicinity, and given that the Xiao Family had their roots at Cyteen and the Mallorys had theirs in the Hinder Stars, it was unlikely that the Xiao family had any history with them, either.

But by reputation—of their two ghosts, Senior Captain Tom Mallory was an honest merchanter, paid his bills, and excepting his allergy to black box installation, wasn't necessarily that willingly tied to EC operations. *Miriam B* paid her bills and had a clean, even a meticulously clean reputation— which *Come Lately* did *not* have. But one could not get around the fact they'd both played fast and loose about the whole Olympus situation. It was a tossup, who of the two ghosts—or both—to try to deal with.

And was Captain Thomas Mallory likely to be happy to be so singled out as the one a Pell ship and a Cyteener wanted to deal with? Hard to say. If station was wondering what had led them here, asking to talk to *Miriam B* might just inadvertently point a finger in the wrong direction.

The Family that ran *Come Lately* was the Bellagios, once actually based at Thule, in pusher days. But given that *Come Lately* had been the ship carrying on a fairly shady set of dealings with Pell, considering it was *Come Lately*'s activities that actually *had* brought them here, there was just a little less baggage with the Mallorys.

Approach one, or approach both?

They always had a conversation-opener with *Come Lately* about trees and sailing ships. But that opener led in specific, potentially distracting directions. One had to wonder whether or not to give station that tidbit of information.

"*Little Bear* has successfully repositioned," Scan 2.1 said. "Now at one minute thirty-one second lag."

Smooth as silk. *Little Bear* and her crew continued to impress. He wondered how station was taking the performance, wondered if they even had a clue.

In the meanwhile, shift-change had happened around them. "She's yours, now," Mum said, passing him. And added, in a low voice: "Keep a little ahead of Min."

That was plain advice. And she didn't mean ship position.

It was, in fact, time to try to talk—if they could get action out of station— before Min dived in for his own say . . . which of a certainty he would want to.

But if *he* could get an exchange going first with the upright, rule-following, and meticulous Mallory, not the sort of man that excited Min's aggressive qualities, he might better avoid side issues. He could at least open the conversation, hoping that Mallory might be their bridge to a productive discussion with the operation's EC component.

The fact was, they *had* information both should be interested in—vitally interested—if only they'd hear it.

JR went to his own seat, forward of the takehold rail, looking out over the rows of Family going through previous-shift reports. Felt like dropping his head onto his hand and shutting his eyes—but everybody out there was likely about the same. News breaking in the first half of a sleep cycle tended to do that.

Fletch arrived with a nutrient mini-bun, "Compliments of Mum," and leaned on the console beside him.

The coffee was beginning to taste off. The bun went down in two mouthfuls and a tide of flat coffee. Fletch waited. JR waited, until Fletch said, "Well, still not clear whether we're dealing with a bot in Central. Is it? Can't tell by the inflection or the answers."

"No," he said. "But with three ships and a pusher sitting there—there's flesh and blood in charge. No way not."

No word from station. No word from the ships at dock. Min had made one hell of a show, and gotten nothing from station that resembled shock.

They sat now at roughly one minute thirty seconds from each other, *Finity* and *Little Bear*. And *Finity* was two minutes fifty-odd seconds light from the station. Fletch remained, doing his own digital chores on his handheld.

Then Len, Com 1.1, sent an advisement to his screen: *LB pending #1.*

JR pushed a button, so Fletch could hear.

"*Senior Captain*, Little Bear," Sarah's voice said over the speaker, "*you are clear, sir. Captain, call is on tight beam.*"

"Min, my friend," JR said. "Welcome to our interesting situation. Glad to see you."

There was a wait. Three minutes and some seconds lagged, which was the way they wanted it. No single action from station or some outlying mass-driver could get them both as they lay, and *Little Bear* or *Finity* could be headed for jump at the least provocation.

"*JR, my friend,*" came back, Min's cheerful voice. "*What is our situation here? It looks interesting. Over.*"

Actual conversation across a solar system was an artform worked out over centuries: you said your say, the other party said their whole speech simultaneously, which saved waiting on the lag, you compared notes and you commented. Answers took the same route. Sometimes you overlapped and interleaved in a crazy way, especially when the lag was over ten minutes, but not too needful over a roughly three-minute gap. Still, you sat and sipped your coffee and took notes and waited, waited. Nobody wanted a time-lagged case of mistaken impression or forgotten point.

"One pusher, unknown," JR said, "sits docked on A-mast. On B-mast, *Miriam B* and *Come Lately* and a third ship that we make out as an FTL whose leading surfaces show stain and whose recessed surfaces look new. We see no markings. The latest images we have follow this transmission."

He'd leave those three vanes without comment. Min's reaction might indicate Cyteen tending in the same theoretical direction, however experimental.

"Our surmise is this third FTLer has arrived by pusher. Station has meanwhile asked our business. We did not answer until your arrival. Then I asked to speak to *Miriam B*'s Senior Captain, figuring there might be some meeting of minds. No response as yet.

"Regarding the pusher, we came on it at dock, as you see, and have had no communication with it or anyone representing it. We have looked for its energy trail: it has sat here a while, so its unloading is likely well-advanced. Its origin is undoubtedly Sol, and we calculate its arrival as not that recent, but within the standard year—which might mark the arrival of all occupants currently in residence; but the station is in much better condition than expected; so we suspect a lengthy occupancy, possibly a sizable population. There is scant outward sign of previous scrapper operations. It appears to have been massively reconstructed since the salvagers stopped coming here, and our two ghosts have been delivering a goodly amount of flour somewhere.

"It's possible this particular pusher was launched in anticipation of *The Rights of Man* going operational. *Rights* did attempt jump from Alpha, but is years behind schedule, something the EC could not have known at the time this pusher was launched. Beyond that, I'm out of guesses. The odds of finding a pusher at dock and the unexpectedly good condition of the station hull both argue that this is not the only pusher serving this station and that repair has been going on here for some time, aided likely by the two FTLers at dock.

"Olympus has been watching us, but not acting, and has not communicated beyond querying our purpose being here and suggesting we're not welcome. Mostly we seem to be dealing with a bot's routines, but I'm betting they're paying attention as we've gotten closer. We did not mention your impending arrival. We imagine that rather spectacular entrance—my compliments to your ship and crew—is now under intense discussion. In my estimation, also, there is no real likelihood that *Miriam B* can or will respond independently to *Finity*'s query—same situation as at Alpha; but I'm still waiting.

"Station's ability to reach us with significant hostile action as we now sit seems limited to insystem miners, which are also likely robots. We've seen no evidence of more spectacular surprises. We are maintaining vigilance in that regard, in the notion some 'drivers may be sitting out there in the dark, but so far we have seen nothing threatening from station or from mining operations. Over."

A delay, but not a long one. Then Min's voice:

"*Such an interesting system you've brought us to, my friend. —We jumped six hours behind you. We had no further communication from other ships or station before leaving Venture and we did not file a course with station. Two ships meeting and then departing on a Thule vector likely stirred some lively talk on dockside and in station offices.*

"*We were very pleased not to find wreckage along your track at Thule and here. We assumed you wished to arrive here first and assess the situation for Pell quietly. We wish to assume that you had no warning of what we see here. Over.*"

Min was more than justified in asking very blunt questions.

"Xiao Min, we take no offense at justified questions. The Neiharts assure you we had no warning at all that this existed, and we have remained here in some measure because—however great our urgency to report—we asked you here and felt obligated to wait for consultation. Having established that Thule was non-operational, we used all speed through that system, because, as we discussed at Venture, we hoped we were on the track of at least one of our two targets. That both are here was a surprise. We assumed a pusher would be involved if there were life at Olympus, but by no means expected to find one in progress of delivery. That Olympus is in good repair was a surprise. The unknown FTLer was a very unpleasant surprise.

"On my honor, Xiao Min, the Neiharts are profoundly grateful to see you. You have deserved our thanks all through this operation. But I ask you— with no ability to call on past favors, since the balance of favors-done is very much on your side—stay and observe while we try to find out the extent of the problem here and make a try at talking to these people. Should any threat materialize, please get your Family to safety without hesitation and with no other thought. We ask you report the situation to Venture and Pell on your way to Cyteen space, and convey my message to Emilio Konstantin, that we now have a serious threat, and that Pell and Cyteen have every good reason to work on this together. Over."

Again the delay for reception, but silence followed. Min had not launched into any immediate message following his initial statement. The silence wore on. And on. They should have the images by now, as clear as they could make them. Possibly it was a consultation.

Then: *"The Xiao Family thanks the Neiharts for this clear statement. We will agree. We ask you advise us in advance of your next actions. What is your assessment of what we see? Over."*

Most of that had been covered in his previous statement—with the exception of the three-vaner . . . and he still held out for Min's opinion before extending his own. As for his next actions . . . he wished he were more confident.

"We will be sending you our images from closer in; and our transcript of communications in its entirety. Olympus will have realized by now that *Finity* is not the *only* observer of their actions. They must also understand that their presence here will no longer be secret from Pell. We hope they will realize that communication with us is the next logical course and that waiting two decades on a policy reply from Sol is not an option here. It's my intention to talk to the merchanter Families present and offer them *and* the EC a better choice than this continued evasion. Over."

There was a pause in communication. The packet was ready. JR ordered it. It went.

"We are in receipt," Min said. *"A moment."*

And after that moment:

"The FTLer in the image is an interesting design. Not unprecedented, but one rejected some time ago by Cyteen engineers. More extensive images would be of great interest to Cyteen, particularly if they claim it to have jumped successfully. It appears, however, to have been pushed here, which means its construction was, at very least, concurrent with the beginning of The Rights of Man. *One wonders what that relation may be. A smaller, more mobile, faster craft, and a megaship—both, one supposes, wanting competent crew. But of a certainty, what is here did not happen overnight or without purpose. Over."*

It *was* a next logical conclusion. "The coincidence of our happening on this pusher and this ship by chance does strain my imagination," JR said, "It does feel as if its arrival is coordinated somehow with the failed launch of *Rights.* Perhaps they intended to bring *Rights*—and her cargo of Enforcers—here. Over."

And within seconds past lag:

"We agree on both. There will surely be other pushers en route. They are rich. They can support more than one or two or even three operations, and we agree: when Rights of Man *attempted a run toward Bryant's, it was surely intending to come here by way of Thule. One in some sense regrets they failed that first jump. A novice at Helm might have made a great spectacle here. Over."*

"Arrival here was an adventure. I concur in that. —As for immediate plans, we'll be making a closer approach to station to get a closer look at the two merchanters, and at that creature without a name. We'll send images directly as we process them. We'll continue efforts to contact the EC authority and explain to them reasonably, I hope, that Pell is willing to talk to them—constructively. If they *have* been coordinating plans with Cruz and Hewitt at Alpha, through the two FTLers, we have an update for them they will not like, things those two ships may or may not have been able to learn at Alpha. Among other facts they will have to absorb, Abrezio will certainly not allow the megaship that has cannibalized his station for decades to defect to another station. Neither will other stations, including Alpha, do business with those two ghosts until this situation is settled amicably and sensibly. Olympus will have to make some decision on its own, even if it's a decision to try to pretend we never found them. We can afford to do that. We can, in effect, ignore them, which would mean invoking the embargo and refusing to deal with their ships. And they can sit here waiting for more pushers, with a twelve-year communications lag. Or we can negotiate their reasonable entry into the region, on our terms. That will be our approach. Over."

"*We shall gather data in the meanwhile,*" Min said. "*And move from time to time, lest they forget us. The Neihart Family is very welcome to claim most of their attention. Over.*"

"We will continue to try for a reasonable outcome. Profound thanks for your support. The Neiharts and the Galways thank you. Over."

"*Dining with the tiger, JR,*" Min said. "*That also is one of our proverbs. Be aware. Over.*"

"We share that one," JR said. "Take care, Min. Signing off, if you are satisfied."

"*There may be fools,*" Min said. "*Always expect fools. Take great care, Captain James Robert. You are more than just your ship now.* Little Bear *signs off.*"

JR drew a long, slow breath, feeling the ironic sting of Min's not-so-subtle *Captain James Robert,* and met Fletch's gaze. "And so it begins."

"He's right, JR," Fletch said. "We need you. The Alliance needs you. Be careful."

He attempted a laugh. "Don't worry. I'm no damn hero."

"I know you, JR. You never go off-duty. Not really. Normally that's not a problem. But in this . . . realize you have support. Trust us. *Use* us."

"I rely on you all too much."

"There you go again. Trust me. Trust *us.* Trust those Galways riding with us, who have economic hope for the first time in their lives. Trust our

Cyteener friend, who for some weird reason actually seems to like you. We're in a hell of a situation, holding the entire damn EC to account, and if they get loose again, if they try to pull a Cruz, well, we've got the pictures and we can lock them out of every extant port."

"God. I can see it now: ten years station-time to file complaints, only to watch them no-show for court dates, until, 'Sorry, our party is taken ill. Heart attack.'"

"A real heart attack."

"And the chargeable one is dead. The EC cleans up its messes that way. Hopefully what we have here are two sane profit-motivated merchanter families and some Sol-born EC at as lonely a post as you could find. We don't need a court date. We need some people to come to their senses and figure out where their interests actually lie."

Another presence arrived quietly out of the executive corridor. Madison, assessing whether he wanted to talk here, or there, or not at the moment.

JR made eye contact and Madison came across the sacred line as Fletch nodded and left.

"I was in the office," Madison said, as another sandwich landed on his desk. "I heard Min. I sent it around to Mum and John."

JR ignored the sandwich. "Good. We can breathe easier now. Min sounded a little taken aback by what we've got here, not to say I blame him. Hell of a surprise to drop into."

"Glad it was Min and glad it was your watch. Xiao Ma and I do not communicate as well."

"I'm always uneasy. Min and I generally understand each other . . . until we don't. But that pusher out there is a shock under any circumstances. Min shares our suspicions that this is the other half of their move at Alpha. That this is where *Rights* would have gone, if it could. *Rights* could have dropped out of sight with a full load of Enforcer recruits and brought them *here,* for a start, maybe for further training. Operationally, they could pick up forces and move them anywhere, trading green Alpha recruits for forces a whole lot tougher. And if they move from here to develop and hold Thule—they could make this quite a little fortress."

"Except no half-assed sim-trained crew is going to get *Rights* into this system in one piece. Thule, yes. Maybe. Here . . . not going to happen. Ask Kate. Part of me wishes they'd made it out of Alpha and tried it. Might have solved all our problems at once, if they got this far."

"Min said much the same."

"Smart man."

It was a sobering thought. One he couldn't share. Death was not something he wanted . . . on either side.

"Castle, huh? What do you think's in there?"

Madison shrugged. "The pushers might deliver Earth-born trainees along with supply and . . ." Madison nodded in the general direction of Olympus and the FTLer. ". . . those. Likely Earth-born. Who'd view us as the aliens. We are—to them. Same as the azi are to us."

A thought worth a shiver. "We've lost so many opportunities in this stupid splitting apart, and it all boils down to the EC's damn insistence on control. Every time they clamp down—humanity fissions. Pell. Cyteen. God knows about its colonies. Time we put some of it back together."

"Soda doesn't go back into the bottle."

"No, and Cyteen's going to expand for a while, until it's satisfied, hopefully without running into anybody else. But it won't be infinite. It's big and dark out there. But we've got our spot in it. Earth keeps trying to manage all this. And it couldn't manage Alpha. We keep hoping it's learned, but here we are, with *Rights* near bankrupting Alpha and now this place having sucked up the pusher traffic that should have been fixing Alpha. They've got two merchanters attached to this, maybe looking to get their hands on that fancy ship, but it's a question whether they're really subscribed to what Earth is selling. I'd like to get their side of it."

"So would I. God knows *I* wouldn't want to take the offer, but *Firenze* was damn sure desperate enough before we stepped in."

"An old warhorse like Giovanna Galli? They wouldn't have trusted her. She's too independent, too ready to tell them go to hell. That's always been the problem. They don't trust the Families. They never wanted them to exist. And so far, they can't figure what it takes to buy one."

"We may be overly optimistic about the Hinder Stars Families. We may be looking at two who may not sell, but they'll hire, if it gets their hands on that ship."

"Certainly two of the most desperate, at least. And the least trusting. It's why I put a call in specifically for Tom Mallory."

"Why not Frank Bellagio? I mean, I've got my own reasons, but I'd like to hear yours."

"Maybe I *should* have sent to both. But the Bellagios are the ones that blew things for this operation at Pell. If it weren't for that trip to Pell, the racket they'd been running in the Hinder Stars, which may date back to his predecessors, might never have been noticed until far too late. It's possible he had equally shady help with his Pell transactions—like what harm are a few trivial seeds and problem dates? What they couldn't anticipate were the Monahans, or the Alliance trying to contact each and every ship. Nobody from Alpha ever comes to Pell. Still, those trades were venal, stupid, greedy as hell . . . and here we are. Mallory, on the other hand, pays his bills with no complaints filed. On that thin thread, I decided to contact the Mallorys and not the Bellagios, to see if we can talk."

Madison said, "We might make trouble for them, the EC being what it is. Might think we have some special relationship with them."

"If they're honest, they'll go to station admin and be open about it. Which is all right. I don't mind talking to station, either."

"Talk. Question is whether the EC relays your request to them in the first place."

"And if they do . . . whether we have *any* innocents involved here."

"You've also got to consider that pusher crew," Madison said. "Pusher crew—we've never dealt with. But their rep is—" Madison left it.

Unpredictable, clannish . . . and alcohol-fueled.

"We've got *them*. Yes."

"Historically, the EC's never been able to maintain a pusher's loyalty in the long haul," Madison said. "Whatever talk they've been fed, a couple of decades on your own delivers reality on a plate. Question is—does *this* crew understand yet?"

"Min's never seen a pusher, either. We do *not* want him leaving here with a doomsday alert for his home port."

"You've got that right."

A short silence, then:

"You're going to make me explain all this to John and Mum, right?" Madison asked sourly.

Madison was the one who'd naturally interface with John, whose shift touched his. "Your shift, your problem." JR yawned and stretched. "I'm off. If Mallory or station decides to talk on your watch . . . improvise."

"Thanks. Eat your sandwich."

"Had one. People keep feeding me."

"You could stand it."

"I'm doing *fine*." He started to leave, caught Madison's look . . . and picked up the plate.

The Galways of First- and Second-shifts, of whom there were five in all, had a table at supper. The fifth of them, Nolan, sat down ahead of Ross on a flipdown seat at the end.

"I should have taken that one," Ross said.

"Us having the honor of your presence and all," Nolan said with a grin and a grand gesture at the cushioned bench.

Ross hadn't regularly had supper with the foursome, Ian and the twins and Nolan. Himself being the youngest and Nolan, Cargomaster, being senior to all of them, it definitely wasn't right. And standing there with a tray in his hands and a proper end-of-bench seat left, he felt damned awkward. He set the tray down and sat down next to Siobhan.

"So where's Jen?" Ian asked.

"Security meeting," Ross said, and looked at Nolan and the rest. "I'm sorry, guys. I know I've been—"

"Suffering the loneliness," Siobhan said with irony, and pressed her hand dramatically to her heart. "Ah, the tragedy. So *nice* to see you, Ross."

That at least justified a scowl and the twitch of an elbow in Siobhan's direction. "Enough."

"Don't take it to heart," Ian said. "You provide welcome distraction. We're watching this all, outsiders that we all are, and thinking too much in the process."

"Thinking way too much," Siobhan said.

Ross began putting together a sandwich out of the pieces on his plate. He wished he'd taken the meatloaf. He still could. *Finity* was rich. *Finity* never minded seconds. And he'd still not made back his jump weight-loss. Distraction. He could understand that. His own mind kept cycling back to that image from the bridge, station with the two masts, the eerie three-vaned FTLer at one end, and on the other, the pusher, so massive that the station would need corrections after it undocked, just from its proximity.

"Captain sent that hail out," Maire said. "What station's going to make of it, whether they've got a stationmaster who actually doesn't like the EC, or whether they do—it's all dependent on that, isn't it?"

"But reasonable people aren't who the EC puts in charge, are they?" Ian said. "Not if Cruz is any indication."

"That pusher itself's a question mark. It was never one of the original lot," Nolan said. "Got to wonder what they're thinking. Damn sure the EC's done everything possible to innoculate them against anything like free thought. Alpha's own *Santa Maria* and *Atlantis*, they're regular old-style pusher-crew, even if they've half-starved us, supplying *Rights*."

"I'll lay bets each thought the other was bringing the foodstuffs," Siobhan said. "It was a pretty slim celebration the last pusher would've had, when it was all near-beer and fish steak."

"They'd have been feeling the chill, too," Maire said, "of all the Enforcers standing around. Spacers see the changes that just kind of creep up on station folk. And God knows pusher-crew sees it all weirder than we do."

"If things go on as they are," Nolan said, swallowing a bite, "it's only going to get weirder for the pushers. All they know is hauling cargo between Sol and Alpha. Even without whatever's going on here, if *Galway* proves the FTL route to Sol . . . what's going to happen to them?"

"If *Galway* gets through the way we hope—" Maire crossed herself. So did Siobhan and Nolan; and said 'amen.' Ross just sat, with his last sight of Fallan in mind.

"If *Galway* gets through," Nolan said, "and Sol gets a jump route—the pushers won't even have much trade left, except the rare real massy load. Never mind they never took the decision of all the other pushers, to go to Cyteen or Pell to be converted. Never mind they've stood by the First Stars, *and Earth*, keeping the Earth goods flowing, keeping us in touch with where we *all* came from. Their day is ending soon. I feel for 'em. They'll get the news on the Stream about the jump-points. Then they'll get back to Sol, and find FTLers being built, that they'll get the order to push to Alpha in hopes of finding a crew willing to take their bargain, and then everything they know is going to change, with that high profit food and printer stuff and the like, all going to FTLers running it. *This* pusher, they don't know it yet, but if there's a route to Alpha, this pusher's day is already done."

"No sympathy from me," Ian said. "Takes more than proximity to forge a family, and I'll bet anything the officers are EC to the core and that crew's going to be handpicked and indoctrinated to the max. *Gaia* took a stand, way back when, and the EC was forced into agreeing. Didn't matter much at the time, but the EC has seen Pell and Cyteen grow up, and spacers go independent-minded. I guarantee they won't allow ownership of a ship, pusher or FTL, ever again. Whoever crews that three-vaner or any other EC-built ship will be EC, no matter their names."

"*That* pisses me off," Ross spoke up at last. "I don't *want* EC ships handling trade to Sol. Who's earned it, if not us? We may be Alpha merchanters, but we're *not* Alpha's property and we're damned sure not the EC's. The Neiharts have it right. Stations are effectively *dead* without us, in spite of the Konstantins and the Carnaths and Emorys and the head high hoodoos of the EC. We need to talk to the pusher crews. We need to send a message down whatever Streams are going, to any pusher that's on that beam, and all the way to Earth. We need to say to pushers and merchanters, we're protecting *your* interests, which aren't theirs. Same as we've got to say to those two spooks on B-mast: the stations can't ever solve this. We let *them* get together, Pell and Cyteen and the EC and they'll be at each others' throats, because their property doesn't move, does it, and they can't change."

"Listen to the young firebrand, there!" Nolan said, laughing, so Ross took a breath and clamped his mouth shut.

"No," Ian said. "He's right."

There was quiet at the table. Nobody was eating at the moment.

"Ross-me-lad," Nolan said, "you're upsetting my appetite."

"These two spooks we've been chasing," Siobhan said, "they're Alpha ships like us, at least halfway. *Finity*'s big, *Finity*'s rich, and that's probably off-putting with these two Families, same as it was for us at first. But *Galway* is a name they're bound to know. We know the same people. The same trade. The same ships. *We* can talk to them."

"Not that the EC is going to favor letting them and us do that," Maire said. "I'm betting station won't let crews stay aboard here. Old rules prevail. I'm betting there'll be no meetings without EC present."

"We might at least give these two ships a hail in *our* name," Ian said. "If the Neiharts will let us have a hand."

There was a moment of silence.

"I'd be for it," Ross said.

"Can we *be* more involved?" Siobhan asked, and Nolan shrugged and said,

"We're the third ship. Damn right we should have a say."

Another message went out from *Finity* to Olympus and the merchanter ships at dock:

"This is Ian Monahan, Helm 2.2 of the merchant ship Galway, *aboard the merchanter* Finity's End, *courtesy of the Neiharts. Our own ship is underway out of Alpha, bound for Sol System under command of Senior Captain Niall Monahan, relying on jump-points as yet unnamed, as we believe you are aware. We understand you have visited Alpha since our departure, and we would appreciate news from Alpha where most of our Family remains ashore. Will you be willing to talk and share a few pints? Awaiting your reply."*

That, delivered in this, the tail-end of Mum's shift, the dividing line between ship's mainnight and mainday morning, was an interesting stir of the pot, in JR's opinion. John and Mum had conferred during mainnight, and then Mum conferred again with him at his wakeup. It was the Monahans' own inspiration, the conclusion was, it was not inflammatory, and well-conceived to imply a lot and give not much.

Send it, JR had agreed at maindawn, at the beginning of First-shift. And later, with Madison taking the conn, he retreated to his office for a scan of reports and a quiet lunch at his desk—actually a second breakfast roll: Pell's speciality, that roll, of which *Come Lately* had also seemed so fond—shipping as a frozen pellet and expanding to spicy deliciousness when thawed and baked. They had taken on a supply of those sufficient for a voyage to Alpha and back. It was not disciplined, a second breakfast, but Madison had said it—he needed his energy. He had thinking to do, a critical decision to make. Sugar helped.

He was *not* going to let station's silence wear on another twenty-four hours. As a ratchet up in this game of nerves, the Galways' message was a fair good try. But by the record of silence since they'd arrived, *nothing* was going to happen in a hurry, and Olympus was prepared for hell to freeze over.

Gentle rap at the door. He moved a foot, pressed the button.

It was Mum. Fourth-shift was about to enter its sleep cycle. And Mum did sometimes drop in for a late word at the turnover.

"Note," he said. "I had lunch, I have supper on order."

"Good for you."

"No word yet on the message. No acknowledgment of receipt, but it's a good try: innocent enough on the surface, plenty of subtext, given everything else we all know. The Mallorys and the Bellagios, if they get it, have something to think about. Maybe they can budge station, granted they've gotten the message. Granted they have access to their ships, and *they* don't have people held hostage."

"Credit the Monahans," Mum said, "for the thought and the asking."

"I do. I will."

"So—do you have a next move in mind?"

"Wondering what they'd do if we just began prep to leave, no further word passed?"

"Nothing they can do about it," Mum said. "They can't just go about their business taking no thought of us. They're worrying over there if they're half sane. Holding meetings."

"All the EC executive things," JR said. "Hoping we're worrying and holding meetings. A case of whose executive cracks first."

"The EC's good at sitting."

"Well, I'm not, and if they won't talk, we'll leave and go warn the rest of human space. I'm not remotely interested in sitting here for the next six months, watching them offload a pusher. —Speaking of which, we've got a new angle on the pusher's tail, thanks to our drift. Got a name."

"*Do* we?" Flicker of sharp interest, Mum being what she had been, pusher captain.

"*Wellington.*"

Instant frown. "*Wellington.* Not sure I like that."

Early pushers were things like *Gaia, Santa Maria, Golden Hind, Beagle* and *Polaris,* explorers and the like.

"So what's *Wellington?*"

"Famous general," Mum said. "Defeated Napoleon. Where's your Earth history?"

"I do know Napoleon."

"Well, Napoleon didn't win. Wellington did. Beat him at Waterloo. And I'm not sure I like the tone of that, myself here, where we are, them doing what they're doing. And I don't mean the sitting. Generals and wars. When they get into books to name important things, it's not a random choice. Committees do it. With a lot of meetings."

"So who's Napoleon, lately, in their minds? Emilio Konstantin?"

Mum snorted. "Hell, no question. Olga Emory."

It might well be. When station-folk spooked about aliens, it wasn't the gentle hisa. It wasn't even the long-ago mystery of Beta. It was the present-day Emorys and the Carnaths and their handiwork, the azi. Likely the EC felt much the same.

"A dedicated pusher, for Olympus, with a general's name instead of an explorer or the like," Mum said with a shake of her head. "They could commission a few more pushers to help Alpha, with names like *Charity* and *Compassion*, but no. Let's borrow trouble. Let's set up a station that's real difficult to get at, just for stockpiling Enforcers, and wait our chance to take it all back. Gotta wonder how long this has been going on here at Olympus, and how many pushers they've sent, with how many people that won't have troublesome loyalties. The station shows no signs of the scrapping that we know took place here. Olympus looks fat and well-kept. This is years this rebuild has been going on. This is people's whole lives."

"Wonder how many of these tri-vanes they've got in Sol System, how many are on their way here on the front of some new pusher."

"That's a question," Mum said. "Also a question how it connects to the *Rights* build at Alpha."

"If that's not all noise to cover what they've got going here. They could have a *hundred* of the tri-vanes built at Sol."

"But no crew," Mum said. "They can't even *test* that crazed vane array at Sol, so they had to bring it here. They had to get some damnfool broke merchanter to set her up and work out her kinks. And God help *Galway*, if they've sailed into what the EC doesn't want us to know about. Let's hope to God the Monahans remember *Gaia* and don't let the EC set foot on their deck."

"If they did get the better of Cruz, the Monahans will at least be armed against boarders," JR said. "As for fuel, they'd have time while they're lazing about mapping those two points, and they'd be crazy not to take advantage of that."

"We hope," Mum said.

"But you know something else, Mum. If the EC can push new-built FTLers here, and sign up failing merchanters, our Alliance, rescuing these Families and getting them out of debt, is not going to make the EC at all happy. They don't *want* Alpha fixed. They want people who will sign their freedom away to keep their Families alive. They want a crew that'll take Company orders for good and all and leave their Families ashore."

"Never attribute to stupidity that which can be explained by really intense malice? Breaking the Families to get their ships crewed is beyond mean." Mum gave him a fast under the brows glance. "You *do* realize, James, if this lot is up to that degree of no-good, they're capable of mayhem. *We* may be tougher-built, but the vanes are vulnerable."

"The station is far more vulnerable than we are, and there are two of us."

"I don't need to say be careful, James. I'm as close to Earth-born as you've ever stood, and I'm saying don't assume. Don't even assume about these two merchanters. They're right out of the deep dark, so far as I'm concerned, because I don't understand them. Our Monahans are different, but they make sense. These two have been playing a long, dark game, and deceiving their own in the process, and profit isn't the only god they answer to. As for that flaming great pusher, straight from Earth, even if this isn't the ship's first trip out, I doubt a single crew member has made more than one trip. Sol learned from *Gaia*. As for these two merchanters we've gone to such great lengths trying to include in our organization—I'm betting they've been serving the lords of misrule for as long as there've been merchanters, and there was never a time these two did not serve the EC, in one form or another. I'm convinced of that, seeing where we've found them."

". . . launched out of *Cyteen*, mind. At least their FTL converts."

"And after that never attaching to any station and refusing the black boxes that would tell their story to the rest of us. The Bellagios' pusher was Thule based. The Mallorys' was Olympus. God knows what deals they made with the EC before going for their FTL upgrades. God knows what they were paid or what the hell ties them to the EC now. Decades of subterfuge is the least of it. At least we know where those black-box-avoiding upgrades were made. And still they played it coy. A couple of runs to Pell . . . probably shakedowns to test the upgrades. Extreme low mass goods, inbound and out . . . at least officially . . . just to make it look legitimate and avoid questions of how did they manage. Venture chits. Boat kits. Trees. In the firmest confidence Pell and Alpha would never compare notes on imports. And didn't, until we did."

"If it weren't for those trees," JR said, "and chance visitors from Alpha, they might never have been found out. One does have to wonder about those trees, whether the Olympus execs knew about them, or if it was an under the table deal even here. It would be something if good old-fashioned merchanter larceny in one of their own brought their house of cards down."

"Even alerted, we could rationalize every other question on *Come Lately*'s condition, her trade pattern, her power upgrade and her merchandise. But dates—dates and trees, with nobody comparing notes until Alpha met Pell. . . ." Mum sighed, as the lights gave three brief flashes. It was the end of her day. "Well, James, Senior command is all yours."

She wasn't talking about the handover. He knew that. It was the middle of Madison's shift and John would be taking over. She meant your debate, your win. Go fix it, James.

The responsibility, dealing with the station, with the ghost ships . . . all of it was his, well, his and Madison's. Before they'd ever begun talking to other ships about the Alliance, they'd hammered it out in odd hours, how to and where to. John and Mum had been far less convinced that the problems of aging ships and Cyteen's colonial push were anywhere near relevant to them. Yes, Emilio had made the suggestion . . . in partial jest . . . but it had taken root and flourished in JR's own mind—that merchanters could be another power, the one that could hold all the competing forces in check. It was his idea. His push.

Now they sat here facing *his* problem, in a shape they hadn't bet on.

"Madison." He sent it on the captains' channel.

"Here."

"Got a message for Min."

"Better coming directly from you."

"Thanks. But you're probably right. —Com 2.1?"

"Sir."

"Resend the last-sent message."

"Aye, sir." A second of delay. *"Message resent."*

The Galways' message had gone twice now.

"Repeat that send to station at half hour intervals, watch to watch."

"Half hour intervals, watch to watch, aye."

"Com 2.2, message for Xiao Min, tight beam. As follows: *JR Neihart to Xiao Min, with respects to Grandfather Jun. We appreciate your patience. Lacking clear communication with the station or the merchanters, we are taking more energetic steps to open a dialogue if any party will take the responsibility. Please carry out our agreement should any hostility follow and keep yourselves otherwise disengaged, for your safety. We urge you to keep Cyteen way out of this, as far as risk. We will be communicating as possible and will have ears up for your input."*

Min might or might not answer. He waited the time out. Then:

"We will abide by our agreement, JR Neihart. The Xiao Family wishes you success."

That was Min himself, and one might read a personal concern into the fact. Min was still actively backing them, this time with no reference to Grandfather. JR tapped into Com directly, bypassing Betty and Aubie both. "We greatly appreciate the support, Xiao Min. We will share what we learn. We thank the Xiao Family. Over."

"We will be watching. Exercise due caution. We will execute our part of the agreement. Over."

"I count this a personal as well as a Family debt, Senior Captain. Thank you. Ending."

"Take care. Little Bear concludes transmission."

Book V   Section xx

"This is the Senior Captain speaking," sounded in Jen's ear. And in everyone's, in the close confines of the Security office. "We are preparing to move ship. In one hour, we will do three successive rapid repositions toward station perimeter. All prepare. Juniors and youngers, be aware, that's three. Count them. Do not move until the third finishes. Punch the alarm if you have a problem, but you will explain it to the captain and your alarm may be ignored, good of the ship. Third-shift, sleep on: you'll get an extra fifteen from Second and another fifteen from Fourth. First-shift Nav and Helm, it's your problem. Second-shift, delay shift-change until notified. All-ship, condition yellow. All stations attention. Condition yellow."

Jen looked at Fletcher. At cousins Parton and Twofer, who looked at Fletcher. Fletcher shrugged. "We're going closer," Parton said. "Aren't we?"

"Not our problem," Fletcher said. "Could become our problem."

"You think we'll be going aboard the station?" Parton asked.

"I think Senior Captain wants to give the other side the chance to do the right thing," Fletcher said. "Doesn't mean any of them will be remotely interested. Or that any of them will take responsibility. They've invested a shitload into keeping their operation here secret. They've been found out and there's no telling what they'll do to prevent us finding out any more. We're not prepared to arrest Olympus Station, but we could do them more damage than they could us, if we have to make a quick getaway. This situation just isn't on the charts."

"You think they've launched something at us?"

"We'd be the first to know," Fletcher said. "And there's been no sign, as of yet. This reposition . . . that's a bit dicey. Three bubbles, three chances to grab everything around us and shoot it out the other side as high-V missiles.

We've got no damn charts that aren't antique, so I hope we don't boost a rock without meaning it. Trust Helm to make sure we won't be aiming right at station—that's the burn we've got coming up. But we're going to get a lot cozier, I'm thinking, and that's bound to give them a little shake up. After the relocation, whether or not we actually dock, we'll be in position to get some really good visuals on the station, maybe get an up-close of that FTLer that shouldn't exist. Cyteen would like that a lot."

"Maybe we *shouldn't* correct vector before we move," Parton said. "A nice little stray rock or three . . . we could give them a major repair issue and solve the whole problem, at least for now. Oops. Sorry about that."

A shiver traveled down Jen's spine. *Finity* wasn't armed, but she *could* throw things station couldn't stop, even if they didn't deploy the otherwise peaceful-use mass-drivers. It was getting scary, when her cousins started talking like that. On the one hand, she wanted them to do something to stop the EC from doing whatever they were here to do, but on the other hand, she didn't want them to be the first ship ever to damage a station on purpose. She really didn't want people to die.

"There's time to get to quarters," Fletcher said, "if you want to. Or you can ride it out here. Take your pick."

They were going to decouple the ring real soon. Wherever they wanted to ride it out, they were going to need to be in that place, that soon.

Parton got up, and Twofer followed. Jen hesitated, third, not sure, and then decided her own bed, her own cabin, was not where she wanted to be, alone, when so much was happening so fast. She wanted to be in this office, with Fletcher, who always answered her questions, who helped her understand, no matter what. She'd left her cabin in good order, everything latched down, no problems. She checked the supply cabinet at her seat. There was juice enough, if something went sideways.

And it wasn't a never-could happen. It was scary, what they were about to do, which was gather way in a hard burn and then bring up the jump engines, forming the bubble for a fraction of a second. It was something *Finity* had done only once in *her* existence, and it was a stomach-heaving experience, first a hard burn, then halfway to subspace and then out, like a V-dump, but not, and without trank in your system, and she didn't like it. What Ross had recalled from Fallan about the spacer who'd seen hyperspace came back vividly, and if ever there was a time you *might* see that sort of thing . . .

To station perimeter, Uncle Jim had said, meaning station safety perimeter, and their motion had a long way to go, toward the station. They were truncating days of travel into three quick folds of the fabric of space, a finesse that ought to impress the hell out of pusher crew and Sol Station officials.

And Ross got to calculate it, got to put in those numbers that, one day, would hold the lives of all his Family in the balance. Kate had trusted his numbers once. That had to spook him now.

Hang in there, Ross, she thought. *I trust you. Trust yourself.*

The takehold sounded for the preparatory burn. Parton and Twofer would have made it to their quarters. She just rested while it lasted, looked at Fletcher, who was calm as if they did this every day.

The lightness increased. That didn't help her stomach.

We're going in, she thought. They were going toward station. And that damn pusher. And the whole situation.

No question. We're going in.

Book V   Section xxi

G was mostly gone. By the time relocation began, the only thing holding them in their seats would be the belts.

Lay course, was the instruction from Kate at Nav 1, which was no problem. The burn had trued them up. Ross shut down peripheral thinking and just worked the numbers. A station in the range of instruments and following a known course was hell and away easier to put in the crosshairs than some invisible jump-point that was all math and relative motion.

Then there was the other calc that was mostly Helm's problem, but Nav supplied the data—like a V-dump, but not—absolute local velocity, vector, stellar mass, target mass . . . all a Nav problem. But—

Fal, they got me calcing a local hop-skip in Foucault's lap. God . . . bless . . .

He could *hear* that star if he listened. Not the cacophony it would be if he was coming up out of trank, but he could hear it, and it was in a restless mood.

The ringing from the Ardaman that had floated in and out of his head was quiet now. The limit for entry was behind them, but Foucault was not going to be happy with their move, and the disruption of space they were about to make would set the star itself to ringing, if they weren't careful.

But Foucault's numbers were old friends now, Kate had seen to that. They'd even run sims on this exact possibility.

Didn't make the real thing any less scary. The clock was running, the ship was moving, the station was moving, the math was shifting even before the hard burn started, and Foucault and its partner were definitely in the mix. But it was only Foucault they needed to worry about now. That crazy-patterned Ardaman was an artifact of both stars, but for this purpose, only Foucault mattered. V-dump was one thing when you were riding into system at high V. You blew energy off in the formation and release of the bubble and, grace of the local star, repositioned. This was a dead-stop to dead-stop show of power; a damnably difficult, intimidating show of power.

James Robert Neihart, damn the man, was stark raving mad.

Numbers, numbers, *numbers* . . .

And, *God!* it was exciting.

"Helm," came JR's order. "At your pleasure."

The takehold sounded. It did nothing for the nerves. Ross input. Other lines popped up on the screen, one, two, three, four. Five, all within a hair of each other, and this time, he registered when his blue disappeared behind Kate's green.

He sat, nerves twitching. Ian, over on his right, was probably in a cold sweat.

The numbers on Nav screens changed in a steady flow. Computers were locked on and adjusting, adjusting, adjusting.

"Three," Helm 1 said. "Two. One."

Reality blinked. Failed. Blinked. Failed. Blinked.

Three flickers, each worse than the last. And with each phase out, it was harder to check the numbers, to make sure they were on point, but he did, and thank God they were, because he honestly didn't know how in hell they'd do anything about it if they—

Then . . . everything was just . . . normal, and screens were flashing with reset and input.

Made it, Fal. Ross reconfirmed the lines. *We're good. We're still alive. We didn't hit the station. Didn't end up in Foucault's belly. We're at relative stop minus a hair.*

"*Spot on,*" Kate said calmly. "*Nicely done, there. All of you.*"

Praise, from Kate. He wondered if the time would ever come when he *didn't* need that validation. Who gave it to Kate? Who gave it to Fallan? Being X.1 of a shift took that kind of confidence.

Confidence. Not arrogance. You *delivered.*

With a faint clunk and thud, the ring began to turn. Within moments, up and down began to assert themselves.

His hands shook a little. He swallowed hard, to manage his stomach, and the screens showed their new reality. They were down to reckoning in kilometers, not AU's. Still carrying some way. The optics were coming up with detail they hadn't been able to see, and Captain James Robert—the whole shift called him that when he wasn't listening—was on his feet as if nothing damn much had gone on, studying that massive display.

So what did he get that they couldn't, from what was in front of them? There was a lot of speculation flying about, what they *could* do about Olympus, and whether they ought just to kite out of here and confer at Pell—maybe pass the word down the line of stations what the EC was up to here, and get a consensus just not to let any trade from Olympus dock at other stations.

But point of fact—and Senior Captain seemed to be thinking down the same track, what was going on here wasn't trade, and they needed proof . . . like pictures. And Captain James Robert having chased those two merchanters from Pell to Alpha and back again—he had business with them, no question. Business and a serious warning . . . because those two were Families.

How they were going to deliver that warning past EC opposition was a question.

Book V	Section xxii

"*Well,*" John said, via com, "*that should stir things up.*"

JR drew a breath, scanning details of the pusher they'd never been able to get at distance, detail right down to the instruction plates on a service access. That fine. Nav had outdone themselves. "We'll see. We'll see whether they see fit to answer. Go back to sleep."

"*Are you going to do anything else interesting?*" That was John when he was off-duty. A wit, when he was half-asleep.

"Do you want me to wake you if we get a message from station?"

"*Only if you get one of the merchanters talking. I already know what station has to say.*"

"I think we can all figure that one."

"*Did anyone think to advise Min what we're doing?*"

"It's all handled. Good night, John. It's all zipped up."

"Hell. As if I'm going to sleep with this going on."

"Take a pill, John. We're going to need someone fresh if we have to move."

"Take a pill," Madison cut in. *"He's going to drop this into my lap, and Mum's tired. I need you sane."*

"Hell if," Mum cut in. *"I'm pouring a Scotch. Take a pill, John."*

"Yes'm." John cut out.

"Keep us advised," Mum said.

He had Madison and Mum to consult with and a Third-shift captain to step in fresh on whatever mess the three of them couldn't handle. That was all he could ask for.

"Station will be consulting at this point," he said on bridge address. "For now we'll continue on course at current rate." Current course was carrying them closer to station and current rate was a brisk clip, which station wouldn't like. Bow-on kept the critical engine section out of their line of fire, but it also put *Finity's* ring and extended vanes in their sights, if they had a mass-driver. And if they had any policy that covered a ship that didn't come in scant of fuel, which they were not—station could issue threats to withhold service—none of which mattered. They were good for an escape, and running lighter the further they went.

JR stood. He sipped a cup and put on an air of confidence. In fact he was too wrought to sit and do routine things. The hindbrain was still processing, still sorting through acts of past EC station admins and what they had gathered at Alpha—the EC regulations file, no less—to figure what the station might feel empowered to do. Various EC rules gave admin the right to curtail movement, restrain certain people, take possession of a ship, a business, a residence, if there was suspicion of subversive activity. It could imprison for thirty days without charges, interrogate under drugs, and it could seize assets. Likely it was the same set of rules here, and its insistence on full access to ships at dock meant there was not a prayer of Tom Mallory getting a communication of any sort unless station gave it to him and stood over his shoulder while he answered.

It also meant, if *Finity* docked, they could have a fight on their hands from the Company men, not necessarily from the Families . . . but that, too, remained possible.

He considered awhile, then said, "Com 1, transmit just the station portion of the Alliance agreement. Let them know *our* rules of station engagement."

"Aye, sir."

That was station's rights under the Alliance consensus, which gave stations the right to their fees, their charges, right of recovery of debt from cargo transport fees or cargo sale before payment of earned monies, which nipped a defaulting ship in the bottom line.

Plus it carried the obligation for stations to revise their charters in certain ways involving ships and crews. A crewman's citizenship was his ship, and ships under the Alliance charter were independent states for all practical purposes. There would be no boarding without permission, and crew was not obliged to leave the ship unattended. A ship was liable for damages done by crew, but a crewman could not be held longer than two hours without notification of a ship's legal representative, could not be imprisoned unless released by the ship, but could be barred from the station for a time to be determined. Et cetera.

That went on for a file of considerable length, and wanted a signature. The other signatures on it went clear across the Hinder Stars and the Beyond as far as Mariner, with an official addendum from *Dublin*, included in the files he'd gotten on Pell, that Cyteen and its colonies would sign once Pell had signed.

The Olympus stationmaster *could* decide to query them as to what the hell this was, but in all likelihood, they'd already heard the gist of it from the two ghost ships . . . unless they'd been holding out on that information, in which case station was probably already asking *them* what the hell it was and *had* they signed it.

"*We have transmission from Station,*" Com 1 said.

"All stations, Com 1," JR replied. First-shift had sat a lengthy, tense watch. What they heard in that order was that many more useful minds would be on the problem as well.

He *hoped* it was an answer to the transmission. Or Tom Mallory, being allowed to call.

"*Finity's End, state your intention. You are not cleared for approach. Please coordinate with traffic control.*"

And again: "*Finity's End, state your intention.*"

"No reply, Com," JR said. Until they had an official voice, it was mere traffic direction. And they weren't complying.

But with that near instantaneous relocation, station's time to think had suddenly run out, and it was past time for any of the ships currently docked, including the pusher, to think about their own position.

"*Finity's End, state your intention.*"

JR lazily beeped Com 1 and keyed in his mic. "This is JR Neihart, Senior Captain, *Finity's End.* Our intention at the moment is to speak to *Miriam B*'s Senior Captain Thomas Mallory, or whoever is currently holding that office."

A lengthy pause.

"We will advise Captain Mallory of your request."

Not a *word* about *Little Bear's* presence in the system. Not a single word. But they damned sure knew *Little Bear* was out there. And station could get Mallory patched through from any bar—there was *always* a bar—on the Strip. If they claimed they couldn't find the senior captain of one of the four ships docked, they were lying.

JR waited, and watched the inputs. Nothing stirred, so far as exterior observation. The station kept doing what it had done, which was nothing.

He *waited*. And waited.

Com 1 beeped his board. *"Station,"* Com 1 said.

"Go," JR said, and immediately:

"This is Tom Mallory." A commanding voice, that. A deep voice. *"Finity's End, you're asking to talk to us."*

"This is JR Neihart, Senior Captain, *Finity's End.* Sorry to interrupt your business, Captain Mallory, but you and Frank Bellagio are the known factors here, merchanters that we've been trying to track for a bit of business. Over."

A pause. A very lengthy pause, and real: there was practically no time lag in the transmission. *"Due compliments to the Neiharts and* Finity's End, *and, we take it, the Monahans of* Galway. *What sort of business?"*

"A mutually beneficial agreement. I understand you heard about it at Alpha. Every station and every ship operating has willingly signed on. *Miriam B* and *Come Lately,* and, we now find, Olympus itself—are our only missing pieces. We've been hunting you from Pell to hell and gone, and you may imagine our surprise when our inquiries led us here. We thought you might be dealing in a little station salvage. I take it that is not the case here."

A lengthy pause. He waited.

"No, it is not," Mallory said. *"What is your business?"*

"Exactly as stated. I've forwarded a document to station. I'm happy to send you the same."

Another lengthy pause. Then: *"Captain Neihart, you will have noticed we have a complicated situation here. Does it take two ships to deliver a document?"*

"We've traveled together to reassure you that this is not just *Finity's* idea. Also, by the agreement, decisions for the Alliance require three signed parties. There are three Alliance ships here, counting the Monahans, and they do count, by all convention of law. I'll send you the ship version of the agreement."

Silence. Prolonged silence.

"Captain Mallory, we have come a long way for your sake. You were at Alpha. You're fairly well abreast of what went on there, let's agree on that. You may have had recent contact with members of the Alliance . . . notably *Firenze,* under Giovanna Galli. The Alliance is providing her with a new navigation system at fair cost, a loan with years to repay. She was in fairly dire straits when we met, and a lot happier when we parted. I understand that operation is now progress."

"They were in anticipation of that when we spoke. I'm glad to know it came through. But I find it very difficult, sir, considering all that you see here, to believe that you've come to this inconvenient station simply to sell us insurance."

"Odd as it might seem, precisely that. Insurance on your cargo, on your mechanical soundness. We can do that. Same as we're refitting *Firenze.* And we've offered Alpha Station a modified version of the same bargain. They are getting desperately needed supplies they asked for. Point of interest, what are you trading here? What's going well?"

"Foodstuffs, mostly. Flour. Prices about standard."

"And exotics? Your trades on Pell are what made us think, perhaps, you were salvaging here. Imagine the luck, happening into dock with a pusher in port. Don't suppose you can liberate a few cases of Scotch."

A pause. Perhaps a discussion on the other end about those *Pell* trade items. Then: *"Depends. Station deals with the pusher. We deal with the station. You might find things of interest. But you have to dock to pick it up here. I'm not running pods out. So what are you hauling?"*

Tom Mallory was after information, same as he was.

"Mostly fuel. This has been a long run for us, with no guarantee of options on this side. But we can take on a little mass, no problem. Especially luxury stuff."

"Don't tell us you came to trade."

"I'd never ask you to believe that. We're offering what I've said we're offering."

"Stationmaster requests you brake, Captain. You are far exceeding ordinary drift."

"We're well within our capabilities. Station needn't worry. Who's operating the new ship? Earth-built, it seems."

A pause. A very long pause.

"Captain, let's not waste time. I know what's gone on at Alpha. We know. Station knows. The pusher knows. We know each other knows, so let's not

pretend otherwise. If you want to discuss the matter, that can happen. The new ship is a freighter, crewed by Family, as the Mallorys and the Bellagios understand is an issue with you. Does that answer some of your concerns?"

"Pushed here."

"Pushed here, sir, arrived a month ago. Her name is Shalleen, *her registry is Sol, and her captain of record is Ella Bellagio. She's new-built, based on an old design, with a few enhancements, and she's just in from her second insystem shakedown."*

"Her purpose being?"

"Supply and trade, from here to Venture, Bryant's, and Alpha."

Well, wasn't that disingenuous.

"And Sol?"

"Remains to be seen."

"Should be possible . . . granted the Monahans' jump-points to Sol prove viable. The need for pushers to Alpha might slow down somewhat if they prove out. But then—there's *here.* Wicked rattle we got out of Foucault coming in. We welcome honest trade, and pusher trade certainly makes sense here, given this point's instability, should Olympus choose to become a major hub for Sol goods. Pushers could move a massive lot of cargo that can't move any other way. And there's absolutely no reason our agreement can't encompass pusher trade—though it would make better sense to open negotiation on that matter with Pell or—"

"Stationmaster would really like you to hammer down the V, Captain."

"We note that. Tell him if he'll make clear the local zoning, we'll comply, but unfortunately we don't have current charts for Olympus."

Charts that would show mining zones, reserved zones, and other things a truly nervous EC station might not like to hand over. But—

"This is Stationmaster Acienne Jiburi." It was a woman's voice, sudden, sharp and crisp. *"What is your business,* Finity's End?"

"Pleased to hear from you, Stationmaster. I'm sure you know we *will* report what we find here to other stations. I hope you'll find it a relief to drop the secrecy and open a constructive discussion with your neighbors—who are not necessarily unwilling to trade openly and fairly with you and your local ships."

"I have no idea what you're talking about. What I am talking about is your rate of speed in a restricted zone. Reduce V and take instructions."

"Stationmaster, you have two ships in port who have been doing business in Sol goods at Venture and Pell, business which has, inadvertently we are certain, broken interstation trust, due to the deliberate obfuscation of provenance of those goods and violation of trade regulations in the last docking.

As the go-between for stations, we have come to mediate that situation. We have arrived to find you have a very large ornament atop A-mast, and we are naturally curious, as merchanters, exactly what goods are about to hit our markets. We would also, in the interest of merchanters in our organization, like to talk to the Senior Captain of the *pusher* you have at dock. Finally, we hope to resolve the question of whether the import of banned goods at Pell was a failure of communication or . . . something else."

"We are not a commercial station, Captain. We are a research and administrative station, we have adequate supply and there is nothing for you here. I repeat. Reduce your speed. We do not appreciate this show or your humor."

"Our course will not intersect, Stationmaster, which I trust your techs have assured you."

"Too damned close, Captain, which I trust your crew has informed you!"

"We saw no need to spend days maneuvering to investigate activity at a mothballed station. But if the EC declares it activated and if, as the trade at Venture and Pell would indicate, you are doing business here, we ask for docking instructions, on the understanding that we operate under the rules outlined in the document we provided."

Prolonged silence. One might believe Olympus had broken off the contact. One did note the loud silence regarding the trade of Sol goods with Venture and Pell.

"We are an EC operation. We are not obliged to sell you fuel or services. We are fueling a pusher. We have none to spare for you. We hope this will not be an issue."

A bit of frankness. And a fishing attempt. "That would be a problem, if we needed it, but we don't. We came here specifically looking for *Miriam B* or *Come Lately,* and we expected no more than a fuel dump and a goods cache, neither of which would be ours to tap. As happens, we have information you should find useful, and we are willing to carry a message *from* you to other stations, who, I assure you, have an interest here. If you should see your way clear to sign that document we have sent you, you would find other stations interested in trading for pusher-delivered goods, which would be very much to the benefit of all concerned, including the EC and Sol System. Should you wish to consult your authority—assuming it will take a while—we are still willing to convey a reasonable message to other stations and deal with your supply issues in the meanwhile, if necessary."

Another silence. Likely the stationmaster was consulting with someone. Or perhaps she was reading the rulebook and considering her retirement options.

Then: "Finity's End, *we can provide you the bottom of B-mast if you will dock. We believe that should be adequate.*"

"We are pleased to accept the courtesy, Stationmaster. Be advised, if we dock, we remain a sovereign nation, under Alliance rules, as do you. We will shut down ring rotation and accept a rotating docking-connect for stability, but we will not tie into station systems, we will not accept lines or bundle, we will not debark, and we will accept no visitors except by invitation. We will ask to be in contact with the captains of ships at dock. And we will be offering them and you information such as we may be asked. So you understand. Over."

Pause. Then, with evidence of tension in the voice: "*You can begin by braking,* Finity's End. *And by identifying that ship hanging out there in the dark behind you.*"

"That is the merchanter *Little Bear,* a member of the Alliance."

"We do not have that name in records."

"Suggest you update your records. The family is Xiao. They're here as witness and support and their presence as witness simply assures your good behavior *and* ours. We will begin maneuvers at this point, Olympus. Thank you. We appreciate your courtesy. Ending."

Thumb-push ended that conversation, at least for his part. He looked out across the bridge, and switched to general address. "We're going in for a stand-off docking at the end of B-mast, cousins and friends. There's some risk to it, but more risk on their side. We'll be watching our surrounds very carefully, and, Com 1, have a message rigged but as yet unsent advising *Little Bear* to go hell for broke out of here. We will not send except under a captain's direct order, or in our incapacity, your discretion, understood?"

"*Aye, sir.*"

"I hope we *will* be able to have a reasonable exchange with station administration, but given this exchange, I doubt it. I want to get as much information as we can, I want to know what we're dealing with, and I want to get on record that we had boots on that deck, faced their officials at their advantage, and made offers, to which they made specific response . . . which I anticipate will be a stall, a counterproposal, or a hell, no, but we will have it recorded that there was an offer and a response. I emphasize we will not put the ship at risk, and we will protect hull integrity and mobility at any cost— *any* cost, including damage to the station. They know *Little Bear* is out there beyond their reach, and we shouldn't find abrupt action necessary, but needless to say, everybody, every shift, on the way in and after we're at dock, keep alert, mind your takeholds constantly and pay attention to what's going on. Got it?"

Nobody, down to the three- and the five-year-old and the three under-10's in the loft, was a total novice in alerts and takehold alerts. The baby was with her minder, still down in medical. Those were the thoughts that welled up first and foremost: the Family, and the presence of the Monahans, who had by no means signed on for what they'd run into.

His responsibility, whatever happened from here out, was to protect them. When one of *Finity's* captains was on the bridge in a developing situation, it was not up to a vote. Next-shift just took it from there and followed the plan the last had set in motion. It was Mum's way. It had been Jeff Neihart's and Winnie's and Torrey's, the original James Robert's, and the way of everybody who had ever held the senior command on old *Gaia*. The active captain couldn't be asking may-I and *Finity* couldn't change course at every shift of command on the bridge, not physically and not mentally.

But damn. *Damn,* he felt alone at this moment. Damned if he'd put crew at risk, but he *needed* station's official stance to take back to Pell, *needed* to know what was happening on this station. *Research and administration* was one thing, but if the EC was looking for something more, if the EC was bidding for a strong return, a fortress in the Hinder Stars—that outbid everything else.

"That's all," he said, and tapped out.

"So, well," Madison said in his ear. "*That was interesting, brother. Well done.*"

He couldn't say *I hope so,* with the Family and the Monahans in front of him. He couldn't show emotion. He'd gotten good at keeping his face a blank no matter what was coming into his ear from Madison and the others—to which not even Com 1 was privy: they had it rigged that way.

"*A good close look at the setup,*" Mum said from somewhere. "*That should be interesting, in itself.*"

"*I vote we adjust our speed to let Fourth-shift dock,*" Madison said.

"*Hell, no,*" Mum said, whose shift routinely handled docking. "*First-shift can deal with station. First-shift is doing right well at it.*"

John, JR decided, had taken a pill, or *John* would have chimed in on the question. Just as well, since Second- and Third-shifts were switching places. That would put John, cold-blooded and decisive if not as imaginative, in charge of a fast getaway if he, JR, ended up in a stationside cell. No matter what Madison promised, Madison was constitutionally incapable of leaving him behind without an attempt at rescue.

John, for all he was a great friend as well as a cousin, wouldn't hesitate for an instant.

"*They want us to soft-dock endmost on the mast,*" Madison said. "*Do you suppose they realize that if they want to play games, we can upset their whole day? Your call, JR."*

They had the invitation. Station might be thinking that their being attached to the station was some sort of protection should *Little Bear* decide to throw something their way. But the greater likelihood was that station didn't want them going away without giving some clue what they were dealing with. Station was hoping to get some time—a margin that they were eating up, coming in as hot as they were.

"I'm about to order our slowdown," JR said. "We've got the time. I'll be calling Min and informing him. Any other observations?"

"We'll manage," Mum said. *"Just wrap it up, James. Madison can explain it to John."*

"We're set," Madison said, *"brother."*

Book VI   OLYMPUS   Section i

To Xiao Min and all the Xiao Family from JR Neihart, Senior Captain.

Finity is on course to dock at Olympus, at my instigation. I am sending you the entire transcript of an exchange with Tom Mallory, Senior Captain of Miriam B, *and another with one Acienne Jiburi, stationmaster. The new ship at dock, we are advised, bears the name* Shalleen. *Mallory states that* Shalleen *has made two shakedown runs in the system under the hands of Bellagio family from* Come Lately *and that she stands fueled. As to her general worthiness we are not informed, but we may perhaps assume she is crewed with at least a single shift of Bellagio crew, who may or may not be aboard at the moment.*

Our conversation with Mallory was interrupted by the stationmaster, who requested we slow our approach and come in. We are invited to tube-dock at the end of B-mast, from which we should have an excellent view of both the merchanters and the new ship at dock. We are proceeding with that intention, having made it clear to Stationmaster Jiburi that we will not disembark more than a few of us.

Without invitation, we have transmitted Alliance registration documents to Miriam B *and to Olympus administration and have now sent the same to* Come Lately *and* Shalleen. *We have little hope that any of these will sign while at dock here, if they are even permitted to receive them. We are hoping to continue dialogue with the Mallorys and Jiburi and will attempt to open discussion with the Bellagios and with the pusher at dock.*

We will continue to stress in all discussion that our mission here involves the presentation of documents for the benefit of all concerned. We have also touched on the events at Alpha, which both Miriam B *and* Come Lately *have apparently reported to Olympus. Whether they are prepared to accept a new reality and talk seriously with us remains a question, but we will not spare the effort and we will have the legal record of the offer and their response.*

It is my sense that Come Lately *is discharging one or two shifts of her*

Family to crew Shalleen, *to which they may be taking title, under what terms and with what purpose we do not know. Certainly should she appear at Venture, she will cause a stir. It is my guess that possession of* Shalleen *is a reward for service.*

Regarding the pusher, we did not make progress on that topic.

Sent from my office, with images.

JR Neihart.

That went out.

Thirty-eight minutes later, by the clock, a message came in:

To the Captains of Finity's End, *the Xiao Family extends greetings. We have your message, the transcript, and accompanying images, and wish good fortune to all the Neiharts and guests in this undertaking. We are maintaining position and readiness. We will observe as agreed, and under terms of our agreement, we will carry news to all ports along our route.*

Sent from the bridge, Little Bear.

Xiao Min.

Book VI   Section ii

They had blown off V. Ring rotation had resumed after the hand-off to Second-shift, and the order now was general Caution. It said nothing against hanging out in the mess area, for those newly off-shift, and Ross was so inclined. A beer would have come very welcome, but bridge crew had to stay clear-headed under yellow, even off-duty. Ian and Siobhan and Maire were there as well, but they all knew the same things, so there was nothing, really, to say. They sipped orange drink and tea and hung about, silent for a time, just happy to not be alone.

"Won't stay docked too long," Ian said, finally. "The Neiharts have that baby to think about: Z-G is hard on them."

They had optics on the screen, fined down to serial numbers on the girders, if it mattered—close enough now to worry station, being as they were on a slanting approach.

There'd be no shore leave here, no safety to be had inside the station, and they all were going to be operating in zero-G, battened down and ready to move hard, for the time it took for those going ashore to do whatever business they could—short business, they hoped. The days coasting in had been their best chance since leaving Alpha to rest and regroup, but things would happen fast, now.

Leisurely from their end, sitting sipping tea and juice, but the Monahans in general had been on the receiving end of *Finity's* last unannounced visit, and *Finity's* approach was a scary thing to watch from the other side, no question. Damned sure that on Olympus, as once on Alpha, pulses would be quickening. Techs would be calling officials. EC offices would be scrambling.

Policy-makers would defend their prerogatives and fight each other . . . if it worked like Alpha. Every ship had its self-interest. Every office had its priorities and procedures and wore them like a shield. Every official and officer wanted *not* to be blamed for whatever happened next, in the close-knit society of ship or station.

"Whoever's in charge is not having a good day," was Ian's word on it.

"That pusher crew's going to be asking station some questions," Maire said. "And they've got to have their own opinion of all this. Pusher crew's got to care about their ship, be it the safety of where they're sitting, or the safety of the ship that gets them out of here. They'll be asking questions about their own future, now, won't they?"

"I'd like once to talk to somebody who's come from Earth, or Mars, or wherever," Siobhan said. "That would be so weird. I'd buy him endless drinks."

"He'd be asking you what does us finding him mean to *his* future," Ross said. "And what do we tell him? That his ship could get him to Earth, sure, but not the Earth he knew. In less time, he could be at Pell—enjoying life."

"And then what with that ship? What good's a manned pusher?" Siobhan asked. "It's too late for converting that creature to much but scrap, isn't it? She's got the value of her metal, and not much more. Is it even worth it to push her up to speed again?"

"The bots were servicing her," Ross said, "which would imply they at least intended to send her back. With what, God knows."

There was a time the crew quarters of the old pushers had been worth converting, the old engine pack detached, the vanes of an FTLer installed. Those converts had had living quarters and some curious amenities, in earliest FTL. They'd hauled far, far less than they once had as pushers, but more often. Eventually, the converts had given way to the smaller purpose-builts, which were faster, more economical, and far more numerous. To handle the purpose-builts the old pusher Families had had to break up, so there were more ships, and related Families. Converted *Gaia* alone had held out until there was *Finity*, a ship large enough for all the Neiharts at once.

The first purpose-builts, like old *Firenze*, which had aged into scary malfunctions, could be rebuilt now and modernized. But, excepting the two that served Alpha, the old giants were long gone, stripped down. The only thing left even of historic *Gaia*, was the crew-ring which had been moved complete to *Finity*. Her steel had gone to the new docks of Pell Station. No new pushers had been built, except the few robotic heavy-movers on set routes.

And now this one . . . and whatever else Sol had built to supply Olympus.

The pusher out there was very likely to be headed for scrap. One had to wonder what was going through the crews' heads. It was one thing to haul an FTLer out to known FTL routes; something else entirely to get there and discover an FTL ship might reach Earth through Alpha. Imminently. That was where their world *really* changed.

So . . . what could JR offer the pusher crew, Ross wondered—them with no training in modern ships?

"What good's a pusher?" Ross echoed the question. "Captain said something about *accommodating* pushers, but did that mean he thought pushers might continue to be used to bring Sol goods in here? That stationmaster didn't sound much interested in trade with *anyone*. The crew, though . . . they might have insights into the EC that Pell'd like to have, and Pell would treat the crew right, unlike the EC. Alpha's proof of that. Retrain them, maybe. I don't see a percentage in them going back to Earth. Can you imagine? Olympus is near twice the run to Alpha. They'd be time-stretched as hell, time they got back."

"They live on pusher-time," Ian said. "And if they go back for another run, how much of a life have you got? Fallan could tell them, couldn't he? Or Mum. Old *Atlas*. And *Gaia*. That's who could really talk to the pusher crew, couldn't they?"

"Hell of a situation for them," Ross said, thinking of Alpha. The hotels. The places built for the pusher trade, that staffed and opened only when a pusher was in dock. The shops with the burst of color and variety they brought, an injection of life that lasted a year or more.

The days of living gods were over. And that was sad. Alpha spacers, if no one else, could feel unaccountably sorry for the crew of the *Wellington*.

Only a couple hours to go. The ring would be disengaging soon for docking.

JR, belted into his office chair and, with the ordinary sequence of *Finity*'s shifts disrupted, sipped tepid coffee from a safety mug and pored over the best images they could get of the end of B-mast and the fittings available—as well as the very accurate files on *Finity*'s own engineering. They hadn't had to worry that much at Hinder Stars stations with a quasi-modern mast dock, but here they were coping with a true pre-FTL mast—a mast-end design made explicitly and exclusively for pushers.

The *Wellington* would be hard-docked up on A-mast, with massive grapples holding it in place to a rotating coupling. Once connected, the ship essentially became a part of the fixed axis of the station. It was an old system, designed for dealing with one, possibly two ships in dock, and in the case of the pushers, for half a year or more at a stretch. Offloading was done outside the hull, with service vehicles, while ship's crew made the twice-per-visit transition through a flexible tube connecting the ship's airlock to one on the mast.

The smaller FTLers in dock on B-mast used, from what he could see, a modified version of the service vehicle docking ports.

Finity had no provision for the pusher grapples, nor would she have accepted them under any circumstances. The modified service ports along the mast were equally impossible, and there was no adaptation such as Alpha had had to handle larger ships. To connect to the Olympus mast, *Finity* would have to use the same tube connection a second pusher would use, but she would have to rely on her own positional thrusters to keep her a steady distance from the station . . . which posed its own kind of danger. The slightest drift away from the station could strain that reinforced passage tube until it snapped . . . with consequences for the station.

Station simply said come ahead, which said station was either completely desperate for answers or completely misjudging the risks involved—which itself was worrying for their sense of operational safety. *Pell* wouldn't have agreed, and Pell was easily ten times the size of this station, far better able to handle the destabilizing effects of huge masses in proximity. But then Pell

knew something about managing mass, and even with its highly sophisti-
cated means of internal adjustment, it wouldn't have agreed to what Olympus wanted them to do. It was possible the senior captain of the *Wellington*
would be calling in objections. A pusher, especially with all her crew de-
bauching on the Strip, was ill-equipped to disengage those massive grapples
and back off, should *Finity* screw the linkup.

But if *Wellington* were making objections, station was overruling them.

Which left JR on his own to assess the dangers.

Straining the physical tether was a problem for station, but not good for
the ship's side of the equation, either. If the tether snapped, the tube itself
could do a lot of damage with the kinetic energy of the parting masses involved, not to mention pieces and parts flying about.

Of course, keeping *Finity* standing off, unlinked but available for personnel transfer . . . should they decide to venture into a small-craft port of
B-mast . . . was also an option. Mum favored that idea, as easiest for a fast,
clean getaway.

JR didn't.

For one thing, station wanted them attached, for whatever reason, and if
that request was, against all odds, a gesture of good faith, he was willing to
play along. But he also favored the tube precisely *because* pulling away while
still tethered *would* cause maximum disruption to station, while leaving *Finity* virtually untouched. If the EC decided to play dirty, sending the station
into a massive wobble would keep them far too busy to attack *Finity* on her
way out, and explosions near the other docked ships would not be an attractive option for them.

Finity was very strongly reinforced about the docking probe. That was a
given. Were there other structures on the probe or the hull at risk from a
bump or miscalculation? On *Finity's* hull, a maintenance hatch, number 23,
was possibly a vulnerability in the area. So was the auxiliary airlock, E-1.
Computer *thought* both would withstand an accidental impact. *Senior Captain* thought the damned maintenance hatch, which was pressure-sealed
into a utility storage, was expendable—if need be. Hell. So was E-1.

There were a lot of expendables on that reinforced airlock at that point,
from exterior communications plugins, to emergency air supply and power
supply for a spacewalker with a problem. All that could go. If it had to. The
whole damn docking probe could go, if it had to, if that would get *Finity*
away from a hostile situation.

Because it was certainly possible that station might attempt some mischief. It was highly doubtful the station itself would have a mass-driver
mounted anywhere, which was the most lethal tool available to ships.

'Drivers were mining tools, not what you'd call a station occupation. But station might well try to position a utility pusher to attempt to cripple the ship and have a go at her folded vanes. Possibly station believed *Finity* at simple tether would be the proverbial sitting duck, and that, damaged, her condition might force *Little Bear* to come in range.

Damage to the docking probe would be possible, but not a good idea, since the damage they could do station in return, partly thanks to that very tether, would not be minor.

Little Bear, meanwhile, would be out of Foucault system like a shot, to tell Pell and Cyteen that what was going on here needed to be shut down cold.

And Pell and Cyteen could do that, possibly long before Sol even knew their little secret had been uncovered. They might be uneasy allies, but they had one common problem. The EC.

It was *not* the outcome JR personally wanted. No one in their right mind wanted to see conflict erupt between the EC and the Beyond—but he had to prepare a response to that eventuality. Engineering was setting up *Finity*'s own 'driver, arming it with scrap metal and other loose items that could cause, when launched at high velocity, damage to an aggressive station's hull. Given the experimental nature of *Finity* when she was built, and the circumstances of the EC pirating the plans, the engineers at Pell had given her a number of options, not all of which they advertised . . . one of those being two 'drivers—for mining uses, naturally—that could be directed from the base of the docking probe.

He hadn't ever really questioned the engees' thinking . . . until now. He'd thought, since 'drivers were designed for aiding in the mining of fuel, that two made sense for the ship's size. Now . . . he wasn't so certain.

He didn't, personally, want the onus of having fired a mass-driver at a station. Last thing he ever wanted to do. But *station* usually described a fragile structure with families and people trying to go about ordinary lives. If there *were* families the EC had intentionally sent here, or that had grown up in spite of plans and orders, a profound throwback to early days—it was a situation that might weigh on what Olympus was willing to risk. But it was not a consideration that would stop *Finity* from protecting its own, not under his command, and he would take the heat for it.

As for the EC's concern for the innocent . . . they had none. Alpha proved that. With its systems in near-collapse, and with intermittent food rationing, work on *Rights* had stayed on schedule, oh, yes, and for the workers on that project, employment with the EC meant exemption from that rationing— never mind the shortages were entirely due to the priorities given shipments and labor for that construction.

And where were additional pushers that could have filled the gap?

Here. Bringing Olympus back to life. Likely with designs for Thule to follow.

He had to wonder if trying to reason with the stationmaster was worth the effort. That a sympathetic and caring human being had gotten through the filters of EC management to run a clandestine operation—he didn't believe that for an instant.

But it was necessary to *try*. Somewhere in the cogs of the machine, there had to be human beings who, once getting out here, once getting in contact with people in the Beyond, once exposed to the thriving network they'd built . . . were capable of understanding that there were ordinary human beings out here—even where it got strange, at Cyteen—human beings that wanted fairly reasonable things, on a human scale, and that in all this vastness of stars and planets, there really was enough for everybody to live a reasonable life.

He likely was, in Acienne Jiburi's view, a merchanter captain that Emilio Konstantin of Pell had sent out here to cause her trouble and wreck her hard work. He . . . had sympathy for her. He *had* to muster a little charity on his side in order to hope for charity on the other. But there was no guarantee Jiburi had not grown up on the motherworld, or in the administrative cloister of Sol Station, ambitious and full of enthusiasm to do this and run it all—no plan ever to go home to Earth, but no lack of loyalty to the motherworld, either.

Much as the first Alpha stationmaster had undoubtedly been. Hard to figure what the EC thought would go differently this time. By the presence of that tri-vaned ship out there, Earth had decided it was going to start operating in a region where jump-points *could* be had from a station without the historical baggage of Alpha. Which established a power beyond Sol System . . . but still beyond the reach of rapid communication, another power that very easily could break free of Sol . . . history endlessly repeating itself. *Surely* the EC could see that.

Whoever was actually behind this long, slow slog of an effort at Olympus, Sol's plan to get a fleet of FTLers out here the hard way—was about to find the whole plan thrown into policy meltdown by a sudden redirect of traffic at FTL, Sol from Alpha. God help *Galway*. They didn't know what they were running into.

Policy this large didn't dance well. The unexpected could paralyze decision-making, meaning decisions wouldn't necessarily make sense, and what was here, at Olympus, might have instructions what to do if found out—but what if the finding-out came not in the form of a random little

Alpha merchanter, but a Pell megaship and a Cyteen merchanter . . . and what no preplanning could anticipate, the Alliance itself.

Could Jiburi be reasoned with, for openers? And who had the power here—the station director, or a pusher who couldn't outrace the lightbound Stream? Was either of them inclined toward Cruz-level violence?

He was already risking more than he wanted to, and while he trusted Min to keep his word and inform Pell on his way out of a disaster—and he truly did believe in Min—Min's greater loyalty was still to Cyteen and Cyteen's views.

And how Cyteen might react to any incident of violence from the EC was another serious question.

Getting *Finity* clear of trouble was number one priority, if EC hell began to break loose here—make sure *Finity* was safe and on her own way back to Pell, priority one, and get Emilio and Min in Emilio's office together, for some rational resolution before the information hit Cyteen—

God. He hoped an incident involving *Finity* would not tempt Min to retaliate . . . before leaving as promised. Min and John . . . had things in common.

Another sip of coffee. The source of which was Pell. It was a synth, but a decent one. There was so much out here that got along so very nicely without Mother Earth. Not that he resented the holy home of mankind or failed to recognize its importance. But the attitudes—

No, cancel that. He would not go into talks with whatever Stationmaster Acienne Jiburi represented, with his mind dead set against the humanity of the other side. Jiburi had the most to lose here. Or to gain. Her station, for her, was her ship.

Would you or a deputy accept a ride to Pell, Stationmaster? Would you like to open negotiations?

Cooperating with Pell would solve so many problems. Turn your whole operation into a supply chain of heavy transport from Sol, so your operation could have a reason to sit only a short hop from Venture. Earth goods could do it for you . . .

Give or take that Sol's fastest route to connect onto the trade network might yet be through Alpha, and given Alpha's trade with Earth, if established, might save Alpha's next neighbor Glory, such as it was—there were still roles for a pusher for the heavy hauling.

If they'd come on this first, ignorant of the Enforcer recruitment at Alpha, they might simply have given Olympus a friendly hail and offered them help.

But *Rights of Man*, a ship deliberately built to move Company Enforcers . . .

Was this the same operation?

Certainly the takeover of *Galway* was one official's action. Was it an action the EC would try to justify, or had Cruz overstepped? It was not anything this administrator had anything to do with.

And there was nothing at this end of the operation that Pell and Cyteen would strongly object to. Unlike *Rights*, this tri-vane, that might or might not be a technological game changer, *was* built for cargo. If she was intended for the Mallorys or the Bellagios, fair game—Families were Families. They could deal.

Challenge the Families with ships run by hire-on crew the EC picked and controlled? The Alliance would have a word about that. But—Mallory and Bellagio were merchanters—and here they were. The EC dealt with those two Families . . . evidently to their benefit. Alpha merchanters were, no question, merchanters. But they weren't Pell-side merchanters. They had different constraints. Different lifestyles, a narrow economy, still living between the feast and famine cycle of pusher-calls . . .

The Monahans had sent that message to both ships, hoping to open talks, Alpha ship to Alpha ship, struggling Family to struggling Family. It was possible the Monahans' statement could reach them.

JR punched into com, said: "Locate Ross Monahan. I want to talk to him. My office."

Book VI   Section iv

Cup of coffee with James Robert Neihart wasn't the most relaxed situation. Ross took a sip and a deep breath after, asking himself what reason there was for him to be in conference with Senior Captain, as *Finity* headed for a confrontation with Olympus. Ian, Helm 3.1, was their ranking go-to for messages and requests, particularly from the senior captain.

Was he nervous? Hell, yes. Was it something to do with Jen? Had she said something to him she shouldn't? He tried to remember what they'd talked of the last few days, and came up with exactly nothing the rest of the ship didn't know about.

Senior Captain, belted-in to an executive desk chair against a slowly lessening G while a Nav trainee tried to maintain his orientation and a semblance of dignity—took his own sip of coffee, and frowned.

"You Monahans sent a message to Tom Mallory."

"Yes, sir. I understood you authorized it. Sent it."

"I did. It was a good thought. Whose was it?"

"I—" Except it hadn't been his idea. Not really, for all the cousins insisted otherwise. "The idea just came up and we all agreed."

Never mind they'd made him write it, standing over him until it was done, something he realized too late might have made it back to JR.

Senior Captain just looked at him a moment, then: "We'll be going into soft-dock. Not for long. Going in to talk with station, and probably the ships, possibly including the pusher. There are things they think they know and things they need to know. I think a Galway's presence could prove useful in that exchange."

Visions of Jen in trouble plummeted away to a dizzying sense of height.

And darkness. And the starkness and shadow of ships lit by a red sun.

Him. Outside the hull. A place he'd been, that nobody else had been, when Galway pulled out of Alpha.

"You're an Alpha merchanter," Senior Captain said. "Technically, so are they."

"Never directly met them, sir. Never coincided in my years."

"But they would know Galway."

"I'd expect them to know us, yes, sir. We were the—" He stopped dead, not knowing why he'd used the past tense. It hit with superstitious, chilling force. "We are Alpha's number one local. No question they know us in that sense."

Senior Captain nodded. "You're from there. More importantly, you were involved in the EC raid on Galway. You're a first-hand witness. Your presence, that Galway patch, the things you witnessed— No matter who's in charge of Alpha at the moment, whether it's stayed free as we left it, or whether the Company here has been told any other story—you personally know what happened aboard Galway. If you're there, it's not just us putting whatever spin we like on the situation. If their facts match ours, fine. If they don't, you can say what did happen."

"I could. I can, sir. On com, you mean, or . . ."

"Face to face. Docking is their idea. We're going to talk. If we can get some support from the two merchanters we've been after, and persuade the station and the pusher to talk with Pell, we might actually pull something good out of this. It could also go badly. Very badly. There is that risk."

"Talk to them here?"

"There, likely. I doubt we can persuade them onto our deck. It will be a short meeting: we don't want to stay linked any length of time. If they're half sane, they know they're under observation, and that our friends the Xiaos will be upset and reporting somewhere if they make a hostile move. Whether they'll agree to sign on to the Alliance—I much doubt. But we can offer them the option. And we'll try to get them to talk with Pell, for starters."

"Yes, sir."

"You also *know* what happened on *Galway*. It's important to establish that. There's also the fact *Miriam B* has been at Alpha recently and has some mental reference for your Family's situation: which might be useful—if you're willing to do this. There's risk in it. There's risk the situation may blow up and us on the wrong side of the wall, so we could end up sitting in a cold cell in Olympus' gut for a good part of a year while Pell sorts this out. That could well happen."

Senior Captain let him think about it. And he did. "Also possible, isn't it, that *Come Lately* might have been at Alpha since *Little Bear*. *Galway* could have come back. They could know that."

"Possible, but I think if they had any such word to give us, station might have told us by now. If that information's available, I'll get it, whether or not you're there. Don't let that be your reason."

"*Galway* is the third ship."

"They know you're here."

"All the more reason. They shouldn't think we're hanging back." It wasn't what he, top of the list, wanted to do, but it was never going to be said that Galways were the batch in the rear. Still: "Should be Ian, however."

"I'm asking you."

"Why?"

"You're level-headed, you think under pressure, and you're not one to flare . . . and you're the one who witnessed."

"Hell, I'm the one with the dent in his skull to prove it." *Finity* was asking backup going out there. Captain James Robert was asking for help. From *Galway*. "I'll go."

"You're sure."

"I'm sure."

"Just being there will say plenty. What we want is to offer this place, and that pusher, assurances they're safe, first; and that, second, they're going to have to deal with a changed situation."

"Yes, sir."

"You're not under my orders. Understand that. None of the Galways owe us anything. Don't think it."

"Yes, sir." It came out automatically, the *sir*, with this man. "I'll be there." He had no idea what he was going to say, what they were going into, or what chance they had getting the EC to see reason, but what was going on here affected *Galway,* and he *wanted* to be part of whatever try this man was organizing.

"All right," Senior Captain said, and looked at the clock. "Assume a tube-connect, light pressure suits . . . in case. Nothing strange for you. *Let* them think we're delicate flowers and can't stand the cold. It'll give us a chance to get back, if the pipe springs a leak or some bastard on their end pulls the plug. Go kit up. That *Galway* patch is the only equipment you'll really need. No weapons, but we will have Security with us."

Jen, he thought. And the thought must have flashed through his eyes, because Senior Captain said,

"Excepting Jen."

He tried not to show his immediate relief, as he drifted free of the chair.

Book VI   Section v

The off-shift lounge, to the rear of the Second-shift bridge, was close and convenient from the offices, and quiet at this remove from shift-change—nobody would likely be there. Ross went toward that, in a corridor eerily deserted, shoving off from takehold to takehold into the darkened cross-passage, with lights turning on as they sensed movement.

While the ship was under minimal push and with the ring shut down, he still had the option to leave a note in system for Jen and his cousins, but they'd try to talk him out of going and there were too many thoughts circulating in his head to want to give them time and focus. He'd made his decision. He didn't want to verbalize the reasons, but his mind said he was right and his gut said it was right—

But trying to explain those reasons to Jen or Ian or Connor . . . no. Not yet.

The bridge crew lounge offered quiet, and bright light from screens echoing the bridge, everything to put him in a working frame of mind, which was where he needed to be, staying out of the way until Senior Captain said to move.

He was ready as he was. No weapons, Captain had said, which meant no roller-chain, no knife. Those staples of a shore leave stayed in his quarters.

He was already wearing a *Galway* jacket, which was all the gear Senior Captain asked him to have.

So he used his remaining eleven minutes until takehold to cruise along the dispensers, harvesting a couple of frozen energy bars and a drink packet that he stuffed into his jacket pockets, as well as half a dozen extra jump e-packets—best not expect junior runners to be risking their necks to fetch them anything if they came back in a hurry. Too many was always better than not enough. If talk suddenly went sideways and station decided to bring a mass-driver to bear, he could find himself riding out jump in the airlock.

In that disquieting thought he hauled himself down into a chair and belted in for a wait and a drink.

Five minutes til burn: alert on the general address. The ten-minute warning flasher had gone off while he was getting the energy bars. In another couple of minutes, the blue flasher in the overhead would go to red. And the ship's automated burn warning, staccato bursts, would wake the dead or the dead drunk.

Final slowdown to match pace with the station. And a slow careful drift into position, acceptance of an ancient tube.

A little scared of the hour ahead?

Maybe. He thought he ought to be.

Go talk to the EC.

He still didn't know exactly why that *yes* had come out of him so fast, but he didn't regret it, wouldn't take it back. He knew there was a lot the captain had been thinking and *not* saying, like—maybe they could get killed, if the stationers were complete fools. It was definitely a risk that they might be detained.

If they were held, it would be the better part of a year before ships from Pell could even get here to begin talking them out of their trouble. That could put him out of sync with *Galway* when she came back, maybe years separated . . .

Which was a stupid thing to think. No matter what, he was already out of sync. If all went as Niall planned, *Galway* could be gone as much as six years. The Monahans waiting on Alpha will have spent all that time on station, realspace time. If all went as planned, *Galway* would spend time at both points, mapping them, and more time at Sol, sorting all that out—while he had strung jumps together with only a week here and there in realspace. A year stuck on Olympus would just . . . even things out a bit.

Would station really lock them away? Try to brainwash them? Or would they be left to wander the station until someone came from Venture to talk them out of trouble? That sounded likely. Had to wonder, did they take

Venture chits here? Not that he had any, but the captain might. Hell, if they got stuck here, they could work on station's attitudes. Senior Captain had the gift of persuasion—sitting face to face with the man, he sounded reasonable no matter what he was saying . . .

Go talk to the EC. More to the point, those two First Stars merchanters.

He could still back out. He could still say no. But—

If he could do *any* good—if there was a chance of getting the merchanters to take a stand here . . . even if *Galway* couldn't talk Sol System into dealing, at least the Monahans would have achieved *something.*

But . . . what good could he really do? Who was he, that anybody should listen to him? The ineffectual idiot who got himself bashed in the head and tossed out the airlock?

The questions that had haunted his nights all the way from Alpha came flooding into his head.

Why had he been the one to escape *Galway?*

And what good was he sitting a trainee board here? What if Fallan had *needed* him, on that first jump to an unknown, untried point, a jump Fallan intended to make as unpleasant as possible . . . a deliberate attempt to twist their uninvited "guests" inside out, which also meant extreme stress on Fallan's frail self? What if Fallan failed and the *ship* needed him? Fallan had had those numbers in his head after one viewing, had sent the paper back to *Finity* with him. Well, *he* hadn't needed that paper either, not after that one look.

And if he truly *had* what Fallan had, that thing they'd always laughed about, if he truly did *feel* stars when he was hyped, sometimes even stone cold sober—if that was a real thing, if ever it would have been useful to *Galway*, it would have been on those chancy jumps into the unknown. Mike, Nav 1.2, was good; but he never *felt* a star, thought Fallan was having him on . . .

And, God, when it came to a fight for the controls, as Fallan himself had promised it would, the EC intruders against *Galway's* rightful crew . . . Fal was so fragile. Very old, very frail. *He* was young, he could hold his own in a fight . . . damn, he could.

The Monahans he'd left behind on the *Galway* bridge were so few, against armed Enforcers. One more Monahan might have made some critical difference. If it would have, if the EC fools won and fried *Galway* trying to make those jumps themselves . . . would he *ever* know?

What if, what if, what if?

Maybe he should have parted company with *Finity* at Venture. Maybe he should have said goodbye to Jen, and all. He could have been most of the way to Alpha by now, where Family, shorebound and living on Alpha's charity, waited for *Galway*.

Sure, the notes from cousins had said Alpha was living up to that promise, were full of optimism and advice of things to see and do . . . someone had found, God help them, digi-brochures from Pell that were only a few years out of date.

No, he'd turned all that down at Venture, thinking he could do some good this way. With the rest, he'd said, sure, he'd go on a hunt for a secret EC contact point . . .

But now that they'd found it, and it wasn't just some lonely, falling-apart station, now that they *knew* that everything was connected, that the Rights build and the failure of supply at Alpha was all one piece—more and more things connected; and it was becoming clearer and clearer that *Galway*, if she had survived, had sailed into a situation completely different from anything they'd remotely imagined. It wasn't Alpha's independence that was potentially threatened by what the EC was doing here. This place was one crazy jump string from *Pell*.

Hell, yes, Captain James Robert was worried.

And Captain James Robert had looked him in the eye and asked, effectively, Will *Galway* back us in this?

While *Little Bear* hung out there in the dark, hair-triggered and ready to run for Pell and on to Cyteen.

We need to show some patches in this beyond *Finity*'s own, says James Robert Neihart.

And God, what was he going to say to that, but, Yes, sir.

Was he a fool?

Maybe, but—

Damn, he *did* want in. *Galway* was the third ship. Meaningfully, *the third ship*. If her future was under threat at Sol, if the Galways that survived were going to have a claim to relevance—most of all, if someone was going to try to argue two wrong-headed Alpha merchanters to reason, and damn the EC on their own deck, who else had a shot at it? He didn't know if *Galway* still existed. He didn't know if she was coming back with anybody he knew in charge. But *Galway* deserved to have done something in this game. He wanted that, for the Monahans. He *wanted* that . . . for himself.

For having missed his berth on *Galway*, and left Fallan and his First-shift cousins to deal without him.

Slow pressure started and braking began in earnest.

This time—this time, he was going. He'd been taken out of the action

once, through no choice of his own. That desertion had eaten at him ever
since. This was a chance to get back in, maybe finish something for his shift
and for *Galway*.

Book VI   Section vi

Olympus B-mast occupied the forward screen in close-up, girder-laced detail. Second-shift was on, everything zero-G. JR paused in the exec corridor
doorway—Madison being in the chair—and scanned the visual on the big
display, listening to the voices of Com 2.1 and station as Madison's shift ran
her into proximity.

Vickie, Helm 4.1, arrived from the crew lounge, at the back. Helm 2.1,
Caplin, had himself made the request, and Vickie, their docking expert, had
vowed herself sharp enough. She slipped into Caplin's seat, all of Helm 2
having shifted down a seat, leaving Helm 2.4 at a trainee board.

Mum was still awake. She was watching from quarters, with a voice link.
Madison was on for approach and docking—after which Vickie would go
off-duty and Caplin and all his shift would take Helm until John, sleeping
the sleep of the uninvolved at the moment, and needing to be fresh when he
took over, would get Madison's up-to-the-minute briefing.

Which they hoped would not involve a problem. But if it did, it would be
John's problem, and all John's problem, to get them disconnected from station and away—*no* negotiating with station: let them simmer for a few
months.

That was the plan. It wasn't a great one. But it left station with damn-all
they could do about it, no immediate use for hostages, and not a damned
thing the hostages could tell station that station couldn't get at any other
station just by asking.

So they'd sit a while. Jim B would step up from Helm to captain the shift
in his absence, Madison's Second-shift would function as main shift until
Finity came back and got them out, preferably before that pusher fueled up
to its return trip . . . himself having *no* desire to spend the rest of his life en
route to Sol.

It was a risk. It would be a damn nightmare if that became a possibility.

The mast was all the view, both real and magnified times ten, and the blinking green light was a come-ahead.

The only way for *Finity* to dock was to do a free-dock, which meant a non-rigid connector to the mast, and utter reliance on *Finity* to manage stability and position. *Finity* could indeed manage it, but without grapples, that meant micro-corrections, which in turn ran up against limitations in *Finity*'s supply of fuel for those systems. Nothing they hadn't budgeted for before leaving Pell, and nothing she couldn't manufacture on her own, given time, but staying connected that precisely would have a definite time limit.

Which meant they couldn't afford to leave the ship for long, they couldn't bend in that resolve, which was in one sense a hurry-up on the visit once it began . . . it meant they couldn't afford trouble, and they couldn't afford to be stalled by EC rhetoric and foot-dragging.

"Permission to join the bridge," JR said on command-com.

"Permission," Madison said. Then: *"Problem?"*

"Not so far." JR moved out, a practiced shove and free-fall across from the executive corridor, a quiet slide of his hand along the takehold rail, to a stable and upright hold with one hand and a foot.

"So far, so good," Madison said, real-voice. "Station ops is cooperating."

"So far. —Do we still have contact with admin?" JR asked.

"Guarded but generally positive," Madison said. "We passed the message, we want to talk with *all* command-level officers, station's and ships'. The Olympus alterday stationmaster is against a meeting and won't join us, but the mainday stationmaster—that's Jiburi—is actually hurrying the process along, agreeing with our linkup and opening up data links to their ops."

"She doesn't want her station dented."

"Very much the case. Meanwhile Mallory's agreeing to meet. Bellagio's not, so they're keeping one senior captain out of it, whether by Bellagio's opposition or just their precaution against our bad behavior. *Wellington* is, however, sending their Second-shift exec."

"Encouraging that they're talking at all," JR said.

"JR. I've been thinking . . . you should stay. *I'll* go. Of all of us—"

"No sale. My decision. My risk. Listen. I'm taking Security. We'll not be spectacularly armed, but Fletch insisted."

"Damned right."

"And we'll have the Galway Navigator, who is walking proof of the extremes the EC is willing to go to. He has his own questions to ask them, and stands to get Mallory's attention just by being there. Mallory has been to Alpha, has heard the whole story. Likely young Ross has become a bit of a legend on the Alpha dockside, among other things. And reaching the merchanters in this operation is more important than anything we can accomplish with Sol-born EC."

"It's Sol-born EC that's got the controls on the station, brother."

"I'll be polite. I'll put as few of us at risk as I can manage. And I'll get the kid back safe and sound."

Madison gave that a thoughtful frown. "I'd rather send John and a thermonuclear device, but I understand the logic. Question is whether the merchanters have any power at all in this."

"They have a choice . . . and choice is power. They'll leave here, eventually. They'll have their own council, in the privacy of their own ships. They'll face an all-new station scrutiny of their trade . . . and they'll draw their own conclusions. Our job is to get in, make our pitch, get the feel of the place . . . and get out. We're depending on station for a tube crossing. And they're depending on us not to dent the station. Which means we both have reason to play fair. If they want to do us in, guns won't help us, and they'll have broken the rules, leaving *Finity* free to show them just how much havoc she can wreak, pulling out. If they try to hold us—well, let John talk to them."

Madison looked away, staring at the screen.

"I could say I was you, brother. They wouldn't know the difference."

"*I* would. You can make the call when *you're* Senior Captain."

Madison's eyes snapped back to him.

"Let's not think about that. *Fletch* goes armed, right?"

"Fletch and his number two. Yes. Nothing too obvious. And I won't be too offended if Olympus also takes precautions, but—" JR shrugged. "Operationally speaking, I've looked at the Olympus schematic on file. It's a bigger version of Alpha. They've been using B-mast for the merchanters, so there'll be a lift from the mast to the ring and the import offices, same as on Alpha . . ."

"The damn schematics are more than a century out, the place has had scrappers and junkers all over it, and a whole damn rebuild."

"There'll still be a point at which the mast lift arrives at the ring, and we will *not* go further than those mast-access offices. I don't anticipate more than an hour for the actual meeting. John's on deck for the event, but I'm asking you to sit in and be another voice and an assist to him, if you can stay awake awhile. Mum is going to take a pill and sleep through—in the very, very remote chance you need to jump out of here."

"The hell she will. The hell *I'll* sleep, until you're back safe."

JR shook his head, but there was no point in arguing. "Listen. Big risk, but big potential gain. I'm not expecting an immediate resolution, but we have a chance to get a dialogue going with at least one element here. They've been here a while. If their two ghosts have been gathering even the most basic data from Pell and Venture . . . they've got to realize the economic advantages of becoming a major part of what we have. If I can play to that, just get them *thinking* about it . . . that will be useful *even* if *Galway's* come back with the EC in full control. If nothing happens, even if station authorities can't be reasoned with, as long as we get back in good order, fine, no problem. We go our way and we head for Pell to report in. But—"

Pause for attention.

"But?" Madison asked suspiciously.

"If anything adverse happens, *forget* about our situation. I want you to back John, signal *Little Bear* and pull back. Just back off—without uncoupling—rock the station and disable the pusher. Take out the Stream. —*Then* talk to station."

"JR, you're *not* setting this up to make this happen. Are you?"

"Of course not."

Madison stared at him a minute, then: "You're taking that kid over there."

JR drew a deep breath, let it go. "Let me tell you something you probably know better than anyone, brother. I'm *not* the good guy. I'm not *that* James Robert. I'm this one. I'll use what I have, and whoever I have, to stop the EC before they push Pell head-on into a conflict with Cyteen. So, yes. I'm taking the kid. To make a point, if nothing else. He's got a real clear idea who he'll be talking to . . . and he *wants* to go."

"And if he starts a bar fight? He's been aching for one since he got thrown off his ship. You know that as well as I do."

"I also know he's smarter than that. Listen. I'm not expecting to have happy talk. Not sure what he might add, but *Galway* should be represented and he's my choice. A little honest accusation from a fellow Alpha spacer might spark some honest response out of Mallory. Frankly, if they're all smiles and agree to everything, *that* would scare me. Bottom line, brother, and listen to me: *Finity* has to get to Pell, Pell will have to talk to Cyteen, and Pell *and* Cyteen have to start paying attention to the Hinder Stars, whether or not *Galway* has shortened the time we have to do it in. We're apparently *here* just in time. With luck we've stopped them crewing the likes of *Shalleen*, one ship after the other, with dead-broke Alpha merchanters. For all we know, Sol has a string of pushers on the way, each one pushing another FTLer with it—intending to offer them to *Miriam B, Santiago,* and *Pearl* and every old, badly-hammered Family out here, all under the EC's rules. If that's the plan, the fact *Shalleen* is here means it's reaching its final stages. Our arrival, the exposure of this place, might just have kicked that plan into high gear. The ships being pushed can't be hurried, but recruitment can. Fortunately, we've given the spacers an option, but they didn't know all the possibilities when they signed. If we don't spread the word about this place fast, the Alliance will fail before it ever really gets started. So I'd appreciate it, if we do get held here, that you do sort of hurry the return."

"For God's sake—"

"It's a different future that branches from here, Maddie. Regardless what happens, we can't go back to the universe as it was. We get this one try at breaking this business up before it gets nasty, or we have Pell trying to deal with the EC alone and Cyteen flaring off sideways and deciding to go on proliferating colonies, which, mark me, is the way it will go. Cyteen *will not* deal with the EC. You know that."

"I know it."

"So if it all blows up, under no circumstances do I want you to come in to pick us up, even if they beg you—not in the stir we'll have made. Get the hell back to Pell fast enough to overtake *Little Bear* if you can, and consult with Emilio. Persuade Min to pull *Dublin* and friends in on the effort to stop this mess before it proliferates into an EC grab for Venture. Let Emilio take it from there, and then come back to pick us up, with at least one other merchanter as your backup."

Madison just looked at him, long and hard. "You just get yourself back aboard for a consultation on any proposal they make, and if central control stalls you, I can start the discussion by picking little pieces off the station right then."

"No. No. And *hell* no. Absolutely no warnings and no argument with them. Either we do have a discussion with this station or we don't; and if they let us walk out, fine. But if they don't let us walk out, you target that pusher, then go. Don't be suckered in on some offer to hand us over. *We* can sit quiet in local lockup for a few months."

"A damned year. And they won't be happy with you."

"If a few ships want to come over from Venture to argue with them in the interim, that would be fine. But *you* do not come in after us until you have Pell backing you up, and above all, make sure Min gets out of here clean and fast without incident. *Last* thing we need is a Cyteen ship taking action in what comes next. Got me?"

"All right. *All right.* John and I will back you up. You know Mum will."

"So get us in, hand off to John, take a pill, and just wait your turn."

"Damn it, brother. This is a *massive* risk."

"Keeping this place from becoming a fortress, peeling away the Hinder Stars, and handing the whole Beyond to Cyteen? Worth it, brother."

It was a soft docking—a tube-connect, and the old tube-connects were simple, universal, and pressurized—*Finity* didn't even need human help to snag the magnetic guides and dog the connecting plate into place—a suit-up-and-swear operation in most Alpha ships. Ross had nothing to do in the prep room of the airlock but watch the screen and wait. No grapples. There might as well have been. *Finity* had the numbers and the tolerances in her system and—a wonder worth watching if he hadn't been so nervous—her positional jets were going to keep her there, free-falling, accounting for the station-effect and her own, and holding position in spite of it all—

Not because she was designed to do this, but there were other occasions when precision mattered, like moving into ring-dock. Damned useful when *Finity* didn't want to tie herself to this place—and a piece of megaship arrogance that sent its own chill through Alpha sensibilities. Because she could. Because she belonged to *this* age, and Alpha and Olympus were pieces of the same outmoded era.

Still . . . it was impressive. The ring was shut down, *Finity* was in Third-shift's hands, and everybody aboard was under Red, meaning snugged down and wary, and very little was stirring aboard, nor would be until they had been aboard station and come back. On the screen above the entry to Emergency Exit 1 was the distorted view from mast-end, with that alien tri-vane foremost in the scene, and above it—*her* seemed too warm a word for the creature—*Miriam B* and *Come Lately* . . . looking, from this perspective, like three half-opened petals of the same flower. And above all, the great ring of the station with its spokes.

Bigger than Alpha. Newer—if you could count anything centuries old as new at all—and massively rebuilt. Beyond the ring, way off—up—there—the pusher. A new-built pusher.

The hatch worked behind him, automated, stop-your-heart noisy. The prep room itself was command territory—*Finity* had four E-ports with suits, pods at five others. Number one was what they were using, and suits stood like sentries in their individual bays, EVA gear in racks alongside; but *don't suit* had been the order.

And who arrived was Fletcher, and Twofer, and Parton. Fletcher wore a regular silver-grey shore jacket. The other two had *Finity's End* and *Security* blazoned in white on black padded armor.

"Ross," Fletcher said by way of greeting.

"Sir."

"No need to give you the beginner lecture." That was humor. Alpha spacers made this sort of crossing as babes in arms. Ross appreciated that. He had a case of nerves developing, not about the crossing, but about where they would be, and who they had to deal with—a consortium of senior captains and EC station admin, who might be asking him questions, every Alpha spacer's nightmare.

"Yes, sir," he said.

"How's the pressure?" Fletcher answered his own question by checking the readout. "Looks good. Coldsuits should be enough. I'd start heating up, though."

Ross already had. It was a good jacket, lightweight—good warming function. The one thing he had from *Galway,* given by the Family before he boarded *Finity* . . . warmth and moral support in one.

So they weren't trusting the tube all the way: a coldsuit with the headgear and five minutes of air could get you through a tube failure; and you could move. He'd not looked forward to a hard suit—not outright phobic about it, but it was a set of memories he really, really didn't want right now.

Finity made a correction. She'd been making them. This one shifted the walls a little while they hung in air.

The lock gave its deafening crash. Senior captain joined them, greeted Security. And him.

"Sir," he said. *Sir* answered all questions, handled all problems. He was safe with *sir.* It was the words he had to come up with on station that terrified him.

God. He hadn't told Jen.

He hadn't told Ian.

Or anybody. He'd been locked in his own head, and he'd thought he'd wait, and then the Red had come on, along with the order for him to get to the number 1 lock, which—

He'd outright frozen for two heartbeats, caught between the captain's order and the Red order. Then realized he was exempted. His job was the object of it.

So move, fool.

He had. He'd been first here.

He was *not* going to shake. The jacket lining was on Heat. He did not need to shiver.

But Jen—God, she was going to be mad.

She wouldn't think about him, wouldn't worry til it was obvious where he was, which it wouldn't be while the ship was on Red, and that status wouldn't change until they were back. And if, for some reason, she *did* try to reach him and couldn't, when the ship was engaged in a problem, sometimes there were conferences and people didn't turn up where they usually did, and she'd take it as that.

Besides, nothing he could do about it now, was there?

But he should have told her. He *really* should have told her.

Access Personal Com? Leave her a note in system?

That was cold.

He hadn't told Ian, either. Hadn't given him or Uncle Connor a chance to confuse him with advice about what to say. Confuse? God, he was a fool. He could *use* a few ideas about now.

Senior Captain was talking to Fletcher, calm as he wasn't. Twofer and Parton had put on sidearms.

Senior Captain said, to empty air, "Com 2.1, advise Olympus we're ready."

"Earpiece." Parton offered one. Ross took it and inserted it in his ear. "Here, Galway," Twofer said, beside him, and offered him a small, flat disc. "Inside pocket, before we kit up. This is so we can track you. We're all carrying them."

"Yes, sir," Ross said, glad of the idea of *Finity* tracking them.

"And this—" Twofer held up a small black disk. "Goes on your collar. — Here." Twofer's huge, surprisingly deft fingers affixed the small pin. "Cameras. Won't fool anyone, but they're not designed to. They let us in with them, or we turn around and come home. They record, we record, no one can question the facts."

Coldsuits were being hauled out of one locker: he began putting his on as Twofer got one out of the locker adjacent. It was a wrestle in zero G, the flimsy transparent stuff, but it was slick, and it wasn't hard to sort out once you had one hand or one foot in the right hole. He hadn't used one since . . .

Galway. Glory's equipment sucked. You used the coldsuits there rather than trust the tube. They'd always joked about it.

"You're clear to go," he heard. Second-shift Captain Madison, talking to all of them, from the bridge, which was confusing: he thought it was Third-shift in charge. *"Good luck, team. JR."*

He pulled the squidgy mask on. Part of it clung to your face. Part was a hard faceplate. The air it gave smelled of new plastic.

"Com check," Fletcher called, and they sounded off in turn.

"*Madison will be in steady contact with station,*" Senior Captain said then. "*Mainday stationmaster has agreed to meet us in B-mast conference A.*"

That was an immediate visual. Right turn from the core lift. Every station from Venture to Glory—same plan, same map. You just changed the signage.

Felt suddenly homelike.

But not.

"*Tom Mallory will be there,*" Senior Captain's voice said in his ear. "*He will have Frank Bellagio on com. Wellington's second in command will be there. Station-com is being cooperative so far. It's also possible they're utter fools and want hostages, in which case John's on deck in about ten minutes and he'll explain to them how much he wants us back. If anything does happen, just go easy. The advantage isn't on their side, and we'll just hope that we don't get into that discussion. Ross.*"

Heartbeat quickened. If that was possible. "Sir."

"*Answer any questions they ask, no clearance from me. Claim the floor as the moment takes you. You're speaking for Galway. We'll back you.*"

"Yes, sir." Equal to a captain he wasn't. But he was resolved not to disgrace his ship.

Senior Captain said. "*It's a go, then.*"

The airlock opened. That sound . . .

Fallan . . .

Oh, he was not doing well.

Senior Captain went. Fletcher did. Twofer and Parton were waiting to go last. Ross caught a takehold and pushed himself free with a vengeance.

Tube passage, same as every voyage, every station he'd grown up in.

Choice made.

Book VI   Section viii

Tube transit was never pleasant, but it was all early stations offered, and certainly not the first time JR had used it. A non-moving grip-line assisted rapid movement. The air, beyond dry, would have burned with cold. The masks and gloves and suit held it off somewhat.

Olympus claimed the access was safe, and pressurized. It demonstrably had nothing better. Deliberately breach the tube? Station might, if they were fools, but a deliberate accident would do nothing good for Olympus. Holding them hostage was easy and potentially useful. And should a legitimate accident occur, the suits should protect them long enough to retreat back to the ship.

"If everything goes well," JR had said to Jiburi, in setting the terms, "that second ship out there will wait for a report from us, and we will leave together, to inform Pell and arrange a meeting and, we sincerely hope, a negotiation to the benefit of everyone. If something adverse befalls us, that ship will leave immediately, carrying a very upsetting message to Pell and all stations. Things will not go well for Olympus at that point. I will be very disappointed if that happens."

"I assure you," Jiburi had returned, *"we are anxious to have a reasonable discussion. You will be safe and free to return to your ship."*

Reasonable, except that Jiburi and Mallory would *not* accept an offer to talk aboard *Finity* instead. *"Being,"* Jiburi had argued, *"that your ship is mobile, and we are not. We do, however, see the advantages of a discussion. Wellington's Captain Lee is less enthusiastic, and she is the ultimate authority, while Wellington is in dock. You, Mallory, and I can continue a discussion of principles and general desires by com, if you wish, which can have no binding effect, or we can talk on Olympus face to face, with a guarantee of safe passage in both directions. Our regulations require the meeting to be recorded under our own protocols, and if you want credibility and official status for our report to Sol, which will be to your advantage, we will do our own recording, as we assume you will."*

So, well, Jiburi finding herself and two of her three supply ships' captains kidnapped to Pell was a reasonable fear. Olympus, on the other hand, clearly was going nowhere.

That was the rational end of it. Slinging oneself as rapidly as possible through a thin-walled tube offered a less rational perspective, but so far the equipment seemed in good order and the airlock ahead was open and lit. JR caught the last takehold, judged an adequate shove toward the inner wall of the airlock, and held position there as the other four made it in—technically *inside* the station, now. Fletch pushed the cycle button, the door shut, the seal hissed, and the inner door opened to a utilitarian space that could have been a core-lift access on Alpha or Bryant's or Venture, same look, same scale: room for twelve, if none were Hank's size, with a similar-sized core lift standing open and ready to zip them up the mast to the core and then out to the rim.

It was all agreed. Parton clipped to a takehold beside the lift access, to stay in the access area and assure that that connection stayed available. JR gently shoved off into the lift. Fletch and Ross did the same, followed by Hank, who then pushed the button that jolted the car into motion toward the rim. Hot air blasted at them. Feet found *down*, relatively speaking, and limbs, gut, and sinuses all settled as acceleration brought a sense of orientation.

"You'd think heat cost them in that damn tube," Fletch muttered, slipping out of the suit.

"Cold, for sure." JR unmasked, clipped the mask to a carabineer on his jacket pocket, handed the thin, rolled suit to Hank. Fletch did the same, then breathed into his hands, filtering the air as the car kept their feet on the deck.

Ross complained of nothing. Having shed his suit, he passed it on, then stood, feet braced, shoulders hunched, visibly shivering in the chill—the one of them that truly didn't have to be here. JR did feel a twinge of blame in that. But it was respect Ross wanted, respect for the Monahans, bottom line, in the whole of their dealing with the EC. That commodity, *Finity* couldn't give him. *He* couldn't give him.

The EC damn well could.

Book VI   Section ix

"Bloody hell," Jen said, switching off her handheld. Nobody was talking. Com might be, but Com wasn't allowing access outside the bridge—possibly not beyond the exec. And she arrived in the Security office, in micro-gravity, having spent considerable physical effort to get between decks, with no Fletcher, with no Parton, with no Twofer, and faced a loose coffee cup drifting across the scene.

The Caution had been in effect. Then the Red. She understood they were soft-docking. She'd sent a bot-call to the Security Office, found no one. She'd waited through all of it, waiting for stability. Waited for the automated voice to announce a permission to move about, until she'd concluded there wasn't going to be one, and because she was Security, and because she was worried, she'd left her quarters.

Still in the lower corridor, she'd heard the airlock.

That had put a hurry into it. She'd manualed the lift, drifted in deserted corridors, the only one fool enough to be violating a Red order and moving through the ship. She'd reached the Security Office, gone in—found no one on duty, pulled herself into a seat and engaged com—the usual where-is-it com that carried routine chatter from the bot that tracked schedule and orders: *find Fletcher*, being her first request.

Then the cascade started. That the office was deserted—not uncommon. But com said, to successive questions, Fletcher was not available, Parton was not available, Twofer was not available.

She'd called Com, which should be 2.1, Betty, bypassing the bot. "This is Jen, Security. Where's Fletcher?"

And Betty had said, *"You don't know?"*

So, in the upshot of things, Uncle had gone to Olympus.

Fletcher had, of course, gone with him.

Fletcher had taken the whole team.

That was good, because she damned sure didn't want Uncle Jim going alone to talk to those bastards.

She called Ross, using the regular bot.

"Ross Monahan has left the ship."

No. *Surely* no.

"ComBot, is Ross Monahan with the Senior Captain?"

"Affirmative. Ross Monahan is with the Senior Captain."

Why? Why in hell?

What in hell did Ross or *Galway* have to do with Olympus?

The station *was* likely laid out the way an Alpha spacer knew upside and down, but they weren't taking a damned tour.

Uncle intended to talk face to face with the Olympus stationmaster, she got that. With the stationmaster and with EC authorities. And the merchanter captains.

It was a major risk having any personnel on that other deck, given EC attitudes, but Uncle could be persuasive—taking on a sharp dealer and getting him to see where his own interest lay in a deal Uncle wanted—Uncle was very good at that. Hell, he had persuaded the Alliance into existence, hadn't he?

The same reasoning might work if Olympus were free to deal and if the people in charge here had the ability to consider and affect their own futures. Station was now in a very difficult situation, exposed, with FTL a new possibility, their whole clandestine operation now under the spotlight; and while messages didn't travel faster than ships, a ship that had just been at

Alpha was sitting right on B-mast . . . so they knew. They *knew* that the map was changing, and that orders from Sol might not be the orders Sol would give now, particularly as, if Sol could reach the Hinder Stars in three jumps, other entities could reach Sol if they were really determined. That was, concept-wise, *very* different for Sol to think about.

Olympus also knew, in its own situation, there was *Little Bear* sitting out there in the semi-dark, not in reach. Had to know if they tried pressure on Uncle Jim there could be a lot of trouble. They might not know how *much* trouble, that ship being a Cyteener, but they at least had to know it was out there watching.

So, yeah, it was reasonable what Uncle was doing, and maybe he wanted Ross to impress on station the reality of the ship that was bound for Sol, and the changes that were coming. Not to mention the attempted takeover of his ship. Yeah, Ross going made sense, but *damn* . . . why hadn't someone told her? Leave her behind? All right, she could deal. But give her something to do! Some way to help!

She belted in, and, though feeling weird because it was Fletcher's desk, adjusted the feed to bring her the various stations ops-com tracked, camera to readout to camera again.

All the people she cared most about in the universe were over there, across an ancient tube-access on a mothballed station. Nobody had ordered her to watch that airlock, but it seemed prudent to watch what she could . . . the airlock was absolutely secured, not in station control.

Outside cam showed *Finity* herself was snugged against a real delicate part of station with that tube-connect not even stressed. She'd experienced *Finity* holding steady for delicate transfers, but this, with the little position shifts, was something else—downright arrogant display of finesse. That transfer tube was hardly moving.

Five minutes of watching the tube do nothing, and her handheld beeped. Her heart jumped. But it was just general com, housekeeping.

"Reminder: Special order. Duty schedule has changed. Second-shift is going off-duty and Third-shift is coming on."

What the— It was still Madison's watch, but *John* was coming onto the bridge. John, whose first impulse to a crisis was neither patience nor peace— *he* was Uncle's choice to be in charge of the ship while Uncle was gone.

Hairtrigger John.

With Madison and Second-shift, the better team to handle jump, gone after half-shift, and then, according to the computer display, coming *back* on after John.

God, she did not like that. It was all mixed up.

If they wanted to break ten thousand laws, *Finity* could wipe out a station if she set about to do that.

Uncle Jim wouldn't do that. She didn't really think John would.

But did Uncle—leaving John in charge with Madison and then Mum to follow . . . maybe for an emergency jump out of the system—mean to create an incident to shine a light on this place? Maybe trigger the whole Alliance to do something about it? Would he really do something that crazy?

Definitely. She told herself that. It was dangerous, what they were doing, but these EC stationers surely weren't wholly crazy. The ships at dock were merchanter . . . of what affiliation remained to be seen . . . but Family ships were not going to risk themselves for the EC's sake. Station had a whole lot to lose if *Little Bear* found it necessary to go off to Pell to report a problem— or worse, go off to Cyteen without even slowing down at Pell, and bring *that* back. If station behaved badly, those merchanters could break dock—doing a deal of damage to B-mast in the process.

No. Station wouldn't want to take on merchanters. Uncle was gambling they wouldn't, but he wasn't betting *Finity* on it—leaving John to make a fast get-away and Madison to make an emergency jump out of the system told her that.

He *was*, however, betting *himself.* And Ross. And everybody with him.

Damn, and *damn,* Ross . . . who had nightmares about his shift going on *Galway,* and felt personally guilty about leaving Fallan to handle all those chancy jumps . . . *He couldn't tell you no,* she wanted to tell Uncle. Damn it all.

Finity adjusted, a microburst. She felt the move, instinctively caught herself against the desk edge, and bent a fingernail. They were in a gravitational tug of war with the station and that pusher up there, and that used resources.

She tightened the belt a little, struggling with anger and wanting to hit something, and utterly impotent. A couple of unsecured datasticks wandered loose, right off the desk, obeying a slight bias toward the floor. Out of reach. She was furiously angry.

Which was of course why, dammit, they'd have worried about taking her, the lightweight, the novice. "The smile that got things done," was Fletcher's word.

The cheerful manipulator.

Well . . . screw that. Damn all a smile could accomplish in this operation. *Think, Jen, think!*

What could *she* do from here? That was the real question, and she had no answer.

But—that was saying she was worried. And outright scared.

Her job was security. She was part of *Fletcher's* team. And there *was* a way she could be useful. She could tap into ship's communication with Uncle, not to say a word, but to track what was going on, so long as Uncle maintained contact with Com. There was no order against *Finity* Security tapping in and knowing whatever Third-shift was hearing. And if something happened, something she could do something about—

She opened Fletcher's desk, took one of the special Security earpieces off the clip, clicked it, and plugged that into her ear.

Its default was its other units.

"Come in," was the first thing she heard, a male voice, and not a familiar voice, which meant some stranger was within a few meters of a *Finity* pickup.

Book VI   Section x

"Thank you," JR said to the security officer—who had noted Fletch's and Hank's weapons without comment—at the lift exit, and with Ross and Fletch and Hank, he entered the first of the core-lift meeting rooms, feet on the deck at a comfortable one *G*, air like a wall of warmth driving away the chill of the corelift.

They faced a semicircular table, a dark-skinned middle-aged woman seated at the apex, with one civilian aide and a couple of armed Enforcers in blue uniforms behind her—that would be Acienne Jiburi. And next to her, a man of about fifty, dark haired and lean, with the ship-silhouette patch of *Miriam B* and the name Thomas A. Mallory blazoned on a blue and grey jacket. Mallory was at Jiburi's right, with two of his own against the wall behind him. Mallory scanned them all, pausing a moment on Ross, before settling on him. On Jiburi's other side, a greying woman in a blue jacket with two EC enforcers at her back. Her jacket patch had a marbled blue planet and said, below that, *Wellington*, in gold letters.

Both captains wore identical silver pins on their collars: the simple circlet of the old Great Circle pusher captains.

And there were four weapons in evidence, four people in EC Security black, representing EC interests, against the wall between Jiburi and the *Wellington* officer, but belonging, by their patches, to *Wellington*.

There were multiple empty chairs to either side. JR took a position standing with Ross at the opening of the semicircle, with Fletch and Hank to the rear. They were definitely outnumbered in arms and personnel.

"I appreciate the meeting," JR said. "I'm JR Neihart, Senior Captain, *Finity's End*, out of Pell. I assume Senior Captain Tom Mallory, Stationmaster Jiburi. May I have the honor of an introduction, Wellington?"

The grey-haired woman said, tautly, "Agnes Lee, Senior Captain, EC pusher craft *Wellington*."

"Captain Lee." When the *Wellington's* number 2 had been scheduled to be here. Noted.

Lee gave one stony-jawed nod, no friendliness at all.

"With me," JR said, "is Ross Monahan, Navigator, *Galway*, based at Alpha Station, representing his own ship, whose name may be familiar to you."

Silence. One had to wonder, were they waiting for accusations?

"I have a question," Ross said, on his own, into that deathly quiet, "whether you saw *Galway* at Alpha, Captain Mallory."

And longer silence.

"No," Mallory said finally. "We did not. We know where she went. Not how that came out." And then added, somberly: "She's still expected, Navigator. Or was, at the time we were there. Bets are laid on the outcome. Your Family is reported in good spirits."

One question answered: mark down Mallory for a decent merchanter—Ross's situation had cut to the bone, and drawn information, and frowns from Jiburi and Lee alike, that answer having been passed for free that they might not have wanted to give at all.

"Fairly answered, sir," JR said. "Thank you. And we assume, that *Rights of Man* is still at Alpha."

"That would be correct, sir," Mallory said. Gaze very direct. "Question for question. Excuse me, stationmaster. Trader to trader, what *brings* you here?"

"Business with you," JR said, pointedly to Mallory alone. "Various ports may have told you that. As to what led us here, extrapolation of information we received at Pell. In specific, various Earth goods that hadn't come through Alpha, which Galway was in a position to know. Not from your ship, be it said. Those goods suggested the presence of a pusher—an Earth to somewhere-not-Alpha pusher."

He'd purposely not named *Come Lately*, her captain not being present to defend himself, but it did seem politic to absolve Mallory of blame to the stationmaster.

A point perhaps not lost on Mallory: his expression did not change much, but it changed. Jiburi and Lee were frowning.

"Possibilities for origin fairly rapidly became Thule or Olympus, all other sources having been eliminated—by time and their stars' ill humor. But by the condition of Olympus, I'd guess that *Wellington* isn't the first pusher to arrive here since Olympus went down in a cloud of lawsuits. I'd also guess that the urgency of resurrecting Olympus is why the EC didn't just add pushers to the Alpha route."

"Keep going," Jiburi said, and faces at the table were grim.

"Not much to add," JR said. "We came here to find *Miriam B* and *Come Lately,* to invite them to join their fellow merchanters in an organization designed to solve some of the problems inherent to the FTL trade. If I may be frank, after *Galway's* disturbing experience at Alpha, we're beyond glad to see that they are still Family ships, in Family hands."

"We are Family ships," Mallory said. "Both."

"We are very glad to hear it."

"These are also ships that do business *here*," Jiburi said. "The Earth Company has its own requirements, and its own contracts . . . which do not recognize a Pell-based organization. We do, indeed, know what happened at Alpha. We've had a full report. Your disruptive operation there, your *organization*, including a Cyteen-based ship, subverted law and order on that station, incited riot and terrorized station inhabitants, putting them in fear for their lives and the integrity of the station. And to top it off, you incarcerated the top EC official on the station, decommissioned the EC office, and disrupted a major EC operation."

Well, that was the EC's view of the situation. And who had given them that report? Mallory? Bellagio? A letter carried from some EC sympathizer on Alpha, doing undercover for Olympus?

But if he could appeal to the merchanters, and move them. . . . "Captain Mallory. You've been to Alpha. You heard what happened. Ship interests are ship interests. And our offer to all parties . . . stands. *Miriam B* and *Come Lately* get the same treatment as any other ship, no impediments. Clean slate with other Families, on whatever side of politics, no matter past record. Cyteen and Pell and the Company can't go at each other if we're how what moves, moves. Bottom line of the Alliance—nothing moves if we don't move it. Come to us whenever, wherever you like. If anybody wants to fight about it—first one that breaches the agreement, or harms a ship, their goods don't move. Get word to us."

He was set then, to walk out.

But:

"We've heard about your demands at Alpha, Captain Neihart," Lee said sharply. "I arrived here with very specific orders, and they in no way include your organization. Understand, your rules will not be honored here."

"Non-signatory stations," JR said, "will receive no trade from signatory ships. Your ban will not be a problem."

"That will not stand."

"You can hardly force ships to come here. And other stations will do business only with Family ships, of which you appear to have two. As I say, not a problem. However . . ." JR paused, debating whether to continue. Then: "I assume, Captain, that your actions are subject to orders from the EC. Those orders may change with the arrival of FTL at Sol, and the need for ports. This place, should Mallory and Bellagio not have told you, has a very bad entry for FTL. It has quiet moments. It has moments it isn't. There's a reason it was mothballed when FTLers came onto the scene."

"Bad entry." Lee's lip lifted in disgust. "Damned lies. *Excuses*. What killed this station was *Pell*. What killed this station was the theft of what became the Pell core and the establishment of an illegal enterprise above an inhabited world, against every law and charter. What killed this *station* was pure politics, a move to cut off the First Stars and trade with Cyteen." She snorted. "And you have the *gall* to impugn a Sol Original."

JR kept his reaction from his face. *Sol Original*. She meant Cruz. According to Abrezio, the Cruz name was near royalty back on Sol Station.

As for the theft of the Pell core . . . that was the Company line from way back. What was disturbing was hearing someone still arguing it in a company of FTL spacers.

"Pusher Captain," he said, forcing calm. "Pushers do fine here. But Foucault is potentially a massive risk. As Captain Mallory can tell you. C being C, you just can't scan ahead to know what it's going to be doing when you get there—or what it may decide to do because of your arrival."

"You claim you speak for Pell," Lee said. "Under what authority?"

JR lifted a brow. "I was speaking for physics, Captain. But I do *not* speak for Pell. I speak for the Merchanters' Alliance."

"Damned grifters. Collecting money, are you? Who holds it?"

"Never leaves your pocket unless someone has an emergency. Then there's a general draw, apportioned to every ship and station."

"Oh, and stations, too."

"The Alliance offers Olympus and all ships the same terms: benefit for ships is assurance of repair and access to ports. Benefits for stations, beyond the obvious of having ships that arrive and leave dependably, also include the kind of discussion we're having now—polite discussion, sensible reports, exchange of non-proprietary information, non-affiliated representation for help solving disputes. As for instance, you will want to know when those Sol jump-points prove out, and if we knew, we would make every effort to let you know—aside from the black boxes that make that automatic. It would be useful *to you* to be in on the agreement and the information flow. Assuming you've got more FTL ships than the one on B-mast . . ."

"Assume all you like."

"Experimental?"

"*Shalleen* is experimental," Jiburi said.

Of course it was. Unless Sol had found safe jump-points in some other direction, there would have been no power-up at Sol.

"Push one of those tri-vanes to Pell," JR said, "and you'd get conversation. I take it there will be more."

"Possibly."

"Advantages of the design?" Minimal hold. No accommodation for ring docking. One could guess its function was not necessarily as a cargo carrier.

"Classified," Lee said.

Lee probably was not an expert on jump-ship characteristics. Probably not even an expert on what moved a pusher. There were techs for that. Lee might be well out of her depth in a discussion of ship design.

"We are not the only side with secrets," Lee said abruptly, both elbows on the table. "What is that ship out there that does not answer our hails?"

God. Min . . . in dialogue with station . . . no. That would not be a good thing.

"*Little Bear*, Xiao Family."

"*Why* has the word *Cyteen* not come into this discussion?"

There it was. Lee was bone-ignorant on some topics. But evidently had others.

"Because it is not relevant to Olympus. *Little Bear* is Cyteen registry, but she's an *Alliance* ship, a Family ship, and has no shipboard connection to the administration of Cyteen, station or planet. *Little Bear* has been with us—as a Pell ship is working Cyteen-side—to gather signatures for the Alliance—because trade goes both sides of Mariner. Is she a friendly presence? Yes. *Little Bear* has made dock at Venture, Bryant's, and Alpha, but since this station has seemed reluctant to accept visitors, she has stood off while a Pell ship asks questions."

"Is that ship armed?"

"I've never seen her specs, but it's highly unlikely. There's no reason to be—absolutely no threat anywhere in trafficked space that weapons could do a thing about, so I don't know why any of us would be. Are we dangerous? When we form a bubble, we can be—but that's just the nature of what we do. *Little Bear* is holding off out of courtesy while a Pell-registry ship asks the EC what its preferences are at this station. Coming closer might be mis-interpreted as a threat, and that would not be our preference."

"A Cyteen-registered ship."

"Captain, so technically, is *Miriam B, Firenze,* and *Come Lately,* all of which were built at Cyteen yards."

"Re-registered at Alpha," Mallory interjected, "as a point of fact, sir. And that ship is Cyteen registry *currently.* It is based there *currently.* It is gath-ering information *currently.* And it does not respond to hails."

Mallory. That was an unexpected fervor.

"*Little Bear* is entirely a Family ship, does not speak Standard as a primary language, and has no affiliation whatsoever with Cyteen adminis-tration."

"That still does not answer—why is *Little Bear* here?"

"*Little Bear* being the nearest Alliance ship not engaged in Alliance business—or looking for your ship, sir, ironically enough—we asked them to join us on a run inquiring about contraband goods at Pell, which, oddly, raised other points that led us here. We do not agree, will not agree, and do not anticipate agreeing with *Little Bear* on Cyteen politics—supposing they support the Emorys and Carnaths, which we have never even asked them. We have never remotely discussed their opinion about Pell. But we can work together to ensure the flow of goods and good will."

"These are issues," Mallory said, "that involve human life."

"So does international *conflict,* Captain, either cold or hot, which is what we, with our agreements, wish to prevent. We by no means approve of all Cyteen does. But while we trade, we are preventing the worst case: the frag-mentation of nations and the demonization of other humans."

"Seems to us that Cyteen is doing all that *while* you trade with them."

"And that ship," Lee said, "will carry what they observe here to Cyteen, engaging *Cyteen* with business that is properly between Sol and its colonies . . . including, as a courtesy, Pell . . ."

"Which, you are correct, sir, they will do, unembellished, and in detail, impossible for any other ship to deny, only supplement. Whether or not *Little Bear* carries that information out of this system or we do, that infor-mation will reach every ship and station in the black box system, including, yes, Cyteen."

"That has the character of a threat."

"This is how the whole industry works, Captain, and has worked for over a century, here, at Pell, at Cyteen—everywhere, everything is known—or becomes known. As for *Little Bear,* I will be blunt. We came here not knowing what we'd find. We brought, prudently, backup, to make sure our report gets out. Would not you? That ship is poised to depart to advise other stations of whatever the outcome here—starting with Venture and Pell—yes. It will not engage with you. It will simply observe, then leave and tell every station it passes that something happened here. We would like that to be a positive report; the EC's image is currently very badly tarnished by the actions at Alpha. *Rights of Man* has made a lot of people very nervous."

"*Rights of Man* is identical with your own ship," Jiburi said.

"Far from it. *Far* from it. And Pell and, by now, Cyteen . . . knows it. *Little Bear,* if alarmed, will depart Foucault with a report that if we do not follow soon—something is very wrong at Olympus. So no, let us *not* have that happen. For our part, we have nothing adverse to report. Pusher-ships can continue from Sol, perfectly useful, since the difficult route *Galway* is exploring cannot deliver near the volume a pusher can haul. As a pusher-port, you have an uninterrupted future. You want to deliver new ships and offer them, free and clear, to merchanter Families? No problem."

"Let me interrupt your fantasy," Lee said. "That Sol should fall in line and become just one more system supplying Pell and Cyteen on their terms; the Mother of Mankind, doing business with two upstart space stations orbiting uninhabitable planets with nothing friendly to human life in the game? Never! We spend our lives at this! We *built* your reality! Who the *hell* do you think you are?"

The attitude was no news. What *was* disheartening was to hear that attitude from a pusher captain. Mum's worst fears realized: this one was EC to the core. And Mallory . . . God help them . . . was on Lee's side.

But . . . *We spend our lives. . . . Wellington* and *Finity's End* had at least history in common.

"Captain Lee, at a certain point in your voyage, when you began to brake, did you not look forward to your destination, even knowing it had its problems? We understand. We were *Gaia.* We were the ship that said no to replacement crew, that gave pusher-ships their rights, and their due from stations—which I hope you will continue to have. You've disconnected yourself from Sol's timeline—I think you realize that now. You may soon disconnect from this one. Your stake in all this is the station you create, but your *world* is your ship. We don't want to destroy that. Captain, Stationmaster . . . talk with the merchanters you trust. Listen to them, on the realities of trade and that star you're wed to, here. There is a use for what you're building, a function and a value . . . a purpose far beyond what the mission agenda designed it to be."

"Spare us your sentiment. *You*, sir, are working for Pell, a station that began in an act of outright *piracy* that handed the precedent on to Cyteen, to the regret of the entire human race. We *are* the authority here!"

"No one questions that. Each station is its own authority. Cyteen is a market you don't need to touch and an entity you don't have to deal with—but one that is reaching *back* for its humanity, Captain, that wants Earth's art and tastes and images, luxury goods and intellectual goods that can work more change on Cyteen's ways than Pell possibly can. You can do that. And it's to the good of all humanity to pursue that connection. They *want* to be influenced by Earth."

"*Merchanters.* You haul *freight*, Captain. You simply move freight around. You don't build. You haven't a damn claim. Your size, and the disruption you've made in this station, doesn't impress a pusher. Neither does your politics."

"Talk to your FTL haulers. Listen to them. Your anonymity is gone. Your operation is not going to work as designed, but it can be far more."

"This is pointless. You are in EC territory, you are under EC law, and you do not get to stand on *our* deck and tell us whether or not our operation works. You are about one move from—"

"*Captain Lee!*" Jiburi's hand slammed the table. "Captain Neihart! You've given us a document. We'll report it on the Stream. Dutifully. In the meanwhile, we have a situation. Captain Neihart, you will appreciate that we are not going to change our orders on a whim and we are not going to abandon Olympus. I'll give this matter some thought. We'll discuss it. We ask you disconnect and pull off sufficient to ease tensions."

JR drew a breath, welcoming Jiburi's intervention. He had no interest in some pointless debate with Lee. He'd made his pitch and was more than happy to leave. Jiburi—was a question mark. One wondered how long she'd been here, whether she'd come with Lee or been established before Lee arrived. She'd said over com that Lee was the authority on the station as long as the ship was in dock, and he got the distinct impression that she was not pleased with that fact. She was trying now to handle Lee, possibly conscious of the fact that Lee was *not* a permanent fixture on the station, and she was. Whatever came of this meeting, *Jiburi* would be left to deal with it.

One thing was clear: there *was* no dominant authority on Olympus.

Which meant it was time to leave. He dipped his head and began to turn.

"Monahan," Mallory said sharply.

"Sir," Ross said.

"*Why* did *Finity's End* take you aboard? Was it to control the narrative?"

God. *Why* would these two not allow them to disengage? He looked at Ross, but Ross's attention was firmly on Mallory.

"I'm not sure what you mean, sir." Ross's voice was steady, respectful. "They took me aboard because I was hammering at their E-port and, fortunately for me, *they* hadn't disembarked their security. I wasn't even thinking straight, thanks to an EC club that split my head open. My Nav 1, knowing Alpha needed to know what Cruz had done, shoved me in a suit and out the hatch and *Finity* was where there was to go."

"Why not the mast emergency hatch?"

"Nav 1 said get to *Finity*. That's all I could keep in my head. We didn't know but what Abrezio was in with Cruz. So I got to *Finity* . . . somehow. I can't really remember that part. But I could've drifted free and never been noticed out there til some lane-sweep picked me up, half dead or worse. *That's* how they took me aboard, and damned grateful I was."

"What exactly happened aboard *Galway?*"

Ross's eyes moved across the table, taking in each of those seated . . . in judgment. They stopped on Lee, and hardened. "Cruz's *thugs* were waiting in ambush." His gaze moved back to Mallory. "They came pouring onto the bridge as soon as the spin was up and began attacking us before we could even get out of our seats. They had lethals, for God's sake! Cruz was pissed because *we* had the coordinates, and he'd been left out of the loop. Pissed because *he* wasn't going to get credit for a discovery that had nothing to do with him. And because he was pissed, he was going to run the ship, *at gunpoint,* all the way to friggin' Earth. And I'll tell you this, sir, I don't know whether my ship's blown to hell or whether she's made it, but it's damn sure if they got to Earth, it's my Nav 1 that's gotten them there, and my Senior Captain that's in charge. And it's my *personal* hope, sir, that the damn Enforcer pirates took a cold walk on the way."

There was a moment of quiet.

"You swear to that."

"*Galway's* honor, sir."

"Well, that's pretty well a given, isn't it?" Lee said. "The ship's gone and we've got one man's word there was a problem."

Ross turned a look on Lee, and the stare was silent and it was deadly. "You've got *my* word, pusher Captain, and the situation of my Family, and you can go to bloody hell, sir."

Time. Time to shut it down. One clear statement of fact. "The EC cannot be the side of the angels, Captain Mallory. The EC on Alpha violated charter, violated station authority, violated shipboard authority, committed an act of piracy, and pushed the population to the edge of mutiny. The EC has no corner on care for its citizens. Pell and Venture have been doing *your* job past Cruz and Hewitt's bleeding the station dry for over two decades . . . while supply came *here*. We'll be taking our leave, now. We've said enough to make ourselves clear. If you want to talk, we'll be here another day."

"Neihart," Mallory said. "Giovanna Galli sang *Finity's* praises at Alpha. And it's a good thing your Alliance is doing for *Firenze*. I read that. I support your idea in theory, Navigator Monahan *and* Captain Neihart, but here's the sticking-point. We will not be part of any organization that includes Cyteen. And whatever your good intentions, and good acts, that's what it comes down to. In the meanwhile, we can co-exist with the *concept* you have. But the EC is the port we'll have, and where we'll trade."

"We'll talk."

"No," Mallory said. "Not until you shed that connection."

"Beyond a doubt," Jiburi said. "We will send the transcript on the Stream. We will report your offer and our observations. We will consider your proposition. We will communicate to Pell in due course. But tell Pell it should reconsider its associations. And it would not be good, Captain Neihart, for your Alliance to continue to feed information to Cyteen—be it the black boxes or word of mouth. The Mother of Mankind will make her own policy, as she always has, and give you an official answer—perhaps sooner than is now possible, respects to the Monahan Family. As for your Alliance functioning here—you will find less fertile ground. We can better your offer. We can supply these aging merchanters with newer, more modern ships and give these ships everything they need. I suggest you disembark now. With all due courtesy."

"Stationmaster Jiburi, Captain Mallory, Captain Lee. We'll decouple and proceed toward system exit at a reasonable rate. We will remain reachable for communications from Olympus for about the next three days if you wish to ask a further question. Or change your minds. Your health. We'll convey your sentiments where appropriate."

"Captain. Your health."

From Lee there was only a stony silence.

First round. A draw. It could have gone better. It could have gone worse.

JR turned. Ross did, and Fletch and Hank fell in behind as they passed the door to the lift foyer.

Mallory was an if. So was Jiburi.

Nothing would budge Lee. That type cited EC holy writ as the only truth. Lee had changed the program, not sending her lieutenant . . . personally to keep a line on what Jiburi said, if he read it right.

No one followed them. The door behind them closed.

The lift at the far side of the foyer opened to a button-push, with a sigh of unequal pressure. The walls inside had stopped steaming in the length of time it took for the meeting. The cold-suits they had left were there, chill, but not brittle. There was time enough on the trip to the mast-end to put them on.

"*Finity,*" JR said, and Com answered, never having lost connection—and probably being read loud and clear in station ops.

"*Aye, sir.*"

"We're back in the lift and moving. Advise Parton. Stand by."

"*Standing by, aye, sir.*"

JR put on his mask, not intending further conversation within any pickup that station might have arranged. Fletch, Hank, and Ross did the same. Internal com kicked in.

Static interrupted something from Com. It wasn't clear what Com said as the car engaged and began to move. The floor rotated to provide a *down* and *up.*

Static. That hadn't been the case with com on the way in. Not even intermittently.

It was, now.

That was *not* good.

"*We've lost them,*" came area-wide from Com. "*Cameras and audio are all out.*"

Jen took in her breath. Fletcher was out there. With Parton and Twofer. Who were out there with Uncle and with Ross, *not* in a safe place. *She* was all of Exec Security that was not over *there*, and there was nobody but John to tell her what to do. John was able to reach her if he wanted to give orders, but John had the whole ship on his hands.

There were trackers on everybody, but those had gone to static at the same time the cameras had gone to interference breakup, and Optics and Tracking would have John on their necks asking for results. They didn't need additional queries from her.

There'd been no seat for her junior self on the bridge on Captain John's watch, no place official for her to wait it out but the Security office—where she was at the moment; and there was nobody she could call up who wouldn't be in deeper confusion than she was . . . operation-level Security, check the badges, watch the locks . . . find the stray kid. She'd passed the team Captain John's orders—lockdown, stay out of the corridors, standing order with the ship even remotely apt to move, and *Finity* right now was still maintaining that tube-connect, doing her own little dance with gravitic attraction.

She'd thought of calling Marcy D and Dave up, maybe, but what could they do, but sit and stew with her? She'd put them on alert. Ready, in the last two minutes, but not breaking takehold orders. And the office had no damn answers.

She made a decision, used her key to open the weapons locker and took out the only serious armament she had ever practiced with, an impact pistol. She buckled it on, then took her life in her hands and made the long run down the exec corridor to the airlock prep for the tube-connect they were using—no orders, no plan, except to avoid being sent somewhere safe and out of it, and to be there if there was any possible thing she could do.

John's orders flashed on red screens and repeated from the coms like a specific accusation: *Stay out of the corridors. Condition Red. Second-shift, maintain regular sleep cycle; we will advise you. We have not yet determined we have an emergency. Do not add problems to Third-shift crew.*

Her com unit was all static, but she kept it on. It should be picking up Uncle's team. The static *could* clear. It might be station's deliberate interference. It might be just some area they'd run into. She took the unit off-channel only for a handful of seconds, onto the red channel, emergency only, all-ship, and notified Com 3.4. "This is Jen, Security. I'm going to E-1. I'm suiting up to stand by inside the lock."

She took it on herself to send out a wake-up call to Marcy D and Dave; but their ordinary emergency post was the loft, at the other side of the ring—there if the kids and the minders needed them. There was damn-all they could do here. But she wanted extra hands if the team came in with a problem.

She didn't wait for an answer to either.

Captain John clearly had his hands full, and the static on her handheld was still the only feed from the team. She sailed to the E-1 turn, pivoted, kicked off, caught a takehold, and aimed for the mid-level ramp that was the way to the access prep the team had used.

Inside, then, a contortion and shove, herself in her workout kit. She grabbed a takehold, righted herself. The suit locker beside E-1 was another set of five buttons and a personal code. *Finity* made one of her intermittent adjustments and she lost the keystroke. She cancelled, then braced herself at the lock, and restarted the sequence, biting her lip in concentration.

The door shot up. She let the pistol hang free, turned about and backed into the smallest adult hard suit, shoved her soft-slippered feet into the hip-high boots, shoved her arms into the sleeves and had those rising and the suit forming around her before the helmet came down and the machine executed the precise half-turn that sealed it. Air began flowing at several points, soft fan noise, and that was the signal to shove free.

She caught the floating pistol with hands far too clumsy to use it, and in desperation just let it go, swung into the lock with way too much energy, rebounded, then engaged the boot magnetics and voiced-on the chest light.

Calm down. Big calm-down. The impact gun was hopeless with gloves on. But she was there.

"*Jen.*" That was not Captain John's voice, it was Second Captain Madison's, half-drowned by the suit's hissing and adjusting. "*Keep that hatch shut. Acknowledge! Stat!*"

"Aye, sir," she said. "I'm here. I'm suited up. I'm at the outside switch."

"*Don't open that hatch! Parton is under attack. We've lost contact with JR. All bets are off. Don't open that door!*"

"Aye, sir. I'm here. That's all."

"*You've got that line-caster in the locker.*"

"Yes, sir." She'd never thought of that rescue line as a weapon. But it threw a tri-filament line hard enough to reach somebody fast, who'd lost a free-fall mooring. Or it could hurt a damn lot, if somebody was rushing the airlock.

"*Don't open that hatch until JR does. Terry and Vic are on their way to you. Expect them. Meanwhile get the caster.*"

"Yes, sir." She reached the locker, pulled the lever with large-gloved hands, and retrieved the line-caster, four times the size of the pistol with no guard on the trigger, and no question what it was, with the line-canister and two lever-fed reloads at the end of it. The label said something about *Caution,* and *Recoil may cause disconnection . . .*

"*Your discretion, Jen. You hang onto that thing and use your head.*"

Static was all that came through JR's com unit, but the core-lift was still moving . . . one assumed on its proper course. Either the station hadn't intended to interrupt it, or they were headed where station wanted them to be. There had been one thump on their course from the rim, just after the redirection to the mast, a little misalignment of the tube. That had been about halfway. JR waited for it, hoped for it as a sign they were actually coming back along the route they should be taking.

For all they knew, they'd been sent into the depths of the station. There remained the possibility station might strand them—just stop the car and make them bargain to get out of it.

Such an approach to *Finity* would, JR had already set it in mind, constitute detention so far as his order to yank *Finity* free and launch *Little Bear* for Pell, neither of which he wanted to see happen.

He was intensely disappointed. He hadn't been prepared, when he'd headed onto the station in the first place, for a merchanter to be the one to utterly reject the deal . . . not even the slightly shady merchanter he'd have bet on as in tight with the EC. *Jiburi* had been more receptive.

Mallory's refusal rode the back of his mind, mingled unpleasantly with the persistent static in his earpiece.

Things were undeniably dicey. Not yet over the edge, but going there; and the only advisement Madison and John would have they could be in trouble was that com breakup. He wondered if their trackers were similarly disrupted, but there was no way of knowing. And there was the greater question of, having seen the interaction of *Jiburi* with *Wellington's* captain, who was actually responsible for the interference. *Jiburi* had shifted course rapidly at the end, practically pushing them out the door. Had *she* gotten some warning, or was she just reading something in Lee? Just how much control over *station* operations did Lee have? *Jiburi* had promised safe passage, but did she really have the ability to guarantee that?

Damn, damn, and . . . damn. Things they would like to know.

Facemasks, static on com, and cold-suit fans made conversation labored. Fletch was frowning, likely thinking the same worried thoughts, and might be passing touch-signals to Hank: the two were shoulder to shoulder. Ross Monahan was braced against the wall opposite, face dead calm, no clue what he was thinking, just the occasional dart of the eyes from the lift position schematic to the door.

Fletch would have briefed Parton and Hank about contingencies. Ross, however . . .

"Ross."

"*Sir.*"

For Ross *and* the listeners, if any: "Easy does it."

"Yes, sir," Ross said, and his expression never changed.

"Might take a while. We'll get it fixed."

"Yes, sir. No problem, sir."

Sensible. Focussed. He wasn't *elsewhere* the way Jen said he could be when stressed. Thank God.

The car kept moving.

Then braked. Acceleration lessened and *down* began to give way to null-G. Full, easy stop.

The door opened onto cold and light, and Parton . . . clipped on and drifting as they had left him, but starfished, not moving, and not right. Frozen dark beads hung in mid-air. And on either side of the lift door and from an open service door, hard-suited figures closed in.

With *Wellington's* symbol emblazoned on their helmets. They were outnumbered—by a lot.

"*Finity!*" JR shouted, dockside fashion, and kicked off, caught a handhold on the exit and slammed a helmeted head with all the power in his knee as he whipped past. A suited body powered toward him, and Fletch fired: the impacted body sailed back the way it had come: suit jets sent it into a spin, but, damn it—unhurt and flailing.

Hard-suits. And them in flimsy cold suits.

Ross and Hank in unison seized on another and rotated him into the wall, releasing him to the rebound, a tumbling missile across the lift foyer that impeded another's try for purchase.

Chaos. Their only real option. JR got a grip and wrenched at the pressure control on one Wellington's suit as another reached past and tried to get a grip on his mask.

"*Get to the tube!*" Fletch yelled, and Hank and Fletch together tore that attacker away. JR's cold-suit fan had stopped, something pulled loose. Heat was dissipating fast from the open, shadowy tube-connect. The air sparkled with frozen moisture.

"Ross!" JR yelled. "*Go!*" And kicked off hard.

First rule, get the captain and the Galway out of reach. Security wouldn't break for their own safety until *they* did.

Ross dived for the tube-connect. An attacker followed him. JR plowed into that one from behind and bounced him off the floor as another shot went off and JR rebounded. Someone grabbed his arm as he tumbled, and pulled: Ross slung him backward and through the hatch, hurling him on ahead as he flailed out to find a surface. There was the lax grip cord along the right wall—the only traction to be had. JR snagged it and rolled as he tried to see what was behind him.

Ross sailed toward him, in the tube-connect. Fletch and Hank were still in the foyer.

"Fletch!" JR called. "Hank!"

"Keep going!" Fletch's answer came. "We're behind you!"

They weren't, yet, but he did that. He and Ross—using the grip-cord to move. No guarantee the Wellingtons hadn't gotten past them into the tube-connect. The hatch was out of sight, a hundred-odd meters of three-meter tube-connect ahead—the tube clear and open, but bending, impossible to see the hatch, but along the glistening white surface, light spread, blinking green, green, green—which meant the damn airlock was open.

They had closed it. And it was open. *Finity* was wide open. At risk.

"John!" JR tried to switch on com with his chin, and was not sure he had it. "John, dammit, we've got incoming! Seal E-1!"

"*JR,*" he heard through the static. But it was Hank's voice, *Finity*-com coming through the static. "*JR, I got Parton, I got Fletch. I'm coming.*"

Hell of a mess. Damn it! A captain couldn't turn back to help him. Damn it, damn it, damn it.

"Hank, do you read? Are you all right?"

"*Fine.*" Strangled, labored reply. Hank wasn't all right and Ross was actively headed back to help him.

Hell with it—JR hauled at the line and sent himself backward ten meters, fifteen, and managed to see Ross intercepting Hank, who was trying to move two inert cold-suited bodies. "*JR, get the hell back!*" That was Hank. "There's more coming in!"

The pliable tube jolted—minuscule movement, but not *Finity's.* Other bodies were active in the tube. Coming from the foyer.

JR maintained position. Ross and Hank reached him, bringing Fletch and Parton with them, one hand on the line, that jerked and tautened to other users—and there was no safety for them but the ship, whatever was in their way.

Behind them, trouble was moving fast. White lights of hard-suits were advancing on the surfaces of the curving tube behind them.

JR grabbed the line with one hand and hauled, one pull after another, Ross and Hank doing the same—

Then a female voice on com. *"Captain! Ross! Keep coming! Keep coming!"* That was *Jen.*

"Jen, seal E-2! Let us in the lock but don't seal E-1 til my say-so!"

"I got a line here!" Jen shouted back.

JR snatched a glance back as best he could and there were at least three after them, who knew they were running out of tube. A shot opened a hole near him—he didn't hear it but wind screamed past and suction pulled at the cold-suit. "A damn line won't help," he shouted into com, as the tube quivered around them—he looked forward to the green glare of the hatch on the tube, and his next hard haul on the cord showed him one hard-suited figure in the open airlock, braced there, armed with something aimed right down the tube-access.

Female voice on com. *"I got a line-gun, Captain-sir—and I see three behind you!"*

"Shoot 'em!" JR said.

The shot went off and the shadowy bolus shot past him, past Ross, and past Hank, down the snaking throat of the tube, paying out reflective filament as it went.

The tube quivered, as the bolus hit something.

Hank, drawing along one of their casualties, grabbed the shining filament. JR snagged it with a sidelong swipe, Ross's grip was only an instant behind.

"Got it!" Hank shouted. *"Anchor, Jen! Reel in! Fast!"*

Line took up, snapped taut, and if Jen hadn't anchored, she'd be flying past them.

The line pulled hard, snatching them along toward the green glare of the open hatch. JR reached the lock, grabbed a takehold, and reoriented beside Jen as Ross made it in, hauling Fletch, twisting to protect Fletch from slamming up against the back wall, and kicking to the side as Hank barreled through with Parton. Two hardsuited intruders' lights showed in the tube. The line-gun, let free on its tether as their rescuer tried to help Hank, racketed about with brutal force.

JR hit the emergency lock-close. The hatch shot across with a force and speed that could cut a man in half. Impacts resounded off the hull. Not the thud of pellet guns. Projectile fire.

"John!" JR yelled at the com system overhead, at his com pickup, whatever was listening. "Back us out. *Now!"*

"Roger that."

Finity moved and *Finity* moved hard, simultaneously howling the Red takehold. JR's back hit the sealed inner hatch, Fletch crumpled up with him. The hatch and hull resounded to thunderous impacts, three, four—the tube itself, likely, snapped, rebounding in freefall chaos.

"Medical," JR said to com. "Get us medical! Stat!"

Parton was moving, however improbably. Fletch, in his arms, wasn't.

JR carefully eased the shattered mask off. The fixed stare said Fletch wouldn't move.

Ever.

A choked sob came from the small hard-suit tucked as tight as a hard-suit could tuck against the hatch on the far side of Fletch, the line-gun cradled in its arms.

What the hell had just happened? *Why?* There was no damned sense in it. The mind twisted into knots trying to find reasons to what wasn't remotely reasonable.

If the station hadn't wanted them to leave, station could have detained them all there. Jiburi had given no indication of murder in mind. She'd talked about next steps. Neither Mallory nor Bellagio would dare stage a lethal attack. And even if they had . . . why would they?

Wellington hardsuits.

Lee. He could well believe that.

Likely against Jiburi's direct orders. Lee wouldn't give a damn about that. Chain of command. Martial law. EC Enforcer. Arrogance. Blind, foolish . . .

And for no damn reason.

It shouldn't have happened.

Fletch shouldn't have died.

Parton shouldn't have been left like that. They could easily have overpowered him, taken him into custody.

But that wasn't what Lee wanted. Lee had created that scene. To shock. To terrify them into submission. Parton, their exhibit, their show of power—had been left bleeding, with no attempt to save him.

"Captain." Hank, fighting convulsive shivers, edged over to him. *"You all right? You hit anywhere?"*

"No," JR managed to say. "Not hit. You? Ross?"

"I'm all right," Hank said. And Ross: *"Fine."*

"Fletch is gone," JR said, past a knot in his throat. "Parton?"

"Still got a chance," Ross said, and to JR's left, Ross was struggling to help

Hank straighten out Parton's twisted body. At least Parton's mask had remained intact. The best JR could do, pressed against the hatch, was bring a knee to bear and give Hank's back a support as he held him.

"Takehold," JR said, on a breath. "Takehold strong and wait. John's got to get us out of here, protecting the vanes. Medics may be stalled. We're all Parton's got. Keep pressure on that wound if you can. We'll get the med kit when we can move."

No apology to his crew could cover the situation, and they were all vulnerable, here in the bare steel airlock. Acceleration crushed them all against the hatch. *Finity* had backed off the mast, clearing the station ring in a bone-bruising hurry, still accelerating. Muscle resisted. Joints strained. For a while it was hard to breathe.

John's in command, JR thought. *Madison's up there, but* John's *in command.*

The hardsuit's faceplate had powered up, revealing Jen's tear-stained cheeks, but her expression now showed only the strain of acceleration.

Damned mess. Start to finish. His fault. His own damned fault.

Fletch. Dead. Trying to protect *him.* Parton—it was a bad one.

Dammit. Damn it all.

The pressure let up, abruptly, wholly gone—as the ship went inertial, zero-G. The takehold sounded again, before they could so much as draw breath, and pressure returned, this time pulling them down against the deck.

Finity was rising. Fletch weighed like unforgiveable sin, and JR hugged him tight and counted the beats of his own heart as vision greyed. He knew where *Finity* was going.

A vibration quivered through the hull. Hatch was opening—below the docking probe. Under the airlock. A second hatch. MD-1.

Machinery whined. Thumped. Sudden shock followed, palpable through the takehold bar.

Mass-driver.

Finity had just fired.

Aimed at the pusher on A-mast.

The unthinkable.

Whine. Thump. Second shot. The pusher was mining equipment. God knew what they were actually firing *at* the pusher. Metal. Spare parts. Containment buckets. Anything that would fit.

The *Wellington's* engines would be the target.

A message would be going out to *Little Bear,* simultaneously. *Go for jump. Advise Pell.*

Com's feed of the meeting would have been relayed real time to Min.

And there would be the vid from Jen's hardsuit and from their collar pins. It was highly possible everything that had just happened would be going with Min, too.

"What's happening?" Jen asked, a faint, small voice on pickup. Ross was looking his way, too. So was Hank, eyes asking solutions. Answers. Prophecy of the future.

"We're taking out the pusher's engines," JR said, as accel stopped and the ship went inertial again.

And stayed inertial. John was giving medical a chance to get to them. Help would be coming, fast as they could move by shove and drift.

"Move," he said, and unfolded out of his position, releasing the takehold, holding Fletch weightless against him, not leaving him behind, no. "Due caution. Med's coming: we take Parton to them. Hank, can you reach the button—"

The airlock panel shot back with no one touching the control, and Terry and Vic were there to help with the wounded. They moved along the take-holds until they were clear of the airlock, drifted up the slight ramp to the intersection of corridors, where the overhead lights blinked red, red, red and the screens all said *takehold in effect.*

"We're out of the lock," JR said on com. "Going to 1-1. Safe to move?"

"Medical will meet you," the answer came. Madison's voice. *"We will hold course. Station is busy at the moment."*

Came a hail from ahead, and Sherry, Jordan, and Sam Q appeared, steering along both cases and gear. Sherry and Jordan took charge of Parton with a positive-pressure IV, a heated wrap, and a quick tow toward a nearby storage room Sam had opened up. Vic followed with a limp and exhausted Hank.

Fletch—just was. That was all. JR pulled the mask off, automatic switch to external pickup. "Jen, Terry, Ross. Can you get him—to his office? Can you do that? Wake Fourth Captain, if she's slept through this. She needs to know. She'll know what to do."

As if there were something. As if there were anything to fix this. He didn't wait for an answer. He headed for the lounge, for that entry to the bridge, bloody and unwashed and with no way to mend that or anything, as things stood. One hand tingled, possibly frostbite, contact with the deckplates— whatever. That wasn't serious. The situation *was*, with the ship holding fire for their sake, delaying acceleration, while Olympus might be trying to marshal some retaliation.

Madison and John were both on the bridge when JR got there, Madison in the backfacing seat, John in the active captain's place, both belted in. Madison unbelted and cast free as JR approached, ceding the place. And momentarily half a hundred pairs of eyes broke discipline, distracted by the freefall move alongside the Nav seats.

JR strapped into the vacated seat as Madison took the observer bench below the big screen, and on that screen and screens all about, rapidly retreating, was a horrifying vision. The pusher and A-mast, reciprocal of what had shaken B, gyrated in a slow motion push and pull, the mast wobbling dizzily, the small utility pushers working frantically to keep the *Wellington* from twisting free of its grapples. The pusher's tail, where the engines sat, reflected Foucault's sullen glow like fire, girders blown askew, the conduits and shielding all jumbled, and the massive block that was the heart of the system exposed to view. Two sprays of unidentifiable debris fanned out, bouncing off each other and parts of the ship in ever-increasing chaos.

"*JR,*" John said over the exec channel, "*good you're back. Heart-hurt about Fletch. Parton's secure. I've one more primed to give 'em.*"

"Fire," JR said.

"'*Driver,*'" John said, audible to the whole bridge, "*fire as you bear.*"

Whatever the mass-driver had loaded, it fired. A few seconds later, the massive block disappeared behind a third disorganized cluster of fragments that ricocheted in all directions.

"*We might take a little chaff ourselves,*" John said calmly on exec channel, "*but minor. We are inertial at half astern. Keep us so.*"

"Your call, Third Captain." Most shrapnel would go off into space above the plane of the station, from their angle of attack. Some *could* hit the core, or the ring. Not enough to do significant damage, but the real damage had already been done. *Finity* would suffer the stain of being the first, possibly the only ship to conduct a hostile act toward a station or another ship. And it was his responsibility, not John's. His order.

Regret? No. But there was, even with Fletch's death, no anger in the decision. It was a thing that had to be done. Whoever had ordered that ambush was *not* going to escape accountability in that ship. Fault him for his judgment that it had become a necessity, maybe, but he had not fired on a station out of anger.

Was the anger there?

Abundantly. Forever. He wanted to know who had ordered the attack and why they had done what they had done. The *only* emblem he'd seen was *Wellington's*, but that didn't totally exonerate the station. Arrest Parton, alone at the lift access? Arrest the lot of them in the conference room? That would have been easily done.

Arrest them all before they entered the lift? Easier still. They could simply have shut down the core lift. They could have shut down the tube-connect from central control and withdrawn the connection. No one had to die. Olympus would have won, at least for the year or so it took for a dozen ships to move in and make clear the operation's plans had to adapt.

Easy . . . unless the perpetrators weren't in authority, and therefore had no control in Station Central. Easy . . . unless explaining hostages to the one who *did* control Station Central . . . was not an option.

Instead, someone had arranged that tableau of Parton drifting and bleeding, and attacked them, shocked and confused, in the mast. Hard-suits against breathing masks and heat gloves.

Why? What they'd done made no sense. Unless . . .

Unless their goal had been to lure Neiharts out of *Finity*—to save their Senior Captain.

Unless their goal had been to take over a megaship that actually functioned.

Unless their goal was to use that megaship to get whatever manpower had come in on *Wellington* over to Alpha and take control.

Damn them. Damn them to hell.

"*Proposing to cease firing,*" John said on the exec channel. "*We're well above the pusher's plane now and shrapnel to the station is a consideration.*"

"Yes," JR said in reply, and found himself shivering, not the sight he wanted to present to the bridge. It was over, it was done. They'd rendered the pusher inoperable, without touching the crew ring, nor anywhere crew might be. They'd made hash of the pusher's engines, and spread debris in a wide field that would trouble station with nuisance fragments until they could clear it out . . . after they stabilized the axis of rotation.

Well, Lee's plan hadn't worked. They'd kept *Finity* out of her ugly, greedy hands. In pulling away, they'd sent a shock through B-mast that was going to affect the station and the merchanters docked there, but minor. It was up on A-mast where they'd left their real response.

"Have we contacted Min?"

"I'm in contact," Madison said. *"Min says he wishes reports down to his departure. He's on an eight minute lag."*

"I'll do that," JR said and drew a deep breath. "John, I'll need Com for Min."

"Com 3, Senior Captain's on your board."

"Meanwhile, Madison," JR said, "compose an official report. Get statements from Hank and Ross. Cruel, they've both been through it, but legally necessary. I'll give mine as soon as I come off the bridge. In short: Parton was attacked while we were in transit from the ring, left wounded and unaided. Fletch and Hank covered us getting to the tube, and Fletch died in the effort. As for the bodycam record of the meeting, Com should have that."

"They do," Madison said. *"Entire. I'll send that first, then the official report on the attack."*

"We are continuing," John said, *"in the established vector. Are we outbound?"*

"Yes," JR said. "Direct-to-Pell via Thule."

Silence greeted that. They'd all known it was a possibility, that utterly untested route only *Finity* had a hope of making.

"Aye," John said. *"Com 1, record it. We are outbound. We will reorient for departure."*

"Wait," Madison said. *"Hell! We've got movement on B-mast.* Come Lately *and* Shalleen *are moving out."*

"Miriam B?" JR asked.

"Not yet. The other two are definitely in motion, moving in tandem. Possibly just assessing damage. Possibly leaving."

"Advise *Little Bear*." He gave the order—not his order to give—it was John's. Technically.

"Com 1," John said, unflapped, "advise *Little Bear*." And on exec: *"JR, I'll pass the com if you need it."*

"No. Carry on. But orient toward those two ships. Not enough to scare them, but if they're heading for jump, I want a closer look as they pass us."

"Reading my mind, cuz. Just observe or take them out? Come Lately's *no threat, but we don't know about* Shalleen."

"No!" Fire unprovoked on another merchanter? Just the thought horrified him. Then he realized what John suggested, that *Shalleen*, built by the EC, who had built a megaship designed to carry Enforcers . . . might be carrying something more lethal than 'drivers, and a different kind of horror took over. "Have the 'drivers ready. In case. We don't *know* why they're moving. Maybe breaking with station, maybe supporting it. Maybe just decoupling until the station stabilizes: that was a carefully timed simultaneous release, and at the moment, they're doing little more than drift out of harm's way. Let's see what Mallory does. He was against us in the meeting, but he wouldn't have supported that attack on us, I'm damned near certain. And he wasn't near his ship. Even if he wanted to join the Bellagios, core-lift may be out. He may be stranded."

"Your trust in any of those ships is greater than mine." It was still exec channel, blunt, but polite.

He drew a breath. "I cede to your judgment."

"Hell, no. Keep it coming. Vote, here, Madison. Do we persist with station? Cripple those merchanters? Or get the hell out of here?"

"Cede to JR. He was there."

Watching the readout on the ships' movement, JR realized: "They appear to be under serious power now, those two, moving away from the station as fast as they can get moving. They could be afraid of a similar fate to *Wellington's*. Or some stupidity from station. Mallory's still docked. Scan, keep eyes on them, get as much on *Shalleen* as you can, but let them go and . . . John—" The last of his energy deserted him. "Just get us the hell out of here."

"Amen." That was Mum, breaking into exec. "Need to know *is our cargo, and a damned precious load. Push it.*"

Book VI   Section xv

Takehold sounded again. There was announced to be a brief but major push. Ross grabbed the bar right where he was, outside the makeshift surgery, where two Neiharts were trying to save the life of a third in zero-G and now about to be under heavy accel. He hoped they had the bleeding stopped.

Jen was in there, holding a strong hand-light. She was *needed* to do that, but there wasn't room in that storage room for one more, and nothing for him to do if he were.

His cousins, off-shift and theoretically in quarters, would be worried, but *Finity* was still under Red, and com for other than official business was shut down. And while he wasn't needed here, he needed to be here. Needed to know. Needed time to get his head straight before . . . whatever happened next.

Parton was dicey, but hanging on. That he had a chance at all was thanks to Jen. She'd saved them all.

God, he loved her. Now more than ever.

He'd helped carry Fletcher's body to his Security office. They'd strapped it into a reclined chair, where it would wait for someone to have time to deal with it. All they could do. He'd liked Fletcher. A lot. Fletcher had taken the personal trouble to explain things and get their opinion on this operation. A kind, decent human being, who'd handled the ship's dockside security situations and occasional admin issues, and gotten caught by some Company hire-on's lucky damn shot—brutal EC force of the sort Ross knew far too well.

He was angry. He was damned angry, as old grudges mingled uneasily with Olympus' senseless, bungled use of force. Angry, with nowhere useful to spend that anger. They were free, they were underway, and leaving this godforsaken place. Bits of the bridge report came through intermittent general address. Two merchanters had undocked. *Miriam B* remained on B-mast.

He hoped *Finity's* pull away had slammed her a good one. Mallory *deserved* to be grounded a while, damn his arrogant face. He'd tried to tell him, tried to warn him the kind of people he was dealing with . . . and for a moment he thought he'd gotten through, but then Mallory had said all the shit about Cyteen being a deal breaker . . .

But Mallory was nothing to Lee. God, what a piece of work.

At least *Finity* had hammered the pusher engine to scrap metal. He'd seen the image on the screen in Fletcher's office. He only wished he'd seen it happen. Hell, he wished he'd been the one to push the damn button.

And the disabling of that pusher was just the beginning. He wondered how long it would take Jiburi to figure that out. Olympus Station was about to learn what the word *rationing* meant, since he doubted, once word got out, that *any* station would do business with the Mallorys or the Bellagios.

Not if *he* had any influence on the decision.

Not even if the station and all three ships groveled and begged, after an apology and a signed declaration of guilt . . . as if *that* would ever happen.

As if an apology could bring back Fletcher.

One wondered when the next pusher was due in, and how much of this one's cargo had been destined for Thule . . . another operation probably on indefinite hold with that pusher out of commission. No, that massive pusher crew was going to sit here, taking up space, living on the supply meant to last them, oh, another ten years or so, for as long as it took to fix the *Wellington* . . . if the pusher could even *be* fixed.

Couldn't happen to a more deserving lot of . . . God, there was no word for such people.

All this . . . all this needless death and betrayal. And for what? The fools had no secrecy left. The plan that might have been, had *The Rights of Man* met expectations, that plan to get *Rights* here filled with Enforcers, ultimately to threaten Pell—that was dead. Even if those Enforcers hadn't been decommissioned and put to work fixing Rosie's plumbing, even if *Rights* had managed to jump and arrive at Olympus in one piece . . . even if all those things happened, the only Navigator outside of Fallan Monahan that might get that monster into this system safely was Kate Neihart, and that damn sure would never happen.

He'd *warned* them, dammit!

He'd . . . warned them. Maybe, he thought with a sudden flare of guilt, maybe that said it all. Maybe what he'd said had tipped the scale and convinced Lee to attempt a takeover of *Finity*, taking a page from *Sol Original* Andy Cruz's play book. Steal a ship to replace the one that doesn't work. Had there been a whole army of Enforcers behind them, waiting for *Finity* to open the hatch? Had she planned to pull a Cruz, load her Enforcers onto *Finity*, and force the Neiharts to take them to Alpha?

Idiots, *idiots*. Had they learned nothing from the whole *Galway* fiasco? Merchanters wouldn't be pushed. *Wouldn't* surrender their ships or their freedom. The lines were clearer with each passing moment. There were some things worth dying for, and stopping the EC from creating a police state was one of them.

Damn them. Damn the EC. Damn Cruz and damn Lee.

And damn the ships that had had a choice and still went on dealing with them.

Mallory worried about Cyteen. The Monahans had never had a day of grief out of Cyteen, but honest ships and stations had had lifetimes of personal grief from the Earth Company—while those two ships had lived high on lies for generations. He wished he'd brought a length of roller-chain to that meeting. Small good it did when the other side brought guns, but damned if he wouldn't have given *someone* a bloody damn scar to match his own before they stopped him.

At least Parton might live. They were trying, in there. And all he could do was hang on and wait, when com announced they were going for turnover.

Good. Good, that.

They'd backed out of the tube-connect under the braking engines, which could handle *Finity* with her holds full. They had gone inertial on that course, with intermittent driver-fire only adding V. Now they were going to turn over and bring the mains to bear for a long, hard push toward, he hoped, a safe and unchallenged jump.

Parton was a consideration. Was he stable enough yet for the push? He guessed that was what Third Captain was waiting to hear. If they had to wait a few hours, hell, a week, a month, they could hang here and stare down station with no worry at all. The medics had to be talking in there, but he couldn't hear anything past the noise of the fans.

General address said, *"We are about to rotate ship, cousins and friends, to orient us for departure."* That was John Neihart's voice. *"Once that is done, we will bring up the ring, and you will be able to move about under Yellow. Junior-juniors, you will stay in quarters until ring rotation is normal and until you receive specific clearance."*

It was surreal and reassuring at the same time, the ordinary business of getting underway, same as every ship, everywhere. Normalcy. But then Third Captain continued:

"We regret to report that we have lost Security Chief Fletcher Alejandro Neihart to hostile fire in leaving Olympus Station. Com has personally notified next-ofs and extended the entire Family's sympathy and support. Security Officer Walter Parton is undergoing surgery as a result of the same incident. We are relieved to report Senior Captain is aboard and safe along with Security Officer Hank 'Twofer' Kulik and Nav 1.5 Ross Monahan.

"Finity has rendered the EC pusher Wellington inoperable if not irrepairable, at dock. Finity has neutralized the Olympus Stream buoy. For those of you juniors, any pushers en route will do well enough without it, provided their crews aren't utterly incompetent. Apply yourselves to your studies. Sometimes the machines fail.

"Finity has advised Little Bear to proceed toward jump to Thule.

"Finity will follow to zenith on her own timetable. We will jump to Thule, reorient, and take the high route to Pell.

"Merchanters Come Lately and Shalleen have left B-mast, but pose no apparent threat to us, and Miriam B remains at dock. We are watching these ships and the station closely and will retaliate if fired upon, so move warily, cousins and friends and do not enter risky situations. Juniors and junior-juniors, this means you.

"The Family's deepest sympathies and condolences, Will, Sayan, and Lela. I am deeply, personally sorry. Tim and Marcy, all of us are with you."

The business of life and the consolation of death.

It need not have happened, damn it. It *should* not have happened.

JR shoved his mind away from that black hole of what-if and focused on the ongoing situation, which, with rotation and a good accel burn behind them, needed one more action to finish with Olympus.

"Com 3, get me *Come Lately*, Senior Captain."

Com acknowledged.

If there was any possibility the Bellagios had now had enough of Olympus, if there was any dawning rationality to be had in them, it was worth a try.

"Captain," Com 1 said then, *"message incoming from* Little Bear."

"Senior Captain," John said, *"will you take* Little Bear?"

"I'll take it," JR said, and Min's voice came through.

"Regards to Finity's End. *We have received the relay of the meeting, and your message regarding the attack. We have recorded observations and initiated course as agreed. We will present the gathered data to Venture and to Pell and stations along our route. Ending."*

God, the damn lag. Min was talking from the past. And he was headed for jump.

But he *would* get a message. There was still time.

"Regards to *Little Bear.* This is JR Neihart. We copy. In addition to the audio relay, you should be receiving footage from body-cams, and soon we will have an official report for you. We cannot thank you enough for helping to disseminate the truth regarding what has just happened. But please delay departure until you have those records and our report. The situation is ongoing with the Bellagios and Mallorys.

"In brief: after being assured repeatedly by Stationmaster Jiburi that we would have safe passage back to the ship, we were attacked in the tube as we were leaving the station. One injured, one fatality on our side. The attackers wore *Wellington*-marked hardsuits, however we are not certain it was a unilateral decision. Stationmaster Jiburi, I read as somewhat receptive to our proposals, though refusing to consider them without input from Sol, and we know how that runs. She seemed sincere in her promise of safe passage and may not be complicit in the attack. Captain Lee and Captain Mallory spoke vehemently against the Alliance, Captain Lee citing old school EC propaganda, Captain Mallory citing the inclusion of anything Cyteen as a deal breaker. Whether the Bellagios share the Mallory's stance is unknown, as the alt-day stationmaster and the Bellagios refused to attend. We are therefore uncertain whether the attack came from a mixed faction, pusher command, or some Olympus executive other than Jiburi, possibly bent on removing her from command.

"While we do not know the authority behind their moves, the murder of *Finity* personnel makes its own statement of intent. The exact nature of that intent, whether we are dealing with a Cruz-style takeover of *Finity*, or simply an intention to use executive-level hostages to restrain *Finity* from leaving, is unknown. It is possible that the vid record we have of that meeting is something the instigator wanted to squelch. They began jamming our audio once we were out of the conference room and returning to the ship. It is possible they did not expect resistance. Possible the attack in the tube was an attempt to hold us to get *Finity* to deal: it would not have worked—as if we would forgive any attack on Family, a simple reality I fear they will never understand.

"We have disabled the pusher *Wellington* to hold the perpetrators here to answer for this breach of faith. Whether there are other pushers en route for Olympus or Thule, at whatever interval they can be offloaded, broken down, or refueled, is a question we are in no position to pursue at this time.

"*Finity* is now clear of dock and headed out, with all of us back aboard, one critical, undergoing surgery as we speak. *Come Lately* and *Shalleen* have both left dock, presumably with Bellagio crew. Intent is unknown. They are proceeding outward at speed but have not yet vectored for Thule. We are tracking their courses and gathering as much data on the energy signature of *Shalleen* as we can.

"One assumes, from the simultaneous attack on us and the departure of those ships, that this move was planned: crew was either already aboard or had to be boarding while the meeting was in progress. Whether those ships contain the entire Bellagio family or only skeleton crews, we have no way to know. Ella Bellagio, declared to be Senior Captain of *Shalleen*, was not in the meeting we attended, nor was Frank of *Come Lately*.

"Tom Mallory was at the meeting and *Miriam B* has not moved with the other two. We do not know whether Mallory has been able to get back to his ship, or if he has even tried. It is possible the core lift took damage in the attack and is stalled at the bottom of B-mast.

"*Little Bear* is now clear to return to Pell and her regular schedule. Go with our most profound thanks. All we ask is that you send the records of what happened here on to Bryant's and Alpha as you pass through Venture, by any ships going.

"Should we hear some acknowledgment and/or apology from station authorities, which I do not anticipate, we will take note and acknowledge. We must delay all maneuvers and hold off on jump while surgery continues on one of our own, but we need to get this information spread through the Hinder Stars as fast as we can. We plan to take a high route from here to Pell. We've been running sims and it appears viable for *Finity*, but very much on the edge for anything other than a megahauler. I can't in good conscience suggest *Little Bear* attempt it. Our timely arrival will allow me to handle the explanation to Emilio Konstantin."

Emilio and Min did *not* communicate well.

"We anticipate an extended stay once we reach Pell: the continued strung jumps have taken a physical and mental toll on the entire Family as, I am sure, the Xiao Family has similarly suffered. In due course, we will return our Monahan guests to Alpha, where we may or may not encounter the Bellagios. One assumes, until we have facts to the contrary, that these two ships will skim Thule, intending to get ahead of the information wavefront at Venture and put their own spin on the attacks, but that will fail: no matter how many vanes they have, they can't possibly get to Venture ahead of *Little Bear.* I count on you to pass the task of courier to Alpha to whatever ship is there when you arrive, and to warn Venture against these two merchanters. *Finity* wishes she could release you from this burden, but we feel getting word to Emilio is imperative.

"Events could, however, have the Bellagios and/or the Mallorys back at Alpha, possibly bringing in enough armed Enforcers to overthrow station management or at least make a try at it. Should this happen, we might well see our first boycott, pending *Galway*'s return—or lack thereof—from Sol. For now, we will monitor their movements and continue attempts to reach an understanding with them; but be assured *Finity* will not agree to a second negotiation with Olympus or the *Wellington.* Not at this time. Proceed as you see fit. But we recommend against trusting any EC facility or office until you are safely home. We wish the Xiao Family all good fortune and hope to find you at Pell. End message."

And as for the Bellagios . . .

"Com 1, transmit to *Come Lately* and *Shalleen* as follows: 'Captain JR Neihart to the Captains Bellagio: *Finity's End* is away and clear. We have no intention of hostile action against you or *Miriam B,* and deeply regret the need to disable the *Wellington*. One of our Family was killed and another seriously injured in an unprovoked attack on Olympus' deck. Our attackers wore *Wellington* hard-suits, and accordingly we have taken action to prevent the pusher from leaving and the perpetrators escaping accountability. At no point have we directed any action toward the station itself, excepting only the breaching of the tube-connect to defeat an attack with lethals against our open airlock. Repeat: we do not hold the Bellagios or the Mallorys at fault here, but we will very much appreciate the courtesy of a reply, and further information if you have it. End message.'"

At current distance there was virtually no lag with the Bellagios. Any delay in answering was human. But the Bellagios and the Mallorys, if not complicit, had to be scrambling at the moment to figure what had happened and likely concluding *Finity* had attacked without provocation. The Bellagios' withdrawal might be a temporary pulloff from the station to protect their ships—clearly they had been crewed while this was going on—while *Miriam B*, if the Mallorys were aboard, might be unable to reach Tom Mallory, up in the ring, and unwilling to release without him. If this was an escape move from the Bellagios, at the very least, they'd wait for *Little Bear* to jump, considering *Little Bear* was standing between the two Hinder Stars merchanters and Thule Point—and taking on *Little Bear* and trying to intimidate Xiao Min in some close maneuver would not be their smartest move.

That the two merchanters that were away had sat manned and ready implied, at least, that *someone* had anticipated trouble.

But had not warned *Finity*.

Why, why, and *why?* Ever since they'd come in at Alpha, every question answered had raised a dozen more.

Had the Mallorys also known?

There was still no communication from the station, no response from *Come Lately*, or *Shalleen*, and still no movement from *Miriam B*. Station had not asked for help. If they called, if there was something they could do at this point, if lives should be at risk—

But no. Station had more personnel than they did, and there was no trust left in Jiburi or anyone aboard.

Hell, there was no trust left in *him*. *Damned* if he'd risk one more Neihart to help that station or anyone aboard her. Let the Bellagios and Mallorys rescue their benefactors.

"*Lay course to Pell*," John ordered, calm, unscathed, and all in order. "*We'll go when Parton's ready to travel. Min's watching over us, still. We're not worried about the two merchanters.*"

The bridge settled to routine business.

JR released a long-restrained breath, and let all ship matters go. His hands and sleeves were bloodstained. He was a terrible sight for crew. But he couldn't leave. Not before the various players had had a chance to answer his last transmissions. Not until he knew the merchanters were leaving. And as he waited, his mind kept reverting to the parting words with Mallory. *Never an organization that includes Cyteen.*

That, from one of the original purpose-builts, creaking with antiquity and history, *designed and created* by Cyteen, for God's sake, and a generations-down descendant of a purpose-built's original Cyteen-registered crew. Absolute refusal. He didn't know why, whether it was something in the Mallory history, or personal, or both, but it was enough to breach all brotherly relations with another merchanter.

One ship with that attitude . . . or two, if the Bellagios shared it . . . or three, if *Shalleen* proved out.

But the EC was trying to create more. Pushing whole ships out as lures to struggling Hinder Stars Families.

Granted *Galway* made it—they wouldn't even need to push them. Just ferry crews in to jump them out.

If the Hinder Stars stations chose to continue to do business with the EC—which well they might: FTL to Sol was every Hinder Stars' spacer's dream, the ships their reward for remaining faithful. And if FTLers brought Sol imports and more EC into the mix—what the hell could they do about it? The Families were signed up, bolted down tight, now a part of the effort to stop the EC from running ships in competition with the Alliance . . . but how long would that resolve last, if the EC threw incentives at them: just sign on the line and abide by EC rules and get EC favors.

Hired-crew, such as the EC had attempted to install at Alpha . . . that hadn't worked. Wouldn't if stations stuck to the agreement and dealt only with Family-owned ships.

But gifts of powerful purpose-builts, a push to return to the old agreements . . . could open a chink in the Alliance before it was even well-launched—and trust in Cyteen always was and always would be a problem, more and less according to what the Emorys and the Carnaths and their expansionist notions were doing out there at any given moment. Trust was always gossamer-thin with an offshoot of human colonization that was growing stranger and larger by the decade. While Pell and the Beyond had no inclination to enlarge their reach—station-based, Pell, orbiting a planet they couldn't expand onto, Cyteen had had no hesitation setting down on their own living planet, terraforming a large section, and producing a population born in labs specifically designed to expand their territory.

Mallory more than had a point.

But was Sol any better?

They hadn't won, here. Min was still a friend—trustable; and Mallory was not. The Galways were still risking everything. The stations that had signed and the ships that had signed would all be against what had happened here—but that disapproval would not be limited to the attack on the Neiharts. He could only imagine how footage from those two ships, of *Wellington's* blasted engines, of the station reeling from *Finity's* pull-away, might read to Hinder Stars stationers who had only a handful of meetings in which to judge JR Neihart.

Min had to get to Venture first, had to get the body-cam footage into the system before the Bellagios got there.

And wasn't that the question of the century? *Could* Shalleen *jump?* Just how fast *was* she? What in hell did that tri-vane system hold secret? It was possible she'd hold back to stay in tandem with *Come Lately,* but what if she didn't? Could Min still get out ahead of her? Was he right to take *Finity* to Pell first rather than Alpha? And could even *Finity* outrun *Shalleen?* It was hard to remember sometimes that Sol wasn't the same place *Gaia* had left centuries ago. Before there was the techo-giant Cyteen, there was Earth. With the basic concept of FTL handed to them, damn straight they were capable of making their own innovations. If he could just get Bellagio to talk . . .

Unfortunately, the two ships now out ahead of them were hellbent on evading contact. Com 3 kept trying, but to no avail.

He wouldn't try to get between them and the stations. Signed or unsigned, they were still Family ships. He wouldn't bring charges, wouldn't use the Alliance to shut them down, not them, not the Mallorys. But once *Finity* and *Little Bear* made port and the black box spread the account, the welcome of those ships at stations and their welcome dockside might become an issue—particularly if they had Enforcers aboard. Rules had been breached, unwritten rules, but potent ones, and charges would fly back and forth—ships that had sided with the EC, a ship that had damaged a station—an EC-run station that had killed one of *Finity* crew . . .

He had to try, still, to convince those three ships. He didn't read Mallory as for-hire, or a scoundrel. Far from it. And Mallory, upright, bill-paying, and by-the-book, might ultimately reach a breach with the EC, once he knew for sure what had happened after the meeting.

But there'd been that bright, shiny silver circle on Mallory's collar, that said old school, and stubborn. The old Circle Trade captain's pin, the same as on Captain Lee's collar. Mum had worn one once, and put it away when they broke up old *Gaia* and made her pieces into *Finity's End.*

The bearers of that pin were a breed apart. An honorable breed. It still meant something aboard *Finity*, who didn't claim it, and could. Probably it meant far more to Mallory than it meant to Lee, who likely read it simply as EC above all.

He didn't recall seeing any of the other Hinder Stars captains wearing one . . . which made him wonder if the Bellagio captains did, and, more to the point, perhaps, when they'd taken to wearing it again . . . or if they'd ever stopped.

Damn. He'd made an essential and regrettable mistake, dealing with Mallory. He wanted that meeting back . . . only in some quiet dockside bar, with time to talk in depth, and without the EC directing the conversation.

He wished, he truly, deeply wished, that meeting had gone differently.

He wished Fletch were here. Wished they could talk it over. Get the sense of it all. Plot a course.

But Fletch wasn't. Wouldn't be.

He shivered and tensed every muscle to keep it from showing. He was cold and he hurt. He needed a shower. Food. Sleep. But he couldn't leave, not until they got a response from Min. And that delayed. And delayed. There was possibly discussion going on, aboard *Little Bear.*

Finity was all right, and the Alliance hadn't lost a ship. The EC was going to have to make a crippled station and a crippled pusher habitable for a good long while. And they weren't going to be any happier with *Finity* than they had ever been.

Get back to Pell, as soon as Parton was clear and they could make jump. That was what they had to do. As fast as they could, via a route only *Finity* could take.

Emilio wasn't going to be happy.

Well . . . neither was he.

Book VI   Section xvii

Ample time passed, and still no answer from *Come Lately* or *Shalleen*.

JR escaped the bridge only long enough to shower and change. He was supposed to be asleep by now, as was Madison, in this, the deepest part of the overturned watch. And yet they were all here, and Mum, who should be following John (but that schedule was now in question) was awake and on exec channel. JR felt himself short of resources, everything expended, but no part of him was inclined to leave the bridge.

God. Schedules in a mess and none of them near at their best, and for what? Nothing gained and so much lost . . .

Miriam B remained fixed to an intact B-mast on a slowly stabilizing station. Rough on anyone aboard her, which hopefully did not include kids and elders . . . but EC rules in this case protected them. The Mallory kids would most likely be in sleepover, up in the station ring, and minders would have protected them. Station, like Alpha, like Venture, like any Hinder Stars station, would have no vast spaces to compare with Pell. People aboard would have gotten through it, one earnestly hoped. Mum thought so. Mum had seen it in its heyday, had walked that deck, been in the bars. Been one of the princes of the pusher age.

"The *Wellington's* going to have some cleanup to do," was her remark, seeing the vid. "The grapples will have blown off under stress, explosive charge . . . supposed to protect the station. In this case, the ship *and* the station. But there's no repairing that engine."

Come Lately and *Shalleen* continued outbound behind them, still generally on the zenith route, but not on a direct line toward them or *Little Bear.* Maybe they weren't leaving the system. Maybe they were just going to draw off further into the dark of Foucault's system . . . intending to become peripheral to the problem. Safe. Non-combatant.

They'd be utter fools to challenge *Finity.* And *Little Bear,* who, not having jumped yet, was currently in their path. Min might as well be saying: Go ahead. Try to jump. I'll beat you to it and we'll see whose bubble wins.

Min was still delaying here. There was urgency about his departure. But he was also stalling-out those two ships, positioned as he was, while *Finity* had Parton's life to consider in what moves she made. Debts to Xiao Min kept piling up.

"Heads up, JR," John's voice came over exec-com. *"Our two ships are on the move."*

JR sought the appropriate screen, the schematic of *Shalleen's* and *Come Lately's* predicted course. It showed new activity. A revised vector that would put them . . .

"Good Lord," he said, "are they planning to ram us?" Granted space was very wide, but that was cutting it too close for anyone's comfort.

"Not unless they've a death wish," John said. *"But it'll give us a nice up close and personal look at that ship in operation."*

"It will that." JR studied that shifting schematic, the telemetry on both ships that had been pouring in since they'd left the station then: "I want to know where they're headed. I also want to know everything we can get about that tri-vane job. I want to know its energy signature seven ways from Sunday, especially if it goes into jump."

"Already ordered."

Still no response. Another boost, first *Shalleen*, then *Come Lately*. The schematic shifted.

"Good God, that's a lot of power," Katrin D, Engineering 1.1, their Chief Engineer, was another of his shift, up here tracking that ship's numbers, no matter the shift.

"John," JR said finally, on exec channel, "it's just nerves has me staying here. I could well be in quarters."

"Hell, no," John said. *"Stay put. Take a nap where you sit. If they call, you talk. I have enough on my hands, playing tag with those two idiot ships. On the other hand . . . since we're stable here for a while."* He switched over to general address. *"Privilege of seniority. All ones, four minute break. Go."*

There was still a Caution on, but the number one posts unbelted and moved, whatever the need. JR took the opportunity to unbelt for a moment in quest of hot coffee—his own cup. Red. And Madison's. Black. "John, you want one?"

"Pass," John said. *"I've still got half."*

"Madison?" JR asked, offering him the cup across the console.

"Yeah, thanks."

JR sipped his coffee. Word came from Med: Parton was back in surgery. Senior Medic, Baynes, was qualified for the procedure, but he didn't get much practice: a baby, a broken bone, a whack on the head, that was the run of need they generally had. He'd be operating with a bot-assist, state of the art, just in case. They just never imagined a just-in-case like this one.

They needed—*needed* to leave Olympus. Urgently. With Parton in delicate condition—they might not have that option for days.

Well enough. *Finity* could still outrun anything station or those two merchanters could throw at them. They could stay here as long as they needed—possibly long enough to have Olympus and the EC *and* the pusher command come to their senses. There was that to hope for.

"Little Bear," Com advised them.

"Exec," JR said. They all needed to hear. "Put it through."

"Neihart Captain," Min's voice said. *"The Xiaos offer profound regret for the loss of one of your own and sincere wishes for the health of your Family member. We are delaying departure until the situation is clarified regarding the two merchanters and until* Finity *is able to follow, which we*

understand. We have also sent a protest to station and all three ships re-
garding this action. This message as follows for the Senior Captain, and all
captains. We bear witness that Finity *has observed extreme restraint in*
withdrawing from dock at speed, and that Finity *has taken no action against*
the station itself despite a lethal attack by station on Finity *personnel. We*
support Finity's *action in rendering the pusher incapable. Data from inde-*
pendent monitoring probe placed in station vicinity confirms Finity's *ac-*
count, and while distance does not permit ship visual of the exact nature of
Finity's *action, we have a timeline of beginning and ending fire which*
demonstrates that fire was never directed at the station, and that fire ceased
as Finity *rose into a position in which the station's hull might suffer damage."*

Data from *independent monitoring?* What *independent monitoring?*

The hell, Min, JR thought. *And God bless your suspicious ass.*

Only one place such a probe—that reported to Min—could be situated.
On *them,* damn it. Limpeted to their front end.

"In this record the Neihart Family has behaved without fault while sta-
tion has used lethal force. Little Bear *offers assistance if needed and will*
bear true witness to Venture, *to* Pell, *to* Mariner, *and to* Cyteen. *We are*
sending our own message to the Mallorys and Bellagios, assuring them of
our intent to deal fairly with them if they will approach us openly and with
proper intent.

"As Finity *is taking the message directly to Pell, from which it will be re-*
layed to all other stations and ships in the Beyond, Little Bear *instead de-*
termines to take it directly to Alpha via a routing Come Lately *cannot safely*
take, and arrange the immediate inclusion of that record into the Alpha
Stream, since the Olympus Stream is no longer functioning.

"We appreciate your offer to deal with Pell Stationmaster. So, I suspect,
will he be better pleased to talk with you. We have run the numbers on the
high route to Pell—interesting option, routing through Thule first—and
would indeed prefer to avoid same. Alpha is covered. Over."

They were still at a long lag. The *'and to Cyteen'* would not sit well with
the Mallorys, still on Olympus, probably not with the two merchanters underway, and certainly not with Captain Lee. But then, they might refuse to
listen to *anything* coming from *Little Bear.*

That attitude would not, could not, survive. Cyteen was a truth the whole
of human space was going to have to cope with.

"I'll respond, John," JR said, and followed with: *"Finity's End* gratefully
acknowledges *Little Bear's* message of support, and thanks *Little Bear* for
the offer to carry the message all the way to Alpha and to message Sol on our
behalf on the Alpha Stream. Our injured cousin is still in surgery. We will

advise as soon as we have a timetable for his recovery. We are continuing efforts to contact the three merchanter ships, but have received no reply. Olympus remains intact and is stabilizing itself. We will not send personnel to assist, since their attack with lethals has taken one life of ours, and threatened another's, though we remain uncertain whether the agency is the station and *Wellington* or the pusher ship *Wellington* alone. We thank the Xiao Family for their remote witness of these events and wish them safe journey to Alpha. Words cannot convey the depth of our gratitude for this action. Ending transmission."

There was another wait. Various stations started giving short breaks at top and bottom of the rankings. There was quiet, quick movement to the lounge facilities and back.

No word from the surgery, except that surgery was still underway.

There was still no word from Olympus or from Mallory.

The coffee wasn't enough. Nothing sounded more attractive at the moment than taking an hour in quarters, horizontal, under standard G. Aches were setting in; his hand, with cold-burns, hurt. And he'd wrenched his shoulder with the force of the retracting filament.

Jen. God bless her self-starting, stubborn soul. When things had blown, she'd moved, assessed, positioned herself where she needed to be—and she'd anchored the damn line-gun, or they'd have gotten it like a missile when she hit *retract*. She'd never used one, never been part of the EVA drill, probably never received training for it. But she'd used her head. Little Jen, Jenniebug, had done the right thing first, or they might have been swimming in cold space, flung out as that tube-connect snapped, with little chance of rescue in time, and then Olympus would be calling it an accident caused by *Finity's* own panicked pull-out.

Jen was pretty well all that was functional of exec Security, now. They'd need her to come up to speed on systems and routines Fletcher might not have passed on to her. Things Parton knew, if he made it. Hank, Twofer—he knew some of it. He was bright, but he wanted specific orders. He always wanted orders on things. And the essentials were all in records: JR could provide codewords out of exec storage.

It wasn't Fletch's fault. They'd gone armed with non-lethals, limit of their license. They'd gone prepared to assert their rights in an executive standoff . . . not to deal with deadly force and an attack on the ship—when merely stopping the core-lift would have been enough. A little cargo light-fingered by a loader, trouble that never got off dockside—*that* was the ordinary mischief Security had ever had to deal with . . . until the Alliance began to push the EC, at Alpha, and now here.

Even at Alpha, with all that had gone on, the EC had observed civilized boundaries.

Right down to the point they turned weapons on *Galway* crew, on their own deck, no less. They'd attributed that act of piracy to one man, Andrew Cruz.

"Captains on the bridge. Mum. Madison." That was Com 3.1 talking. Relaying to the bridge and all the executive. *"Medical says—Parton didn't make it."*

The stone face was automatic. Bridge did *not* react. But the shock went right to the gut.

His decision, his call, his idea. And Fletch and Parton were gone. Just—gone from their posts aboard ship, gone from the future, gone from all ability to say, Sorry. Sorry I took you there. Sorry I didn't bring you back.

To no damn advantage. Nothing won there. Nothing gained.

"Com," John said, *"give me shipwide."*

Com did that, and John made the quiet, solemn announcement. The silence aboard was heavy.

And all JR could think was: the whole damn division lost, in those two men. Security settled dockside quarrels, dealt with station enforcement to get a drunk cousin out of hock, and kept the random drunk stationer from wandering up the ramp to have a loo—that was what they routinely did. And he'd taken them with him into a situation where somebody—and he didn't even know who—had wanted the situation to blow beyond recovery.

And damned if they hadn't almost succeeded. God, he wanted to give it to them, everything *Finity* could throw at them. He hadn't, but only because he'd planned before leaving the ship exactly how to retaliate, should the meeting blow up.

And now he had to wonder, who on that station *wanted* bloodshed? And not just bloodshed, because that attack had been more than murder, more than attempted piracy. It was deliberate sabotage of any rational settlement, an attempt to *shatter* any possible arrangement between the station and the Alliance . . .

God. Why hadn't he thought of this before?

"John, Madison," JR said sharply on exec, "I do not believe Jiburi planned this—or even knew. Station could have stopped that lift car, held us hostage, maybe, wanting me to persuade you to afford access and turn over the ship."

"That would have been a cold day in hell," Madison said, *"much as I love you, brother."*

"And I'd space myself before I let you. But that didn't happen. Instead, we had a serious overkill attack, a dozen or more hardsuits and lethals against five in coldsuits and two impact pistols. I don't think they intended any survivors."

"Not sure this is news, brother. Where are we going with this?"

"I think they were trying to *provoke* an incident. That pusher captain, Lee . . . she was like nothing I've met. Military, maybe? Certainly cold blooded and hard core EC. They're *not* us. Do what they're told. And not just the ambushers, but any of those who might have ordered them. Different mindset. They don't remotely understand us or know what we'll do . . . and that goes both ways. The point is, we've been too focused on the Bellagios, and not enough on the chaos we left behind. We need to assume it was *not* Jiburi behind it. *Jiburi* might think we set her station to wobbling, fired on her docked pusher for no reason. She needs to know, in case she's being undercut; *Mallory* needs to know."

"Got you," John said. *"We have your body-cam footage. We have footage from the airlock monitors. I'll send it on endless loop along with your message to station and to the Bellagios . . . hell, I'll shove it into every damned com from here to Fargone, Cyteen-side, if I get the chance. Every black box that touches dock. Meanwhile, cuz, you and Madison get some rest, Madison because he's going to need to spell me in not very long and you because you need medical attention. Mum, if you're listening, go back to sleep. We're on our way, we're stable, we're spun up, and we'll just watch the pieces settle for a while. We'll see* Little Bear *clear system, then hightail it behind them."*

What John didn't say was that they were free, now, Parton being dead, to advise *Little Bear* to go for jump. They would follow, when personnel had gotten a little rest. No more need to linger here.

Two dead. An absolute disaster. JR unbelted and got up, headed toward the exec offices. The hand wasn't that bad. The muscles were going to ache. He wasn't anxious to try to sleep, not yet, not with Fletch and Parton on his mind. He needed to change clothes. Get the blood off his hands. Like washing away the last trace of Fletch.

He decided he'd go to the exec office a while. Just sit.

Neither was he surprised when Madison joined him.

"Mind?" Madison asked, and: "No," JR said, and they went in together and sat down, in long silence.

Twofer Neihart, the big man who'd fought the attackers to get Ross and the captain through the exit, and stayed to get two apparent dead men back to *Finity*, had just slid down against the wall when they'd gotten the news about Parton, and sat there still opposite Ross, staring at nothing, tears running down a cold-burned face. Jen, who had delivered the news, knelt beside him, telling him he'd done all he could.

What could anybody say? Twofer, Hank, as the First Captain called him, had risked his life for *Finity's* dead, and thought he'd saved one of them. But he hadn't. Both dead.

"Why'd they do that?" Hank asked finally, sounding . . . lost. "Why'd they do that at all? It makes no effin' sense. They could've just stopped the lift. Locked the hatch so we couldn't get out. And Parton was all alone there, and God-many of them. They could have taken him without killing him. Easy."

"Maybe they couldn't stop the lift," Ross said. Alpha was in his mind, after the EC had gotten total control of the station. That world. That time. "Maybe they couldn't get into controls."

"Doesn't make sense," Hank repeated, as if he hadn't heard. "What for? Why? Did they think we'd just fold?"

Maybe they would've, in our place, Ross thought.

Then other Finitys appeared in the distance at a run, maybe Parton's next-ofs, or Fletcher's. Caution had lifted. Crew could move.

Maybe one of Hank's own, Ross decided, as two of the group gathered big Hank up from the deck and hugged him and commiserated. Jen got up on her own, and just stood there watching that group, exhaustion in every line of her body.

Ross thought he should get up and take the two steps toward her. She'd fought too, and none of the arrivals were for her. She just looked stricken. But before he could muster the strength to move, cousin Ian arrived from . . . somewhere . . . grabbed his arm all unexpected, pulled him to his feet, and hugged him hard.

"What in hell, kid?" Ian asked him, and he just had to say,

"I don't know. I don't know anything." And how did he explain why the

Senior Captain had snagged him along? Or why he hadn't told the others, or what in hell had motivated Olympus to try to kill them instead of just—doing something rational, like holding them and trying to deal.

He just couldn't find the words. He was, he decided, still in shock. And Nav should *never* be thrown off track like that, no matter the circumstances. He felt divorced from everything—from time, from the star, from the ship—Sound echoed.

"Damn it. You still got all your fingers?"

He looked. None were black. Just red. Ian felt his fingers, checked his ears, ran a rough hand over his head like Ian felt—he didn't know . . . responsible. Disrespected. He wasn't sure.

"I'm fine," he managed to say, and that was way short of covering Ian's distress. "Captain . . . wanted a Galway with him," he fought to find the words, to explain. "—for the merchanters. And I was there. Or maybe it was because of *Galway* and Cruz. That, I—" A sudden case of the shakes took him, and Ian pulled him into tight embrace, anchored him in blackest space.

"It's all right, Ross. Doesn't matter. None of that matters. I'm just glad you got back."

"Th–there was no damn warning, Ian. We walked out of the conference and everything was fine, and when we got there, they'd taken out Parton and just . . . left him drifting there. Then they came after the rest of us. They weren't trying to stop us. They were trying to *kill* us. It makes no sense, Ian. Like Alpha. Like—one group was like this, halfway reasonable, and the other—the E-damn-C was just *hell* no."

He was babbling. He bit his lip to stop the words, and just let Ian's arms keep him on his feet until his knees stopped giving way.

Finally Ian let him go, pushed him back enough to stare at him.

"You're all right." It was a question.

Ross nodded. "Yeah. I'm fine."

"Fine, hell. You're back where you were on Alpha. You're looking into—*look* at me!" Ian's hands on his shoulders shook him, then held him. "Damn the EC. *Damn* them all!"

He pushed away, and tried, hard. Saw Ian's face again. Hadn't for a moment. Hadn't seen anything. Ian grabbed his face and looked at his eyes. Frowning.

Ross thought about the universe a minute, and could say, with some confidence: "No. No, I'm not b-b-back on Alpha. I *am* all right. Just . . . shaken up. I w-wasn't alone this time. That was the w-w-worst, at Alpha. But . . . I-I-Ian . . . they're doing the same thing all over again. Wanted to force their way in. Bloody damn EC pirates!"

Another hug, gentle, soothing. "Fuist anois, deartháir. Easy."

"Bastards are forcing us to fight back." He pushed away again, and this time Ian let him go. He drew a huge breath and steadied himself with a hand to the wall. "They're saying—they're saying, even Mallory of *Miriam B* was saying—they won't deal because there's a *Cyteen* ship with us. And what the hell good is an agreement across space if Cyteen isn't a part of it?" The corridor around them was out of focus, distorted, and cold despite the blast from a vent directly over them. "Fletcher's dead. Parton's dead. They were good people, Ian. They didn't fire on anybody, no way did we start this. And whatever Cyteen is, the Xiaos are damn good people!" Anger surged up out of the last well of strength he had. "Damn the EC! *Galway's* risked every-thing trying to give them for free what they never won on their own, and they don't deserve it. I want *Galway* back, but I don't want *them* with her, hell if, Ian. I don't want anything to do with them, ever again. Hell with trees. Hell with boats and booze and three-vaned ships. Who *needs* Earth?"

"You're not alone there either," Ian said. "Unless *Galway* comes back with a whole lot better report on the EC than we've had."

"I'm not sure I can believe it, even if they do," Ross said. "Twice nothing's still nothing. —Damn it. Just . . . damn it, Ian."

"Yeah," Ian said. And after a moment. "I should get back to the cousins. They're anxious about you, but when we heard about Parton . . . Do you need to stay here? Shall I tell them you're all right? Or can you come?"

He didn't know. Didn't know where he could be. Where he had to be. Where he *needed* to be.

"Come on," Ian said, laying a hand on his shoulder, "before we get an-other takehold."

Jen, Ross thought, suddenly clear on that one thing. She'd saved him . . . saved the captain . . . and lost Fletcher. Fletcher, who meant as much to her, maybe, as Fallan did to him. And now Parton. She had to be hurting. He needed to go to her, hug her, tell her he was sorry.

But Jen had disappeared. He didn't know where she was. Not even where she'd go. To the captain, maybe. Duty. They were tight, those three. Her. Fletcher. The captain.

A glance around was all grieving Neihart crew, people he didn't know, mourning people he barely knew.

And he was in the way of more Neiharts gathering.

He went with Ian.

Debrief was simple: Fletcher was dead, now Parton was, and Jen recorded the report, verbal input, because she wasn't up to more. Twofer ... Hank ... was worse. He'd just hugged his mother and stood there numb. And when they'd all broken down at the surgery, she'd gone with Hank into the office, and they'd sat down in a place now with too many chairs. That was how it was. They'd gotten Uncle Jim back, they'd gotten Ross back. It had all gone to hell, which was not the way Jen expressed it in the duty log.

Her amplified version had, from the moment of ambush, one critical point that had to be made: *Finity* had tried to protect the station lift system from hard vacuum.

Attempt to secure the hatch on the station side of the tube, in consideration of human lives on station, was not successful. Fletcher tried, but was fatally shot by Wellington *personnel in the attempt.*

She'd gotten that from Hank's body-cam footage. She'd snatched that on remote, made herself watch all of it now, all the way through, looking for every detail.

"Third Security, Hank 'Twofer' Kulik Neihart, was able to recover unconscious Second Security Walter Parton Neihart, and the body of Security Chief Fletcher Alejandro Neihart from the core-lift foyer and entered the tube access with them. Fletcher was killed by a Bowman-12 projectile gun fired in the lift foyer by Wellington *personnel. Hank 'Twofer' was able to get himself, Fletcher, and Parton into the tube connect with Senior Captain and Galway Navigator Ross Monahan.* Wellington *personnel gave chase into the tube-connect still firing, until all Finitys and Monahan reached the airlock and sealed it. The tube-connect was breached as* Finity *pulled away. Whether the attackers were able to seal the stationside hatch and protect the core-lift system is not clear on any vid record."*

Her voice was steady up to that point. Hank listened, and finally moved, opened the cabinet of Fletcher's desk and grimly took out a bottle of Scotch and two glasses. He poured two shots, then put the bottle back into its slot in the cabinet and latched the door.

She'd rarely drunk the hard stuff. Once, the prized Scotch, when they'd

finished their run at Alpha. Now she took the little glass offered. Hank's face
was white under the reddened burns: his hands, however, didn't shake. Only
his voice did, when he said, "For them."

"For them," she said, and took a sip. "Hank, you got them back. They're
home."

"You got us in," Hank said, jaw muscle struggling for control. "Good job,
that. Good job. Captain's safe, because of you. You put yourself into that
record. Hear? The Galway kid—yours—he made it all right? Got all his
pieces?"

"He's fine," she said. "His Family came for him." And it was like a curtain
going across, a change in things, and she didn't know what, except that here,
in the office where Fletcher wasn't, there was a change in circumstance, a
change that made *here* the right place to be, and *Finity's* loss, her team's loss,
suddenly paramount in her gut.

She'd been there in the lock, at least, done the best she could, and maybe
if she'd been faster, met them halfway—

But no, she couldn't have anchored the line-gun if she had done that, and
it had pulled them in faster than they'd ever have managed on their own.
Gotten them away from the Enforcers. She'd done the best thing. There just
wasn't a better thing to have done, given that people on Olympus deserved
worse than they'd gotten, and if *Finity* pulling away had blown the people
that killed Fletcher and Parton into cold space, she only wished she could
have shot them first.

They finished the Scotch, one and the other, and tucked the empty glasses
into safety-hold.

"That boy of yours," Hank said, which hurt, but just for a moment. That
was how Fletcher and Parton had seen Ross *and* her: as kids. Which they
were. But Hank added, before she could respond: "Young man gave a fair
account of himself, both to Mallory and in that fight. I could've gone down,
too, except for him. He was first into that tube and he pulled the captain
with him. Got *him* out safe. Gave me a chance at least to save the others.
Even if it didn't work. That was the priority, your young man and the captain, you understand that."

"Absolutely." She had seen some of it on the body-cam, had heard the
exchange with Mallory on the com. It was good to know Ross had kept it
together, done exactly what he should have done. Any other action would
have gotten in Hank's way. Pulled Senior Captain away. Maybe saved his
life—

"He was proud of you, you know," Hank said. "Fletcher, I mean."

She inhaled sharply, wished she had the Scotch back.

"Laid odds you'd be next in line soon and joked he'd have to watch his back."

He'd never said anything, not to her. Nothing like that.

"Said he learned a lot, just watching you handle stationer folk. He loved you, Jennie-bug. We all love you."

Her throat was too tight to speak . . . so she just got up and hugged him . . . as hard as she could.

Book VI   Section xx

Third-shift had changed off, Second-shift was on, with Fourth to follow, likely to take them through jump to Thule . . . now that Parton's safety was no longer an issue.

It all depended on what the two Bellagio ships did.

First-shift was scheduled to come on after jump for that tricky first jump to Pell—but Ross wasn't about to go back to his cabin. None of the Monahans were so inclined. It was a gathering of the clan in the exclusively Monahan space they'd been given, Training-B, where new information would always come. Fletcher had promised that.

Information was damned slow coming, when it involved ships traveling huge distances through system, and a station not inclined to talk, but little drops of it were precious. Ross, exhausted, intermittently dozed off in a reclined chair, counting on his cousins to wake him.

The Xiaos had not bolted from the system when *Finity* had come under attack. They were supposed to have, but they hadn't, being at a safe distance and having options. When *Finity* had broken dock . . . closely followed by *Shalleen* and *Come Lately* . . . *Little Bear* had helpfully canceled her jump but maintained her course, occupying the general direction of Thule Point and effectively blocking the exit.

Little Bear was a major Cyteen merchanter ship. There was not much *little* about her, and while not nearly as potent as *Finity's*, her jump bubble would pose no small deterrent if those two tried to muscle past her. When the time came to jump, *Little Bear* would go first, and these two, if they planned to jump, and it increasingly appeared that way, would just have to wait.

Finity would wait until they'd *all* gone . . . *Finity* wanting very much to record that tri-vane's departure.

Miriam B remained at dock, for whatever reason—Ross had renounced trying to figure Mallory's motivations—and Olympus Station was intact, though still working on its stability. *Wellington* had come free of two of her grapples, trailing one, and taken serious damage: scan showed fragments outbound in various directions, and her engine nacelles were likely beyond repair.

Finity had sent station the body-cam footage and station had responded with a series of insane statements somehow blaming *Little Bear* and Cyteen. Argument on the point would gain nothing. *Little Bear* had commented in ship-speak, then launched a vehement response to station, regarding the standards of civilized behavior, their utter disgust, and the promise to distribute both the body-cam vid and station's response at every station call. Xiao Jun, Grandfather himself, had made the statement, in barely comprehensible Standard.

"Ross?"

Ross jerked awake, blinking.

"Ross." Ian's voice got his attention, and Ian was looking past him toward the door. He turned—

There she was, ramrod straight, in *Finity* grey. Dark hair neatly braided. Gold bands, now, on the collar. Exec. Security patch on the sleeve.

Her eyes were bruised with weariness.

He swept a hand across his face and through his hair, and pushed himself out of the chair, not knowing what he should do. They stood and stared at each other, until finally, Jen's hand twitched. He took it, just the fingertips. It was Jen who interlaced them.

"Sorry," he said. "I'm sorry. I wanted . . . couldn't . . ."

She interrupted gently. "I saw you with Ian at E-1. Figured he could do more for you than I could. And . . . I had a report to write, while it was straight in my head."

He knew which one. "Wish I could have helped. Really wish it. I deserted you."

She shook her head slowly. "Were there when we needed you. Hank says you saved Uncle Jim. In the tube."

Not what he was expecting.

"Hardly. Just grabbed him when he rammed one of the attackers that was coming after me, and bounced the wrong way."

Her hand tightened on his. Hard. "Wasn't a little thing. For any of us."

The silence grew long. Finally: "What can I do, Jen? Tell me. I'm at a loss here."

She sighed, and leaned into him, wrapping her arms around his waist. "Just . . . hold me a minute."

That . . . he could do.

Book VI   **Section xxi**

The numbers shifted and shattered . . . reformed and shattered again. A tide of monkeys swarmed the elephant. Foucault flared and rippled, raged and shouted . . .

While the tiger lurked.

Tiger, hell, it was *Fizeau*.

Ross shuddered awake.

Tigers, elephants, and monkeys . . . God damn Purple Pagoda and their stupid holos, mucking with his head again. He reached for the stars, that *awareness* that had been with him since he entered the system, hoping to drive the stupid dream out of his head.

He blinked until his eyes focused on the numbers scrolling across his console screen, trying to find in them some reflection of that edge-of-sleep dream.

Sans monkeys.

But for once, the numbers failed him. It wasn't numbers making him dream of monkeys, it was the churning in his gut, reaction to the constantly wailing energy of this crazy system. It went beyond feeling just the stars, it was the wind, the planets . . . and a hell of a lot more he'd yet to figure. God, he wanted *out* of here.

Awake, he barely noticed it, thank God.

Jen was gone, likely back to her Security station. Time had passed. Surely time had passed. His cousins were still here, at various stations, some watching, waiting, some sleeping, others stirring.

On the screen, change was happening. The merchanters had moved past them, at an angle, and were already deploying vanes. *Come Lately* was an aged purpose-built updated with middle-aged tech: she spread her two vanes, and was nothing more than they'd expected. *Shalleen* and her tri-vane arrangement, simultaneously unfolding, was, however . . . weird. The vanes seemed apt to touch, making a circle.

The vanes weren't active yet, thank God. They had safely passed *Finity*, but numbers at screen bottom said *Shalleen* was still close. *Much* too close to make a jump.

Ross watched his second display, now devoted to the tri-vane, an image that fluxed as disturbing dreams and his waking mind kept skipping back and forth. On the secondary screens in Training-B were numbers and graphs, electronic representations of the space-time around those two ships. Power-up of the vanes had begun, created minor ripples in the numbers as well as his gut . . . but nothing like that dream . . .

Thank God. If they jumped, if they just got out of here—

But they were still too damn close. *Wait, dammit, just . . . wait. You have time, Bellagios. We aren't chasing you. Don't be fools . . .*

From Thule, the Bellagios had their choice. Venture or Bryant's . . . Bryant's, that would take them to Alpha. And the *rest* of the Monahans.

Don't you dare touch my Family, you traitors. Stay the hell away from them . . .

Blink.

He shut his eyes. Not a damn thing they could do about it. Trust the Family to see through Bellagio's EC lies . . .

The wind howled, the lightning flashed . . . and monkeys lurked . . .

Dammit. He forced his eyes open, wondering would he *ever* sleep, so long as they were in this system, and sought the readout on *Shalleen*. Time *had* passed. Those numbers from the vanes continued to rise.

The idiots were going to jump early. Not willing to run closer to *Little Bear*, maybe.

Finity needed to brake. Give them room.

But they weren't doing that.

Blink.

He needed to say something. But it wasn't his shift. Fourth-shift Captain Mum. Surely, *surely* she'd brake soon.

Finity wasn't out of the danger zone, yet. Fizeau was kicking up. The instruments showed the solar wind, the energy fluctuations. Sure, a departing shockwave was nothing to incoming, but still—

God . . . playing chicken with hyperspace. They were all of them fools. *Brake, Senior Captain-sir, before it's too late . . .*

And there was Kate, the Senior Captain, his own console . . . was he dreaming it? Maybe he'd only dreamed Training-B, the flux—

Dammit. Dreams. Reality. *Get it straight, Nav 1.5.*

No. He *was* awake, he *was* in Training-B, and those ships—those *ships* were too damn close. He could *feel* that.

The numbers on the big screen had stopped rising: it was just a partial power-up, a systems test, maybe.

Finity could outrace them, if *Finity* wanted—but *Finity* was keeping her steady acceleration. Not toward jump. Not yet.

Keeping *Shalleen* in real time sight. To *watch* that jump.

Let them go, Captain-sir. It's not worth the risk!

They couldn't go on accelerating as they were. They had *Little Bear* ahead.

Don't challenge them to jump early, Captain-sir. They're crazy. Apt to do anything. Let them get out. Far, far out.

Hands wanted to work, dreaming or not, but his keys were dead, every control he had was dead, his screens only reflected what Nav 4.1 was inputting. And on the screen at the head of the room, the dreadful progress of jump-prep from the ships—focused now on *Shalleen*'s image. Beyond her, they could actually see *Little Bear.*

His stomach twisted into knots.

"Damn," Maire said, suddenly, voice to his side. "Just how close *is* she?"

"Camera effect," Connor said. "Foreshortened. Extremely."

Didn't matter. Didn't matter. Still too close, they were all too *damn* close.

The view tightened. Numbers spieled. The big screen and the Nav console display shifted, not by his doing.

Distance seemed the least reliable datapoint.

"If she intends to play games with *Little Bear*'s bubble," Ian said, dropping into the Helm seat, "she's a fool."

The cousins gathered behind Ian. Helpless. All of them. No buttons that did anything real. Nothing to be done if they were. They were irrelevant, able only to wait and watch.

Little Bear was still in the lead, all of them moving toward the optimal jump range, still hours ahead.

More than hours, if he'd had any say. A day, maybe more, before they were safely beyond . . . what he was feeling.

But nobody was pushing. There was still time to talk, if the Bellagios *would* talk.

Maire and Siobhan and Patrick settled at their consoles, just watching the numbers.

Netha and Connor were talking with Ian, who was on his feet now, surreal sight—you didn't stand up on the live bridge, not without orders. A situation was going on ahead of them. Nobody ought to be leaving their console.

But it was *not* the bridge. They weren't in control of anything. And there was leisure to get up. To get a drink. Even a sandwich. *Finity* was no longer in crisis. The two merchanters had gone past them, and were moving away. *Finity* was *not* giving chase—thank God.

Vanes had run a test cycle. But sanity appeared to have prevailed aboard the two merchanters as well: they were in ordinary acceleration now, giving themselves room, and *Finity* was letting them run. *Little Bear* was likewise holding steady, but not—not, from the data he was getting now—in their direct path.

Likely communication was going on between *Finity* and *Little Bear*, but none of that was coming through. Somebody should bring the Com consoles live, so they could hear as well as see what was happening on the bridge. He thought that. But he didn't personally need another channel of input at the moment. He just needed to calm down, get that overpowering sense of unease out of his system.

There was Foucault: in an uproar . . . winds whistling out of a bottomless source in waves; nearer than Fizeau, who was too near for comfort . . .

He could feel them, but those sensations were back under control.

Muted chatter of Monahan cousins, the soft *tap-tap* of someone crossing the room, the hiss of a drink from the dispenser . . . safe, as safe as it was possible to be, cousins around him, no takehold in effect.

He could see Fizeau with his eyes shut, once he actively sought the feeling. He knew the precise direction—felt it lurking like that damned tiger in the Pagoda's wall, not doing much . . .

But making Foucault dangerous. He knew that. *Knew* it.

He rubbed his eyes, flashing ever so briefly on the sleepover, the immovable elephant, and the cascading monkeys. There, but not. Separate. Millions of kilometers separate, Foucault and Fizeau, but traveling forces of nature . . . waves of solar wind that sometimes whispered, sometimes shrieked. Constantly changing as the stars moved in their ancient dance, churned in the outer reaches of the system by three gas giant planets. Fizeau . . . you couldn't pick it out of the starfield, it was so small. Yet moment to moment, the effect of one stellar output on the other was scarily potent. Unpredictable. He'd dealt with binaries all his life, both at Bryant's and Venture, but Groombridge 34 was a certifiable hell hole.

He'd never had this feeling of . . . waiting to be pounced . . . a feeling that had been there since the moment they'd dropped into the system.

Dueling Ardamans. Intersections of solar winds and gravity wells. Resonances that rang like bells when a ship's incoming bow wave hit them, that rushed and swirled in the wake of an outgoing jump-bubble.

Equations began to dance across the darkness behind closed eyes, flowing with the solar winds, stretching, distorting—

"Here." Connor Dhu set a glass of ice water in front of him, on a console where it shouldn't be—but with a cloth napkin to sop up the condensation.

Water was probably a good idea, no matter he wasn't thirsty. He should be hungry, too, but he wasn't. He emptied the glass and set it back on the napkin, eyes still on the screens . . . where *Shalleen* had started accelerating again—maybe wanting to get out ahead of *Little Bear.* He sought the numbers for *Little Bear,* waiting for their response, praying they, too, just let the Bellagios go unchallenged. . . .

Connor settled beside him at Helm 1, pulled up an engee overlay. Gave a low whistle.

"That *Shalleen?*" Ross asked. Not his field. Not remotely. He wanted to know. Wanted some other assessment. "What are you reading?"

"Just an insane spread for a ship that size. Normal-space, normal space acceleration, but I'm wondering what purpose that three-way assembly might serve. Doesn't immediately say anything to me about how far or fast she can jump. Total surface area isn't that much different from a two vane, but that curvature . . . the three could almost act like a single vane . . . but how *deep* a ship goes, that's the power thrown into them. By the distance between those three vanes . . . it's got to be a smaller bubble than ours. But how much power she's already thrown into them, just warming them up—raises all sorts of scary questions. Gotta wonder whether Thule can pull her down."

"What will happen, do you think, when she gets to Venture? I mean, she's weirder than hell. They won't know what they're looking at. Won't trust her, no matter what she says, will they?"

"Scare hell out of station, that's sure, with that energy signature. Worse, if they get a look at her. Maybe think Beta's invading for real."

"God," Ross said. His skin prickled. Vision became dark, became Connor again saying:

"Let's hope, if they get there first, they've got sense to wait for *Come Lately.* Once station knows what she is, she'll get a lot of attention, not all of it positive. With Earth rumors swirling about, and that design—there may be a rethink. Like maybe a new deal with the EC."

Ross turned away, staring at the screen, but seeing Fletcher's dead face, wondering how many of his own First-shift had ended up the same. "Never again. Not if I can help it. I'll run the numbers to carry Company cargo for the sake of Family, if that's the future we come to have, but I'll not deal with them, not them, not the Mallorys or the Bellagios, either."

Connor's hand pressed his shoulder. "We can't ignore all of Sol. Maybe *Galway* will come with a different solution."

Ross drew a deep, shaking breath. "I hope to God you're ri—"

"What the hell?" That was Netha. "Are they going for a tandem jump? How insane are they?"

Ross turned to the big screen, grabbed the table edge as a dizzying wave passed over him. Serious burn going on *both* Bellagio ships now. *Come Lately* going all out, *Shalleen* just keeping pace.

Tandem jump? They had plenty of room, but, God, that was pushing it, especially with a ship that had never jumped. Who *knew* if that tri-vane could even hold a stable bubble?

There was no damn reason to hurry. *Little Bear* wasn't threatening them. *Finity* wasn't. But there they were, pushing it. Just those main thrusters pushing those vanes through space were making the scrolling numbers squirm, and while they hadn't yet powered up the vanes to full business mode—

—a rippling protest from Foucault traveled from his gut to his fingers and toes.

The system . . . or space itself . . . did not *like* that ship.

Shalleen's actions just . . . didn't make sense. If they *were* only testing, if they were waiting to get a safe distance from the star before jumping, why not just retract the vanes? Or was it all part of their plan? To jump with virtually no warning? Nasty, nasty trick to play on every other ship in the region, if that was their game.

One part of him, a crazy stupid part, intensely wanted *Finity* to accelerate, to stay in range and watch that Sol-built mystery function. Another part wished *Finity* would show them *real* power, run past them and get out first. Just . . . go. Thule. Pell. Wherever. Just get the hell out of this entire mess, along with *Little Bear*, before *Shalleen* . . . did whatever she decided to do.

Minutes, a quarter hour, a half hour crawled past.

Connor brought him a second glass of water, and a third. *Keeping you hydrated,* Connor said.

He drank obediently . . . and watched the screens.

Camera view switched from one fugitive merchanter to the other, stabilized each time as the system knit the image together. Both ships—*Come Lately* with her standard rig. *Shalleen* with that circular tri-vane—pulling steadily away.

Finity hadn't unfolded yet. *Little Bear* hadn't. They offered absolutely no challenge to the Bellagios. *They* offered no challenge, but the Groombridge system . . . He felt the power and anger of Foucault at his back. He had Fizeau over his shoulder, slightly to the side. And thanks to the localized disruption that was *Shalleen*, he felt in his gut the trajectory the two ships were aiming for.

He hoped, *God*, he hoped, that they would jump separately.

And even as he thought that, he felt the disruption that was *Shalleen* begin to shift. On the screen, the numbers showed *Shalleen* pulling away, opening the distance between the two ships . . . and the knot in his gut relaxed a degree.

Good. That was good. He *didn't* wish the Bellagios ill, no matter they were EC-connected. He didn't blame them for what had happened. Not them and not Mallory. Families protected each other and whatever deal they'd made with the EC might well have been made long before the EC's *The Rights of Man* had destroyed the economy of the First Stars.

Didn't mean he'd ever trust them. But he didn't want them dead.

Did the Bellagios even *know* that Finitys had *died* at *Wellington* hands? If they did . . . would they care? Had Senior Captain's message gotten through to them? If they knew that, if they had a clue what had happened to make *Finity* break dock and attack *Wellington*, wouldn't they at least, before leaving, have accepted a call, or made one themselves?

Maybe they'd just seen the destruction of the pusher and thought they were next . . . never mind neither *Finity* nor *Little Bear* had made a single threatening move toward them.

Crazy, Ross thought. The EC just did that to people—he knew that now, in a way he hadn't before meeting Tom Mallory. Insane lies, repeated often enough, just . . . turned people crazy. And those crazy-making, lying people had built *Shalleen*, a design that challenged everything he understood about FTL.

He wanted to see it. He dreaded seeing it. *Shalleen* had enormous power, no question. She carried more of what looked like engine, more than was ordinary for a ship that size.

But not yet. Please, God, not yet. They were still too damned close to *Finity* . . . and if they went much further, he was worried about *Little Bear*.

Another line joined the graphs, though there was no change yet on visual. Small bursts of power, three different profiles in turn . . . cycling. Was it one vane, and then the others in sequence? And was that warm-up or was that pre-jump function?

Whatever it was, Foucault *really* didn't like it. The solar wind shuddered, scattered like the Garden fireflies escaping his moving hand.

Not yet, Bellagios! God . . . not yet. Wait.

On the screen, then, those vanes began to pulse, a blue light, slightly different for each vane.

"Vanes are *cycling* on *Shalleen*," Connor said. "Weird . . ."

He didn't need Connor to tell him. Didn't even need the image on the screen.

"What's our lag on them now?" Connor asked Scan.

"Eleven seconds." That was Siobhan.

Fairly close. A shiver went down his spine. Hell, it was still too *damned* close.

"Only a fraction of their power so far," Connor said.

Connor had his instruments, solid, rational numbers—

His *gut* said there was a predator lurking, vibrating with energy, waiting to pounce. And it wasn't manmade.

Dammit! He tried to drive that feeling away, but the waves of energy persisted, rising, swirling, sudden collapse, only to rise again. And that was *only* Foucault's output reacting. Eventually—soon—Fizeau would react. It *had* to.

"They may want to give themselves plenty of time to balance the field before jump," Connor said. "Maybe they're just running tests."

"I sure as hell would," Ian said. "They've never jumped that thing. And for God's sake, they pick Foucault!"

Netha snorted. "No damn choice, have they? Unless they want to grow old here."

"If they pushed it here," Ian said, "they could push it to Thule, test jump from there."

"And lose their audience?" Netha snorted again. "*I* think they're outright showing out. They want to scare us. Warning, to force us to back off. 'Take a ringside, Finitys, and watch some *real* power.'" She made a rude gesture at the screen. "Bastards."

"Maybe," Ross said quietly, and paused when his voice shook, but the cousins all turned to look at him. He struggled against the angry waves churning his stomach, and when he could trust his voice: "Maybe they think *Shalleen* is their best chance of beating *Finity* to Alpha. Maybe they want to make sure *they* control the story about what happened here."

A small silence, then Ian said, "Damn. Point to Nav."

And Netha: "She just might do it. All that power, and her vanes not fully employed? Just how fast could she be?"

Ross took a deep breath. "Guess we're going to find out."

Never mind it would be months before they actually *knew* who got to Alpha first. *Finity* was headed for Pell. By the time they got back to Alpha . . .

They watched as that pulse increased, creating a constant shimmering blue circle around *Shalleen*. Pretty ship, Ross thought involuntarily, even as that sense of being watched made him glance over his shoulder . . . toward Fizeau.

Come Lately's vanes came full up, *Shalleen's* grew brighter . . . which began to argue against tests—and for Netha's tandem jump.

But not *this* route. Not this damned ship!

They had to know forming two fields that close together in a *normal* system would send crazy shockwaves. They *had* to get further downrange.

As *Come Lately*'s field began to form, Ross felt that twisting ripple of disturbance build exponentially. *Shalleen*'s field alone had had Foucault in an uproar. A combined field . . . could rip this region of space to shreds.

Were they insane?

Unless . . . they *wanted* to set it off. Wanted to jump out and leave *Finity* and *Little Bear* to suffer whatever fate decided to throw at them. Dammit, they knew neither *Little Bear* nor *Finity* was challenging them. Senior Captain had told them so, directly.

Numbers popped up, taking the right third of the image.

"What's this dataflow?" Siobhan asked.

"Numbers," Connor said, the obvious, but his voice was tense. "*Crazy* numbers. Their fucking field's coming up. *Idiots.*"

Crazy was right. What jumped to the main screen was unlike any field they'd ever seen. The pattern began to dance, rippling one vane to the next to the next. It was astonishingly complex.

A second image appeared; an image that looked for all the world as if it were from *inside* that rippling field.

"*How* in hell are we getting this perspective?" Nolan asked, from the drink counter. "Not to mention Connor's numbers?"

Netha, watching over Connor's shoulder, said: "We might have tucked a little present onto her hull, while we were coming into dock. There was a lot of that going on while we were there."

"God damn," Ian said. "Us clever people."

Siobhan said. "Illegal as hell. But, yeah, clever."

The number-dance was steady. Then wasn't. Now and again a tick. Now and again a *big* tick—that jolted like an electric shock. *That* would sort out as the field built. Ross hoped.

Just when he thought he couldn't take another of those shocks, the vanes stopped cycling and engaged in a different dance, a seemingly random firing. Having no idea what *normal* might be, considering the amount of power involved, it was beyond scary.

"Balancing the field, I'm betting," Connor said. "Engees didn't like those ticks."

Neither did Foucault. The reaction from the Ardaman had become buffeting waves, pushing one way and another. Ross closed his eyes, swayed with those gravitic forces. A little off on the left, compensation from the right. Damn . . . it was surreal . . .

"Too close," he muttered. "Too damn close."

"She's done two test runs," Patrick said. "Even if they haven't jumped her. Surely they know the limits of her bubble. And *Come Lately* is closer than we are."

Come Lately had the protection of her *own* bubble—

Where the *hell* was the Fizeau Ardaman? Ross wondered, suddenly, as Foucault's ebbed and throbbed around him.

What was happening to *it* with these two bubbles forming? He felt it, then. The wind was there. It had *been* there all along, just masked by Foucault's.

He could feel it, feel them both twist and contort as force met force, solar winds, gravity wells, and two very different space-warping bubbles.

"Fuck," he said under his breath, eyes skipping between two columns of data on *his* console screen, echo from the bridge, where Fourth-shift was active.

Numbers that finally, *finally* began to make sense with his gut feelings. "I wouldn't *do* that. I really wouldn't do that."

As *Shalleen* . . .

Relocated.

Book VI   Section xxii

"*Finity's End* to *Come Lately*," JR said, third time, channel 1, seated, belted in, in his office now. Mum was the captain on the bridge.

Incredibly, they had not gotten a physical jolt from that tandem relocation, but the *readings* were extreme.

It was *not* a good place or time to pull a stunt like that. Foucault was flaring, had been since *Shalleen* had begun accelerating, and while there was no reason to suspect cause and effect, *because* of that flaring, the associated outpouring of solar wind and expansion of the Ardaman limit . . . he didn't want to think what shock waves that crazed field might be sending back to the star.

Dammit. Get farther out, you idiots. A hell of a lot farther out.

"*Finity* is not in pursuit. The Neiharts have absolutely no quarrel with the Bellagios. Delay jump. We *need* to talk, Bellagios. Over."

Telemetry had *Shalleen* back in view—only thirteen seconds-light from her last location, short drop.

Scary short. The kind of move that landed you in your own bow wave.

Fools. If they wanted to get out ahead, get the *hell* out ahead. A good minute. *Two* for God's sake, with that unknown array.

On the right of the screen the numbers cycled again—one, two, three—but no longer equal in strength. Balanced, one had to assume.

One damned well hoped. *Shalleen*'s three-vane circle continued to glow on the screen.

Come Lately's bubble was all the way down. Her vanes dark.

The jagged graph on the right margin of the screen was back to pattern—one-two-three . . . cycling faster and faster. It acquired a beat. Clockwork even . . . until it hiccupped.

Spike. Big one.

Slight adjustment to the numbers, then. Another spike, and another.

Just like before. But this time, they didn't cycle down. Didn't rebalance, if that had been the purpose of that last down-cycle.

Maybe, *maybe*, the spike itself was the goal.

He didn't like that. Didn't like that one damned bit.

"*JR.*" Com pinged him, live voice. It was Kate, like him, off-duty. "*Are you seeing this?*"

Abruptly, midway between one heavy pulse and the next, *Shalleen* . . .

Disappeared, in a flaring sun of blue vanes.

"Fuck!" JR gripped the counter edge, knowing, *knowing*, dammitall, what was coming.

The takehold blared.

And *Finity* yawed abruptly to intercept the wave head-on.

Book VI   Section xxiii

Takehold!

Ross gripped the console edge. Foucault's anger slammed into his gut.

Fizeau pounced.

And the world went grey. His ears buzzed. The takehold blared: "Take-hold. Ring-accel. Takehold. Ring-accel . . ."

The words pierced his head like knives, but made no sense, as wave after wave, from *Shalleen,* from Foucault, from Fizeau—twisted his innards. He lost the stars. The elephant was back . . . and the monkeys were racing around it, *through* it. The tiger pounced—yanked space *flat.*

The buffeting vanished. Sight and sound returned . . .

And in all that violence, the empty glass, the red napkin had stayed on the console, one corner of the napkin hanging, as before, off the edge. God. *He'd* been turned inside out.

Charts registered. Scan came back. Around him cousins staring at screens, same as before.

Come Lately had been at about twenty-five seconds-light from *Finity.* She was now at 1.71 *minutes*-light. Displaced. No matter *her* vanes were dead. *Shalleen's* bubble had pulled her. That was the only expla—

Where *was Shalleen?*

"She's jumped," Maire breathed.

Jumped? *Come Lately* had just been forcibly relocated, out ahead even of *Little Bear,* but *Shalleen* . . . was nowhere to be seen, not on visual, not in telemetry.

Jumped? His gut screamed otherwise. Foucault was beyond angry. Fizeau had pulled back into its den. The Ardaman was ringing with that fluxing dent in spacetime that had been—*was* dammit—*Shalleen.* A dent that squeezed and pulled and ripped everything it could reach: matter, energy, gravity itself. The elephant had blasted through spacetime, pulling everything in its wake.

Like a manmade black hole.

Ross pressed knuckles against his mouth, trying not to throw up. *Shalleen's* gravity wave hurled monkeys that were there and not . . . dragged them back as space *shook;* and then what might be Foucault itself . . . slammed him in the gut. Angry. So very, *very* angry.

Vision blurred.

Pressure on his shoulders, pressure that *wasn't Shalleen* or Foucault: Ian's hands and Ian asking was he all right—chasing away the visions. At least for a moment. They'd be back, he was dead certain, in this room of live screens and virtual keyboards.

Ross staggered out from under Ian's hand, left the chair, found his balance and raced for the numbers. Needing . . . reality. Not *those* impotent numbers on an impotent screen. He needed the real thing.

He *needed* the bridge.

He hit a wall, had a shocked glimpse of reality: the outer corridor.

He ran.

Ran.

Shalleen jumped? No, no, and *hell* no.

Silence. A vast silence, except his own pounding footsteps, racing the curve of the ring.

Center of the universe—Foucault was still mightily, *mightily* pissed, a whistling roar of wind drowning out Fizeau, a torrent swirling into *Shalleen's* hungry mouth. *That* was the monkeys. Subatomic particles trapped in that gravitational pit.

And he had stared right into it. Deep. Twisting and ringing.

Two Finitys in the corridor flattened themselves against the wall. He ran past without slowing. He reached the bridge and seized the takehold beside the lounge-side entry, gasped after breath, then slung himself on through, staggering as the chairs and floor warped up and down and around him.

Foucault was *still* reacting mightily, never mind the star was light-hours away. The wavefront, speed of gravity, speed of light, time itself—were in chaos. Realspace healed itself in fits and starts between the waves. *Shalleen* there and not, then back again.

There. Gone. There. Gone, gone. There . . . too long. *Far* too . . .

She was gone. There . . . but not.

Nav 5 Console was an island, *his* chair empty in this shift. He dropped into it, heard Captain Mum's voice sharp and real, but the words made no sense. He reached out, keyed the sleeping Nav 5 station awake, laid fingers on keys that *worked*, and pulled up the numbers *he* needed as his screens came to life.

Little side screen was frozen. The spybot attached to *Shalleen* had stopped transmitting. Lost. Sent trans-C. Blown. Out of range. Another star, another universe. Who knew, in the abyss *Shalleen* had skimmed?

Numbers in the data columns had frozen.

But the gravity wave, the kinked Ardaman, the resonances of Foucault and even distant Fizeau: those numbers were there. They were real. These buttons all worked. These buttons gave him reality . . .

The stars came back.

"*Query* Come Lately," *Senior* Captain's voice came over main ops, cutting through the buzz in his ears, sane and realtime. "*Do they need assistance?*"

And he heard/saw/felt JR enter the bridge as yet another mobius warp, whether from the first disturbance or the second, passed through the ship, milder than the last, but enough to make him gag. Foucault whistled and roared, hairy with prominences.

Ross gritted his teeth, fingers on keys, tried to focus past the chaos as the disturbances continued to come. Random monkeys bounded past, only to be sucked back down in the elephant's wake.

Suggest we don't jump, sir. Strongly suggest no one jumps for a few hours.

"Hush, Ross!" Ian's voice, low, right in his ear, hand pulling at his shoulder. Crazy cousin: he'd said nothing. Couldn't, until the numbers made sense of elephants and monkeys.

A voice said over the general com: "*Nav 1.5, leave the bridge, please.*"

Fizeau's going to feel this. The wave's rolling back. The tiger's going to pounce if we try to leave now. Won't make it, sir. Never make it . . .

"*Ross!*" The grip on his arm was insistent. He shook it off.

"*Nav 1.5, leave the bridge immediately.*"

Com 4.2 said: "Come Lately *is not responding to hail, Senior Captain. Scan is continuing to look for* Shalleen."

"*Acknowledged,*" Senior Captain said over com, wherever he was.

"*Definitive on jump,*" someone said, nearby.

And another voice on com: "*She's left.*"

Book VI   Section xxiv

"*Bullshit!*" Ross's shout rang across the Fourth-shift bridge, and JR, reaching the area, held Ian Monahan from another attempt to pull the kid out of the chair.

Ross was clinging to the console edge, protesting: "She's still *here.* The god damned monkeys've killed the elephant. —Dammit!" Ross pressed his fists to his temples. "*Get out of my head!*"

God. Psychological break. Major. They needed medical up here. Fast.

"C'mon, Ross." Ian's voice was anguished. "Let's get out of here."

Ross grabbed the console, watching the Nav screen, eyes intent and calculating. Ian in desperation looked to JR.

JR shook his head. Leave him be. It was racket. It wasn't destructive action. It was a trainee board, linked to Nav 1, nothing that could *do* anything . . . except give a cracking mind a much needed physical anchor.

"Little Bear *is expressing concern for* Finity's *welfare,*" Com 2.1 said in JR's ear, exec channel. "*They report themselves as safe.*"

"*Your call, JR,*" Mum said.

"Reassure them," JR said, still watching Ross. "Try to raise *Miriam B.* Advise them what happened. Advise them *Come Lately* may need assistance." And recalling that crazed warning from their Monahan guest: "Inform *Little Bear* we will continue in normal space. We ask they stay with us. Jump is delayed to First-shift at earliest."

"*That*," their Monahan guest muttered, pickup being live, "*is a fucking good idea.*"

Mum hissed, but JR didn't think for a minute that the kid realized he was speaking out loud. Whatever had him in its grip was nothing to fool around with, not for the kid, not for *Finity*. —Not on the bridge.

A First-shift Navigator having a mental break—he needed to get Kate here. If anyone could pull the kid back from wherever he had gotten to, if anyone could save that mind and get something rational out of this kid who felt stars—it would be Kate.

And no, they weren't going to jump. Foucault was not one to mess with under normal circumstances, and *they* had just had an experimental FTLer go . . . somewhere not immediately discernable.

"Get me Nav 1.1," he said to Com over channels, only to look up and see Kate already working her way through the cluster of worried-looking Monahans that had gathered in the lounge-side entrance. Kate's eyes went straight to Ross as she reached the scene.

Ross paid no attention to any of them: his fingers were now flying on his keyboard.

Kate watched the kid's screen silently . . . then shouldered past JR to get a fast consult with Anya, Nav 4.1. A brief discussion, a nod, and Anya windowed Ross's screen on the main display, the giant screen at the front of the bridge.

Mum, current captain of record, crossed the exec line and came back as far as Nav 1.

"Let him be," JR said to Ian, and went to join Mum and Kate, beside Nav 1.

"On to something?" Mum asked, and Kate shrugged.

"Kid's figuring. I don't want to interrupt him if I don't have to. That trivane had a problem. He felt something. He's looking for the numbers. I can tell you personally, it's nasty out there."

"Damn nasty," Anya said. "I agree with the kid. Sit tight. Observe. We don't need to go anywhere at the moment."

JR looked at Mum. Mum's Nav 1 and his were saying no-go, and it was a good moment to listen—which meant not disturbing a Navigator launched on a problem only he, at the moment, seemed to see.

"Permission to talk to Scan," Kate said.

Mum gave a curt nod. "Go."

Kate went. JR looked back at Ian, still beside Ross. Gave a short nod. "Just stay with him."

There was quiet for a moment, no movement but Kate coming back to talk to Anya, with Mum listening in. It boiled down to, *Scan's got nothing.*

Kate leaned against an empty chair . . . and waited. Ian remained behind Ross, hands on his shoulders. Comfort. Stability.

There was maybe five minutes of utter quiet, stations going about gathering what data they could. JR waited. Sweat glistened on Ross's forehead.

Five minutes.

So very much could happen in five minutes. A whole life could come and go in five minutes. Play this wrong . . . and they lost Ross Monahan.

Ross half-turned and talked to Kate. Earnestly. And not, from Kate's expression, any nonsense about monkeys. Kate nodded. Ross turned back to his screen.

Massive things could change in five minutes. A navigator stressed to the max . . . began making sense.

Kate stayed put. Mum went back to her official place, head of all the sections. Nav 1 through 4 continued to function. Nav 5 continued on his own business, with anguished cousins gathered at the door. Eventually, Ian retreated to that group to give what reassurance he could, leaving Kate to stand with her hand on Ross's shoulder.

They were approaching shift-change. They were worn down, battered, no one at his best.

Come Lately had not responded, despite Mum's efforts to contact her. Eventually, her vanes came back up and she disappeared, leaving completely normal telemetry ticking through local space. *Come Lately* was gone. Jumped. Normally and safely. On a heading for Thule.

New numbers made a split-screen with the system schematic now on the big screen: *Engineering* was running the numbers again and again on that strange three-vane array.

And on Anya's own display, JR could see that screen, Science and Nav together were going over numbers—maybe trying to figure what Ross saw, and why a Navigator who felt stars had such a strong, strong feeling *Shalleen* was still here.

But if Ross was right, if *Shalleen* was still here and had just relocated . . . possibly to Fizeau's region, the chances of finding her were slim to none. Groombridge 34, Foucault and Fizeau, was a *big* place. Twenty-six hundred years for that pair of stars to complete one pass.

Com came on again, announcing shift-change, and reversion to normal shift sequence.

First-shift was up. Mum called it, resuming com. Crew would begin reporting.

And they had a problem sitting in Nav 1.5 that wasn't budging. A problem now in his own shift, with ample time to work his numbers. Which was not necessarily, in JR's opinion, a good thing. Sleep, drugged if necessary, and time away from the problem, would be his advice.

But Kate said *leave him*, and Kate would be there. Several Monahans would be not that far away.

People started moving in. Fourth-shift began moving out to showers, each as a First-shift came in to take his place.

"Permission to stay here," Ian Monahan said, meaning with Ross rather than at his post at Helm 1.5, which was no trouble to grant.

"Stay with him," JR said. Security might want to come in, but he sensed that was the last thing in the universe good for Ross Monahan at this moment. "Just let him do what he wants to do. Stay with him."

"Yes, sir." From Ian.

From Ross, no response, no attention. It was all keys and numbers . . .

. . . until he stopped. And sat back.

Book VI   Section xxv

Shift had changed. Kate and Bucklin, Ty and Jim . . . *they* were in the stations in front of him.

As they ought to be.

Everything looped back to the beginning. They were coming in . . .

No. It was *not* Pell. It was Groombridge 34.

Things had happened.

A lot of things had happened. Fletcher. A line shooting through the dark. Monkeys, shadows, tumbling over one another, refusing order.

A touch on his shoulder. He panicked. Held it in.

"Ross." Ian's voice. "I'm here, kid. You're all right."

He was here. He *was* here. At his post. On *Finity's End*.

"Ross? You're excused from the shift. You can leave. It's all right."

Shalleen had disappeared. They said she'd jumped, but he knew she hadn't. *Knew.* He'd . . . he'd run to the bridge, to a board that would give him *answers.* But . . . he'd done something wrong. Something irrational. Kate had asked him questions and he couldn't get a word out to answer.

Except he had. Elephants and monkeys. God, he'd cracked. Here. Of all the places in the universe. A place filled with people he respected beyond calculation.

And now he was dismissed from shift. Maybe dismissed from the bridge for good. He thought . . . hell, he *knew* . . . he'd said things he shouldn't. Crazy things.

But the wind kept coming, a tiny portion still funneling into the pit that was *Shalleen.* Yes, the figures on the screen kept moving, but those numbers were not telling the whole story.

He could hear Foucault's occasional shriek, and Fizeau muttering in the distance. But the wind was not as bad as before. Not as upset.

Not nearly.

God . . . how long had it been? How long had he been lost?

At least the monkeys were gone. Out of his head. He saw Foucault. *Felt* Foucault.

"Ross?" Ian reached to unfasten his belt. No. His shift was on. Hours yet before he could leave.

But he was dismissed. Ian had said that. And Ian urged him to his feet, but his legs were jelly and he couldn't begin to take his own weight. Connor took the other arm, and they moved him out, toward the lounge, and beyond, to the corridor. All his cousins waited there, touching him, commiserating with him, telling him he'd taken a knock in the head . . .

Damn EC enforcers had done that, hadn't they? Cruz's thugs. But that was a long time ago. At Alpha. He'd been on *Galway.* This was *Finity's End* and they were at Groombridge 34 . . . Olympus was behind them.

Not a knock in the head. Not this time. It was the wind that had ripped him apart. He was, over all, numb, not particularly in pain, except inside, where it hurt not physically, but emotionally. Being wrong. Being that far off.

Except—damn it, he was *right.* Don't question your gut. *Kate* had told him that. Work til the numbers explain what that gut feeling means, one way or the other, but don't question the feeling.

Kate felt stars, too. Kate might think he'd cracked, but she might feel at least some of what he felt and keep looking, might find the answers he hadn't been able to find. He wanted to—

"Come on," Ian said, and urged him down the corridor.

"You're on shift. Get back there!"

"I'm excused," Ian said. "It's all right."

Excused? Because of *him?* What *he'd* done? What *he'd* said? Dammit, enough was enough!

"It's *not* all right." He jerked his arm free. "I'm fine. I can walk. I can take care of myself."

"The hell," Connor said, and to the others: "Suppose we ought to call Jen?"

"No!" The word escaped in a shout and he forced it down. "No way, cousins. I'm fine. *Fine.*"

"You're off your head," Patrick said. "You took a hit, all right? You took too many hits. Just come on. We'll go back around to B, we'll have a sit. Get you some water. Some calories. Maybe get the medic—"

"*No.* Damn it, Pat, I don't need a fucking medic! I need—" What the hell did he need? "Sleep. That's *all* I need. Just let me go. I can find my own bunk."

"The hell no, cousin. You're using language you never use—you cursed at Captain Mum, f'God's sake—and we're not leaving you on your own. You'll be having a sit and a beer or something stronger with us, and a bag of ice for the bruises. Warm blanket and all. We'll be sitting with you, and if you go on with this *I'm all fine* stuff like that, we'll be putting a gag in your mouth and taking you *straight* to the medics without a by-your-leave. Beer and a sit, or medics? You got no third choice."

He froze, staring at Pat. *Cursed at Captain Mum?* God. No. He even vaguely remembered doing it. A lot of what he'd done began to snap into clarity. His eyes hurt from staring unblinking at the screen. The rest of him hurt from being slammed around when *Finity* blasted away from the station.

Headache. That much, he certainly had.

He wasn't sure a beer would help that part, but the rest . . . hell yeah. Numb . . . sounded real good.

Book VI   Section xxvi

"Request to approach." Jen's voice, over JR's exec Com. Jarring, for all she had the absolute authority. Now. JR looked up, saw her standing at the painted line.

"Granted," he answered, and she came.

"I heard what happened," she said, very quietly. "I think I have . . . useful observations."

"Regarding Ross?" he asked, and she nodded. "Should I call in Kate?"

A frown, then, "That would probably be useful."

Kate was watching. Kate likely suspected Jen's reason for coming to the bridge, and had passed her primary to Bucklin. He lifted his chin and Kate joined them.

"Ross?" Kate asked, and Jen nodded.

"I think . . ." Jen said, paused, and continued. "I'm sorry, Senior Captain, sir, but I think I'm at fault, at least partially."

"Just tell us, Jen," JR said.

"It's . . ." her head ducked, then rose to meet him squarely. "It's about Ross's monkeys."

"Go on."

"At the Royal, they have this big gold elephant."

"I remember."

"Well, they've added holos to the foyer. Monkeys that trigger randomly and run all around the room. They really spooked him."

Kate folded her arms and took a deep breath.

Jen continued: "He was already having orientation problems, then these things come running at him, *through* him."

"Reality," Kate said grimly, and Jen nodded, looking relieved.

"It was more than just surprise. It's the . . . there but not there, as he puts it. Later, at the Garden, he really, *really* didn't like the virtual tree in the special exhibit. Anyway, after the incident, he began kind of obsessing on those monkeys. I tried to tease him out of it, but . . ."

JR looked at Kate, who was nodding slowly.

Kate said: "He's still sorting out his sensing stars . . . an interesting time for those of us cursed with the ability. I'm here to say, I can sense it to, but I can't describe what I'm seeing. And I'm by no means as sensitive as he appears to be. Whatever happened when *Shalleen* tried to jump made *me* queasy, and I've had decades to get it under control. Ross was already stressed and exhausted. The meeting, the pullout from Olympus, hours in B watching numbers . . . and he's hit again. The universe has gone crazy on him. He's had far too much New, and nowhere near enough time to process it."

"I . . ." Jen said, "I'm so sorry. I just . . . didn't anticipate . . ."

"Not your fault, Security," JR said. "Not remotely."

"*I* didn't see his break coming," Kate said. "But your account helps me understand why it did. I'll talk with him. *Shalleen* . . . I felt it, too. I think he . . . needs . . . to hear that most of all. —This place, Senior Captain, is *not* good for us."

"No argument," JR said grimly.

"I . . ." Jen looked a bit at a loss, wanting, JR was certain, to get off the bridge to somewhere private.

"Well done, Jen," he said, with a nod toward the doorway. "Well done."

Book VI   Section xxvii

"Finitys and Galways, this is Senior Captain. Shalleen *and* Come Lately *are no longer within scan. We assume they have jumped and not merely relocated.* Little Bear *remains in system, waiting for us while we sort out and attend to our own.*

"The memorial for Fletcher Alejandro Neihart and Walter Parton Neihart will take place in chapel, at Second-shift end. Will, Sayan, and Lela, Tim and Marcy, we love you so much.

"Our situation: best estimation, Come Lately *has made jump toward Thule, from which we assume she will lay course to Venture, and probably Bryant's and Alpha. We assume* Shalleen *will take that route as well, where she may attempt, with* Come Lately, *to become a problem . . . possibly again involving* Rights. *Remote possibility involves a try at the high route to Pell, but we strongly doubt that. We doubt she or* Come Lately *know it exists, though we cannot say for certain. We especially doubt it if the relocation we witnessed is the best she can do. She clearly, as we can attest, has a wide area of effect. We cannot say definitively whether that was crew error, a malfunction, normal operation . . . or simply a first attempt. Her exit from system was certainly impressive. We have a very large amount of data to process in the coming days, which we will share with* Little Bear *before leaving.*

"Sol has paid very high to find a crew capable of getting this prototype ship out of Olympus—setting up all this, over a lengthy period of time— but these two merchants are, whatever else, Family ships and not EC hire. Until proven otherwise, we will deal with them separately and on different terms than we regard EC Enforcement.

"The Captains have been advised—and I think it worth listening to that

advisement in an abundance of caution—that the local star is in a disturbed state; the risk in an exit now is higher for a ship of Finity's mass, and very high for two ships in close succession. For safety's sake, we will wait til conditions improve.

"What is good: Little Bear has offered, at considerable sacrifice of her time and resources, to further delay her return to Cyteen space and wait for us at Venture, as we make the fastest possible time to Pell. At Pell, we will report the situation—and there set ashore our youngest, their minders, and those Family members that Medical reports need shore rest. Then we will set out for Alpha, picking up Little Bear at Venture—and take our Galway friends home. What situation we will find at Alpha we do not know. But we all know the local EC operation out there, with all that is at stake. We are, with the Monahans, still hopeful that Galway will make a safe return and prove the Sol-to-Alpha route for ships of conventional design; but in the meantime, we will see to it that stations from Pell to Alpha are aware of what happened here.

"If you have comments or requests, the exec office will receive them with understanding and compassion. If you feel a need to ask medical relief from duty, you will be met with understanding. Junior-juniors, all of us have been scared. Please don't be embarrassed about that. Should you feel panic or just need to talk, please ask your group minders to help you contact your mothers and olders about it as soon as possible, whether on-shift or off.

"As a further note—if any of you—and this includes the juniors—are experiencing unusual dreams or spookiness, please talk to medical. It's not you, it's this place. So do not hesitate to seek help.

"I regret to say we are once again delayed from trade. But the captains unanimously feel the risk is warranted, and that our capabilities, with Little Bear, make us the ship best able to deal with whatever we find.

"So . . . we have at least two days while Foucault calms down. Take care, rest as you can, and keep those takeholds in mind. Watch the young ones and be safe.

"General announcements: the ring has returned to normal rotation. Report any problems. Meantime, continue to keep your gear tight-stowed. This is not a friendly system.

"First-shift will release in thirty-three minutes. Second-shift, you have thirty minutes til shift-change, starting now.

"Good morning, Captain Madison.

"Expect the regular sequence of duty shifts. First-shift will make the proximate jump to Thule and we will take it very easy on this passage to Pell, family and friends.

"Olympus Station continues to be upset with us, but if they should send something substantial our way, it would take a long time to get here. Consider that we are essentially out of danger."

Book VI   Section xxviii

Two full days, and *no* sign of *Shalleen.*

Foucault did settle. Finally. Ross had feared, truly feared, that the feedback from that failed jump might permanently destabilize the star. But stabilize it did.

He'd talked with Kate. He'd apologized. He especially apologized to Captain Mum. Sleep helped. Food helped. Reviewing tapes and sorting through the data helped; but going over *Shalleen's* numbers with Connor only confused him, pushed him—too far. His hindbrain was still processing, still trying to fit numbers to feelings. While occasional output from Fizeau still sent waves through his nerves, at least the panic, the desperate grasping at sanity, had eased.

There *was* an explanation, he was increasingly sure of that. There was a rational answer, if only, somehow, he could find it.

Kate believed him about *Shalleen* . . . sort of. That was both comforting—and a re-balance on the edge of the pit. She *believed* him. She was sane and *she* was working on it.

To prove him wrong. Maybe.

Or maybe she had her own misgivings. She *said* she'd felt it, too, if not so much. He wished he could believe that, but he feared she sometimes said things just to make him feel . . . not that different.

He tried to come down from it. He sat two shifts, reading an irritable star, finding no ghosts, no pit, no sign of another presence. Not, at least, in the numbers. He spent time with Jen, talking about anything other than what had happened.

This shift-end, *Finity* had even regained the luxury of a sit-down meal, and the galley had produced a proper supper, last before jump. Jen, of course, had grabbed the two of them a little three-seat table all to themselves. No strings attached, she insisted. No heavy implications. Just a little quiet time such as they hadn't had since . . . ever, really. Even the time at Pell had been more about getting tickets for the Garden than it had been about them.

Just relax, she said. And: Dress. She wore the silver jumpsuit. Ross wore the good jacket.

So relax it was, as relaxed as he could manage since the incident. The bruise on his cheek had gone various colors. But it would be gone by Thule arrival. Things would be a lot better once they got to Thule—where there would be no Foucault urging at him; where, most of all, there'd either be two traces of passage—or three: beyond *Little Bear*'s—either *Come Lately*'s track alone; or with *Shalleen*. They would know reality from guesswork, at last. And for that resolution . . . he was anxious to get underway. He would know, then, how sane he was. He would either find he was right; or otherwise; and from there—

From there, it was on to Pell via that tricky high road. Get word to Pell . . . then get back to his Family.

He was willing to accept an answer, *any* answer: either prove he was right without knowing *how*—which was almost as unsettling as not knowing; or prove he had just—as Connor said—taken one too many jolts to the head. Medical had strongly urged him to stand down from ops entirely til they were back at Venture, but hell with that. He'd wanted to continue, and considering he was only a trainee, having no live controls under his hands, Medical had relented.

That helped more than anything. Routine. Running exit sims according to Kate's very sane parameters. Prepping for that unique run to Pell . . . damned if it didn't heal the soul to have his line meld with the others of his shift.

He worked hard on reality today, on calm, on meticulous attention to here-and-now details, having ventured the limit into chaos. He tried not to think about the tri-vane. Tried not to work on the *how* or the *why* or the *where*.

Yet it persisted, that feeling that *Shalleen* was both *here* and *not-here*.

Kate said she'd believe both of his states of mind until proven otherwise—Kate's humor; and loyalty to her people. She'd actually sat off-shift and talked with the Engees about how *they* thought those engines and vanes worked, and what the readings they had from her showed . . .

She hadn't said she had any answer, or any idea, and from hoping she would come up with an answer, and her saying not yet, he just tried not to think about it . . . while from time to time the sensory illusions urged at him: Foucault, with another dig at his attention. Fizeau, not to be forgotten. Awareness hit him like that, from time to time.

He tried right here and now *not* to listen to Fizeau, who had something to say, overriding Jen's remark, something about their time at Pell.

No. He did *not* want to hear the star. *Any* star. Not at the moment. Didn't want to *think* about Groombridge, or Olympus, or *Shalleen*—or *anything* to do with this place. He sat down, poured them each a generous glass of wine from the carafe. Pell wine, not synth. Two shift-changes more, and they entered in countdown for jump . . . and escaped this system. First-shift would be taking them through—*his* shift, and he was determined to be in that seat, laying course, and riding through it.

Leaving this place, leaving Foucault, where everything that could possibly go wrong . . . had.

They had to wait for their main course to be delivered, just like a fancy restaurant. Easy, companionable silence. Fingers lightly interlaced, with the occasional, feather-light stroke to keep things interesting. Jen talked about Pell, about the game shop, as staff on duty moved about the tables, some distance away yet. Their tabletop was vacant, but for the wine, the silverware, and a huddle of little items in the center. . . .

He found himself looking at those items, head tipped first one way and the next. A salt and a pepper. A water carafe. A clear vase with a sprig of greenery.

They became a solar system. Olympus system. God, *no*. But—

He reached for the water carafe. Moved it. That was Foucault. Moved his wine glass. That was *Finity*. Moved his water glass. Slightly. *Little Bear.* Salt and pepper were the two Bellagio ships.

He shouldn't be thinking about that. Jen was sitting there, saying something and he couldn't hear it . . .

The wind from Foucault was quiet now, safe, a whisper in the leaves of the green sprig. Back then, facing them—it had roared. Shrieked.

The vase was Foucault's wind. A single bit from the leaning sprig was Fizeau's. Shift of the angle . . . he rotated it with a push of his finger. It had been *that* way.

And the pepper shaker that was *Shalleen* was too small. *Shalleen's* field had been massive. He stole Jen's water glass and replaced the pepper shaker. Jen said nothing.

Two ships, one riding quiet in the wind, while the other—its vanes vastly overpowered, cycling, creating a vortex of overcharged particles—feeding, taking in particles from that unusually dense solar wind . . . he could *hear* particles streaming into that blue circle. Wind from Foucault. The wind from Fizeau meeting the force of Foucault . . .

Shalleen was the gilt elephant sinking through the floor, the monkeys were those charged particles, falling after.

He shut his eyes. And in that darkness, wine glass, vase, sprigs—became . . . not elephants and monkeys, but stars and ships and solar winds, particles. Opened them again, on Jen's dark eyes, filled first with concern, then relaxing as he took her fingers again and squeezed.

It wasn't Fizeau's fault. The answer wasn't in either star. Not in the combination, either. The Ardaman was weird enough, as weird as he'd ever felt, but *it* wasn't the reason.

It was the damned elephant: *Shalleen* herself.

Jen didn't say anything. Just watched as he shoved back from the table.

"I've got to talk to Kate," he said, laying a hand on hers. Sanity demanded, that look of hers demanded. "I'm all right, Jen. I swear I'm all right."

"You've got an answer." It wasn't a question.

"Maybe *the* answer. Kate's just over there. I'll be back. I'll be *right back*."

Book VI   Section xxix

Little Bear had left the system, Foucault was quiet, and *Finity* was once again prepping for jump. First-shift was coming up, slowly replacing Fourth, and JR had taken his usual seat on the bridge. The four Monahans on his shift came in together, laughing at some private joke, before scattering to their various posts.

That was good—seeing Ross settle into vacant Nav 1.5. Ross put in his code, brisk, sure movements. Focused. Relaxed. Ready to go. *With* them, a hundred percent, bright-eyed and full of purpose.

It had been three days since Ross had interrupted Kate's dinner with talk of vortexes, solar winds, black holes, and supercharged particles, and for three days, on Kate's insistence, Scan, Longscan, Engineering, and Physical Science had been working non-stop to find the evidence to support the kid's theory.

A theory predicated on that kid's *gut feeling* about a region of space some five light years across. Navigators: spooks, the sanest of them.

Granted, the kid had the training and the intelligence to analyze those *feelings* into a coherent theory—a theory Kate had taken seriously enough to stop her dinner and start investigating—but still . . .

Elephants and monkeys. He'd truly feared the kid would never recover, the hour he'd been definitively escorted from the bridge. But God-willing, he'd not only recovered, but come out of the experience stronger. Kate said he had, swore that she'd turn his board live in a heartbeat if it became necessary; JR could only take her word for it and hope it didn't *become* necessary anywhere this side of Pell.

He'd had his own talk with Ross, early on, but a mere Senior Captain wasn't up to finesses of particle physics with a strung-out Navigator, and when *Kate's* early explanation also referenced Ross's monkeys and an elephant, he'd thrown up his hands in defeat.

Stand-ins for, among other things, the solar wind and *Shalleen* herself, was what Kate had said, associations triggered by the bizarre experiences Jen said the kid had met on Pell, and JR was more than willing to take her word for it. However it had come about, those elephants and monkeys had led them to a solid theory on what had happened to *Shalleen*.

A theory he was damned if *he'd* ever be tempted to test.

"It's the design," Kate had said, "the ship design's at fault. It's in the numbers. Some of the data we need to absolutely confirm what happened to her is out of reach, too far cross-system for our instruments to pick up for months, maybe even years. We had eyes on her, we had that bug on her, and once we looked at her numbers, combined with Scan's standard system telemetry—with the kid's theory in mind—there's no question the attempt to jump took her out. Consensus is, she wouldn't be safe to jump anywhere, let alone out of here. It's *not* the place. Groombridge was the cap on it, but she'd have blown anywhere."

The last he'd heard, the numbers hadn't combined to make total sense yet, but the ship's design, the cycling tri-vanes . . . that eerie imbalance as she was powering up—he could easily believe that was the key, and very glad he was to have cousins to solve the details.

Ever since they'd seen *Shalleen*, debates on the design had permeated Engineering's every off-hours conversation. Advantages proposed, detractions proposed . . . What they had now was those numbers in operation. The numbers said the bubble had formed. And *Shalleen had* gone. Somewhere. They'd not been able to find her signature in system. Neither had they caught a whisper of a distress call or detected the kind of disturbance a ship dropping back down should create.

Logic would say she'd simply jumped. Spectacularly. Noisily. But still, jumped.

Except for a kid hallucinating about elephants, who insisted she never left the system, that she was still here . . . and a senior navigator who insisted it was worth their effort to try to find her.

Engineering and Nav of several shifts had been looking at the telemetry, the field, the solar wind—data on the Ardaman and gravitic fluctuations before, during, and after that blazing departure. There had been still another of those conferences going on, back in Conference-1, Senior Engineers, Science, *and* Nav, during the last hour of Fourth-shift. Kate had been part of it. And she arrived now on the bridge with Bucklin *and* Madison, who had no business being up at this hour.

JR caught Madison's eye and waved them over.

"So?" JR asked.

"Still theory," Kate said, wasting no time, "but damned if I'm not a believer. That three-way design is meant to pull in whatever mass it encounters. Ross's vortexes and black holes aren't a bad analogy. Bubbles warp space. That circle of vanes amplifies the gravitational effect, captures solar wind particles and anything else available, and turns them into energy which in turn feeds the bubble. Free fuel, and a lot of it."

"Turbocharger," Madison said.

"For want of a better word. Physically, the bubble she made rivaled *Finity's* . . . big, but a whole lot nastier. Whether or not it would function safely in a normal jump is still under debate. *I'd* sure as hell not want to be aboard. But *Shalleen* began accelerating and powered her vanes up *inside* the Ardaman, aiming to over-jump *Little Bear*. Passing *through* her, *over* her, in jump-space—so she pushed it. That bubble of hers pulled all that flaring solar wind in with her and twisted it into spaghetti."

"Spaghetti." God. But he could see it. The Ardaman, that ever-shifting mathematical boundary around a star, that point at which a star's outgoing energy was dispersed enough for an FTL ship's space-warping bubble not to wreak havoc, was inviolate. To jump inside that boundary—was beyond crazy. He didn't care what size ship you had. To do it safely would take massive power to form the bubble *and* jump fast enough, which maybe that turbocharged array could have done.

Maybe it was possible, but it wasn't without threat to everything around you . . . like three other ships. Disruption of ship systems was the least of the possible outcomes. Getting sucked inside out was theoretically possible . . . and maybe, unpleasant thought, the Bellagio captain had aimed to do just that to a Cyteen ship—to *Little Bear*.

God only knew what might have happened had *Little Bear* had her vanes out, powered up or otherwise.

"The numbers indicate *Shalleen did* go up, but immediately overloaded," Kate said. "We got data from *Little Bear*, and that monster bubble never touched them. *Close*, but not close enough. *Shalleen's* systems failed just as they initiated jump. Her field, when it went, collapsed in less than a nanosecond, as we now think. She came *down*. Sort of. Massive, *massive* localized energy flux pushing out on her vector at full C showed up on *Little Bear's* data . . . because *Little Bear* was ahead of her. We'll never catch up to it." Kate paused, took a breath, then: "She's still here, JR. Ross was right. She's still here, pretty well where she went up, but gravity—at lightspeed— didn't pull much of her down as matter."

"The other state," JR said, "being—energy. That pulse *Little Bear* caught."

Kate nodded slowly. "Without more information we simply aren't in a position to get, we can't even guess how much, if anything, recognizable came down or where. We're still looking, but realistically . . ." She shrugged.

"Bottom line," Madison said abruptly, "we've just witnessed a trial of that three-vane system, and for whatever reason, it didn't go well. They bid to make a hyper-ship to out-do our largest and best—and now *Come Lately's* mourning a sizable number of their Family, God help them. Question is . . ." Madison looked at Kate, who frowned and looked away, shaking her head. ". . . do we tell Olympus?"

"Or . . . what?" JR asked, trying to read that exchange. "Let them— Olympus—assume for a while that she made it, and their plans, whatever they are, are on course? Seems only right to at least send them what data we have, let them know their ship is gone. *Come Lately* won't know, couldn't have warned Station before they left. They were behind her, same as us, and they don't have that data from *Little Bear.*"

"*But would they love us for pointing out their weaknesses?*" John said out of nowhere, eavesdropping on JR's exec com. "*Hell, they won't believe our analysis. Not for a nanosecond. If she's gone, can't possibly be superior EC engineering at fault. They'll say we're responsible, tossed a bomb up her ass, interfered with her, or something, never mind it's impossible. That's the way their brains operate. As far as they're concerned, only reason we could possibly have in sending such a message is to stop their precious program. And . . . hell, again . . . do we want to help them out by explaining it? We don't need to help them set up here. Hell, I'd prefer they left altogether.*"

Damn.

Madison said: "It would give us months, maybe years to get word out to the rest of the stations about what's happened here. *Everything* that's happened. To people who will believe us, who will take the time to look at *Shalleen's* numbers and the tapes of that meeting. Only thing we get if we warn this lot now is Mallory heading out to spread lies about us blowing up their ship. Who knows when another of those tri-vanes is due to make it out from Sol? Maybe tomorrow, maybe a decade. So *Galway* headed for Sol, and if, God forbid, it turns out she doesn't make it, Abrezio's transmission of the data points will be there in a couple of years. For what we know, there could be dozens of those tri-vanes stockpiled at Sol, crew salivating to test those points, to get to Alpha along the *Galway* route, but without proper training, without proper testing. If we're lucky, they'll blow themselves up along with a hell of a lot of EC enforcers. And if they insist on being that stupid, damned if I'll cry for them."

God. He could see where this was headed. And he understood *why* he hadn't been called in. His gut churned just thinking about the lives that could be lost. There were times, his fellow captains frequently reminded him, when words weren't enough. And maybe he *was* too soft. Not so many years ago, he'd accepted the Senior Captain position because he'd been un-deniably the best suited, physically and mentally, for the job. He'd never, ever expected the job to include a political situation like this. No one had. No one could have predicted it.

"*Miriam B* would be next on the list to get one of those tri-vane ships," he said. "Not some EC crew. I'd hate to see that. Our whole goal is to *save* Family ships."

"You're kinder than I am, brother," Madison said. "I'm not sure I *want* them signed on with us. And say we do send Olympus the telemetry and warn them. Who gets it? *Wellington?* Fat lot of good that would do. Would station even pass it on to Mallory, who might have at least some hope of un-derstanding it? Even if he didn't, if he's worthy of his Captaincy, Mallory isn't stupid enough to jump an untried ship until he's gotten a report on *Shalleen* from the Bellagios. When that doesn't come, *maybe* he'll be ready to listen to those who *saw* what happened."

"*Senior Captain decides,*" Mum said, intervening from the speaker over-head. "*Do we tell station what we know before we leave? More to the point, do we tell the Mallorys?*"

Not to mention, ultimately, the Bellagios of *Come Lately* when and if they caught up with that ship. God . . . there were times . . .

But Mum was right. It was *his* decision to make. Madison and John had made *their* views clear and made massively good points. Mum . . . was an expert at keeping her opinion to herself, if she was certain about the argu-ments JR himself would raise.

And there was one big one. There *was* an obligation to another mer-chanter Family, whether or not that Family returned that consideration.

That obligation was part and parcel of *everything* they were trying to accomplish. And the Mallorys, without a warning, might be getting one of those ships, possibly within months. A Family that might, if the next free ship had the same issue as *Shalleen,* take their own three-vaned ride to hell.

Hairtrigger John he might be, but John was right: send them the data and they'd find a way to twist the numbers into a *Finity* plot to destroy their FTL program, or worse, use the data they now had to fix their program, if such a fix was possible. *Finity* engineers said "no," but "not possible" was only a challenge to the creative mind. And the Company would believe what the Company decided it was profitable to believe.

Would Tom Mallory take offense, once the truth was common knowledge? Once he discovered Captain James Robert had known, and chosen *not* to send the warning? Captain Mallory, who sat there and rejected everything JR had tried to offer?

At some point, when dealing with willful self-deception, reason failed.

No one spoke. JR took several long, calming breaths, thinking of time, and a warning that *they* had to get to Pell and Cyteen, if they were going to unify the Beyond against all that might come at it from Sol. Of the *millions* of lives that could be destroyed, if the EC succeeded in their militarized takeover.

Of the endless battle for truth, if Olympus had time to spread a twisted version of a warning from *Finity* . . .

Time. Everything was time. And there was no buying back a wrong choice.

"*So do we tell them?*" Mum asked again.

He took a deep, deep, *deep* breath . . . and released it, along with his doubts.

"No," he said.